PERFECT
DEAD

Jackie Baldwin practiced as a solicitor in a rural town for twenty years specialising in family and criminal law. She then trained as a hypnotherapist and now works from home. She is married with two grown up children and loves to walk with her two dogs in local forests. She is an active member of her local crime writing group. *Perfect Dead* is her second novel.

 @JackieMBaldwin1

Also by Jackie Baldwin

Dead Man's Prayer

PERFECT DEAD

JACKIE BALDWIN

KILLER READS

Broughton House and Garden, in Kirkcudbright, is the Edwardian home and studio of Scottish artist, E. A. Hornel, one of the early twentieth-century Glasgow Boys. It is owned and operated by the National Trust for Scotland. Any and all mentions of Broughton House and the National Trust for Scotland, beyond the mere fact of their existence, in this novel, are entirely fictitious

KillerReads
an imprint of HarperCollins*Publishers* Ltd
1 London Bridge Street
London SE1 9GF

www.harpercollins.co.uk

This paperback edition 2018

First published in Great Britain in ebook format
by HarperCollins*Publishers* 2018

Copyright © Jackie Baldwin 2018

Jackie Baldwin asserts the moral right to
be identified as the author of this work

A catalogue record for this book
is available from the British Library

ISBN: 978-0-00-829432-8

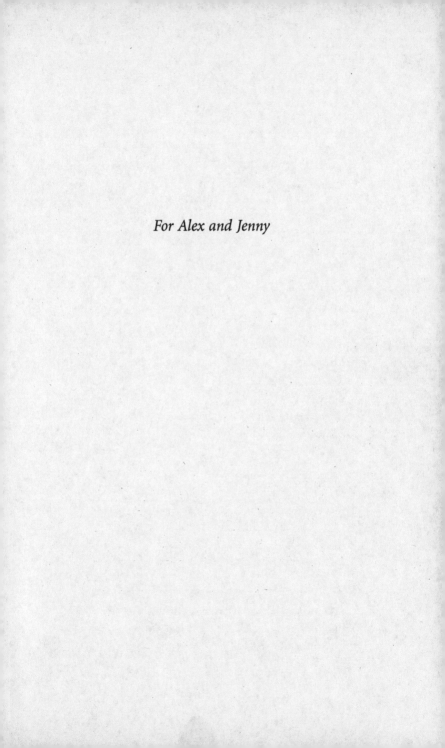

For Alex and Jenny

Prologue

Ailish opened her eyes then closed them again as her head started to throb. She stumbled to her feet, fighting the urge to throw up. Unwelcome flashbacks of the night before painted her face in disgust. Looking at her slight form in the mirror with yesterday's make-up blurring the lines of her face, she felt older than her nineteen years. She glanced at her phone and tears prickled. It was her mother's birthday. She could picture her sister and father laughing and chatting as she opened her presents in Ireland. It was as if she had ceased to exist, such was the disgrace she had rained down on them when she ran off with Patrick, three years ago. He had completely turned her head with all his big talk. She had fancied they would live in London, not the tiny harbour town of Kirkcudbright tucked away in a corner of south-west Scotland. Instead of the romantic existence she had pictured for them, they had wound up living in this glorified hippie commune or, 'The Collective', as they liked to be known. At first it had been fun, exciting even. A world away from the parochial narrow-minded community she had left behind. She had been proud to be Paddy's muse and loved nothing more than to bask in the warmth of his regard as he painted her from various angles.

1

Lately, she had felt Patrick's love receding like an outgoing tide. He was preoccupied and distant and hadn't asked her to pose for him in ages. The atmosphere in the house was different as well. She had a feeling they were all keeping secrets from her and each other. They had always used drugs but lately the drugs had become harder and the parties more forced and a little weirder. There was a powerful undertow dragging them all down to God knows where.

Suddenly, as she looked out of the window, she knew with unusual clarity that she didn't want to be part of this toxic environment anymore. She would lay it on the line with Patrick and ask him to leave with her. He had been holed up in his studio for days now. She'd been warned off disturbing him as he was working on something new. Well, tough! This couldn't wait. He would see sense. He had to.

After a quick shower she threw on her favourite dress and swept up her long curly hair, just as he liked it. A slick of lipstick and a touch of mascara and she was ready to do battle.

She flung open the door to the studio and stood, open mouthed, tears spilling from her eyes as she took in the scene before her. A beautiful young girl stared back at her insolently, maintaining her pose. She was reclining naked on a velvet chaise longue, one arm positioned behind her head. Only the blush of colour staining her chest betrayed her.

Patrick turned round, and their eyes met. He dropped his gaze. There was nothing left to say. Wordlessly, Ailish spun on her heel and left the studio. She was done. It was time to go home and beg for forgiveness.

Standing at the bottom of the drive, her eyes misted with tears, she looked back up at the brooding Victorian house with no sign of the maggots crawling within. She texted her elder sister, Maureen.

'I'm sorry. Please forgive me. I'm on my way home. Ailish. x'

Walking towards the bus stop, she heard her name being called.

Surprised, she glanced behind her. When she saw who it was, she smiled and walked towards him. The bus wasn't due for another hour. She had time.

Soon she was ensconced in a comfy armchair, knees drawn up under her, a warm mug of hot chocolate clasped in her hands. As she poured out her woes he leaned forward attentively. The drink was comforting, strong and sweet.

She paused. She didn't feel so good. Her eyes couldn't focus. She struggled to stand up, but her legs wouldn't support her and she collapsed back onto the chair. Alarmed now, her heart flopped in an irregular rhythm as she tried to make sense of what was happening to her.

'Help me,' she whispered, looking up at him. This couldn't be happening. She didn't understand.

He remained where he was, a creeping malevolence revealing itself to her. She was on the verge of losing consciousness when he picked up her unresisting body and carried her into another room. He laid her on a thick plastic sheet.

A last tear tipped from her eyes.

She would never see her home again.

Chapter One

7th January 2013

DI Frank Farrell glanced across at Mhairi as the police car slid and bumped its way along an icy farm track towards a small stonewashed cottage. It was 10.10 a.m. and the sky was bright with a pale wintery sun. A young police officer who worked out of Kirkcudbright stood in front of the blue and white tape and walked towards them as they parked alongside the SOCO van.

Farrell exited the car with a feeling of dread in his stomach. In his time as a practising Catholic priest, suicides, in particular, always had a profound effect on him. The thought that someone might be driven to die at their own hand was unfathomable.

'SOCO nearly done in there, PC McGhie?'

'Yes, sir, they reckon it's fairly cut and dried. The police surgeon is in there too. Didn't exactly have to look for a pulse. Blood and brains everywhere.'

Farrell quelled him with a look.

'Do we know the name of the deceased yet?'

'Monro Stevenson, according to the opened mail, sir.'

Silently, Mhairi and Farrell suited up in their protective plastic coveralls and overshoes. Even if it was suicide, care had to be taken not to contaminate the scene, just in case.

'Right, let's get this over with,' said Farrell.

He opened the door and entered with Mhairi.

A middle-aged man in a tweed jacket and cords was packing away his stethoscope in a brown leather satchel in the hall. He straightened up as they approached. Farrell noticed that he had an unhealthy greyish tinge to his face and that his hands were shaking.

'Morning, Doctor. DI Farrell and DC McLeod.'

'Dr Allison. Cause appears to be suicide. A terrible business,' he said. 'A patient of mine, as it turns out. He was only twenty-seven.'

'It must be difficult when you know the deceased,' said Mhairi.

'Yes, if only he had come to me. I could have got him some help. Anything to avoid this,' he said, gesturing towards the other room.

'Any chance you can give us an indication of the time of death?' asked Farrell.

'Well, as you know, my role here is restricted to pronouncing life extinct. However, given that rigor is at its peak, I would hazard a guess, strictly off the record, that he died somewhere around fifteen hours ago. However, you'll need to wait for the preliminary findings from the pathologist for any degree of certainty.'

'Thanks, Doctor,' said Farrell. 'I appreciate the heads-up.'

The doctor turned to leave. Farrell approached the two experienced Scene of Crime officers, Janet White and Phil Tait, who were gathering their stuff together at the rear of the hall.

'Janet, what have you got for us?'

'It looks like a suicide,' she said. 'Gun placed in the mouth and trigger pulled. We lifted prints from the gun. Gunshot residue on the right hand of the deceased matches that scenario.'

'There's a note,' Phil said. 'It's in a sealed envelope. We'll get you a copy once we've done the necessary checks back at the station. We've also removed the gun for ballistics analysis.'

'What was it?'

6

'A PPK 380 mm. We recovered the bullet from the wall behind the chair.'

'How on earth did he get hold of one of those in this neck of the woods?'

'Your guess is as good as mine,' shrugged Phil.

'A suicide note,' said Mhairi. 'That means it's unlikely to be a murder?'

'Unless he was coerced, or it was staged,' said Farrell.

A thought occurred to him and he popped his head out the front door.

'PC McGhie, were the lights on or off when you arrived at the scene?'

'Off, sir,' he answered.

Everyone left but Farrell and McLeod. They stood in the doorway to the sitting room. A malodorous smell hung in the air, the coppery scent of blood mingled with gunpowder, faeces, and urine. Not for the first time, Farrell railed at the indignity of death. Wordlessly, he took a small jar out his pocket and offered it to Mhairi. They both smeared menthol beneath their noses to enable them to complete their observations without losing their breakfast; though he figured it might be a close call as he glanced at Mhairi's white face.

There were two wingback chairs either side of an unlit log fire, with a large rectangular mahogany coffee table between them. In one of the chairs a body was slumped. The face was intact, but the back of the head was a tangled mess of hair, blood, and brain tissue. The corpse was stiff, like a mannequin. On the table there was a half-full bottle of malt whisky. An empty glass lay at the deceased's end of the table. Farrell walked into the room and crouched down to examine the table's surface.

'Look,' he said. 'There's a faint glass rim on the opposite side as well. Could suggest that he'd had company earlier in the evening. Look in the kitchen and see if there's a matching crystal glass anywhere. The two rims are the same diameter.'

Mhairi left for the kitchen, and he heard the sound of cupboards opening and closing. A short while later she returned.

'No sign of it, sir.'

'Now, that's odd,' said Farrell.

'Couldn't it simply be that the same glass was moved across the table for some reason?'

'Be a bit of a stretch from his side. No, I reckon he may have had company last night.'

Farrell stood up and turned his attention to the rest of the living room. It was furnished traditionally, with a walnut grandfather clock in one corner, and a carpet in muted greens and gold that had clearly seen better days. There was a photo of a dark-haired smiling young man holding a glass trophy and shaking hands with someone in a suit. Another of him in the middle of two beaming parents. A third showed him with an attractive blonde girl, posing at the top of a snowy mountain in ski gear.

'He looks so happy in those,' said Mhairi. 'Hard to believe he killed himself.'

'Appearances can be deceptive,' said Farrell. 'Whatever happened here, we owe it to his family to determine the truth, however painful it may be to hear.'

'I feel sorry for the cleaner that found him. Imagine happening on this with no warning?' said Mhairi.

'It's as well she did,' said Farrell. 'It doesn't take long for a body to become infested.'

'Where is she now?'

'She's waiting for us at her home. I thought we could pop over and interview her when we're finished here. Give her a chance to calm down and gather her wits together.'

They heard the sound of the mortuary van bumping slowly along the track. Leaving the room, they had a quick look round the rest of the cottage. Mhairi opened a door into a bright and airy studio, which contained a jumble of brightly coloured canvasses.

'He was an artist.'

Farrell studied the works in the room intently. He was no expert in modern art, but the canvasses were visually appealing.

The bedroom was plain with no feminine touches. Only one toothbrush in the bathroom and no prescribed medication to be found.

The sound of muffled voices heralded the arrival of the mortuary van. It was followed by a car that discharged a young officer who looked unfamiliar to Farrell. As he'd been down in the Dumfries area less than a year, there were still plenty of officers sprinkled around the smaller towns and villages he hadn't happened across yet.

'Hey, Paul,' Mhairi, greeted him. 'You here to accompany the body?'

'Drew the short straw for the last waltz,' he said flippantly, before catching sight of Farrell.

Not for the first time, Farrell envied Mhairi her natural ease around people. He nodded awkwardly at the younger man, silenced now by his presence.

Sombrely, the three of them watched together as the corpse was zipped efficiently into a black body bag and loaded into the van. The young officer climbed in as well and the van departed, bumping back down the track bearing the ruined remains of a life.

'And that was …?'

'PC Paul Rossi, sir.'

'We'd better go and interview the cleaner who found the body while it's all still fresh in her mind.'

After a last look round, they locked the door and left.

As they reached the car, Farrell noticed a small cottage on the same side as the one they had just left, about one hundred metres away. It looked fairly rundown, but he could see the flicker of a TV screen through the front window.

'Has anyone interviewed the occupant of that cottage?' he asked PC McGhie.

'No, sir, I didn't even notice it when I arrived because it was still fairly dark then.'

'Right, Mhairi and I will pop by now, just in case the occupant saw or heard anything suspicious.'

'You'd think they'd have heard the gun go off at the very least,' said Mhairi. 'Yet, nobody called it in.'

Chapter Two

They walked along the icy lane to the cottage, the frost biting into their extremities. On the way up the path to the front door, Mhairi's legs shot out from under her and she'd have fallen if Farrell hadn't grabbed her.

He rang the doorbell. An old man opened it and peered out at them from beneath several layers of clothing. He was small and wizened with sharp eyes.

'DI Farrell and DC McLeod. I'm afraid we have some disturbing news.'

'Sandy Millar. I figured as much. You'd best come into the warm,' he said, motioning them through with arthritic fingers to a small lounge where a coal fire was putting up a valiant battle against the frost clinging to the inside of the windows.

DI Farrell and DC McLeod perched on the edge of the hard, threadbare couch while the man settled himself into the chair opposite.

'I'm afraid to tell you that your neighbour, Monro Stevenson, died last night,' said Farrell. 'Did you know him well?'

'I didn't even know his name,' he said with a grimace. 'Though, I'm sorry he's dead. Kept himself to himself, he did. When the snow came last month, he didn't even bother to clear my path or ask if I wanted a bit of shopping.'

'Were you here last night from 5 p.m. onwards?' asked Farrell.

'I'm always here,' he shrugged.

'Did you hear or see anything unexpected?' asked Mhairi.

'I did, as it happens,' he said. 'A car came down the lane around 5 p.m. I looked out the window, as I thought it might be my daughter come to check on me. A big bugger it was. It went by, and I went to make my tea.

'Later, when I was eating, it came back up the lane heading for the main road, but I never paid it no mind.'

'Any chance you could hazard a guess at the make and model?' asked Farrell.

'It was dark, lad.'

'Did you hear anything unexpected?' asked Farrell.

'Not a thing. I had the TV on, mind.'

'Nothing that could have been a gunshot?'

'The lad was shot?'

'A shot may have been fired,' said Farrell.

'No, I definitely didn't hear anything like that. You'd have thought I would have done. The telly wasn't up that loud as I was waiting for my programme to come on.'

'What programme would that be?'

'The six o'clock news.'

'Thank you,' said Farrell, rising to go.

'You've been really helpful,' said Mhairi. 'If anything else comes to you, please contact myself or DI Farrell,' she said, passing him her card.

'Will do, lass,' he said, hobbling to the door to show them out.

'Probably someone got lost and came down here by mistake,' said Mhairi, as they got back in the car. 'Once in the lane they'd have to keep going. The only place wide enough to turn is right at the end.'

'Perhaps,' said Farrell.

* * *

The address Farrell had been given for Fiona Murray was a one-bedroom flat in the centre of Kirkcudbright. The block looked rundown and as if it needed a coat of paint.

Farrell rang the bell and a portly middle-aged woman opened the door. She was as white as a sheet.

'Fiona Murray?'

She nodded. Her eyes were hooded and expressionless.

Still in shock, thought Farrell.

'DI Farrell and DC McLeod. We decided to pop round and save you the bother of coming in to the station,' said Farrell.

'Thank you. That's most considerate. Please, come in.'

She swung the door back and motioned them inside.

The interior of the flat was spotless but spartan in the extreme. There were no personal photos or ornaments, except for a wooden, framed picture of the Virgin Mary on the mantelpiece. Probably the last thing she felt like was dusting round knick-knacks in her line of work, thought Farrell. He sat beside McLeod on the hard sofa, and Fiona Murray dropped straight onto an upright chair facing them.

'It must have been very distressing coming upon a scene like that this morning,' said Farrell. 'Can you confirm what time you found the body?'

'I go in every Monday morning at 9 a.m., set him straight for the week. As soon as I opened the door I could tell something was badly wrong. I found the body and called you lot right away.'

'Was the door locked?' he asked.

'No, it wasn't, now you mention it. Even when he was in he usually had the door locked but not today.'

'Were the lights on when you went in?' asked Farrell.

She stopped to think.

'No, they weren't. I put them on myself when I went in but turned them off when I left. It didn't seem right to light up … well, you know.'

'Were the curtains in the room that you found the body open or shut?' Farrell asked.

'Shut. And I left them that way. I didn't want anyone looking in and seeing him like that.'

'How close did you get to the body?'

'I went right up to him but I could see there was no hope … that he was gone,' she said, her voice flat.

Farrell changed tack, bringing up a photo on his phone of the crystal glass from the table.

'Do you recognize this glass?'

'It looks like one of Monro's. He didn't use them often.'

'How many did he have of this type?'

'Only a couple.'

'Are they both still intact as far as you know?'

'Well I haven't broken one. If he did, I wasn't aware of it.'

'How long have you been working for Monro Stevenson?'

'Just under two years. I answered an ad in the local paper.'

'How well did you know him?' asked Mhairi.

'Well enough. I was his cleaner, not his friend. I'm not the chatty type. I think he liked that. I didn't disturb his concentration when he was working. He kept out from under my feet, paid me on time. It was a suitable arrangement.'

'Were you aware that he owned a handgun?' asked Farrell.

'No, I certainly was not. I never set eyes on such a thing.'

'Had you noticed any shift in Monro's mood of late? Did he seem depressed or worried at all?' asked Farrell.

'Quite the contrary. He seemed in fine fettle. He was very excited about being in the running for that big art prize.'

'What art prize?'

'The Lomax Prize. He said it could launch his career if he won. It's Edinburgh based, I think. A big deal, apparently.'

'What about the girl in the photo on his desk? Was he in a relationship?'

The cleaner shrugged.

'That, I couldn't tell you. I certainly never met her.'

'When you were cleaning, were there any signs that a girl had stayed over?' asked Mhairi.

'I was his cleaner, not a tabloid journalist,' she shot back. 'I wasn't in the habit of snooping around.'

'I wasn't suggesting that,' said Mhairi. 'Please can you answer the question.'

'I never saw any evidence of someone sleeping over,' she replied, her lips compressed as though to hold back the angry words threatening to spill out.

'Did he have any visitors in the past few weeks?'

'I have no idea. None that I was aware of.'

'Thank you for your time, Mrs Murray,' said Farrell standing up. 'I know this has been a difficult morning for you.'

'It's the parents I feel sorry for,' she offered, as she was seeing them out. 'The loss of a child is hard enough to bear without all these unanswered questions.'

Chapter Three

Back in Dumfries, Farrell made his way to DCI Lind's office on the first floor. He walked in with a cursory tap on the door and surprised his boss and old school friend in a look of misery. It melted into a smile so quickly that Farrell wondered if he had imagined it.

'Frank, come away in. What's the score with that body then? Terrible business by the sounds of things.'

'Well, it looks like a classic suicide,' Frank said, taking a seat opposite Lind's desk. 'He appears to have pulled the trigger all right. There was a note.'

'But?'

'Something about it seems off. By all accounts he had everything to live for.'

'Maybe so, but that's no defence against mental illness. He could have been depressed and nobody realized.'

'Possibly. There was also a car passed down the lane a short while before the likely time of death. It stopped too long to have been turning. He may have had a visitor.'

'Maybe they told him something that pushed him over the edge?'

'Or maybe he was murdered and the whole thing was staged?'

'The Super's going to love that theory,' said Lind with a grin.

'He'll go nuclear,' said Farrell.

'You got that right.' DSup Walker wasn't renowned for his calm temperament. 'So, what does your gut tell you?'

'I think we should consider it a suspicious death meantime.'

'Agreed. Get the Major Crime Administration room set up and fix an initial briefing for noon. I'm appointing you as Senior Investigating Officer on this one. Assemble your team and let's get cracking.'

'Right you are,' said Farrell, rising to his feet. He remembered that unguarded look when he had walked in. 'How's Laura?'

'She's doing well, joined a support group.'

'That's good to hear,' said Farrell. Laura and Lind were his oldest friends; their marriage had taken a hammering last year when she had lost a baby at five months.

'I'll hear what you've got so far in a few hours,' said Lind.

Farrell took the hint and left him to it. His next port of call was Detective Sergeant Mike Byers, who was working at his desk in the pokey room he shared with DS Stirling. Personally, he couldn't stand the man. He was casually misogynistic with a gym-sculpted body that spoke to his vanity. However, he had done a solid job of running the MCA room during the Boyd murder case a few months earlier.

'Byers, I need you to open the MCA room and post a briefing there for noon. The death in Kirkcudbright is being treated as suspicious for the time being.'

'I thought he topped himself, sir?'

'We've reason to keep an open mind,' said Farrell.

His stomach growled just as his phone beeped. Time to refuel and take his medication. He headed down to the canteen where he managed to find a limp cheese and pickle sandwich and the muddy dark sludge that passed for coffee. He retreated back to his office and closed the door before sliding out his pill box. Ever since he had come within a whisper of having another breakdown he had been meticulous about taking his maintenance dose of lithium. During their last major case the spectre of insanity had felt his shoulder once more and he had no desire to be reacquainted with that part of his life.

A photocopy of the suicide note was on his desk.

Please forgive me. I have tried to fight this darkness. When I found out about the Lomax Prize I thought it was a lifeline to cling to. I see now that it changes nothing I cannot go on.
    Your loving son,
    Monro

The note was typed and signed in blue ink. The signature was ragged and uneven, which could suggest heightened emotion, Farrell thought.

There was a knock and Mhairi popped her head round the door. He pushed the note across to her, and she sat down to read it in silence.

'How do you feel about being the Family Liaison Officer on this one?'

To his surprise, she was silent, looking torn.

'Spit it out, Mhairi.'

'I would, sir, if it wasn't for what happened to my brother.'

Farrell recalled seeing a picture of a smiling young man in uniform at Mhairi's flat a few months earlier.

'The soldier?'

'Yes. He wasn't killed in Afghanistan.'

'Oh?' The penny dropped.

'He died … later.'

Her face flamed red, and she looked on the verge of tears.

'Suicide?'

'Yes. PTSD, they reckoned.'

'I'm sorry, Mhairi. I'd no idea. Would you prefer to be off the case altogether? It's not a problem.'

18

'No, sir, that won't be necessary. I can work the case. I just don't think I could handle being up close to all that emotion.'

'No worries, there's more than enough work to go round.'

After Mhairi left he pondered who he could appoint as FLO in her place. DC Thomson had recently been made detective but, although hard-working and keen, he didn't yet have the people skills for such a dual role. He had a lot of growing up to do. PC Rosie Green came to mind. She had recently flowed in to the PC-shaped hole left by DC Thomson and seemed fairly robust and sensible.

He phoned downstairs and, five minutes later, there was a brisk knock on the door.

PC Rosie Green was around twenty-five. She had an air of calm competence about her that Farrell felt would be reassuring to the family. Other than that, he really knew very little about her. As far as he was aware she didn't seem to be particularly tight with anyone in the department but was well enough liked.

'Rosie, take a seat,' he said. 'I take it you've heard about the suspicious death in Kirkcudbright early this morning?'

'Yes, sir, only I thought it was a suicide?'

'That remains to be determined,' he said. 'The reason I asked for you is that I'm looking for a FLO for his family and wondered if you might be interested in taking on that role?'

She paused before answering as if she was thinking it through. Farrell liked that quality. Some might mistake it for slowness, but he would rather have a measured response than an off-the-cuff one to be regretted later.

'Yes, sir,' she replied. 'I would definitely be interested.'

'Excellent. I'll make that a formal request then and you can get up to speed with everyone else at the briefing. If you find DS Byers he'll give you a copy of all the information we've gathered to date, which isn't much.'

The phone rang. The parents were here. He asked for them to be shown into the small conference room.

'As it happens the parents have arrived to speak to us. I know you're not yet in possession of all the facts, but could you join us in the conference room?'

'Of course, sir,' she said, rising to her feet.

Chapter Four

He allowed them a few minutes to settle then entered with Rosie. The couple looked to be in their mid-fifties and introduced themselves as George and Doreen. Doreen's eyes were red raw with weeping.

Farrell was pleased to see PC Green immediately took the lead, taking Doreen's hand in hers and offering her condolences. Once the couple had been given their tea, Farrell sat opposite them at the oval table and gently began.

'When was the last time you saw your son?'

'He came for lunch on Wednesday, Inspector. He was on top of the world,' said Doreen, her mouth twisting as she held back tears.

'Any particular reason for that?'

'He'd received word the week before that he'd been shortlisted for the Lomax Prize, a major art award. His career was about to take off. It was all starting to happen for him.'

'How many people knew he'd been shortlisted?'

'Probably half of Dumfries by the time she'd done shouting about it,' said George, giving his wife an affectionate pat on the arm. 'She was that proud of him.'

'When did you last speak to him?' asked Farrell.

'He normally phoned on a Sunday evening, no matter what,' Doreen said. 'But we didn't hear from him last night. Now we know why.' A thought occurred, and she turned to her husband, her hand over a mouth stretched in agony.

'Oh God, George, maybe if we'd phoned him, instead of letting it go, we could have stopped him, changed his mind.' She broke down once more, and PC Green put her arm around her making low soothing noises.

'You mustn't think like that,' said Farrell.

'We thought he must be out celebrating still with friends, didn't want to cramp his style,' said his father.

'Could you give a list of his friends' names and addresses to PC Rosie Green, as soon as is convenient? They might be able to help us with filling in a timeline.'

'Well, the thing is, we've never met any of them,' said Doreen. 'Not his artist friends anyway. There are a couple of lads he was at school with in Dumfries that he saw once in a blue moon.'

'I see,' said Farrell. 'Did Monro have a girlfriend?'

'He'd been seeing a Dumfries girl, Nancy Quinn, for a couple months,' said Doreen. 'We met her once and she seemed nice enough. They went skiing together in December.'

'Had he ever suffered from depression?'

His parents looked at each other.

'You might as well, tell me,' said Farrell. 'We'll have to request his medical records as part of our enquiries.'

'He suffered from depression a few years ago. He got in with a group of artists,' said Doreen.

'Bloody hippie commune, more like,' said George. 'From what I could gather they spent as much time on sex and drugs as they did on their art.'

'It didn't suit him,' said Doreen. 'He wasn't brought up to that kind of lifestyle. He became very low and so we fetched him home. A few months later he was right as rain. He never looked back, did he George?'

'How long ago was this?' asked Farrell.

'Three years or so,' replied Doreen.

'Painted up a storm ever since. A new girlfriend as well. For him to kill himself now? Well it doesn't make any sense, does it?' said George.

Farrell was inclined to agree with him, but kept his counsel.

PC Green leaned forward.

'Doreen have you been in touch with Nancy yet?'

She shook her head, eyes welling with tears once more.

'Not yet. We thought it best to come in first, so we had some proper information to give her. She lives in Dumfries, so we'll head there after this.'

'We'll need her contact details,' said Farrell.

Doreen rooted about in her handbag and wrote them down on a scrap of paper, which she then passed across.

'The note,' said George. 'We need to know what it said.'

Wishing he could spare them this pain, Farrell opened the file in front of him and passed a copy across.

Doreen burst into tears and leant against her husband for support. George, however, kept staring at the letter, his brows drawn together as though puzzled.

Farrell leaned forward, sensing his hesitation.

'Something's not right about the signature. It's like it is his writing but it's not his writing at the same time,' he said. 'Sorry, I'm not making any sense. Doreen, love what do you think?'

She visibly pulled herself together and stared at the words again.

'I know what you mean but I can't put my finger on it.'

'There was an almost empty bottle of whisky found beside him. It's possible he'd been drinking,' said Farrell.

'No way!' said George. 'He loathed the stuff. Our son was raised in a working-class home, Inspector. He was a beer drinker. He might have had the odd nip to be sociable, but I don't see him sitting there, knocking it back on his own.'

Farrell noticed it was close to noon. Time to wrap things up.

'I can promise you one thing,' he said. 'At this stage we're keeping an open mind and considering all possibilities. I'll leave you in the capable hands of PC Green, who has now been appointed as your Family Liaison Officer and will keep you advised of any further developments.'

'Once you've seen Mr and Mrs Stevenson out, I'd like you to come straight back up for the briefing,' he said to PC Green.

'Yes, sir.'

Farrell walked along to the briefing with a heavy heart. He knew he should be relatively immune to the suffering of parents after all these years in the force, but their grief always burrowed its way under his skin.

Chapter Five

Farrell walked in to the MCA room and held up his hand for silence. He noticed a few puzzled faces wondering why they were investigating an apparently open-and-shut case with such vigour. The crime scene photos had been put up on the wall. They showed the deceased slumped over in the chair with the gun on the floor beside him. A copy of the suicide note was up there as well, together with a picture of the whisky bottle and glass on the table.

'This may or may not be a case of suicide,' he stated. 'Although there are some aspects that support a theory of suicide, there are certain elements that don't fit with that scenario.

'The preliminary time of death suggests that he died around fifteen hours before he was found by Mrs Murray, at 9 a.m. Rigor was at its peak when the doctor examined him thirty minutes later. That would suggest he died at around 6.30 p.m. the night before. It would have been pitch-black, yet the lights were off and the curtains closed.'

'Was there a lamp near the body that he could have switched off at the last minute?' asked DS Byers.

'There was a standard lamp beside the opposite chair, but not at the one he was sitting in. The other seat was also more worn,

25

which tends to suggest it was where he normally sat. In addition, there were two rim marks on the table, but only one glass. According to the cleaner he had two crystal glasses, but we only found one.'

The faces before him still looked blank.

'It could be suicide, but we need to exclude foul play and, at the moment, I feel far from being able to do that,' he said.

'Did he have a history of depression?' asked DS Stirling.

'Once, a few years ago, according to the parents but nothing recently. Can you requisition the medical records? Phone the police surgeon, Joe Allison, Kirkcudbright. Monro Stevenson was his patient as it happens.'

Stirling nodded and made a note. The oldest officer in the room, he was counting down the months to his retirement.

'A neighbour also mentioned a car going down the lane not long before the likely time of death. There's no way out from that lane but, rather than doubling back straight away, it didn't return for a while. So he may have had a visitor in the hour leading up to his death.'

Farrell noticed PC Green slipping into the back.

'I've appointed PC Rosie Green as FLO, everyone. If you need anything from the family, try and go through her as much as possible.

'His parents indicated that he had been shortlisted for a major art award, the Lomax Prize. DS Byers, can you run that down? Get a list of the other shortlisted candidates and see if they might think it was worth their while to kill the opposition? Find out how much prestige and/or cash was up for grabs?'

Byers nodded.

'We also require to track down a handwriting expert. His parents seemed to think there was something a bit off about the signature on the suicide note. We need to obtain some samples of his normal handwriting, including his signature. DC Thomson, can you deal with that?'

26

'Yes, sir.'

Newly made up Detective Constable Thomson was so eager it was painful to watch. Tall and lanky, he looked like he was still growing in to his body. Despite his enthusiasm, Farrell still wasn't sure that the lad had what it took to be a detective. Time would tell.

'Did he have a laptop, sir?' asked DS Byers.

'Yes, we recovered one from the cottage,' said Farrell. 'It was password protected so it's been handed in to the Tech boys.'

'Be interesting to see if he saved a copy of the note,' said Byers.

'If not, then it might suggest the possibility that it was brought there by someone else and he was coerced into signing it. Good thinking. Let me know the outcome. We'll reconvene at 6 p.m.'

Byers nodded.

Farrell had no sooner got sat behind his desk when DS Walker marched in. It was like being visited by a short, red-haired Darth Vader, he reflected, as the air temperature seemed to drop a couple of degrees.

'What's this I hear about you fannying around with this suicide and whipping it up into a murder investigation?'

Never one for the social niceties, the Super. Preoccupied with the massive changes being wrought by the centralization of the Scottish police force, his bad temper was permanently bubbling under the surface. Judging by the smell of stale whisky that had preceded him into the room, he might be drowning his sorrows in alcohol. Officers like him, who had joined straight out of school and bludgeoned their way up through the ranks, were something of a rarity now.

'It's not a murder investigation, yet, sir,' said Farrell. 'However, there are some unanswered questions.'

'Well, get on with it, man. I don't want this case turning into the same Horlicks that we had last year. I want it wrapped up, pronto.'

Farrell became aware that he was grinding his teeth.

'I'll do what I can, sir,' he snapped.

The two men looked at each other for a long moment before the Super turned on his heel and left. Farrell knew that he was partly to blame for their antagonistic relationship, but the man never missed an opportunity to rile him. Walker harboured a deep mistrust of him, due to the fact he was still a Roman Catholic priest, albeit no longer practising. A bigot through and through, he couldn't trust what he didn't understand. The events of last year hadn't helped matters.

There was a light tap at his door and DI Kate Moore popped her head round it.

'Got a minute?'

'For you? Always,' he said. 'What can I do for you, Kate?'

She sank gracefully onto the chair in front of his desk, her lovely grey eyes regarding him. They had grown closer of late, but he still felt he had barely scraped the surface, as she was so reserved.

'I heard about that poor young man this morning,' she said.

'It may not be what it seems, Kate,' he said. 'My gut's telling me there's more to it than a simple suicide.'

'You suspect foul play?'

'Possibly. Can't rule it out yet.'

'Odd that it happened in Kirkcudbright. You know that case I'm working on, the forgery one?'

'Vaguely,' said Farrell.

'Well, the latest intel from Glasgow is that the forger may be somewhere in the Kirkcudbright area. We caught a break a couple of days ago. A tractor and trailer was involved in an accident on the A75. The driver legged it from the scene, but a forged Hornel painting was recovered beneath the hay bales.'

'Hornel? Isn't that the post-impressionist artist that lived in Broughton House, in Kirkcudbright?'

'The one and the same. I didn't have you down for an art buff?'

'I'm not,' he said. 'Took my mother for lunch in Kirkcudbright in December. She wanted a whirl around the house and garden. Not my cup of tea,' he said.

She smiled at him, and he felt those level grey eyes stare right into his soul. After so many years of estrangement from the indomitable Yvonne Farrell, Kate knew that a day trip marked a significant thaw on both sides.

'The man from this morning,' he said, suddenly diverted by a thought that had just struck him. 'He was an artist, a pretty good one by all accounts. You don't think he was involved in your case at all, do you?'

'I highly doubt it. Throw a stick in Kirkcudbright and you'll hit an artist. That's what it's known for. It's officially designated as an Artists' Town.'

'True. I might want to poke around in your files at a later date, though.'

'Be my guest.' She stood up to go. Cool, elegant, unreachable.

They heard a commotion further along the corridor with muttered apologies and the sounds of files clattering onto the floor.

'That would be Mhairi back then,' she said with a raised eyebrow.

'I'd put money on it,' Farrell muttered, striding to the door and opening it.

Mhairi came charging in, laden with folders, almost cannoning in to DI Moore.

'Oops, sorry, ma'am, didn't see you there. Is this a bad time?'

'We should really put a bell around your neck to warn of your approach, Mhairi,' said DI Moore, as she left the room.

Mhairi looked offended and stuck out her tongue at Kate's departing back, then swung around abashed as she remembered Farrell.

'I saw that,' he said.

'Sorry, sir, I like DI Moore. But, she's always so perfect and unruffled. Shows the rest of us up.'

Farrell suspected that DI Moore's apparent serenity, rather like his own, had been hard won; although he didn't share that thought with Mhairi.

'When's the post-mortem, sir?'

'Tomorrow at nine. You volunteering?'

'No, sir!' she looked horrified.

'I'll take that as a yes, then. Seriously, Mhairi, you have to get used to them. Once you're made up to sergeant, you'll be expected to attend.'

'Fine,' she sighed. 'I'll come.'

'I reckon we should nip back out to Kirkcudbright for a look around the scene again. It'll be easier to be objective now that the body's been removed.'

Chapter Six

Less than an hour later they were driving back down the country lane to the cottage. The pale watery sun had done nothing to melt the icy ground. Farrell groaned as he rounded a bend and saw a media truck blocking the way. Sophie Richardson from *Border News* was trying to sweet talk her way past a bewildered Sandy Millar. A young man was holding a fuzzy microphone aloft while another was laying down cables. Trying to keep the lid on his temper, Farrell slid to a halt and sprang out the car.

'Ms Richardson, your truck is blocking the way to and from a crime scene. I need you to move it. Right now, please.' He stood and glared at her with folded arms.

'Mr Millar, I suggest you get back inside out of the cold.'

The old man scurried indoors looking relieved.

The reporter scowled then reassembled her features into a winning smile.

'Here we go. Full charm offensive,' muttered Farrell out of the side of his mouth to Mhairi who had joined him.

As she walked towards them, he felt an answering smile appear on his face. But only because he was amused to see that beneath her designer baby pink suit there was a pair of matching pink designer wellies.

'DI Farrell, how lovely to meet you again, but in such sad circumstances. A tragic loss of a young life. I believe he shot himself?'

Farrell noticed the man with the fuzzy microphone again, this time it was hovering overhead.

'As I'm sure that you're aware, all I am at liberty to say is that we are treating the matter as a suspicious death and our enquiries are ongoing. Now, unless you and your team wish to be on the news for obstructing police officers in the execution of their duty, I suggest you leave the vicinity at once. You have ten minutes to go down to the turning area and get away from this lane.'

They jumped into the Citroen and followed the news truck as it attempted to navigate the potholes.

'That woman is such a pain,' said Mhairi.

'Once *Border News* have run with it, the nationals will be circling like vultures,' said Farrell, with a sigh, pulling up in front of Monro's cottage.

He fancied the garden had wilted a little since their last visit. Mhairi shivered beside him.

'It always gives me the creeps going back into where someone has died violently. I get the feeling that part of them is still hovering, watching us.'

Farrell turned the heavy key in the lock, and the door swung open. They entered. He looked behind the door, frowning.

'Don't you think that's a ridiculous amount of security for a country cottage in the middle of nowhere?'

Mhairi glanced at the series of locks and raised her eyebrows.

'Definitely overkill. I'll ask PC McGhie to get on to the landlord and see if he put the locks there or if it was the deceased.'

The miasma of death still hung in the air. Farrell tried to ignore it as he slowly walked around, looking for anything that might have been missed. There was no sign of the second crystal glass. It was always the small things he found so poignant. A half-finished packet of biscuits, the milk in the fridge, a library book waiting to be returned. A life with its forward motion cut short.

Mhairi shouted to him from the bedroom.

'Sir, come and have a look at this.'

She was rifling through a notepad.

'He had started working on an acceptance speech. According to his diary, the awards dinner for the shortlisted candidates was due to take place on the first of March.'

'Doesn't exactly square with him killing himself,' said Farrell. 'Most people in his position would want to stick around and see what happened. If he'd shot himself afterwards, in a fit of artistic pique, that would be more understandable. Bag up that notepad as evidence. We can compare the handwriting with the suicide note to check that it's genuine.'

Mhairi turned to the antique chest at the foot of the bed and opened it. She pulled out a framed photo of a young woman with long dark hair and an engaging smile. It had clearly been taken in summer. She was wearing shorts and a halter-neck top. Wrapped in an oilskin cloth was a canvas containing a nude portrait of the same woman, executed with considerable skill. It was unsigned.

'I wonder who this is?'

'Well it looks nothing like the girl he was seeing recently,' said Farrell. 'She was blonde, if she's the one in the skiing photo. Possibly a previous girlfriend? I'm guessing she ended it rather than him, or he might not have hung on to these mementoes.'

Their final stop was in the spare room, which was flooded with light reflecting off whitewashed walls. Several canvasses were mounted on the walls and there were many works in progress stacked around the room. They both stared at the riot of colour.

'He was good, wasn't he?' said Mhairi. 'Even though I know nothing at all about art, they kind of take your breath away. What will happen about the competition now, sir?'

'I don't know, depends on the rules. You might want to ask

DS Byers to check that out. If his entry is null and void then it could provide a motive.'

Sombrely they locked up and returned to the car.

'How's the studying going, Mhairi?' asked Farrell.

She groaned and shook her head.

'Don't ask. As if I wasn't depressed enough.'

'It's not that bad, surely?' asked Farrell looking worried, as they got in his dumpy Citroen. He turned the ignition, it spluttered into life, and he coaxed it back down the icy track to the main road.

He had encouraged Mhairi to put in for her sergeant's exam, as he felt she was more than capable. If she had a focus it might help her curtail her chaotic private life. She was in her late twenties which he'd thought was the ideal age to be going for the promotion. Maybe the added pressure was making things worse?

'It's not the work, exactly. It's just that between job and studying I hardly have time to see Ian.'

'Ian?'

'I met him back in November.'

'You kept that quiet.'

'I know. Didn't want to jinx it.'

'Good guy, is he?'

'The best. Perfect gentleman. A rare breed these days, present company excepted,' she said with a glance at her boss.

'That's great! What does he do?'

'He's a freelance writer, and he's taking a sabbatical to work on his novel.'

He worried about Mhairi more than he should but ever since her fiancé had dumped her, when she missed their rehearsal dinner because of work, she had tried to bury her heartbreak in meaningless flings. It had been tearing a hole in her soul not to mention causing gossip around the station. This new chap sounded promising.

'We're going out tonight for a meal, if I manage to get away on time.'

'Make sure you scoot off straight after the briefing then.'

'I'll try, but I've got a "To Do" list longer than my arm,' she said.

'You've still got to make the time for things that are important,' he said.

'I love how you don't practise what you preach, sir,' she said.

He contented himself with an enigmatic look.

It was true. Since all that business last year, he had become something of a hermit, but that was also because he felt the lure of his long-dormant vocation, tugging him back to active service as a priest once more. He had shared these feelings with no one. Not even his spiritual adviser and dear friend, Father Joe Spinelli. He needed to be sure he was returning to his vocation for the right reasons and not simply hiding from the pain and trauma of recent events.

As they reached the outskirts of Dumfries, where the River Nith wound along like a serpent beneath the bypass, he was jolted from his reverie.

'Actually, I bumped into Laura on Saturday night in Spoons.'

'Oh yeah?' said Farrell. 'There with Lind, was she?'

'No, she was out with some woman. A right party animal. Do her good to get out and let her hair down, what with all she's been through after losing the baby and the stuff with the twins. I took it as a good sign,' said Mhairi.

Farrell wasn't so sure.

Chapter Seven

Once back at the station, he logged in the extra evidence bags and headed down to the MCA room to prepare for the last briefing of the day. The small investigative team had started to filter through.

He'd put DS Stirling in charge of HOLMES in the MCA room, as much to keep him out of harm's way as anything else. He was just months off retirement and so risk averse he was useless in the field, as Farrell had discovered last year. His experience would be useful in here.

A few minutes before 6 p.m., Mhairi slipped in, causing Farrell to do a double take. She must *really* like this bloke. She was wearing a red jersey dress that fell to her knees, with navy heels, and a dark wool coat over one arm. He wasn't the only one to look twice. Mhairi was known for vamping it up when she went out. This signalled a change of gear.

'You must be Mhairi's classier sister,' said DS Byers, attracting glares from everyone. It was no secret that he had the hots for Mhairi, and her continued rejection made him spiteful.

Mhairi ignored him and lifted her chin.

'Right then,' said Farrell. 'Let's get started.' He nodded a greeting as DI Moore slipped in at the back.

'Stirling, can you find out what details you can about a group of artists going by the name of The Collective, in Kirkcudbright. The deceased was involved with them a few years ago. Ascertain where they were based? If they're still in existence?'

'Sir,' Stirling replied.

'PC Green, can you arrange for the girlfriend, Nancy Quinn, to come in and be interviewed? Apart from the picture of them both on a skiing holiday, there was no sign of her presence in the cottage. Seems a little odd in this day and age,' said Farrell.

'DS Byers, have you managed to obtain a list of the shortlisted candidates, and is the prize worth killing over?'

'Fifty grand, but the prestige attached to this competition is immeasurable. It's launched the careers of quite a few well-known names into the stratosphere. Turns out another two of the six shortlisted authors live in Kirkcudbright, Hugo Mortimer and Paul Moretti. I've got addresses for them both from the organizers.'

'Good work. McLeod and I will track them down tomorrow. Stirling, any joy with the medical records?'

'Dr Allison wasn't in the surgery. The practice manager was a bit reluctant, at first, but I banged on about the public interest, and then the deceased's mother got on the phone. I have them here.'

'Anything relevant?'

'Well, no terminal illness or the like. He did suffer from a major bout of depression about three years ago. There was a fairly half-hearted suicide attempt with some pills, but he appeared to recover well and was on no current medication.'

'OK then,' said Farrell. 'Good work, we'll wrap it up there for tonight.'

He paused as DI Moore raised her hand and walked forward.

'If I could say a few words, Frank?'

'Be my guest,' he said, standing aside.

'As some of you will be aware, I've been involved in an investigation into a forging racket being run out of this area. We

37

suspect that the forger may be hiding in Kirkcudbright, camouflaged within the many artists there. I know that it will involve an increased workload, but I'd like a couple of volunteers to straddle both investigations in case there is any overlap.'

Both Mhairi and DC Thomson stuck their hands up.

'Excellent, can you spare a few minutes after the briefing to get you started?'

Mhairi looked tense and glanced at her watch.

'Actually, on second thoughts, let's make it my office at eight, tomorrow,' said DI Moore.

It had been a long day. Farrell felt weariness settle in his bones like sediment as he headed back home to Kelton. The full moon illuminated the frost in the fields and hedges giving the countryside an ethereal air. Despite the cold, he opened the window to clear his head.

As he pulled in to the space in front of his cottage, he nodded and smiled at a small group of neighbours, bundled up against the cold, standing chatting a few doors down. He knew he should approach them, but had never found it easy to insert himself into conversation with others.

As soon as he opened the door, Henry was there to greet him, doing his best imitation of a fat, hairy anaconda as he wrapped his plump black-and-white body around Farrell's legs and squeezed, purring loudly.

'Is it you or your tummy that's pleased to see me?' asked Farrell, bending down to pick him up. Henry had been one of Mhairi's more hare-brained schemes to help him recover from the traumatic events last year, but they had settled into a comfortable routine now. He was undemanding company.

Last year he had fallen heavily for Clare Yates, a forensic psychiatrist consulting on the case, but it had not ended well. Since then, he had been retreating deeper and deeper into himself, feeling the tug back to a more ascetic life.

After he fed and made a fuss of Henry, he shed his suit and pulled on his winter running gear. The cold air hit him like a slap as he ran up the lane, turning right along the road towards Glencaple. His stride lengthened as his long limbs uncoiled from hours of desk work and the adrenalin fired up his muscles for a last explosive burst of energy. He pushed away the images of the lifeless face that kept appearing in his head like some macabre pop-up advert. He couldn't believe that Monro Stevenson had taken his own life. It didn't make any kind of sense. He'd been murdered. He was sure of it.

Back at the cottage, he had a steaming hot shower to soothe his aching muscles then pulled on faded jeans and a sweatshirt and padded through to the sitting room. Upstairs he had stunning views over the estuary. Tonight, he shut the darkness of the night out by drawing the curtains and lit the log fire to take the chill off the air. Pouring a small whisky and putting on some Gregorian chants, he stretched out on the sofa. Henry promptly joined him, purring contentedly. He stroked him absentmindedly.

Another murder investigation then. There was none of the thrill of the chase he used to feel while working in Edinburgh. Had the events of last year burnt him out completely? His mind shifted to Lind, married to Laura, the girl he had reluctantly left behind when he set off for the seminary. She had recently lost her baby and was taking time to come to terms with it. Lind was worried about something and hiding it. He should offer to babysit, enable them to get out more. That might help. They had been so happy together when he first arrived back in town. He fervently hoped that his return had not acted as some kind of catalyst for the problems they were experiencing in their marriage.

Chapter Eight

Mhairi walked from Loreburn Street to The Caven's Arms, where she was due to meet Ian. As she entered the pub, the warmth hit her after the cold outside. Ian waved from a table at the back, and she made her way over to him. He greeted her with a kiss, as she shrugged off her coat. There was a glass of white wine already waiting for her. She picked it up and took a large swallow.

'God, I needed that,' she said.

'Bad day?' he asked, eyes crinkling in concern. 'I caught *Border News*. Kind of weird to turn on the telly and see your girlfriend looking all kickass,' he grinned.

'That Sophie Richardson is a monster,' Mhairi said. 'Underneath that baby pink exterior beats the heart of a pirate.'

Ian laughed.

'I mean it!' she said.

'I know. That's what's so funny.'

'I hate bloody journalists.'

Ian looked taken aback by her vehemence.

'What have they ever done to you?'

'Shortly before you moved down here, I was involved in a couple of high-profile cases. Despite us all busting our chops to catch those responsible, the press turned public opinion against us and made our job ten times harder.'

'That must have been tough,' he said.

'So tough, my boss nearly had a nervous breakdown.'

'Frank Farrell?'

'I didn't say that,' she said, glaring at him. 'Anyway, when I saw Sophie Richardson today, it brought it all back to me.'

Ian squeezed her hand.

'It must have been tough seeing that poor bloke this morning.'

'It goes with the job. I reckon traffic has it worse than we do. The things they have to deal with …'

'I can't imagine ever being in such a bad place that I'd consider killing myself,' said Ian.

'If he did,' muttered Mhairi.

'But, I thought …?'

'Leave it, Ian. I don't want to talk about work.'

'Then let's not. Hurry up and decide what you're having. I'm starving!'

He was entertaining company, with a wicked sense of humour, and the rest of the evening flew by. A few short months ago, she would have felt the need to get steaming on a date. With Ian, she could simply relax and be herself.

You're getting in too deep, a little voice whispered in her ear. He'll let you get close and then abandon you. Everyone does.

Chapter Nine

Mhairi almost skipped along the corridor to her meeting with DI Moore the next morning. Ian was such a gentleman. He had insisted on paying for dinner but, unlike a lot of lowlifes out there, he hadn't thought he was paying for something else as well. A goodnight kiss that made her go weak at the knees had rounded off the evening nicely. In fact, Mhairi had had to exercise supreme willpower not to drag him into her flat and rip his clothes off. Even Farrell would approve of Ian, she thought.

DI Moore was sitting behind her desk. She took in Mhairi's fresh eyes and appearance and welcomed her with a wide smile. Dave Thomson was on the edge of his seat, notepad and pen at the ready.

'Thank you for volunteering, both of you,' she said, handing each of them a folder with summaries of the case to date.

'This art forgery investigation began in Glasgow but has effectively ended up on our patch. Not much is known other than the fact that there appears to be an incredibly talented forger hiding out in Kirkcudbright. Up until a couple of days ago we had no idea of how the paintings were being moved around, though it would seem that they make their way to Ireland and from there are transported all over the world. When the operation started they probably simply smuggled them on the ferry in cars, but since the Port Authority has been taking an active interest, it's likely that they are employing other methods.'

'Bit like looking for a needle in a haystack, ma'am,' commented Mhairi. 'There's about a gazillion miles of uninhabited coastline they could launch from. Not to mention all the sailing clubs in the area.'

'You said that a forged Hornel was recovered, ma'am?' said DC Thomson.

'Yes?'

'Well, isn't it likely the forger took the opportunity to visit Broughton House on several occasions to study his work?'

'Possibly,' said DI Moore.

'I know there's not much CCTV coverage in Kirkcudbright, but what about at the museum itself? There could be innocent reasons why someone might visit multiple times, but it could point us in the right direction,' said DC Thomson.

'Perhaps you could contact the museum and ask? It's owned by the National Trust, I believe.'

'Yes, ma'am,' he said, scribbling once more.

God, was I ever that keen? Mhairi smiled to herself.

A thought occurred to her.

'How do we know that the Hornel recovered is a forgery and not the real deal?'

'Because luckily the National Trust had a restoration team working at the museum and they confirmed that the original was still there and undisturbed. They did comment on examining ours that it was a very skilful copy and that only an expert would be any the wiser.'

'If the forgery ring is operating out of Kirkcudbright, is there anyone who can give us the low-down on any potential suspects?' asked Mhairi.

'I was coming on to that. Fortunately, we have Lionel Forbes, art historian and critic, in the locality,' DI Moore murmured,

43

going a little pink. 'He's extremely knowledgeable regarding the local art scene, and the Super has authorized his use as a consultant as and when necessary. However, he's also indicated that we're not to reveal operational details to Mr Forbes for the time being, given that he lives within the community that we are investigating.'

'Could I have his contact details in case we need to ask him anything in relation to the Monro Stevenson case?' asked Mhairi.

'Certainly,' replied Moore, rattling them off without consulting her notes. 'He's very generous with his time. A real asset to the investigation.'

Is he now? thought Mhairi her antennae twitching.

After the meeting was over, her next stop was Farrell's office. Through the open door she could see him writing furiously, lost in what he was doing. She waited a few seconds until he sensed her presence and looked up with a start.

'Mhairi McLeod, are you trying to give me a heart attack? If you're not bowling along corridors like a wrecking ball, you're materializing out of thin air like a ghost.'

She glared at him. Honestly, there was no pleasing some people and there was her trying to be considerate. She felt her rosy glow start to dissipate.

'Hadn't we better get off to the post-mortem, sir? Bartle-White said he was planning to start at nine sharp.'

Farrell glanced at his watch and sprang up out of his seat as though electrified.

'I hadn't realized the time! After the PM, I think we should head straight to Kirkcudbright and take a look at the other two local shortlisted artists.'

'You really think someone would kill to get closer to winning that prize?'

'People have killed for a lot less, Mhairi.'

'While we're there, sir, it might be worth speaking to Lionel Forbes, art historian. According to DI Moore, he's a big cheese

44

in the art world. He might be familiar with the artists on the list.'

'Good idea. Maybe you can phone ahead and arrange for us to look in on him?'

'Will do.'

Farrell stood up and put his jacket on.

'Nice meal, last night?' he asked.

Mhairi knew that wasn't what he was really asking. She knew he worried about her. In fact he had made her worry about herself.

'Excellent, went to The Caven's Arms. Have you been?'

As soon as the words were out of her mouth she regretted them. She knew her boss never went anywhere except round to DCI Lind's for the odd meal. She suspected he was lonely.

'No, I'll have to check it out,' he said.

'Maybe DI Moore would like to check it out as well?' she blurted out.

Farrell's jaw tightened.

'I'm sure DI Moore is more than capable of organizing her own social life,' he snapped. 'As am I.'

Ouch, message received loud and clear, thought Mhairi, subsiding into silence. He never used to be this grumpy.

45

Chapter Ten

Farrell and McLeod entered the mortuary via the back entrance to Dumfries and Galloway Royal Infirmary. They nodded at one of the local undertakers who was leaving as they arrived.

Once inside, they were shown into the well-equipped examination room where Bartle-White was already positioned beside the body. As always, he cut an imposing figure.

'Excellent! I can't abide tardiness,' he said, glancing at the clock, which showed one minute to nine o'clock.

The room smelled of formaldehyde with unpleasant undertones of blood and other bodily fluids.

Bartle-White, a tall but stooped man with a taste for bow ties, wasted no time on small talk and got straight to work.

'Gunshot wound to upper palate is clearly the cause of death. Far more effective than a shot fired into the temple, as it targets the cerebellum resulting in immediate death,' he said. 'I believe the gun recovered was a PPK 380 mm?'

'Yes, that's right,' said Farrell. 'A single bullet was recovered at the scene.'

Bartle-White busied himself once more on Stevenson's ruined head.

Farrell glanced at Mhairi and saw that she was pale but composed.

'As I expected,' muttered the pathologist.

Farrell bit his tongue. Bartle-White was old school and did not tolerate interruptions to his train of thought.

After a few more uncomfortable moments, he suddenly stood upright.

'The exit wound is consistent with a single shot having been fired. I assume that will be the one recovered from the scene?'

'The bullet and the gun are both with ballistics,' confirmed Farrell.

The rest of the post-mortem revealed nothing untoward. As expected for a young man of his age, his organs were healthy and no other possible cause of death was found. His stomach contents were sent off for analysis along with all the other samples taken.

'There was a near-empty bottle of whisky beside him,' said Farrell. 'I'd like to know if there's any evidence that he consumed it? Also, if there's any evidence of drugs in his system?'

'I can't help you there until we get the results back from toxicology. Currently, they're taking around four weeks to process. However, judging by the healthy state of his liver, I would doubt very much that he was in the habit of drinking to excess. Are you saying he was a drug user? I saw no evidence of that.'

'No, I was more wondering along the lines of whether his drink could have been spiked and then the suicide staged while he was unconscious or incapacitated.'

'Good heavens, isn't that a bit of a stretch?'

'Perhaps,' said Farrell. 'Perhaps not.'

'I'll try and put a rush on the toxicology results, but I can't promise anything.'

'Appreciated.'

'It seems pretty clear cut to me,' said Mhairi, glancing at her boss as they got back in the car.

'It seems that way,' said Farrell. 'There's just a few things about it that feel wrong to me.'

47

Chapter Eleven

Less than two hours later, Farrell parked his car at the harbour in Kirkcudbright, opposite the Tourist Office. The tide was in and the fishing boats bobbed gently up and down with an attendant mob of hungry seagulls screeching overhead. There was a strong smell of fish mingled with the salty tang of the sea. Mhairi consulted the map on her phone and started walking.

'I think it's over here.'

They stopped in front of a whitewashed building with the words 'Kirkcudbright Art Gallery', painted in eggshell blue on a piece of driftwood. A bell tinkled as they entered. Inside, a middle-aged woman, her face wreathed in smiles, got off the stool, where she had been knitting, and came forward to greet them.

'Janet Campbell, gallery owner, how can I help you?'

Farrell produced his warrant card, and the smile disappeared.

'Is this about that poor boy, Monro?'

'Did you know him?' asked Farrell.

'That I did. I have one of his paintings in the gallery.'

'When was the last time you saw him?' asked Mhairi.

'Let me see, now. It would be a week past Monday. He popped in to let me know he'd been shortlisted for the Lomax Prize. He was so excited. That's why I can't believe he would've wanted to kill himself. It makes no sense.'

'Aside from last week, how was his demeanour generally?' asked Farrell.

'He seemed happy enough. Like most creative types, he would hit a slump from time to time but, in the main, he appeared to be fine.'

'Could you show us his painting, please?'

She led them upstairs to a light-filled space and over to a corner. The canvas depicted the same dark-haired girl as the picture they had found wrapped in the deceased's bedroom. This time, she was sitting in a field of poppies, oozing vitality, smiling into a hand-held mirror as she brushed her hair.

'Look closer,' said Janet.

Mhairi exhaled as they realized that the reflection in the mirror didn't match. It showed the same girl but looking haunted, with bruised eyes and sunken cheeks.

'Do you know anything about the model?' asked Farrell.

'I met her a few times; she came in with Monro.'

'Were they ever an item, as far as you know?' asked Mhairi.

'They were just friends, I think. He was obviously keen on her, but she was involved with Patrick Rafferty up at Ivy House.'

'Is she still there?' asked Farrell.

'No, she disappeared into thin air. Ran off one morning three years ago and no one has seen or heard anything from her since. Her folks reckoned something bad happened to her. The sister came over, put up posters; the family even offered a reward for information, but nothing came of it.'

'I see it has a "Sold" sticker,' said Farrell, pointing to the red dot.

'Yes, it sold a few months after she went missing. The owner requested that it should remain on show here in the gallery in exchange for a modest annual sum.'

'Who is the owner?' asked Farrell.

'I'm afraid I couldn't tell you. It was all arranged through an Edinburgh solicitor.'

'Isn't that rather unusual?' asked Mhairi.

'Yes, I suppose it is,' Janet smiled. 'Can't afford to look a gift horse in the mouth though.'

'The main reason we came here was to speak to Paul Moretti, and this was the address given for his studio?' said Farrell.

'He used to rent the studio flat from me, at the back of the gallery, but he left over three years ago.'

'Did you know him well?'

'Not at all, really. Our paths rarely crossed. He's allergic to sunlight, poor chap. Breaks out in burns and blisters if he goes out during the day. He had his own key.'

'Did you know he's been shortlisted for the Lomax Prize too?' Mhairi asked.

'My, he's a dark horse,' she said, clearly surprised.

'Is any of his work hung in here?' asked Farrell.

She grimaced a little.

'No, it's not really my cup of tea. To be honest, I find it distasteful. I believe he sells a fair bit to foreign collectors. Certainly, he always paid his rent bang on the nail, so he must do all right out of it.'

'Distasteful, how?'

'He likes to paint dead things, animals, birds, that sort of thing. He showed me one once, wanted me to sell some in the gallery. It was all I could do not to shudder in front of him. There's a big market for it abroad, he said. I gave the studio a wide berth when he was in it. Worried about what I might find in there. He did leave it spotless when he left though, so I can't complain.'

'Do you have his home address?' asked Mhairi.

'Yes, he lives at Lavender Cottage. Head back out of town then take the third turning on the right into Silvercraigs Road. The cottage is at the top of the hill on the left.'

Farrell handed her his card.

'If anything else occurs to you in relation to Monro Stevenson then please don't hesitate to get in touch.'

'Mike Halliday, the man who lives in the studio now, is an artist too. He might be able to help you. I think he was quite friendly with Monro.'

'Thank you, we'll swing by on the way out.'

Chapter Twelve

They walked around the side of the building and found the studio entrance. A tall, muscular, clean-shaven man in his early thirties was sitting on a rustic bench against the wall, in a small garden that was overflowing with snowdrops and crocuses. A small blue and white fishing boat sat on a trailer, adding to the charm. He drained the dregs of his cup and stood up as they approached. He smiled at Mhairi, and she smiled back.

'DI Farrell and DC McLeod,' Farrell said, leaning over to shake his hand.

'Mike Halliday, pleased to meet you,' he said. His expression became grave.

'Are you here about Monro?'

'Yes,' said Farrell. 'Did you know the deceased well?'

'Well enough,' he said. 'I would never have had him pegged to do something like that in a million years, though.'

'Why do you say that?' asked Mhairi.

'He was really sound. Cheery enough whenever I came across him. Mind you, I hadn't seen him for a while. I used to meet him in the pub for a beer now and then, but he'd been off the grid for the last three or four months I reckon.'

'Were you aware he'd been shortlisted for the Lomax Prize?' asked Mhairi.

'I'd heard that. Funny time to check out.'

'Did you enter as well?'

'Me? Heck, no. I'm just a jobbing artist painting pretty pictures for the tourists,' he said. 'I've come to terms with my place in the pecking order.'

Something about the way his mouth twisted made Farrell suspect he hadn't come to terms with it at all.

'I understand he used to be part of a group of artists known as The Collective?'

A flicker of anger flitted across Halliday's face, so quickly Farrell couldn't be sure it had ever been there.

'Aye, well, nobody's perfect,' he said. 'It was a long time ago.'

'Hugo Mortimer was shortlisted as well. Are you familiar with his work?' asked Farrell.

'He made quite a name for himself a while back. Even the critics loved him. But, as far as I'm aware, he hasn't exhibited for years. I was completely gobsmacked when I heard he'd made the cut. I would've thought his brain would be completely fried by now.'

'What do you mean?' asked Mhairi.

'Well, he's into all that hallucinogenic crap, isn't he? Fancies himself a modern-day Byron. Be laughable if it wasn't so pathetic.'

'So you're not a fan, then,' said Mhairi.

Halliday laughed.

'Sorry for sounding all bitter and twisted. I'm not the only jobbing artist around here who's had to put up with that lot lording it over us. They act as though they're at the forefront of the renaissance instead of some sad middle-aged swingers.'

'If they're not commercially successful then what do they live on?' asked Farrell.

'Rumour has it that Penelope Spence keeps them all afloat with a family inheritance. I've certainly never heard of any of them doing a day's honest graft for a living.'

Halliday glanced at his watch then got to his feet.

'If there's nothing else?'

'Just one thing,' said Farrell, 'I don't suppose you know the remaining local artist shortlisted? Paul Moretti?'

'Can't help you there,' he said. 'I've never seen any of his work, but I believe he's a committed artist, all right. He'd have to be, to be holed up in that cottage day in day out, painting in the dark. Enough to drive you quietly insane, I should think.'

'Known associates?' asked Farrell.

'None, that I'm aware of.'

'Does he show his work locally?'

'No, I'd have heard. I don't even know what kind of stuff he's into.'

'The gallery owner, Janet, said he painted dead stuff, animals and birds?' said Farrell.

'Did she now?' he said, his expression unreadable. 'I would take that with a pinch of salt. He probably just didn't want Janet poking her nose in.'

'Thank you,' said Farrell. 'Appreciate you helping us out.'

'Any time,' he replied with a warm smile, disappearing off back into his studio.

Chapter Thirteen

Ten minutes later they were picking their way up an uneven garden path to the front door of a dark cottage, overshadowed by the looming granite cliff behind. Closed shutters stared sightlessly into the distance, paint peeling like some scabrous disease.

Farrell hammered on the door. The blinds were down but given what they had been told, Moretti could still be in. They were on the verge of giving up when the door opened a crack.

'Give me a couple of minutes to get away from the light then come in closing the door behind you,' said a disembodied voice.

OK, this is creepy, thought Mhairi as she followed Farrell in to the dim interior. The house smelled cold and damp.

'Turn right,' called the voice.

They felt along the wall to the doorway.

'Please, come in and take a seat,' said the voice.

Gingerly, they felt their way to two wingback chairs and sat down. Across from them, the owner of the voice was a darker blot in the gloom.

'I apologize for the lack of light but, as I'm sure has been explained to you, I cannot tolerate it. How may I help you?'

'Could you confirm your name and date of birth?' asked Farrell, hoping he was writing on the correct page in his notebook.

'Paul Moretti, 2nd August 1973.'

His voice was hoarse, and he was muffled up in many layers to withstand the freezing temperature inside. He wore a hat with flaps over the ears and dark sunglasses.

'DI Farrell and DC McLeod from Dumfries,' said Farrell. 'We're investigating the death of Monro Stevenson.'

'Yes, I heard. A shocking business.'

'Did you know the deceased?' asked Mhairi.

'In a manner of speaking,' said Moretti. 'The art community in Kirkcudbright is very incestuous.'

'When did you first meet him?'

The figure in the gloom changed position. There was a pause. 'I didn't say that I had met him. We've never been introduced. However, I knew who he was.'

'Congratulations on being shortlisted for the Lomax Prize, by the way,' said Mhairi.

'Thank you.'

He didn't sound that happy about it, she thought.

'Did you know that Monro and another local artist were short-listed as well?' asked Farrell.

'Yes.'

'When was the last time you saw Monro Stevenson?' asked Farrell.

'I don't see much of anybody. However, I do remember seeing him one night about two weeks ago.'

'You can't be more precise?' asked Farrell.

'It was the first half of the week, not long after the weekend. So, a Monday or a Tuesday.'

'What time of day?'

'It was late, around 10 p.m. I had been out for my nightly walk.'

'What was he doing when you saw him?'

'He was having an argument with someone at the top of a close on the High Street.'

'Who was he arguing with?' asked Farrell.

'I couldn't say. I was some distance away.'

'Could you describe the man?'

'He was tall, powerfully built.'

'Anything else?'

'He was smoking a cigar. I could see the tip glowing; that's all I can tell you.'

'How can you be sure it was Monro Stevenson?'

Again, Moretti paused and shifted in his seat.

'I'd seen his photo on leaflets in the area and also the local paper.'

Mhairi exchanged a glance with Farrell. She could see Moretti more clearly now that her eyes were adjusting. He was sitting on the opposite side of the room where the darkness seemed even more impenetrable. However, she could tell that he had long legs, suggestive of height, and despite, all the layers, she could see that he was quite slight, possibly even emaciated.

'Have you always had to live in the dark like this, sir?' she asked.

'No. It's been seven years since my condition first manifested.'

'May I ask what your condition is?' asked Farrell.

'Polymorphic Light Eruption. Basically, an allergy to sunlight.'

'Did you live in Kirkcudbright, before you developed the allergy?'

'No.'

It was like pulling teeth, thought Mhairi.

'Would you say Monro had any enemies?' asked Farrell.

'I wouldn't have thought that he was sufficiently interesting to make enemies,' said Moretti. 'Anyway, I heard he killed himself?'

Wow, thought Mhairi. Say what you really mean, why don't you?

'We're looking into all possibilities,' said Farrell.

'I see,' said Moretti. 'Perhaps he was interesting after all?'

They stood up to leave.

'Thank you for your time, sir,' said Farrell. They left the way they came and returned to the car.

'That was one seriously creepy guy. And before you jump onto the moral high ground, it's got nothing to do with his condition,' said Mhairi.

'I agree. It felt like he was hiding from more than the light.'

'I don't know about you, but I got the feeling he knew more about Monro than he was willing to let on. But why?'

'That's what we've got to figure out,' replied Farrell.

Chapter Fourteen

Their final port of call was a handsome stone building in the High Street, a few doors down from Broughton House which held the Hornel Collection.

'Not short of a bob or two then,' said Farrell.

'Must be nice,' sighed Mhairi.

Farrell looked for a bell, but there wasn't one, so he lifted the heavy brass knocker and let it drop. Moments later the door swung back and a familiar face appeared. It was Fiona Murray, the housekeeper who had happened upon the body of Monro Stevenson. Dour as ever, she didn't crack a smile but simply stood aside to let them enter.

'Mr Forbes is expecting you,' she said, gesturing to a door on the right of the handsome wood-panelled hall. 'He'll be down shortly.'

The door led into a study, exquisitely furnished with antiques. Mhairi wandered over to the marble fireplace and inspected the photos. Her eye then alighted on an embossed invitation to a weekend shooting party at some big toff's house. So he was a fully paid up member of the hunting and shooting brigade? She loathed that crowd.

Lionel Forbes entered the room and strode towards them

exuding bonhomie and more than a hint of expensive cologne. Tall, broad and muscular, he was wearing fine tweed trousers teamed with a lilac shirt and purple silk waistcoat. He definitely had charisma, thought Mhairi. A wee bit too much finesse for her taste though. Somehow she couldn't imagine him eating a fish supper in front of the telly like her Ian. Mind you, she couldn't imagine DI Moore doing that either.

'DI Farrell and DC McLeod,' said Farrell stepping forward to shake his hand.

'How can I be of assistance, officers? But first, where are my manners? Can I offer you some tea?' he asked, gesturing to a rich brown leather couch, which made Mhairi want to kick off her shoes as soon as she sat down.

'Thank you, no,' said Farrell.

Mhairi resisted the urge to glare at him. Her stomach was starting to rumble. Farrell had no conception of what low blood sugar could do to a girl.

'I understand that you've recently been assisting DI Moore with an art fraud investigation,' Farrell said.

'Yes, a challenging case from what I can gather.'

His interest sounded purely professional. No warmth towards DI Moore that she could detect. She gave herself a mental shake. Concentrate! This was what happened when she got hungry. Her mind lurched all over the place like a drunken sailor.

'As someone who is very well connected to the art world we were wondering if you could give us some additional information about a number of local artists?' asked Farrell.

'In relation to the fraud case?' Forbes asked, looking puzzled.

'No. In relation to the death of Monro Stevenson,' said Farrell.

'But I thought that was suicide? That's what everyone is saying.'

'At this stage we must consider all possible avenues of enquiry,' said Farrell.

Was hunger causing paranoia to set in or did Forbes look a

little startled, wondered Mhairi, detecting the aroma of something delicious seeping under the door.

'What do you want to know?' Forbes asked, settling back on the couch opposite.

'What can you tell me about The Collective?'

Forbes grimaced.

'A bunch of dilettantes. They live in that crumbling mansion, Ivy House, heading out towards Dundrennan.'

'One of them has been shortlisted for the Lomax Prize,' said Farrell.

'Hugo Mortimer. I was rather surprised when I heard. Don't get me wrong. His early work showed great promise. Twenty years ago, he was the latest rising star in the art world. Instead of knuckling down and cementing his reputation, however, he succumbed to the wildest excesses and fetched up here. A broken down dissolute has-been.'

His colour had risen as he spoke.

'A bit harsh?' ventured Mhairi.

Forbes gave her a charming smile.

'Perhaps. I simply hate to see real talent squandered. He could have been one of the best artists of his generation. I shall view his work with interest once it is released for public consumption.'

'Are you aware of any particular connection between him and the deceased?' asked Farrell.

'Other than the fact that they were both artists, you mean? Well, Monro used to be in cahoots with that lot. He lived with them for over a year. Fortunately, he came to his senses and finally saw them for what they were.'

'How many of them are there up there?' asked Farrell.

'Currently three, although the place used to be stuffed with hippie types. Looked like most of them needed a good wash,' Forbes said, wrinkling his nose.

'So, Hugo Mortimer and who else?' asked Farrell.

'Penelope Spence and Patrick Rafferty.'

'All artists, I take it?'

'Yes, all talented in their own way, particularly Penelope, but broken. They live in their own squalid bubble and have a rather inflated sense of their own importance.'

A lot of that going around, thought Mhairi.

'How familiar are you with their work?' asked Farrell.

'I used to be, until around three years ago when that young Irish girl ran away. After that, they rather dropped off the radar. Mine and anyone else who matters.'

'Until now,' said Farrell.

'Yes, I have to admit my curiosity has been rather piqued as to the nature of the work that so impressed the judges.'

'What about the other shortlisted candidate?' asked Farrell.

'Paul Moretti?'

'Yes. What can you tell us about him?'

'Bit of an enigma. He keeps himself to himself. I've never even seen his work. Rumour has it that it is rather out there, even by Turner Prize standards.'

'What do you mean?'

'I believe he is sought after by private collectors who are looking for something a little more exotic. Of course, that's only a rumour. Nobody knows for sure.'

'Did you know him prior to his allergies developing?'

'No. He moved here from elsewhere. I had never heard of him. It could all be a cunning marketing ploy of course, creating an aura of mystery.'

'And the deceased, Monro Stevenson?'

'Very talented. Tragic to see an emerging artist cut off in his prime like that.' Forbes sighed with what seemed to be genuine regret.

'When was the last time you saw him, sir?' asked Mhairi.

'Let me think … It would be two days before the body was found. I walked past him down by the harbour sitting on a bench and staring out to the sea. He looked rather wretched, which I thought was odd given recent events. I didn't wish to intrude, so I bade him good morning and continued on my way. I believe he may have suffered from depression in the past?'

Farrell didn't answer the question, rising instead to his feet, followed by Mhairi.

'Thank you so much for your time, Mr Forbes. May we contact you, if we have any further questions at a later stage?'

'Certainly,' Forbes said, standing to usher them out. 'Happy to help in any way that I can.'

'Could I possibly use your bathroom before I leave?' asked Mhairi.

Forbes paused a fraction too long, then smiled.

'Yes, of course, let me show you. These old houses are a bit of a maze.'

'Thank you,' said Mhairi, and walked with him upstairs.

'In here,' he smiled, opening a door into the most lavish bathroom, Mhairi had ever seen. She took her time, applying the expensive hand lotion once she had finished. So this was how the other half lived?

She was a little disconcerted to see him standing outside the door waiting for her and wished she hadn't been quite so free with the scented toiletries on display.

'I could have found my own way down,' she said.

'Nonsense, I like to take good care of my guests,' he said with a smile that didn't quite reach his eyes.

Jerk, she thought. Probably thought I'd run off with his fancy aftershave. They walked back downstairs in silence.

'Thank you for your time, sir,' she said formally as he opened the front door. Farrell was already in the car with the engine running.

'Goodbye, DC McLeod,' he replied. 'I'm sure we'll meet again.'

'Not if I can help it,' she added silently, as she jumped into the passenger seat.

'What did you think of him?' she asked.

'He seemed all right,' said Farrell. 'Bit full of himself but probably an occupational hazard for an art critic.'

'I thought he was a pretentious poser, but DI Moore certainly seems to rate him,' said Mhairi.

Farrell visibly relaxed.

'Oh well then, he must be fairly sound. I trust her judgement,' said Farrell.

Honestly, for a smart bloke he could be so dense at times, thought Mhairi. Well she wasn't going to spell it out for him. He'd only take her head off. DI Moore could take care of herself.

'Are we going to see The Collective now?' she asked.

'No, I reckon we'll hold that over until tomorrow. I want to check back in with the team. These artists. Quite an intense lot, aren't they?'

'You can say that again! When all's said and done, it's only splashing a bit of paint around, isn't it?'

'I'd keep that view to yourself in Kirkcudbright or they'll run you out of town,' said Farrell.

The radio crackled into life. The remains of a body had been discovered on Dundrennan Firing Range just a few miles from Kirkcudbright. They were to attend the scene and secure it at once.

'I don't believe it,' Farrell muttered as, glancing at his mirror, he swung the car around in a U turn.

Chapter Fifteen

Back in Dumfries, Lind sighed and, with a heavy heart, picked up the phone. The remains might not be those of Ailish, but he knew that her sister Maureen would want to be told of the grisly find at the earliest opportunity.

'Hello, can I speak to Maureen Kerrigan, please?'

'Detective Lind, is that you?' asked the soft lilting voice. 'Dear God, have they found her? Is she …?'

'We've found the remains of a body. There's nothing to say it's your sister yet, but I wanted you to hear it from me first.'

'I see,' she said with a catch in her voice. 'You'll keep me in the loop?'

'Always,' he said and heard the tears start to come as she replaced the receiver.

He had been the officer in charge of the investigation into her disappearance over three years ago. Given the kind of life she had been living back then, the most likely explanation was that she had simply run off after a tiff with her boyfriend. However, when her elder sister, Maureen, had come over from Ireland to report her missing, he had thought that theory did not sit very well with the text Ailish had sent the morning she disappeared. He had persuaded the Super to let him launch an investigation that had turned up precisely nothing. As with all missing person cases, there had been a number of alleged sightings, but none had turned out to be concrete. He had been left with a niggling feeling of failure. Beyond the bare fact of her disappearance, there had been no evidence then or since to suggest that she had come to any harm. Of course, it might not even be her.

His mobile rang. It was Laura. There was a time not so long ago when unexpectedly hearing her voice lifted his spirits. These days, he was so perplexed and unsettled by her behaviour that his stomach would flip with dread. He accepted the call and frowned as Laura's voice announced that she was unable to collect the children from school as something had come up. He could hear laughter and music in the background. Her speech was slurred.

'Laura, I can't simply drop everything.'

'But you expect me to?' she snapped.

'A body has been found,' he said, attempting to remonstrate with her.

'So? If it's dead, what's the hurry?'

'Have you been drinking?'

'And what if I have?'

He could tell this was an argument he wasn't going to win. Someone was egging her on in the background. Probably that new so-called friend of hers.

'Fine. I'll pick them up,' he said and terminated the call, feeling the first opening salvo of a killer headache.

At least he knew that Farrell was en route to the new crime scene. He could rely on him not to stuff things up. It wasn't the first time recently that Laura had phoned him out of the blue to collect the kids from school and nursery. He had a feeling she was pushing the self-destruct button. Ever since she had lost the baby last year, she had been various versions of the person he married, but never the same one. He had hoped that the worst

66

was behind them but since she had met that woman at her support group things had deteriorated.

He glanced at his watch. There was a scheduled briefing for the Monro Stevenson case at 4 p.m. He would need to take that in Farrell's absence, which would still give him time to collect the kids and deposit them somewhere. But where? They were too young to come into the station.

As if in answer to his prayers, DI Moore popped her head around his door. There were deep shadows under her eyes. She looked exhausted.

'Kate! Shouldn't you have been away hours ago?'

'I'm just heading off, John. Been going through the forgery case files forwarded by Glasgow with a fine-tooth comb, but we have so little to go on. I'm still trying to get hold of the CCTV footage from Broughton House. DC Thomson's idea. Smart lad.'

'Yes, he's shaping up nicely. Actually, Kate, I don't suppose? No forget it. You get along.'

'John, if you need me to do something, get to the point. I can always say no,' she said.

'It's more in the nature of a personal favour,' he said.

'Go on,' she said.

'Could you possibly pick up the kids from school and nursery?'

'I would LOVE to!' She beamed, looking suddenly less tired.

'Really? You honestly don't mind?'

'Your kids are adorable, John. It's hardly a hardship.'

Only to their mother, thought Lind.

'Brilliant! I owe you one, Kate. I'll give the nursery a ring to let them know you'll be collecting them.'

'What about car seats and whatnot?' she asked.

'Both Laura and I have them, and I'm insured for any driver,' he said, handing her his car keys. 'I'll get back as soon as I can.'

'Take your time. I'm not due on until the morning.'

'I need to cover the briefing at 4 p.m. then I should be able to relieve you and work from home for a bit.'

'Is Laura all right? She's not unwell, is she?'

'No,' said Lind. 'Maybe … to be honest I don't really know,' he sighed.

'Give it time, she's been through a lot.'

'You're right. I need to try harder.'

'If you ever want a weekend away, I'd be happy to look after them. I could rope Frank in. They love running him ragged.'

'Thanks, Kate. I might take you up on that!'

'I hear they've found some remains out at Dundrennan?'

'Frank and Mhairi are down there now, to secure the scene with SOCO. Given where the remains are located, I suspect foul play has been involved. It's on MoD property, the firing range. They'll no doubt be sending a couple of officers to breathe down our necks.'

'Another body, though, in that general area? Could be pertinent to the forgery ring?'

'Could also be that missing girl from three years ago, Ailish Kerrigan. I had to phone her sister and warn her of the possibility.'

'That can't have been an easy call.'

'No. Her family have been to Hell and back. Anyway, no point in speculating until the pathologist has had a chance to inspect the remains. What with Monro Stevenson and now this? We're keeping him busy.'

'I'll get off then,' she said. 'Take as long as you need.'

Chapter Sixteen

Farrell sat in the car fuming beside an equally twitchy McLeod, with her mobile clamped to one ear. In front of them was a barrier with the words:

No entry by order of Ministry of Defence. Danger. Unexploded Ordnance.

Behind them was a car containing a couple of officers from Kirkcudbright.

'This is ridiculous. We need to get in there now and secure that scene. How long are these jokers going to be?' said Farrell.

'You're not going to like it,' she said, ending the call.

'Tell me anyway.'

'The MoD are sending someone down from Glasgow. It's going to be around two and a half hours.'

'Well, there's no point hanging about here for that length of time. Did you get the details of who discovered the remains?'

'Yes,' she said, scrolling through her phone. 'Ted Jarvis, tenant farmer. Lives down a track beside the range. As such, he's authorized to go on the land at his own risk for farming purposes.'

'Right, that settles it. We'll head off there first.'

Farrell got out and approached the car behind. It was being

driven by the officer who had attended the death in Kirkcudbright, PC Calum McGhie.

'I'm sorry but we can't advance any further until the MoD arrive, which won't be for another couple of hours. I'm going to need you guys to wait here until then.'

'Yes, sir,' PC McGhie responded, looking glum.

They made a U turn for the second time that day and headed back out to the main road, with Farrell keeping one eye on the satnav. It was so incredibly remote out here that it was nothing short of a miracle the remains had been discovered at all. It was a vast area and ran right alongside the rugged coastline. A thought occurred to him.

'That forgery case you're working on with DI Moore, Mhairi, if they've disappeared off the radar they may be using this land to smuggle the forged pieces out. It's so desolate they would have virtually no chance of detection.'

'It's possible. Look, there's the turning there!'

The road was so narrow, Farrell had almost missed it. Little more than a dirt track winding down to a whitewashed farmhouse that had seen better days. A sheepdog ran out barking followed by a wizened old man clad in so many layers he could have passed for a scarecrow. He bade the dog come to heel and stood waiting for them while they parked in his yard, taking care to avoid the clucking disapproval of the hens. A cockerel that reminded Farrell of DS Byers strutted in front of them.

'Mr Jarvis?' Farrell said, taking the old farmer's wrinkled hand in his own. The man's grip was strong. He wasn't as frail as he looked.

'Aye, that's me, lad. Gave me a fair turn, seeing what I did. Best come in. I'll stick the kettle on. You too, lass.'

Once they were settled at the kitchen table with mugs of hot sweet tea, he began.

'I was out with Jess,' nodding at the dog lying by his feet, 'looking for a stray sheep, when she raced up that yonder hill into a bit of woodland and stood there barking. I shouted at her, but she wasn't for budging, so I hauled myself to the top to see what she'd found, thinking it was a dead deer or a fox.'

He paused, relishing the telling of it. This told Farrell that the remains weren't much more than bones, or he would have been more upset. He figured the old man was lonely, didn't get the chance to talk often, so let him continue at his own pace instead of trying to hurry him up. He could see Mhairi's foot jiggling impatiently on the worn tiles, but she too bit her lip.

'Well, I got up there and could immediately see that the bones were human, so I called off the dog, fetched back here and called you lot. Seemed an odd place to dump a body. Giving yourself all that work slogging up the hill? Didn't make sense when you could've heaved it over the cliffs. It wasn't even as though the bones were dug up. Just sitting on the surface they were. Mind you, they might have been buried at one point. We had some mighty wild storms this winter.'

Farrell stood up, followed by Mhairi.

'Can you take us to the remains?'

'Aye, lad, that I can. It's a fair way mind. Might be best to take the tractor?'

Farrell ignored the pleading look from Mhairi. He couldn't run the risk of destroying any trail of evidence. Shanks's pony it was then. They set off, struggling to keep up with the farmer, who was as fit as a flea. The land was very exposed to the elements, but with spectacular sea views. They could hear the roar below as the waves pounded into the cliffs.

'What about the unexploded ordnance?' asked Mhairi, looking as though she expected to be blown to smithereens at any moment.

'Och, never you mind about that, lass,' the farmer chortled. 'More likely to be hit crossing the road.'

After a couple of miles, Jarvis stopped, pointing to a straggly copse of trees on top of a hill.

'Straight up there. You can't miss it. Will you be able to find your own way back? I've got plenty of stuff to do at the farm.'

Farrell thanked him. He handed a pair of plastic shoe covers to Mhairi and put on some himself. They climbed cautiously up the hill trying not to dislodge any stones or rocks as they went. On reaching the summit, they were breathing heavily. It had been steeper than it looked from a distance. As they moved carefully through the trees they could see the exposed bones lying in a small mossy clearing. They had clearly been placed in a shallow grave.

'That's odd,' said Farrell, frowning. 'The soil seems to have been turned over recently, but the bones are old.'

'Look at those marks,' said Mhairi, pointing to some indentations in the soil.

'Someone has been up here not long ago, which means the bones were either brought here from elsewhere ...'

'Or someone wanted to take a little trip down memory lane,' finished Mhairi. 'About three years ago a girl went missing from this area, an Ailish Kerrigan. It was one of DCI Lind's cases. He always felt that something bad had happened to her.'

They retraced their steps carefully back down the hill and sat overlooking the sea, while they waited for SOCO. Mhairi perched on a rock and turned her white face up to the winter sun, which was now beating down on them with more fervour than normal for a January afternoon. A buzzard looped lazily around, silent and deadly. The seabirds squabbled endlessly on the cliffs.

Farrell sat awkwardly on another rock. There was something rotten in this sleepy little town. Evil had burrowed under its skin and he was going to have to excise it using all means at his disposal. Comfortable in the silence, he closed his eyes for a few moments and prayed.

'Sir!' Mhairi shook his arm, startling him. He should have known better than to think she would give him five minutes' peace.

'They're coming! I can see them in the distance.'

They both scrambled to their feet and waved at the procession of bodies marching determinedly in single file towards them. As the group got closer they could see that there was an army officer leading the two SOCOs, Phil Tait and Janet White, followed by the two Kirkcudbright officers, DS Byers and another army officer bringing up the rear.

As the army officers advanced, with their military bearing very much in evidence, Farrell had to fight the urge to stiffen to attention. He could hear a stifled giggle from McLeod and shot her a quelling glare, which if anything seemed to make her worse.

The leading officer approached Farrell with an outstretched hand. He had been half expecting him to salute.

'Lieutenant Benjamin Wood, at your service,' he said.

'DI Farrell, and DC McLeod,' answered Farrell. 'Sorry to drag you all the way here. How did you get down so quickly?'

'We were at a training course nearby.'

'What about the risk of unexploded ordnance, Lieutenant?' Farrell asked.

DS Byers looked worried. Nobody had filled him in then. Mind you, if he ran true to form he would be more concerned about ruining his expensive shoes than getting blown up.

'Is this part we're in at the moment safe?' asked Byers.

'As far as we know,' the lieutenant replied. 'Shells can veer dramatically off course. Don't touch any suspicious objects, look where you're placing your feet, and you should be fine.'

'I'm going up there now with SOCO and, once they've done the necessary, the remains can be removed to the morgue at Dumfries and Galloway Royal Infirmary,' said Farrell. 'I'm afraid we won't know much until the pathologist has carried out an analysis and we've obtained the results of the lab tests, soil samples etcetera.'

He returned up the hill with Phil and Janet, shrouded in their white plastic overalls and shoe covers. From past experience he didn't dare to offer to lug Janet's heavy kit bag for her. The scathing retort the first time he had tried had been enough. She might be small but she must pack some muscle.

He pointed out the salient features of the scene then carefully retraced his steps, leaving the SOCOs to carry on with their work unimpeded. By the time he reached the small group, he saw that relations had thawed to the extent that the younger of the two military men was passing his card to Mhairi. Byers looked like a thundercloud. Farrell wished he could just move on. It was never going to happen.

'Any further forward, sir?' Byers asked.

'Not really, there are markings in the ground that might suggest someone was up there recently.'

'DS Byers, can you wait here, along with the two local officers, and manage the scene until the remains are removed? DC McLeod and I need to get back to Dumfries and take stock in relation to where we are with the other investigation.'

Byers nodded. Farrell might not like the man but he was efficient and thorough when called upon. Solid backup, unlike DS Stirling, who wouldn't blow his own nose without a risk assessment.

As they returned to the car, at a brisk pace, Mhairi looked at the gadget on her wrist and announced: 'That's me done 20,000 steps so far. Not bad, eh?'

'I refuse to be drawn in to this insanity,' said Farrell.

'You should get one, sir. After all, we do have to be able to catch criminals, don't we?'

'Usually, using our minds rather than our bodies, but I could still leave you standing, DC McLeod, so don't get too cocky.'

Chapter Seventeen

Lind pulled into his driveway and turned off the ignition, leaning his head back against the headrest. He lowered the window and sucked in a lungful of freezing air as if it could push out the blackness that was threatening to engulf him. He couldn't give in. He had to stay strong for his family. Laura had pulled far away from him and he was at a loss as to how to fix things between them. The stars twinkled remotely, indifferent to his problems.

Sighing, he climbed out of the car, the frosty air stiffening his bones. Hiding out here would solve nothing. Straightening his shoulders, he pasted on a smile in readiness and tried to inject some energy into his steps as he let himself in. The silence was unusual this early. He went into the living room.

DI Moore was sitting on the sofa with his youngest child, Adam, cuddled into her. He was fast asleep. Not for the first time he noticed how comfortable she was around children and thought she would make a wonderful mother. She was reading her Kindle and looked up and smiled as he entered, holding a finger to her lips.

'He wouldn't settle,' she whispered. 'He was wanting his mum. I've only just got him off.'

After he had taken his sleepy son from her and tucked him in to his cot without protest, he returned downstairs.

DI Moore was putting on her jacket.

'Sorry, I kept you longer than I said, Kate. I thought Laura would have been home by now. I should have checked. Did she phone?'

'Sorry, no. I expect she was caught up in something and didn't notice the time,' she said, ever the diplomat.

'Kids behave themselves?'

'We had great fun,' she said, looking like she meant it. 'It was a pleasure, John, honestly!'

He imagined coming home to her calm tranquillity every night and pushed the thought away before it had time to take hold. What was wrong with him tonight?

'Things are certainly hotting up at work,' she said, as she was leaving.

'So it would seem. I have a feeling that tomorrow is going to be a very long day,' said Lind.

He checked in on the kids and found them all fast asleep. Molly was the spitting image of Laura, with her long dark curls spilling over the pillow. However, she wasn't a tomboy like her mother had been when they were growing up; she was a quiet bookish child who took her role as big sister very seriously. He removed the book from her bed and carefully saved the page, before putting it on her bedside table.

His four-year-old twins, Luke and Hugh, were sprawled in their bunk beds. Since the events of last year they had ceased to dress alike. Their matching duvet covers had gone. Lind felt sad that even that innocent pleasure had been taken from them.

Finally, he looked in on Adam, who was still fast asleep in his cot. Satisfied, he went back downstairs. A murder and the remains of a body all within the space of a few days. Nothing to link them, but it was Kirkcudbright, for goodness' sake! This was far from normal. There was also a forgery ring running out of there, if intelligence was to be believed. Much would depend on the identity of the bones as to how things went from here. He had a bad feeling about it all that he couldn't shake. It didn't help that he knew nothing whatsoever about art. Unless it was a nice watercolour, he was completely at a loss. Fortunately, DI Moore had a fair grasp of the subject. The house felt even emptier now she was gone. Where on earth was Laura?

He decided not to wait up as he knew from recent experience that she was likely to come in spoiling for a fight. He fought the temptation to crack open a couple of beers and took himself off to bed even though it wasn't yet ten. Things would seem better in the morning.

The sound of laughter woke him. He glanced at his watch and saw it was after three. Laura was clearly drunk, and she had company. This just wasn't on. If he didn't get them to call time now, next thing the kids would be awake and it would be a wailing match all round.

He entered the living room and stopped short. Laura was dressed to kill in an electric blue dress he had never seen before, but the make-up had slid off her face giving her a clownish appearance. She was absolutely steaming. There was no point in having it out with her now. He narrowed his eyes as he looked at the brassy blonde sitting sprawled beside her on the couch, legs akimbo, her short skirt leaving little to the imagination.

'Get a good look, did you?' she said, catching his gaze, giving him a nasty stare.

This woman was trouble. He had met her type before. And now Laura, his gentle sweet wife, was in thrall to this creature. He stifled his rage and said as mildly as he could manage: 'Laura, aren't you going to introduce me to your friend?'

'Her name's Selena,' she muttered, as if to say it wasn't really any of his business. Well, tough, he was going to make it his business. If she wasn't prepared to fight for their marriage he would have to fight hard enough for both of them.

'My name's John,' he said, forcing Selena to take his outstretched hand. 'Sorry, I didn't catch your second name?' He leaned towards her, trying not to wince at the stink of stale alcohol and fags on her breath.

'MacRae,' she said, now looking wary and sitting up straighter.

'Well, Selena, can I offer you a cup of coffee?' he said pleasantly, but she caught the hint of steel in his eyes and stood up, gathering her coat and bag.

'No thanks, time I hit the road. I'll see you, pal,' she said dropping a kiss on the top of Laura's head on the way out.

Laura sat stony-faced until she left then turned on him.

'I don't see what your problem is. Am I not allowed to have friends round now? Is that it?'

'Of course, not,' he soothed. 'But it's three o' clock in the morning.'

'Don't try and "manage" me, John.'

'I'm not!' he snapped.

'We were only having a bit of fun,' she shouted.

'Keep your voice down, the kids …'

'The kids, the kids … that's all I ever hear about. What about me, John? What about ME?'

He looked at her helplessly. She was in a place he couldn't reach, and he knew better than to try when she was in this state. Turning on his heel he left the room and went back to bed. He lay on his side, brooding, until she lurched clumsily into the room an hour later. He pretended to be asleep.

He knew his work was beginning to suffer as he was so distracted by all the drama at home. Prior to the events of last year, he had thought they had a good marriage. Deep down he wondered if it was seeing Frank again after all those years that had unsettled her. He had worried when they first got together after Frank had left for the seminary. Wondered if he was simply the rebound guy? But they had built a solid, loving marriage, or so he had thought.

Chapter Eighteen

Farrell rose from his knees and genuflected on the way out of St Margaret's. He had been up since 5 a.m., having already fitted in a run to Glencaple. Racing against the clock he'd wolfed down a hearty breakfast, finishing the requisite one hour before receiving Holy Communion. Catholics had to be nothing if not organized. He waved at his friend, Father Jim Murphy, on the way out, the poor man already knee-deep in the Catholic faithful.

Twenty minutes later, he walked into the morning briefing, nodding at DI Moore and DCI Lind as he joined them at the front. They had decided to have joint briefings on all three major cases, since Kirkcudbright seemed to be the common denominator. Whether the cases were linked remained to be seen but, given that Kirkcudbright was hardly the crime capital of Europe, Farrell wasn't yet ready to buy the coincidence theory.

The room was packed out as they had also drafted in additional uniforms from outlying stations in the region to help with the investigations.

DI Moore held up her hand for silence, and the chatter immediately died down.

'As most of you will now be aware, this station has become involved in the investigation of an art forgery ring which originated in Glasgow and has now moved onto our patch. The forger is likely based in Kirkcudbright. Therefore, we need to do what we can to smoke him or her out, without alarming them to the extent that they shut up shop and move elsewhere. Recovering the forged painting was a stroke of luck, due to the tractor carrying it being involved in an RTA. Unfortunately, the driver had legged it well before we got to the scene. I doubt very much that he was the brains behind the operation. More likely some local rent-a-yob who was looking to make a quick few bob by smuggling the painting to the drop site. Given the mode of transport, I suggest that we start by looking at any local farm workers with convictions for dishonesty. The tractor has been impounded. The plates were false, so until it's reported stolen, we can't trace the owner. DC Thomson, can I leave that with you?'

'Yes, ma'am.'

'Oh, and have you got hold of the footage from Broughton House yet?'

'Not yet. I've had to go through the National Trust. I'm hoping to hear back from them later today.'

'Don't let them give you the runaround. We need that footage ASAP.'

With that, DI Moore stepped down and DCI Lind took her place.

'As you all know, human remains were discovered on the Dundrennan Firing Range yesterday.'

'Any idea how long they'd been out there yet, sir?' asked DS Stirling.

'All I can tell you at the moment is that it's been more than a year. There was no flesh left on the bones.'

He hesitated.

'There's a possibility that it might be a young Irish girl, Ailish Kerrigan, who went missing from the area on 15th of June 2009 and hasn't been seen or heard from since. Her family have been informed of the find. The remains have been recovered and sent to the mortuary. I believe Roland Bartle-White is arranging for a well-respected forensic pathologist from Glasgow to come down and assist with identification and try to determine cause of death. It's likely that once the remains have been identified this will be a murder investigation.'

'I remember that case,' said DS Stirling. 'She was tangled up with a bunch of artists in Kirkcudbright. What was their name again? Sounded like something from *Star Trek*?'

'The Collective,' replied Lind.

'That's it,' said Stirling.

'You might want to familiarize yourself with the case again, in case we get a positive ID on those bones.'

Stirling nodded assent.

Lind stepped to the side to make way for Farrell.

'Moving now to the suspicious death of Monro Stevenson,' he said, 'The Collective also has ties to the deceased.'

There were a few murmurings. Farrell held up his hand for silence.

'Don't get too excited. Monro was an artist, and the missing girl was involved with an artist who lived there. There may be no more to it than that; it's important not to jump to conclusions.'

'Wasn't another of the shortlisted artists from that lot as well?' asked DS Byers.

'Yes,' said Farrell. 'In fact you can come along and help out with the initial interviews, today, if you're free? However, I absolutely do not want to put the wind up them. The emphasis must be on routine enquiries.'

Byers nodded enthusiastically, making Farrell feel guilty. He was aware that he didn't give Byers as many opportunities to get involved, due to his personal dislike of the man. Overcompensating he gave him a warm smile, which caused a flicker of surprise, followed by suspicion, to shoot across Byers's face.

'The preliminary results of the post-mortem on Monro

Stevenson have come in. Cause of death is by gunshot wound. No surprises there. Hence the gunshot residue on his right hand. The time of death is estimated to be around 5.45 p.m. We're waiting on toxicology results as it appears he may have been visited by someone in the hour prior to his death. There were two rim marks on the table and only one glass. Furthermore, the lights were off and the curtains drawn. It would be unusual for someone to shoot themselves completely in the dark. We are looking into the possibility that he may have been drugged and the suicide staged.'

He could see a few sceptical looks. Maybe some of them thought he was losing the plot.

'DC Thomson, how's that handwriting report coming along? I need to know if the signature on the suicide note was written by the deceased or a third party.'

'The expert, David Williams, has said he'll be able to start work on it tomorrow, sir.'

'PC Green?'

'Here, sir,' said a voice from the back.

'How are the family holding up?'

'The press has been proving a bit of a nuisance. Since the piece went out on *Border News*, a few stray reporters have been turning up at the door, calling repeatedly, the usual nonsense. They've also had hate mail from a few religious fanatics banging on about how the deceased will be rotting in Hell, that kind of thing.'

'Swing by and speak to the civilian press officer, Andy Moran. Get the Stevensons to refer all callers to him, meantime.'

'Yes, sir.'

'Have you spoken to the girlfriend, Nancy Quinn?'

'No, sir, I haven't managed to catch her in at all,' PC Green replied.

'Don't you think that's odd? Can you track down her current whereabouts and arrange for her to come in and help us with our enquiries?'

'Will, do, sir.'

'Right, everyone, snap to it. We've got three critical investigations here that I don't want to see get away from us. It's only a few months since the press were last picking over our bones. I don't want to give them reason to do so again.'

Chapter Nineteen

Farrell was marching down the corridor when DI Moore caught
up with him.

'A word, Frank?'

'Sure, Kate. What's on your mind?' he asked, surprised when
she looked unaccountably furtive.

'Not here.'

They walked to her office in silence. Once the door was closed
she gestured to him to take a seat.

'This is really rather awkward …'

'Best just to spit it out, Kate. I'm no mind reader.'

'It's John.'

'What about him?'

'I think he's having domestic problems. No one else knows. I
thought with you being such good friends you could maybe have
a word with him, see if you can do anything to help? I think he's
really struggling, Frank.'

'Have you tried talking to him about it?'

'No, I couldn't.' She coloured. 'And people generally don't find
it easy to confide in me. I know I come across as a bit aloof.'

'Och away with you, Kate, you've got a warm heart and most
folks round here know that. I take it you mean problems with Laura?'

'He hasn't said anything directly. John is loyal to a fault. However, she keeps demanding he go and pick up the kids when he's working, that sort of thing. I get the impression that she's out drinking with this new friend to all hours and that her and John are not getting on at all.'

Farrell was worried. He'd sensed something was up. However, given his past relationship with Laura, he felt sure that he would be the last person John would choose to confide in. In no way did he want to come between them.

'I'll try and broach the subject, but I may not be the best person.'

'I know about yours and Laura's previous history. I think that if anyone can get through to them, it's probably you.'

'I'll have to pick my moment. Maybe we should team up and offer to babysit? I find them a bit of a handful on my own.'

'Yes,' she brightened. 'They could go out for the evening, or even away for the weekend?'

The weekend? He wasn't sure about that. Wouldn't it be weird to spend so much time in each other's company away from work? He squashed down the feelings of panic her suggestion had elicited.

'Sure, why not?'

'I take it you're heading off to Kirkcudbright shortly?'

'Starting to feel I could drive there in my sleep.'

'Let me know if you hear anything pertinent to my investigation,' she said, professional mask in place once more. 'I've prepared a summary of what we already know for distribution to the key members of your team.'

'Excellent, I'll pass that round. By the way, Mhairi and I questioned that art consultant, Lionel Forbes.'

'Oh?'

'He was helpful enough but by the finish I thought Mhairi was going to bite his ankle. Mind you, she was hungry.'

'Mhairi should learn not to be so judgemental,' she said,

looking annoyed. 'He's an incredibly accomplished man and very well thought of in the art world.'

Farrell stood up to leave.

'I'm sure he is. I'll keep you posted on any developments.'

His next port of call was Walker's office. The Super had been extremely quiet of late apart from the odd snarky comment. He took with him summaries of the three cases.

He knocked on the door, and the voice inside bade him enter.

'Have a seat, Frank,' he said.

Okay, this was new, thought Farrell, doing as he was told.

The Super looked even paler than usual. His red curls, normally kept in check by a local barber, had grown into a fuzzy red halo that only served to highlight his bald patch.

'Thought you'd like a written update on all three investigations, sir,' said Farrell, placing them on the desk.

The Super glanced at them listlessly but made no effort to pull them towards him. Normally he crackled with energy, much of it malevolent, but today, nothing.

'I suppose we should savour these,' he said with a sigh.

'Sir?'

'Well, after Police Scotland comes into being in April, that'll be it. We'll be lucky if we're allowed to investigate a stolen cat without the city slickers tanking down from Glasgow to stick their nebs in. Impotent, that's what we'll be, son, bloody impotent.'

'It might not be as bad as you think, sir,' he said.

The Super gave a snort of laughter.

'I know the kind of cases you've been working on, laddie. Stolen cats aren't going to hit the spot. You'll be away back to Edinburgh in the twinkle of an eye.'

'See, sir, every cloud has a silver lining.'

The Super smirked. That was better.

'I'm getting too old for all this upheaval, Farrell. Reckon I'll grab my pension and run for the hills. Let them get on with it.

It's the likes of DI Moore and DCI Lind I feel sorry for. Bloody fine officers, but there's going to be nothing left here for them to get their teeth into.'

Farrell could find no crumbs of comfort. The imminent amalgamation of all the regional autonomous police forces in Scotland into one centralized force was going to completely change the way Dumfries and Galloway was policed.

'Don't let me keep you, Farrell, best get out there and solve these bloody cases. Show the bastards what real police work looks like.'

Chapter Twenty

As they reached Kirkcudbright, having had to suffer the frustration of being trapped behind a line of lorries bound for the ferry at Cairnryan, Farrell turned to McLeod and Byers.

'These are going to be challenging interviews. The impression we want to convey is that we are just dotting the I's and crossing the T's. Everything routine, verging on boredom, that's the way we want to play it. Let them think Monro's death is suicide, for now, without saying as much.'

'It could still be suicide,' said Byers.

'Assuming no one has blabbed, hopefully they will be unaware that bones were recovered yesterday. If you get a chance to see inside their studio space, take it. Look out for evidence of any copied art works, particularly Hornel, who has a very distinctive style.'

'DI Moore has been giving me and DC Thomson a crash course in fine art,' Mhairi grumbled. 'It's pure torture. I was rubbish at it in school. As for that Hornel? I wouldn't have his stuff up in my flat if you paid me.'

'I'll take the lead with Hugo Mortimer, the other shortlisted candidate. He knew Monro from his time at Ivy House. Perhaps he was the one seen arguing with him not long before he died.'

'Byers, can you take the lead with Penelope Spence? Check not only her whereabouts on the night Monro was murdered, but also Hugo's. Remember to ask about the missing girl.'

'What about me, sir?' asked Mhairi.

'I suggest you take Patrick Rafferty, the missing girl's boyfriend at the time. He might open up more to you as you're younger.'

They left their car by the grass verge outside and walked through a pair of massive sandstone pillars with twisted gargoyles leering down at them. The driveway wound round a large walled garden that had gone to seed. An imposing granite townhouse with flaking paint stood at the end of the drive. It too had gargoyles peering down with sightless eyes. The whole appearance was suggestive of a gradual decline into poverty. Beyond the property, the wind howled through the trees in Barrhill Wood.

Mounting the well-worn steps to the front door, Farrell lifted the faded brass knocker and let it fall with a thud that reverberated throughout the house. His eyes widened in surprise when the door swung open to reveal Fiona Murray. A brief expression of annoyance, perhaps fear, flickered across her face.

'Can I help you, officers?' she asked, looking like she was fighting the impulse to slam the door in their faces.

Farrell smiled at her.

'Sorry, Mrs Murray, I'm afraid we keep turning up like the proverbial bad pennies. We're simply here as part of our routine enquiries into the death of Monro Stevenson.'

'It's a sad business, to be sure. Is there anyone in particular you'd like to speak to?'

'I'd like to start with Hugo Mortimer and then work my way round everyone who lives here. I've brought DC McLeod and DS Byers with me, so we can move things along quicker and be out of your hair as soon as possible.'

She motioned to them to come in.

'I'll tell them you're here.'

They stood inside the vestibule. Mrs Murray approached a tall patrician-looking woman at the end of the hall. They had a muttered exchange in low voices then the woman glided up the stairs without acknowledging them, her spine rigid with displeasure.

They were led in to the kitchen and sat down at a refectory-style monk's bench and table. Farrell hoped in vain for a cup of coffee. Suddenly his eyes were drawn to some scales and a baking tray on the counter top. Following his gaze, Mrs Murray walked over and threw them in the sink, running the tap and squirting washing up liquid over the top. Interesting. What else was she willing to cover up for her employers?

'Mr Mortimer will be down shortly,' she said, looking flustered and almost running out of the kitchen.

Maybe it was time to look in to the ubiquitous housekeeper further, mused Farrell.

They heard brisk footsteps coming across the parquet flooring in the hall, heralding the arrival of Hugo Mortimer, whose presence seemed to quickly expand to fill the room.

'Officers, delighted to meet you. I wish it wasn't under such distressing circumstances.'

Tall and broad-shouldered he was dressed in Levi's and a cotton open-necked shirt with a red neckerchief tied at the throat. A thick shock of unruly jet-black hair and piercing green eyes set off his handsome though slightly louche face. He looked to be in his early forties.

He held Mhairi's hand just a touch too long for propriety, staring deep into her eyes with a small smile that betrayed he was quite aware of his effect on the opposite sex.

Farrell and Byers glanced at each other and shared an unusual moment of complete accord. Mhairi gently detached her hand and sat at the table, all business.

'I understand that you knew the deceased?' said Farrell.

'Yes, in fact, as I'm sure that you already know, Inspector, he used to be part of our household. Until he became, how shall I say it, unwell?'

'You mean, had a breakdown?' said Farrell.

'Yes. I blame myself of course,' he said, with a sigh that Farrell was fairly sure was more down to theatrics than any genuine regret.

'Oh, how so?' said Byers.

'I didn't realize how sensitive he was. I should have known that someone from such a conservative background could never fully integrate here.'

Farrell had a fair idea of what he meant by integration and tried to keep his expression neutral.

'Who was he closest to when he lived here?' asked Mhairi.

'Let me see. I would say he got along with everyone but, if I had to choose, I would say Ailish Kerrigan.'

'The missing Irish girl?' said Farrell, his pulse quickening.

'Yes, they were very close.'

'How close?' asked Byers.

Mortimer laughed, sounding faintly patronizing.

'Let's just say, not as close as he would have liked. Ailish was strangely conventional to be living in a fluid situation such as ours. She couldn't seem to break the "mind-forged manacles" of the Catholic Church.'

'William Blake,' said Byers, surprising his colleagues.

'Quite,' said Mortimer, shooting him a glance. 'He became unwell shortly after she left. Delusional, in fact. At first I thought he'd taken something illicit, had a bad reaction. After a couple of months of his behaviour becoming increasingly erratic, I called his parents and they came to get him. Salt of the earth types. Hard to believe the soul of an artist flourished amidst such pedestrianism.'

Mhairi was looking less enamoured by the minute and sat back in her seat with a stony expression.

Farrell changed tack. He was too damn cocky by far this guy. He needed to shake him out of his comfort zone.

'I gather he was an extremely talented artist,' he said.

'He showed early promise,' said Mortimer. 'He wouldn't have been admitted to The Collective otherwise. It was a serious artistic endeavour.'

'Was? How about now?' said Byers.

'That goes without saying,' snapped Mortimer.

'Were you aware that Monro was shortlisted for the Lomax Prize?' asked Farrell.

'I was delighted to hear it.'

Were you though? wondered Farrell.

'Did you have the opportunity to congratulate him in person, before his untimely demise?' he asked.

'No. I hadn't seen him for around three months before his death. I rarely venture out these days. Too busy working on my new exhibition.'

'When was the last time you had a major exhibition of your work?' asked Farrell.

Mortimer shifted in his seat and bared his teeth in an attempt to smile.

'Not for some time. The artistic life ebbs and flows, Inspector. Fashions come and fashions go.'

'Be a welcome boost for your career if you win this prize then,' said Byers.

'Indeed. Even to be shortlisted confers prestige,' he said.

'Thank you, sir, you've been most helpful,' said Farrell.

Mortimer got to his feet, looking relieved.

As he left the room, McLeod leaned over to Farrell.

'He could be the person Moretti saw having an argument with Monro in the High Street. He's tall, powerfully built and reeks of cigars,' she said, screwing up her nose.

'I don't think that was cigars,' said Byers.

'Alleged argument,' Farrell said. 'I didn't want to put him on his guard. I'm also not entirely convinced that Moretti himself is a credible witness.'

'True enough,' she replied.

'Mhairi, I need you to have a poke around while ostensibly searching for the ladies. If you can get into any of the studios, keep in mind what you're looking for.'

Byers, who was facing the door, gave her a nudge with his foot and she got up and left.

Chapter Twenty-One

Mhairi climbed the stairs slowly, her senses heightened as she listened intently. The sound of music playing drew her along the upstairs hall to a half-open door. Giving a light tap she stuck her head round, prepared to ask where the loo was if necessary.

The door opened into a bright, cluttered studio space. Standing in front of an easel, daubing at a canvas, was an absolutely gorgeous man. He greeted her with a smile which made her momentarily feel the need to sit down. He wouldn't have looked out of place in a Diet Coke ad. Get a grip, Mhairi, she told herself firmly. You're on the job here.

'Mind if I come in?' she asked flashing her brightest smile.

'Be my guest,' he said, pointing to a wooden stool. She perched on it as he kept painting, wondering how to best engage him in conversation.

'So, what can I do for you?' he asked, putting down his paintbrush and pulling up a stool opposite her, too close for comfort.

Her mouth went dry, and her hands became clammy. This is so not happening, she told herself fiercely. Think about Ian.

'I'm up here with a team of officers from Dumfries.'

'Police?' he asked, his warmth fading.

'Yes, DC Mhairi McLeod at your service.' She stuck out her hand, and he shook it slowly, almost mockingly.

'Patrick Rafferty. So, why are you lot here? Come to crack down on the wacky baccy?'

'Hardly. No, we're looking into the death of Monro Stevenson.'

He frowned.

'But that was a suicide, wasn't it?'

'All I'm at liberty to say is that we're investigating all possible avenues of enquiry.'

'I see,' he said letting out a low whistle. 'Should I have a lawyer?'

'Why? Do you think you need one?' she asked, widening her eyes and sitting up straighter.

'Nah, just messing with you,' he said, a gleam of mischief in his eyes.

He really was very charming, thought Mhairi, feeling like she had a devil perched on her shoulder.

'Did you know him when he was here before?' she asked.

'Sure did.'

'And?'

'He was a nice enough bloke. Talented painter. Worshipped Hugo, used to follow him around like a puppy. Hugo said jump. He asked how high. A bit tragic, really.'

'You sound lukewarm. Did he replace you as the boy wonder around here?'

Rafferty looked annoyed and the smile flickered.

'I might have had more time for him if he hadn't had the hots for my girlfriend.'

Mhairi glanced at the walls. She spotted two paintings of nudes, both very beautiful young girls. She did a double take. One of them was the same girl she had found on a canvas wrapped in oilskin in Monro's flat. The painting looked virtually identical, except that this one was signed. The other girl was a stunning redhead. Both of them looked to be in their teens.

95

'Which one was your girlfriend?' she asked, pointing at the paintings.

'At the time it was Ailish,' he said, indicating the dark-haired girl. 'Thereafter it was Beth.'

'They look very young,' she said, trying, and failing, to keep the note of censure out of her voice.

'Hey, lady, I was very young too,' he said. 'I'm only twenty-five now. Besides, I'm an artist and back then my main passion was exploring the female form on canvas.'

I'll bet, exploring them in bed, more like, thought Mhairi.

He gave her a slow once-over that made her feel he was undressing her with his eyes. She stared coolly back at him, refusing to be intimidated.

'You might be a suitable subject, if you're interested?' he said, the flirtatious manner replaced by a detached professionalism.

'Great bone structure. It's about time I painted a mature model, a woman, rather than a girl,' he said sounding enthusiastic. 'Please say you'll consider it? I haven't come across anyone suitable since Beth. It would be all above board. My interest is strictly professional, I assure you.'

Mhairi was unable to stop the blush staining her cheeks.

'I'm afraid I'll have to pass,' she said.

She slipped off her stool and wandered round the studio. As well as the nudes there were many other canvasses, some of which were downright disturbing in a way she couldn't put her finger on. Tortured phantom images that made her feel a bit queasy.

'No chocolate boxes?' She turned to him with a smile.

'I'd shoot myself first,' he said, then looked appalled. 'Sorry, I didn't …'

'I know what you meant,' she said, sitting back down.

There was an awkward silence. She pointed to one of the nudes.

'The dark-haired girl, Ailish, was she the one who went missing? Hugo mentioned her downstairs.'

96

'Yes. I still can't believe she ran off like that. I often wonder what became of her.'

'What happened?'

'Beth happened.' He pointed at the picture of the redhead. 'Up to that point I had only painted Ailish, but I wanted to explore other female forms in my work. I made the mistake of trying to hide it from her. She burst into my studio one morning, caught Beth posing for me and stormed off.'

'Didn't you go after her?'

'What was the point? I realized from her reaction that she wanted a more conventional set-up than I could give her, so I let her go.' He shrugged.

'Did you ever make any effort to track her down?'

'No, she clearly didn't want to be found. Mind you with that family of hers I'm hardly surprised.'

'What do you mean?'

His lip curled with contempt. 'They were hard-line Catholics. Narrow-minded people living a narrow life. They lived more for the next world than this one. The best thing I ever did was get her away from them, before they choked the life out of her. I set her free.'

'Did you ever meet them?'

'God no, they wouldn't let me darken their door. The only one I met was the sister, Maureen. She turned up a couple of months after Ailish left. Got quite the tongue on her, that one.'

'I suppose you can hardly blame her.'

'No, I suppose not.'

'Her last text suggested that she was running back to the fold,' said Mhairi.

'I refuse to believe it,' he said. 'I reckon she came to her senses and didn't get on that ferry. Took off somewhere else instead.'

'Did she encourage Monro?'

'Not deliberately, but she had this ethereal quality about her that drew you in. I reckon he mistook her friendliness for something more.'

'Did he ever paint her like that?' she asked, pointing to the nude.

'Not to my knowledge. As far as I'm aware, she only posed for me. She liked to feel that she was my muse. And I suppose she was … at first.'

'At first?'

'She couldn't accept it when I moved on to another girl.'

'You expected her to?'

'I suppose you can take the girl out of the small town, but you can't take the small town out of the girl.'

'Weren't you from that same small town?' she asked.

'Only in body, never in spirit.'

'How did Monro get along with the other members of the household?'

Rafferty paused, considering.

'He applied to join us about four years ago; I remember they were really excited about it. Hugo was all fired up about reinvigorating The Collective, drawing in some fresh talent, and making a big splash in the art world. Penelope couldn't decide whether she wanted to mother him or corrupt him.'

'Penelope? Not the woman I caught a glimpse of a few minutes ago, surely? She seemed so upright.'

'Appearances can be deceptive, Detective,' he said mocking her. 'We're artists, we like to experiment, transgress, push the boundaries. We don't live in your safe, regulated little world.'

Mhairi stiffened, suddenly seeing herself through his eyes. Dull, unadventurous, a plodding tool of the state. She had to turn this interview around. Put him on the back foot. But how?

'Did you enter the competition that Monro and Hugo were shortlisted for?' she asked.

A flicker of annoyance flashed across his handsome face.

'Yes.'

'Were you disappointed not to make the cut?' she asked.

'Not especially. I'm not a recognition junkie, not like Hugo. He would kill to win that prize.'

There was another awkward silence.

'I don't mean literally, of course.'

"Course, not,' said Mhairi, heart thumping nevertheless.

'For me, it was all about the dosh. Unlike Hugo and Penelope, I have no lake of cash in which to float.'

'So how do you keep afloat, if you don't mind me asking?'

'I have my ways and means,' he replied.

'Legal?'

'Now, I'm starting to feel like I need a lawyer,' he said.

Mhairi abruptly changed tack, jumping off the stool once more.

'I must say you're very talented,' she said, walking around the studio, browsing the canvasses, looking for any sign of paintings suggestive of Hornel. There were none.

'Know much about art?' he asked.

'A bit,' she said, praying he wouldn't ask her any penetrating questions.

'I visited the Hornel museum recently.'

'Oh, what did you think of it?' he asked.

'It was interesting to wander round, and the garden is gorgeous. To be honest though, the paintings didn't really float my boat. I can see that they're clever and have taken skill, but would I want one on my wall?'

'Don't tell me, you aren't one of those philistines that choose their art to match their sofa, are you?'

'No!' said Mhairi, feeling her cheeks turn pink. Rumbled.

'Don't take this the wrong way, but, I have to ask, just as a formality of course, otherwise my boss will kick off. Where were you on the night of Sunday, 6th of January?'

Rafferty rolled his eyes and scrolled through his phone.

'I was where I normally am. Here.'

'All night?'

'Yes. We all ate together as usual, but then I came back up to the studio.'

'Thank you for your time,' said Mhairi, turning to leave.

'Wait!' he called after her.

She turned to face him.

'If you won't model for me, then at least let me buy you a drink? Unless I'm a suspect that is?' he said, with a cheeky grin.

'I'll think about it,' she said.

He passed her his business card, and she took it from him with what she hoped was a Mona Lisa smile and left the room, closing the door behind her.

She then quickly walked along the landing. None of the other doors were open apart from the one to the ladies, which she cast a longing glance at. She really did need to go to the loo now, but she would have to return to the others, to avoid attracting suspicion. She was really torn about meeting Patrick. On the one hand she knew it was a golden opportunity in relation to the investigation. However, she didn't want to mess things up between her and Ian. Patrick Rafferty was just the kind of bad boy she was trying to leave behind.

Chapter Twenty-Two

Farrell flicked his eyes towards Mhairi, as she slipped back into the room. Penelope Spence had kept them waiting for goodness knows how long, while she took some supposedly important phone call, and then marched in with an air of authority and requested tea to be brought before they got started. She was an odd one. Try as he might he couldn't seem to get a handle on her. According to her date of birth she was forty-three, a year older than him, but she had that indefinable fine-boned elegance that could have allowed her to pass for years younger. Although slender, she was tall and wiry. She was wearing a tight-fitting olive tunic, which showed the muscle definition in her arms. Her voice was loud and imperious. Someone who had a clear sense of entitlement. He would wager that she'd been born into the upper classes.

'I hope that this isn't going to take long, officers. I am working on a commission.'

'We'll keep it as brief as possible,' said Farrell, earning himself a wintery smile.

'How well did you know Monro Stevenson?' asked Byers.

'Not as well as I would have liked. He was a sweet boy and tremendously talented, but a little fragile. Over time, he became rather too attached to a girl living here. It was amusing at first, but after a while, it caused a bit of friction. He became sullen and resentful, paranoid even.'

'Could the paranoia have been triggered by drug taking?' interjected Farrell.

'Artists have long had a tradition of enhancing their creativity by partaking of the odd illicit substance, Inspector. I don't expect *you* to understand.'

Oh I think I understand only too well, thought Farrell.

'Just answer, the question please,' he said, striving to keep the irritation out of his voice.

'He may have done. I wasn't his keeper. What we get up to in our private rooms is our own business. After a while we did start to notice that he was behaving a little oddly. We tried to be supportive, but he was undermining the whole ethos of the community. Eventually we realized he had become mentally unwell and contacted his parents. I seem to recollect that the father in particular was most unpleasant. The way he spoke to me.' She shuddered. 'Brute of a man.'

'Am I correct in understanding that none of you residing here are what might be termed commercial artists?' asked Byers.

Farrell was starting to think that he had underestimated Byers.

'Perish the thought,' she snapped, her face flushing. 'Commercial artists are effectively the tradesmen of the art world. We, on the other hand, strive to be at the cutting edge, opening up the frontiers and exploring what it is to be truly human,' she said.

'So, I assume that you are all independently wealthy?' asked Byers.

Penelope shifted uncomfortably in her seat. Farrell saw a glimmer of fear in her eyes.

'I hardly think that our financial position is pertinent to your enquiry, officer,' she said.

'I'll take that as a yes, then,' said Byers. 'Easier to have lofty principles when the wolf isn't howling at the door.'

She scowled, suddenly looking her professed age and then some.

'I mean look at this place! It's hardly the stereotypical image of the artist starving in a garret, is it?'

'Did you enter the art competition yourself?' asked DI Farrell, taking over before Byers went too far and alienated her completely.

'No. However, I was delighted that Hugo's talent had been recognized.'

'Forgive me for asking,' said Farrell, 'but are you and Mr Mortimer a couple?'

She gave him a condescending smile.

'Such a quaint term,' she said. 'I suppose you might define us as that … loosely.'

'What can you tell me about Paul Moretti?' asked Farrell.

Penelope's cup rattled in its saucer as she returned it to the table.

'Very little. He has never been associated with this household.'

'Were you aware he too was shortlisted?'

'Yes, Hugo mentioned it. Is that everything, Inspector? I really must get on,' she said, standing up, as though itching to be on her way.

'Please, Ms Spence,' said Farrell gesturing to her seat.

Reluctantly she sat back down.

'I understand that you had a young Irish girl living here three years ago?'

'Yes, that's right. Ailish something or other. She was involved with Patrick, one of our artists. Pretty young thing, not much substance to her. Very conventional at heart. I knew her little rebellion would soon blow itself out. She had a tiff with Patrick over some girl and disappeared off.'

'According to her sister, she texted that she was on her way home but never arrived. That didn't concern you at the time?'

'Good heavens, no. I reckon she met someone else and sloped

off with them. After all she had pulled the disappearing act on her family before.'

'Were she and Monro ever involved, or was it simply a harmless crush on his part?'

'They never got together so far as I'm aware. The way he used to look at her. I don't know how Patrick tolerated him for so long. It became even worse as his mental health started to deteriorate. He would stare at her as though he wanted to devour her,' she said, an inappropriate smirk turning up the corners of her mouth.

Farrell felt a creeping distaste for her walk up his spine.

There was a crash from the hallway. The housekeeper poked her head round the door with a grimace that passed for an apology.

'Sorry, tripped over the rug.'

Penelope rolled the whites of her eyes but said nothing.

'Just a final formality before we let you go,' Farrell said.

'Where were you on the evening of Sunday, 6th of January, the night Monro died?'

She flicked through an elegant leather diary she had pulled from her bag.

'It seems I was here, where I am most nights.'

'Who else was with you?'

'I imagine we all ate together, as usual. After coffee, we invariably go back to our studios to work.'

'You imagine?' said Farrell.

'Well, we generally eat together at around 8 p.m.'

'Didn't think free spirits would be such creatures of routine,' commented DS Byers, earning an ugly glare.

'Will that be everything, officers?'

Farrell stood up.

'Thank you for your time, you've been most helpful,' he said. 'Patrick Rafferty, next?'

'Done and dusted,' said Mhairi.

They walked back down the long driveway in silence, saying nothing until they were seated in Farrell's Citroen.

'Something rotten in the state of Denmark,' opined Byers.

Farrell and Mhairi exchanged glances. What the hell was going on with Byers? Since when did *he* quote *Hamlet*?

'What?' he said. 'Just because I'm one hot dude, I can't have a brain too? I've embarked on a course of self-improvement. Ask me why?'

'Why?' asked Mhairi.

'Because I'm *worth* it.'

Mhairi looked at Farrell and saw his jaw muscles tighten to avoid laughing.

She could see Byers smirking in the mirror. He really was the absolute limit.

'Mhairi, how did you fare with Patrick Rafferty?' asked Farrell.

'Well, he certainly had motive to kill Monro Stevenson, sir. He was besotted with Patrick's girlfriend, Ailish. Didn't make much of an effort to hide it either.'

'That fits with what Penelope told us,' said Farrell.

'Bit of a slow burn if it was him,' said Byers. 'Three years later?'

'Revenge is a dish best served cold? Could the fact Monro was shortlisted for the prize have pushed him over the edge?' asked Farrell.

'Possibly,' said Mhairi. 'I doubt it though. He was certainly keen to win the prize but for him it was more about the money than the prestige. I think he struggles a bit financially but, art wise, he just wants to do his own thing. He did strike me as a genuine free spirit. A lot of charisma, but he had an edge to him as well, like if you pushed the wrong button he might flip. Hard to read.'

'Any sign of forged art?'

'No, but he did get a bit twitchy when I made an oblique reference.'

'One to watch then,' said Farrell.

'Oh, er, there's something else,' she said, feeling the colour rise in her cheeks.

'Spit it out,' said Farrell giving her a sideways glance.

'He asked me to model for him. Er, he does life drawing.'

'Absolutely not!' said Farrell.

'Bastard chancer,' muttered Byers in back.

'I said no! What do you take me for? He then asked if I wanted to meet up for a drink. He could give me the low-down on the art scene in Kirkcudbright, not to mention get my foot in the door at Ivy House.'

'Mhairi, there's a limit to what I expect my officers to do for the job. Aside from other considerations, of which there are plenty, this man could potentially be dangerous,' said Farrell.

'I know that, sir! I'm not stupid,' said Mhairi. 'But, I don't see what harm a drink could do?'

'Let me think about it,' said Farrell.

Both men maintained a tight-lipped silence all the way back to Dumfries.

Chapter Twenty-Three

Farrell had a banging headache by the time he got back to the station. He needed food and plenty of it. A fast metabolism and a lean physique meant he was universally loathed by dieters. The staff canteen was buzzing, as it was still the tail end of lunchtime. He stood in the doorway undecided. His stomach grumbling with rage forced him over the threshold. Loading up his tray with macaroni cheese and chips he searched for an empty table, before he spied Lind, huddled in a corner with his back to the room, at a table for one. He looked bummed-out and as if he was withdrawing into himself. This couldn't be allowed to continue. Breezily he nudged Lind's tray with his own and pulled up a chair with his other hand. Lind appeared anything but pleased to see him.

'Hey, mind if I join you?' asked Farrell, sitting down before his boss and old friend had a chance to open his mouth.

'Frank,' Lind said, a wan smile flickering across his face. 'How did you get on this morning?'

OK, now he was worried. Something was definitely amiss. But this wasn't the time or the place to get into it.

'There's a briefing scheduled for 4 p.m., so I won't bore you with all the details. Suffice to say that The Collective seems rotten

107

to the core. They've obviously got plenty to hide, but whether it's stuff pertinent to our investigation or just general drug taking and debauchery, I haven't a clue.'

'They identified the bones,' said Lind, his voice flat. 'Stirling and Thomson attended the post-mortem while you were away.'

'And?'

'They belong to Ailish Kerrigan, the girl who went missing. It's now a murder enquiry. She was stabbed, apparently. At least twice. That's how many times the knife nicked her ribs. Her sister Maureen is on her way over from Ireland. Ailish visited a local dentist with an abscess, so we were able to identify her from his records.'

'I can tell that case really got under your skin,' said Farrell.

'I suspected foul play. She was a nice kid by all accounts, if a bit misguided. I didn't have her pegged for someone who would put her family through the anguish of not knowing if she was dead or alive.'

'It appears that the deceased artist, Monro Stevenson, had developed quite an obsession with her.'

'Wasn't a nude painting of a dark-haired girl recovered in his cottage?'

'Yes, but according to Mhairi, Patrick Rafferty maintained that she only posed for him. Quite adamant about it he was. There's also the fact that the painting was unsigned.'

'Maybe he copied it?'

'That would be creepy,' said Farrell.

'Any sign that she reciprocated Monro's affection?'

'None yet, but we'll keep digging. I suppose that given what we discovered about Monro's obsession with Ailish, we also have to consider the possibility that he was the one who killed her three years ago and the guilt is what caused his breakdown back then.'

'That would mean that he did commit suicide,' said Lind.

'Or that someone found out and dispensed summary justice,' said Farrell.

He paused, wrestling with his conscience. They had a potential in at the house but he was letting his concern for Mhairi get in the way of the case. She was a dedicated and capable officer and he should not be standing in her way like this.

'Whatever it is, just tell me,' said Lind pushing away his half-eaten tray.

'Mhairi went off on her own to interview Patrick Rafferty and got a nosey round his studio. We thought he might be more forthcoming if she appeared to happen upon him by chance.'

'And was he?'

'It would seem so. He asked her to model for him. She said no, of course! He then invited her to meet up with him for a drink.'

'It would give us the ideal opportunity to monitor what's going on in there if you think any of them might be implicated in the two deaths or even the forgery ring. It's the one thing that connects Ailish and Monro, after all.'

'It's a regular viper's nest, full of strong, egotistical characters.'

'What does Mhairi say about it?'

'She's all for it.'

'Leave it with me. I'll get Kate to discuss it with her. Make sure she is fully aware of the implications.'

'Something else occurred to me,' said Farrell. 'If he knows she is police and invited her into Ivy House, it could mean he's completely innocent.'

'Either that or a dangerous egotist who gets off on taking risks,' said Lind.

'Are we going to run Ailish Kerrigan's murder as a separate investigation?' asked Farrell.

'Given that we now have three ongoing cases based in Kirkcudbright and the potential overlap between all three, not to mention our modest manpower, I reckon we should conjoin them. Each investigation requires a Senior Investigating Officer; therefore I will assume that role for the Kerrigan murder. If we conjoin briefings and have regular side meetings between the three of us that should ensure that all bases are covered and nothing is overlooked.'

Farrell nodded agreement.

'We can start the ball rolling at the 4 p.m. briefing,' he said.

Lind stood up and left, his shoulders hunched and his eyes cast downward. He seemed to have aged somehow, or maybe he had lost the spring in his step. For whatever reason, Farrell had the feeling his friend was headed into choppy waters. With a sigh he continued to eat his macaroni, but his appetite had deserted him and he had to force it down.

Grabbing another carton of the gut-rot that passed for coffee in these parts, he was on his way up the stairs when he saw Kate leaning over the top bannister.

'Frank, I've been looking for you. We've had a breakthrough in the forgery case. I need your input on this.'

The normally unflappable DI Moore was hopping from one foot to the other with impatience.

Wishing his stomach wasn't bouncing with macaroni like a rubber ball, he ran up the stairs, trying to avoid the scald from coffee splashing over his hand.

'Do hurry!' she called down from the third floor.

Crikey, was she trying to give him a heart attack? he thought, as he increased his pace. Next time he was having a salad.

Breathing hard and trying to disguise it, he followed her departing back to her office and gratefully sank into a chair.

'The person who was driving the tractor has been apprehended, hiding out in a barn near the town of Newton Stewart, name of Shaun Finch.'

'Was he a local man or higher up the food chain?' asked Farrell.

'Localish. Family hails from Annan, so a fair distance from Kirkcudbright. Bent screws the lot of them.'

'Is he talking?'

'Oh, yes. Surprised you didn't hear him singing in the canteen.'

'No solicitor?'

'Nope. His family don't have the greatest respect for the legal profession. Something to do with his brother being banged up and the sentence increased when his solicitor inadvisably appealed.'

'That would do it,' said Farrell with a smile.

'He's visited his brother in Barlinnie and is wriggling like a fish on a hook not to join him there.'

'What's he been able to give you so far?'

'He's confirmed that the forger lives in Kirkcudbright.'

'Who is it?' asked Farrell, leaning forward.

'He doesn't know. He would receive a text telling him where to pick up the package and transport it to a layby on the outskirts of Stranraer. He then had to go to the Black Heart pub on foot and wait there, until he received a text that he was to return. The money would be in a locked metal toolbox that was bolted to the floor of the tractor.'

'So what now? Did he confess he left the painting behind when he legged it?'

'No, he didn't dare. As far as they know, he took it and ran. He's been told they'll contact him to arrange a drop off in the next week.'

'Sounds like he's in over his head,' said Farrell.

'We have him for another five hours. I was hoping you would join me for the next interview?'

'Of course, Kate, be happy to,' said Farrell. A thought occurred to him. 'You're not planning to have this lad wear a wire, are you?'

She sighed but said nothing.

'What age is he?'

'Twenty-two,' she folded her arms.

'You'd be placing him in considerable danger,' said Farrell. 'If he gets caught wearing a wire, he's most likely a goner.'

111

She slumped down in her seat.

'You're right. I know you're right. This case has been driving me crazy. I'm desperate to crack it. I needed someone to rein me in.'

'Has he ever met any of his contacts face to face?' asked Farrell.

'No, not as far as I'm aware.'

'Well, we'd have to explore that further, but have you considered the possibility of sending someone in undercover to replace him?'

'It would have to be someone who's a good fit in terms of age and accent. What about DC Thomson? He's already involved in the investigation and he's keen as mustard.'

'I don't know, Kate. He's still fairly green. Do you think he could handle it? If anything happened to him …'

'He's local to Kirkcudbright, got the right accent, give or take. And he's the correct age as well.'

'Let me think about it. Wasn't Dave sent away to boarding school? Maybe he would sound too different?'

'I've heard him on the phone and he switches back into the local accent without thinking twice about it.'

'We'll see what transpires in the interview.'

'I'm planning to resume questioning him in a few minutes. We took a comfort break. One of the artists you've been speaking to may be implicated, so you might pick up on something I could miss.'

112

Chapter Twenty-Four

They walked down the stairs to the interview rooms.

'How do you want to play this, Kate?'

'I reckon you make a much better bad cop, than me,' she said.

'Thank you … I think. We should lay out Shaun's choices. Either, go back in himself wearing a wire and have his communications monitored, or he can give us sufficient information to send someone else in undercover. The lad would have to stay in a safe house for the duration though. We can't have him running amok, blabbing to his meathead friends and family.'

'Agreed. There would have to be a total ban on contacting his family for now. If they interfered with the investigation in any way, it could put DC Thomson in severe jeopardy.'

'We'll need a cover story that will appease them, and it can't be that he's helping us, or he'll be banished six feet under,' said Farrell. 'I know how these types of family operate.'

They reached the interview room on the ground floor. As they swung open the door, the smell of pine disinfectant fought for supremacy against that of sweat and stale body odour and lost. Farrell sat at the table and glowered at the pimply faced young man opposite him. Shaun Finch tried faint-heartedly to glare back at him, but soon dropped his gaze.

DI Moore switched on the tape recorder and video.

'Resuming interview at 15.33. Please identify yourselves for the tape.'

'DI Frank Farrell.'

'DI Kate Moore.'

'Shaun Finch,' the lad mumbled, his sulky mouth turned down in a frown.

'Can you confirm again for the tape, Shaun, that you've been advised of your right to a solicitor and choose to proceed without one,' said DI Moore.

'Aye, let's get this over with,' he muttered, squirming in his seat. A restless ball of energy with no place to go.

Farrell leaned forward and stared at the youth, who flinched away from his gaze.

'Have you any idea how much bother you're in here, Shaun?'

'I was only the driver, that's all you can pin on me,' he said, slouching further down in his seat.

'That's as may be,' said Farrell. 'But what I think you've not quite grasped is that you are art and part liable in the whole criminal enterprise, not just for your wee bit in it.'

'What's he talking aboot?' Shaun asked DI Moore.

'You've been engaged in a joint criminal enterprise, so you're liable for the forgeries, their delivery and resultant fraud. In other words, you'll be up the road to Barlinnie and they'll throw away the key. Make the rest of your family look like regular pillars of society,' said Farrell.

'No way!' he spluttered, flecks of saliva spraying out through misshapen teeth.

'How else did you think this was going to end?' asked Farrell.

'I thought I was going to cut a deal, like,' he said.

'Trouble is, Shaun, you don't have much to bargain with, do you?' said Farrell, his tone slightly more conciliatory. He glanced at DI Moore, and she took his cue, leaning forward as Farrell settled back in his seat, looking like he needed to be convinced.

'Come on, Shaun,' she said. 'Do yourself a favour, lad. Nobody wants to see someone as young as you wasting their youth locked up in that nuthouse. There must be something else you can tell us.'

Shaun's low brow frowned in concentration. Farrell felt like he could almost hear the cogs turning slowly. He wasn't going to get there on his own.

'Surely, even if you haven't seen any of the players, you must have some idea of who could be involved locally or what else is being planned?' he said.

'Would it make a difference, like? I don't know anything for definite.'

'When you said before, in the earlier interview, that the forger is in Kirkcudbright, how did you know that?' asked DI Moore.

'Well, it made sense given the pick-up site.'

'Which was?'

'Behind one of the graves in St Cuthbert's Kirkyard. Only somebody local to Kirkcudbright would think to put it there. Stands to reason,' he said, growing bolder now.

Farrell weighed up his options. The last thing he wanted to do was lead the witness and have the tape ruled inadmissible at a later date in court.

'What pub do you drink in?' he asked, changing tack.

'The Smuggler's Inn,' Shaun said.

Farrell was aware of it though had never been in. It was the local watering hole in Kirkcudbright for anyone remotely shifty, where they could shoot the breeze with kindred spirits.

'Have you heard any rumours in general about dodgy artists?' he asked.

Shaun scratched his head. It was torturous to watch.

'There was meant to be a big heist going down. The theft of a priceless painting from one of them posh houses. Proper gentry like.'

'Which one?'

'Kincaid House. The kitchen maid from there was in The Smuggler's wi' her man a few weeks back. He gave her the evils and dragged her away. Never heard nothing else. Never seen them since.'

'Do you know her name?' asked Farrell.

'Poppy something.'

'What about him?'

'Not a local boy. Sounded like he was from Glasgow.'

'What about the artists that live in Ivy House, on the edge of Kirkcudbright?' asked Farrell.

'Right bunch of mingers that lot.'

'Aside from their lifestyle, have you any reason to believe that any of them is involved in the forgery ring?'

Shaun scratched his head and thought. The clock ticked on. Farrell ground his teeth together but bided his time. They needed his cooperation.

'What's in it for me?' he eventually asked, his shaking voice belying the bravado of his words.

'A free pass out of jail, if the fiscal's willing to come on board,' said DI Moore. 'You would have to be placed in protective custody until the conclusion of the operation.'

'What? Like in the films?' he asked, looking not displeased by the idea.

'Exactly like in the films,' said Farrell.

'But for that to happen, for that free pass to be issued, we're going to need you to cough up every bit of information you know,' said DI Moore.

'If you can't or won't give us what we need, then there's no deal,' said Farrell, looking as severe as he knew how. 'You'll be staring at serious jail time. Tick Tock!' he said, gathering his papers together as though about to leave. DI Moore did likewise, started to stand.

'Aw right, keep yer hair on,' Shaun scowled. 'I'll tell you everything.'

116

Farrell and Moore sat down again.

'The Collective?' said DI Moore.

'I know at least one of them is involved.'

'How do you know?' asked DI Moore.

'Well, I wanted a bit of insurance like, so I went to the pick-up site early and hid.'

'The pick-up site? Is it always the same?' asked Farrell.

'St Cuthbert's Kirkyard, up past Ivy House and turn up to the left. You go through the gate, turn left following the wall and it's the grave tucked right in the corner.'

'Who dropped off the parcel?' asked DI Moore.

'I couldn't make them out. It was nearly dark, and they were all muffled up.'

'Male or female?'

Shaun shrugged.

'Couldn't say.'

'How do you know it's someone from The Collective, then?' asked Farrell.

'Cos I followed them, didn't I?' He sat back with a smirk. 'I figured I would leave the package where it was for the time being and tail them for a while at a safe distance, but whoever it was turned in to that posh house they live in. That's how I knew.'

'Have you any information that anyone else in Kirkcudbright is involved, apart from that one person?' asked DI Moore.

'Their top man is meant to live in Kirkcudbright. He's the one behind the forgery ring.'

'Says, who?' asked Farrell.

'Says Billy Ryan, the barman at The Smuggler's. Said he over-heard some out-of-town boys talking. Proper hard nuts they were. By the accents, he pegged them as being from Glasgow.'

'When was this?' asked DI Moore.

'Not a clue. You'd have to ask him yourselves. Don't mention my name either. Billy Ryan's not someone I want to mess with. He'd stab you soon as look at you, that one.'

'So tell us, Shaun,' said Farrell, 'how did you come to be mixed up in all of this?'

'Someone contacted me by text. Said they'd heard I could drive a tractor and might be willing to put a wee bit of delivery money my way.'

'Who owned the tractor you were driving?'

'The farmer I was working for at the time. They said to text back if I was interested in taking it any further. Then, they were going to arrange a dummy run and, if it went well, there'd be a couple of hundred quid in it for me.'

'Did you know you were delivering forged paintings?' asked Farrell.

'Not at the beginning, though they did tell me it wasn't drugs when I asked. That's the one thing I didn't want to be mixed up in.'

'And later?'

'Well, it wasn't rocket science. They were wrapped in oilskin and packed in cylinders. Light, not heavy. I thought at first they might be stolen, but when there was no fuss in the papers, I figured they were forgeries.'

'How many deliveries did you make?' asked DI Moore.

'Nine, until I was caught. It was on the first Monday of every month. I was on my way to Stranraer for the last one, when some numpty cut in front of me and caused the accident. I had no choice but to leg it.'

'Did you contact them to say what had happened?'

Shaun nodded.

'They gave me a burner. I texted them when I got away.'

'You're sure that you didn't let on that you'd left the painting behind?'

'No, I didn't dare. I was playing for time till I could scratch some money together to do a runner to Ireland. They said to lie low until the heat dies down then they'd put another burner at the drop site when I got back to it.'

'Have you still got the original phone?'

'No, I dumped it. I didn't manage to get back to pick up the new one.'

'So, to the best of your knowledge no one you've been dealing with knows what you look like?'

'No,' said Shaun.

'Interview suspended,' said DI Moore as they both got to their feet.

'We'll get you something to eat, Shaun.'

They left the room and moved along the corridor.

'I'll take a run out to Kincaid House tomorrow and bring in that kitchen maid,' said Farrell. 'If she's been shooting her mouth off, she could be in grave danger.'

Chapter Twenty-Five

DCI Lind put the phone back in its cradle with a sigh. Maureen Kerrigan was on her way up to his office. It had been at least three years since he had seen her, though she always phoned him around the anniversary of her sister's disappearance. The case had weighed heavily on him.

There was a light tap on the door and a young woman with a long mane of dark brown curls entered. She was the spitting image of her sister Ailish. A walking monument to her loss.

Lind stood up and smiled at her.

'Maureen, come away in and sit yourself down.'

She attempted to smile but her skin was chalk white, and she had purple shadows under her eyes that gave her a bruised look.

A young PC brought a tray with tea and biscuits then left. Lind waited until Maureen had raised a cup to her lips, with shaking hands, before saying anything further.

'How was the trip over on the ferry?'

She groaned and looked queasy.

'That good?' said Lind.

'I'm no sailor,' she said.

'I thought your mother might have come over with you?'

'She left us about a year after Ailish went missing.

120

Broken-hearted she was. Left a note saying she needed to get away from all the reminders. Said she wouldn't return until she was able to bring Ailish home. We've heard nothing from her since. Dad lost heart himself after that. He started drinking, withdrew into himself.'

'I'm so sorry, Maureen, I had no idea.'

'There's been times I've hated Ailish through the years,' she said with a twisted smile. 'If she hadn't been so selfish and ran off with that no-good Patrick Rafferty, my family would still be intact. It's been … hard, you know?'

'Those feelings are perfectly normal,' said Lind. 'You're bound to have felt conflicted.'

'When I got the phone call to say that all this time my sister had been lying in an unmarked grave, I …' She broke down in tears.

Silently, Lind passed a box of tissues across to her. She took one, blew her nose loudly, and gave him a watery smile.

'I want to arrange her funeral in Donegal. How soon can her remains be released for burial?'

'It'll be a while yet,' said Lind. 'We've managed to establish that the cause of death was most likely that she was stabbed more than once. However, due to the length of time that has passed and the exposed nature of the burial site, we can't be more precise. Given the remote location of the remains, and the text that she sent to you immediately before she disappeared, we are most definitely treating Ailish's death as a murder investigation.'

'Thank you.'

'For what?' said Lind.

'For using her name. For talking about her as if she was a person and not just a dead body, a pile of bones. You're a good man, DCI Lind.'

He reached across and enfolded her small pale hand between his two large ones.

'I'll do everything in my power to get you answers, Maureen.

121

You can count on that. In the meantime, where are you staying?'

'I've booked a B&B in Kirkcudbright.'

Lind looked worried.

'Are you sure that's a good idea?'

'Don't worry, DCI Lind, I'm no Nancy Drew. I simply want to walk in my sister's footsteps, feel the essence of her in the last place that she walked the Earth. I'm not about to do anything rash. I've got a friend in the area. I'll be fine.'

Lind wasn't sure that he believed her, but there wasn't a lot he could do about it.

'Promise me you'll be careful,' he said.

'I promise,' she replied.

'In the meantime, here's all the numbers I can be reached on,' he said, handing her his business card, to which he had added his own personal mobile. 'I'll keep you posted on any developments in the investigation.'

She handed over her own contact details on a slip of paper for the duration of her stay.

Lind escorted her down to the front door of the station and had just waved her off when Laura got up from one of the seats in the waiting area. He had walked right by her. The smile froze on his lips, as he took in the stormy expression in her eyes. What he was meant to have done this time was quite beyond him, but he was not going to have a ding-dong in reception, that was for sure.

'Laura, I wasn't expecting to see you here.'

'Evidently,' she snapped.

Lind ran his fingers distractedly through his thinning hair. He had to get her out of here before she blew. A wave of fatigue rocked him on his feet. It had already been a helluva day and now this …

DI Moore appeared from behind the public information counter with her coat on, her face wreathed in such a warm smile that Laura was left with no choice but to return it.

Lind felt the tension ebb from his body as she hugged Laura and turned to him.

'John, do you think I could borrow your lovely wife for half an hour? I'm due a break and I'm hoping she'll join me for a coffee at Mrs Green's Tea Room. I have an unholy craving for a piece of their delectable carrot cake. Laura, what do you say?'

'Far be it from me to stand between women and their cake,' he said, aiming for jovial but falling somewhat short.

Laura allowed herself to be led away by Kate, who was succeeding in being unusually chatty, and a relieved Lind retreated back upstairs. No doubt he was only postponing whatever grievance, real or imagined, had propelled his wife in here.

He knew that Frank, and probably Kate too, had twigged that they were going through a hard time, but he had never been comfortable talking about his private life. It felt disloyal somehow. He was fast running out of ideas though. Frank would be the obvious person to turn to, yet to do so would feel like an admission of failure. He had always known that if Frank hadn't gone off to the seminary, in all likelihood, he would have married Laura. Knowing that his friend had been her first love had been difficult at first, but he had made his peace with it a long time ago.

He forced his dark thoughts down. He wished Maureen hadn't come straight over. Her presence complicated things. The killer could well still be living in the area. There was no way of knowing what had drawn him or her to Ailish, but Maureen was the spitting image of her sister, and he couldn't help but worry that might stir the appetite of the killer.

Chapter Twenty-Six

Farrell took his place at the front of the small lecture room, nodding a greeting to Lind and Moore. Such was the scope of the investigations now they had had to move the last briefing of the day here. As it was, every seat was filled and the clamour of voices and rising heat made Farrell undo the top button beneath his tie. The various investigations were growing arms and legs, but they were now stretched to breaking point, with officers drafted in from tiny police stations all around the region to assist with the legwork. The Super appeared in the backlit doorway and paused before briskly walking down to the stage with a jaw set like granite. The civilian press officer, Andy Moran, sat in the front row, with his notepad open, oblivious to the jostling going on around him.

The Super stepped on to the stage and held up his hand for silence, which was immediately forthcoming.

'As you all know, there appears to be something of a hornet's nest in Kirkcudbright. There's the murder of the artist Monro Stevenson, headed up by DI Farrell, the murder of Ailish Kerrigan, led by DCI Lind, and DI Moore's looking into the operation of a forgery ring. To what extent these investigations are connected is not yet known but it seems likely that there is at least some overlap.'

'How many of you hail from Kirkcudbright or have grannies, cousins or friends who live there?'

A sizeable number of hands were raised.

'Excellent, I want you all to mine those connections for information and report back to one of the three investigative heads. I want anything relating to The Collective, from when it was first set up to the present date, and everyone who has been associated with it. I also want any and all information in relation to Monro Stevenson, Ailish Kerrigan and their known associates. If anyone has some dodgy relatives who drink in The Smuggler's or swim about in the shallows of petty crime, work out how you can extract information from them that might feed into our investigation.

'At this stage of the investigation, we're looking to subtly utilize our connections so that, hopefully, we can identify potential witnesses. It goes without saying that I expect you all to exercise the utmost discretion. And do *not* put yourselves at risk! Is that clear?'

The Super then sat down and gestured to DCI Lind to take the floor.

'Ailish Kerrigan was only nineteen years of age when she texted her sister Maureen to say she was on her way home to Ireland. This text was received at 9.15 a.m. on the 15th of June 2009. The next bus to Stranraer to catch the ferry would have been at 11 a.m. She didn't get the bus. Nor, as far as we are aware, did she ever make it to the ferry port. She simply disappeared into thin air. Sometime after 9 a.m. she left The Collective. There, she was involved in a relationship with Patrick Rafferty, who also hails from Northern Ireland. Her remains were found on the Dundrennan Firing Range, in a shallow grave, within a patch of trees at the top of a hill.'

Lind pointed to the image on the whiteboard. 'There were some as yet unidentified marks beside where her body was found that are suggestive of someone visiting the site after she died.'

'I wonder if someone might have been sitting there with an easel? I've done a bit of work outdoors with an easel in the past. The marks don't look dissimilar,' said DI Moore.

You could have heard a pin drop as everyone took in the horror of her words.

Lind studied the marks closely.

'I suggest you liaise with SOCO, Kate, and see if that theory is consistent with their findings.'

'Do we know if she was killed at the burial site or moved there from somewhere else?' asked DS Stirling.

'Not yet determined. The body has been in an exposed position for some time. Cause of death is likely due to stabbing, as evidenced by two nicks on the ribs. The body was positioned on its back with the hands by its side, as you can see from the scene photo on screen. Extensive soil samples have been sent off for analysis, but they will take a few weeks to process.'

'Again, we need to look into the members of The Collective around the time Ailish went missing. It is necessary to establish whether there were people we don't know about, who left between Ailish's arrival in Kirkcudbright in 2006 and the present day. These people, if any, need to be traced, identified and interviewed as soon as possible.'

'You should also be aware that Maureen Kerrigan, the younger sister of the deceased, is over here just now staying in The Cormorant B&B, Kirkcudbright. I want every courtesy to be extended to her if any of you come across her.'

Lind moved away and motioned to Farrell, who stood up to take his place.

'Turning now to Monro Stevenson. We received the toxicology results back this morning, which confirmed that he was drugged with ketamine. This is now a murder investigation. There was none in the bottle of whisky left on the table, so it must have been added to the glass tumbler. The pathologist has confirmed that there was no apparent puncture mark on the body of the deceased. After the briefing Andy Moran will be releasing an update to the press.'

'The handwriting expert has confirmed that the signature on the so-called suicide note was very similar but not identical to Monro's. It was a skilled imitation. The Tech boys have confirmed that there was no trace of it on Monro's laptop. It was probably brought into the cottage, already prepared, by the killer. This was not a spur-of-the-moment attack, but a carefully premeditated murder.'

'It doesn't look like standard printer paper, does it, sir?' asked PC Rosie Green.

'That's correct. The note was printed off on high-quality cream stationery. Unfortunately, not sufficiently high-quality as to be considered bespoke. There were no other such sheets of paper in Monro Stevenson's cottage.'

'So, if we find the stationery, we find the killer?' asked PC Green.

'Possibly,' said Farrell. 'DC McLeod could you contact all the stationery shops in Dumfries and Galloway to ascertain whether they stock this particular paper? If so, try and ascertain whether there is CCTV coverage. It's a long shot but you never know.'

'Will do, sir,' said Mhairi, making a note.

'That reminds me, we still haven't heard a peep out of his girlfriend, Nancy Quinn. PC Green, I asked you to bring her in?'

'No one's heard from her. The parents did call on her the day the body was found, but she wasn't there, and she hasn't responded to the note they put through the door asking her to contact them. I called round a few times too.' She coloured. 'Sorry, sir, I should have said something sooner.'

Yes, she should have done, thought Farrell. Mind you, he should have been all over it as well. They'd just been spinning a dizzying number of plates.

'No harm done,' he said, hoping it was true. 'We must tie up this loose end, though.'

Another hand shot up. One of the Kirkcudbright coppers, PC Calum McGhie.

'I managed to get hold of the landlord to the victim's cottage, sir. He's been away visiting family. He confirmed that when the cottage was rented, there was only a basic Yale lock on the door. The deceased had asked if he could upgrade it at his own expense.'

'So, either he was hiding something valuable, or he felt under threat. I want you to trace the locksmith and interview him. See if he gave him any indication as to why he needed the extra security.'

'Sir,' said PC McGhie, writing in his notebook.

The heat in the room had risen to an intolerable level, with so many bodies crammed in to the small lecture theatre combined with the heat from the storage heaters. Farrell glanced at DI Moore, and she gave a small shake of her head.

'That's given us enough to chew on for one session. DI Moore will be holding a separate briefing on the forgery ring same time tomorrow.'

Everyone surged out of the two exits to catch up on their paperwork before heading home for the night. Farrell felt the energy drain from him, as if it had hitched on to the tail end of the departing bodies. It was his body's way of informing him he had been overdoing it. Wearily he ran a hand through his hair. After his near breakdown last year he wasn't taking any chances. He needed an antidote to the baser side of human behaviour that was threatening once more to engulf him.

Chapter Twenty-Seven

Grabbing his overcoat, he left the building and headed for St Margaret's. It was so cold it took his breath away. Lengthening his stride, he could feel his cramped muscles start to loosen, and ten minutes later he was dipping his fingers into holy water and entering the church. There was only a smattering of the Catholic faithful there for evening Mass on a weeknight. Genuflecting, he made the sign of the cross and slipped in to a pew at the rear of the huddle; his natural reticence making him more comfortable in his own space. He could see his mother seated near the front, in the middle of a row of women, the ones who got things done. She too had switched from St Aidan's and was doing the best she could to expunge the terrible memories of what had occurred there. As if she sensed his presence she turned round and stared, acknowledging him with a nod and a small smile. He did likewise. They had been long estranged until last year, and it was with slow cautious steps they were exploring their rapprochement.

As Father Murray entered from the far left, moving towards the altar, Farrell reflexively stood, taking comfort in the familiar patterns of the Mass and drawing sustenance from it. As he moved seamlessly with the others to take Communion from the priest, he felt a rare moment of peace. Kneeling afterwards, he lost himself in prayer and sensed the layers of time fall away until he was once more at one with God.

Pulled from his almost meditative state of prayer by the rustle of the congregation rising to its feet, he hurriedly followed suit. It was as if the slender thread connecting him to the Divine had once more been sheared away.

He waited on the steps outside for his mother, glad to see she was smiling and laughing with her new Catholic brethren. She would be in the thick of things here in no time. Her grief had been raw and unexpected. He had thought she might snap under its weight. He had thought that he might too.

She came to a halt and scrutinized him from head to toe.

'You look tired,' she said. 'And you've lost weight.'

This last was pronounced with more than a hint of accusation.

'You are still on your meds, aren't you?' she hissed under her breath.

Farrell felt a familiar flare of irritation and tried to squash it back down.

'Stop fussing. I'm hardly likely to make that mistake again.'

The mistake that had allowed the demon of psychosis to make its presence felt after an absence of fifteen years.

'I'm your mother, I'm allowed to fuss,' she snapped. They both fell silent, overwhelmed by the subtext lurking behind the ordinary words.

Father Murray relieved the sudden awkwardness by choosing that moment to appear. His mother re-joined her friends who had been waiting for her. Farrell noticed a couple of them shooting curious looks in his direction.

'Pint?' asked Farrell.

'Too right,' said his priest and friend, Jim Murray. 'If we head up to the Bruce, we can grab a bite to eat as well. I'm starving.'

A fifteen-minute walk took them to the fluted columns of the Robert the Bruce pub. Farrell felt his mouth begin to water as

130

the sign outside announced it was curry night. That would do nicely.

Although he had only known Jim since the tail end of last year, they had quickly become close. The life of a Catholic priest was a lonely one, and Farrell was glad to provide a listening ear, understanding the pressures only too well. In turn, he could talk to Jim about his growing dilemma of whether to seek a return to active service as a priest, leaving behind the career he had worked so hard to carve out for himself after his breakdown.

As he wiped the last piece of naan bread round the sauce left on his plate and drained the dregs of his beer, resisting the temptation to give a satisfied belch, the revolving door swung open and in walked a couple of women, dressed to impress. He glanced at them idly. Then he did a double take. One of them was Laura, and she was very drunk.

'What's up?' asked Jim, looking puzzled by his reaction. 'Do you know them?'

'It's Laura, Lind's wife. I don't know who the other woman is, but I can guess.'

'Ah, the one who …?'

'Yip,' said Farrell, feeling his jaw clamp tight.

He had no right to interfere. Laura was none of his concern. Keep telling yourself that, said the niggling voice in his head. She had lost the baby weight and had killer curves to prove it, which were much in evidence in her tight-fitting purple dress.

Farrell tried to move the conversation on to other things, but his eyes were continually drawn back to Laura.

Eventually, his friend sighed deeply and turned to him.

'It's like having a beer with a robot.'

'Sorry, Jim, I'm just worried that some predatory nut job is going to take advantage of her in the state she's in.'

'If I didn't know you better, I'd say you had feelings for this woman that went way beyond platonic,' said Father Murray.

'I don't!' said Farrell. 'John is my oldest friend. I would never do anything to come between them.'

'All right, keep your hair on. What about phoning John? Get him to come and take her home?'

'He's got his hands full at work, and I don't want to trigger another row. Their marriage is under considerable strain as it is.'

'Uh oh,' said Father Murray.

Farrell turned round to see two guys in rumpled suits approaching the women. They too looked somewhat the worse for wear and were exuding that air of fake bonhomie that men assume when trying to pick up women in a bar. He tensed, waiting to see if Laura would shut them down. Dammit, she was accepting a drink. At this rate he was going to have to intervene.

The four of them went to sit in a booth. Laura still hadn't clocked him. Maybe she was just chumming her mate, had told them she was married.

He turned back to his friend and confessor.

'Sorry, Jim, I'm sure it'll be fine. Where were we?'

'Debating the merits of chicken bhuna over chicken madras, I think.'

'How's my mother settling into St Margaret's? She's been through a lot, and it's been a wrench leaving all her old cronies behind.'

'I don't think you need worry on that score,' Father Murray said with a chuckle. 'She's scything her way mercilessly to the top of the pecking order. Westminster politics has got nothing compared to the machinations of the Catholic faithful. Her arrival has really shaken up the inner circle. They're all running around like headless chickens trying to outdo one another. I can't remember the last time I've had so many baked offerings. I've put on half a stone,' he said, patting his expanding tummy with a rueful smile.

'Sounds like she's being a bit of a handful?' Farrell said.

'Not a bit of it. Most of our more involved ladies are widowed, not always with the most attentive of families. It keeps them on their toes, therefore happy and engaged.'

'And how are things with you?' asked Farrell.

'Me? Rushed off my feet, as normal. What I wouldn't give for an extra pair of hands some days! If your hours weren't so insane and unpredictable I'd have conscripted you already.'

Farrell fell silent. He would love nothing better than to help out at St Margaret's, but the Super would have a fit if word got back to him. He was feeling more and more conflicted about where his true vocation lay. Where was he of most use? In the Church or fighting crime?

Father Murray nudged him, and he glanced back over at Laura. One of the sleazy characters had his arm around her and looked to be getting ready to make a play. Her mate was already indulging in some tongue action with his friend. As he leaned in to seal the deal, Farrell sprang to his feet and approached their table, struggling to keep his temper in check.

'Laura!' he announced loudly, causing her to spin round in shock. 'How lovely to see you. How are the kids? John mentioned he might join me here later. Aren't you going to introduce me to your friends?'

His manner was mild, but there was no mistaking the menace in his tightly coiled bearing as he looked at the creep now surreptitiously sliding his arm back along the seat.

Laura glared at him. Then the fight went out of her, and she started to cry.

As if reacting to an unspoken signal, both men stood up, muttering about having to go as they had an early meeting in the morning. Farrell glared at them with unconcealed contempt, his copper's eye taking in white bands on ring fingers and the stench of stale booze leaking out of their pores.

The other woman stood on wobbly heels and squared up to him.

'Who the hell do you think you are, crashing our party?'

133

'I'm Laura's and John's oldest friend, DI Frank Farrell,' he replied, a hard edge to his voice. 'And you are?'

'Oh, for fuck's sake,' she muttered. 'I don't need this shit in my life. Laura, I'm off. You okay if I leave you with this fucking charmer?'

Laura waved her away, struggling to get her emotions under control. Farrell passed her a hanky and sank into the seat beside her. Now what? He hadn't a clue what was going on in her head. Crying women weren't his strong suit.

Steeling himself, he waded in.

'Look, I'm sorry, Laura, but I couldn't let you do something I know you would regret in the morning.'

'Don't pretend you know what I'm thinking, Frank, because trust me, you haven't got a fucking clue,' she hissed through her tears.

Two women swearing at him in five minutes! He was on fire tonight. He could do with Mhairi here, she'd have the whole mess sorted out in double-quick time.

'Okay, hands up, I haven't a clue what you're thinking.'

'Some things never change,' she snapped.

'Those weren't good guys, Laura. You know that! Married, the pair of them, looking for a cheap lay. Is that what you want? To be a cheap thrill for some loser?'

'How dare you, Frank Farrell,' she hissed. 'Just who do you think you are? You're such a hypocrite, hiding behind the robes of the Catholic Church when it suits you. Any time things get too intense, you run for the Church. Like with Clare, last year.'

'I seem to recall, *she* dumped me,' he said, striving for a light tone, though the wound had only partially healed.

'Look, your friend has bailed,' he said.

'Whose fault was that?'

'So, you might as well let me take you home.'

Grudgingly, she fumbled for her coat and bag and allowed him to help her out the pub. He shot an apologetic glance back to Father Murray, who had witnessed the whole scene, and whose expression was unreadable.

As soon as the fresh air hit her, she swayed and would have fallen if he hadn't caught her.

'Frank, I'm going to be ...' She bent double and vomited over the pavement, narrowly missing his shoes.

By the time he got her home she was pale and clammy. He called out as he opened the door with her key, but no one was home. The kids must be off staying with Lind's mother.

Once she was in the hall she slid down the wall like snow off a dyke. He had to get her into bed, so she could sleep off the worst of it before Lind saw her in the morning. Farrell lifted her to her feet, but her legs were like cooked spaghetti. Grimacing he hoisted her into his arms and staggered upstairs, nudging open doors until he found the master bedroom. He pulled off her coat and shoes then felt under her pillow for her nightie.

'Here, put this on,' he said, turning his back.

'Help me,' she muttered.

Rolling his eyes skywards he reluctantly helped her remove her dress. He was shocked by how thin she had become, her bones jutting out at sharp angles. Hurriedly, he pulled her nightie over her head. Suddenly, she locked her arms round his neck.

'I love you, Frank. I've always loved you.'

For a split second, he thought about yielding to her embrace. Horrified at himself for even entertaining the idea, he peeled her arms from around him. Nothing but the drink talking, he muttered, as he tucked her in on her side. She fell asleep right away, and he felt his heart lurch. It was as if the years had melted away. She looked so young and vulnerable, like the girl he used to know.

Before he slipped out into the night, he placed a glass of water and a couple of painkillers by her bed.

Chapter Twenty-Eight

Mhairi was in the shower by six a.m. Ian was still fast asleep. She smiled to herself as she remembered what a great time they'd had last night. It was the first time he'd stayed over, and it had felt so natural to have him there. He'd even managed to sweet talk Oscar, who had abandoned her knee for his. She dressed as quietly as she could, to try and avoid waking him. Before heading out, she tiptoed to his side of the bed to leave him a note.

Suddenly, his phone rang, causing her to jump a foot in the air. In one fluid movement he grabbed it, rejected the call and flopped back on the pillow, groaning.

'What is wrong with people? It's the middle of the night.'

'Not a morning person then,' she said.

'For you, I might be prepared to make an exception,' he said, trying to pull her back onto the bed.

'Oh no, you don't,' she said, nimbly evading him. 'Some of us have to work!'

'Some of my best work has come to me in a dream,' he grinned.

'Is that a fact?'

She blew him a kiss on the way out the door.

* * *

As she arrived at Loreburn Street, she saw Sophie Richardson and her crew of reporters, setting up outside the station, ready to pounce on anyone entering or leaving the building. It was starting to feel as though they were under siege. She flipped up the hood on her parka as she approached. The news thus far had been critical of the investigative team, attempting to turn it into a political debate about the merits of police centralization. She put her head down and marched past them in to the station.

The mood in the conference room was sombre. DC Thomson was sitting forward on the edge of his seat. Mhairi tried to look more relaxed than she felt.

The Super had a selection of newspapers in front of him. His normally pale face was red and mottled. He didn't look well and had a bit of a wheeze.

'Have you seen these headlines?' he demanded. 'Bloody journalists using us as a scapegoat to further their utopian fantasies of Police Scotland.'

He picked up two papers and read the headlines out loud. '"Local bobbies painted into a corner over murdered artist. Dumfries police clueless".'

DCI Lind, DI Moore, and Farrell exchanged glances.

'We need to get on top of these cases,' the Super sighed. 'I don't want a monumental cock-up to be the lasting legacy of this station.'

'No one wants that, sir,' said Farrell.

'This scheme you've cooked up, DI Moore. I don't like it,' said the Super, shaking his head. 'I don't like it at all. DC Thomson has no experience in undercover work.'

'He was heavily involved in the murder and abduction cases last year,' DI Moore said. 'He's been working closely with me on the forgery investigation and knows all the ins and outs. He's one of the few serving officers we have from Kirkcudbright; therefore his accent is a close match for the driver. Plus, he grew up on a farm, so he knows his way round tractors and the like. We've obtained permission to use an empty farmhouse for his base, and DS Stirling can be the alcoholic farmer DC Thomson works for. Another two uniforms will be there as farm workers, so backup is never far away.'

'How do you feel about this, son?' asked the Super.

'I'm happy to give it a go, sir,' Thomson replied. 'It'll be good experience and I reckon I can pull it off.'

'DI Moore, once he's out in the field I want regular updates, is that clear?'

'Yes, sir, of course,' she said.

'Very well, I'll sign off on it,' said the Super with a sigh.

'Now no heroic bullshit,' he said sternly to DC Thomson. 'If it all goes tits up, I want you out of there pronto. Do we understand each other?'

'Yes, sir,' said DC Thomson.

'Very well, dismissed.'

DC Thomson left hurriedly.

'Now, then,' said the Super, turning to Mhairi.

She felt her face colour. To be talking about this with the Super was beyond embarrassing.

'What you're proposing is to meet Patrick Rafferty for a drink?'

'Yes, sir. He's offered to fill me in on the local art scene.'

'And then what?'

'Well, ideally, if I succeed in ingratiating myself, I might end up gaining access to Ivy House and be better able to do some digging.'

'We still don't know his position in relation to all this. He might be just as interested in mining you for information as you are him,' said the Super.

'Yes, sir. I'll be on my guard at all times. If I establish a good connection with him it might even be a useful way for us to feed false information back into The Collective at some stage. I've thought it through and it seems to me that the only viable way of getting inside The Collective is to take this opportunity. It'll hopefully give me a chance to ferret around behind the scenes and see if any of them are involved in either of the murders or the forging ring.'

'And if someone behind those high walls is involved and, God forbid, finds you poking around?'

'I can handle myself,' she said firmly. 'I was in dangerous situations on a number of occasions last year and I kept my nerve at all times, didn't I, sir?'

This last comment was addressed to Farrell, who seemed to be developing some frown lines.

'I can't dispute that, Mhairi, but I can't pretend I like this either. At all! Are you quite sure about this, DC McLeod? No one will think any the worse of you, if you decide to pull out,' said the Super.

'Thank you, sir, but my mind is made up. I'm looking forward to the challenge.'

'Very well,' said the Super. 'You have his number. I suggest you phone him and arrange to meet up tomorrow night. We'll take it from there.'

'DI Moore and DI Farrell, I'll expect to be kept in the loop at all times. Is that clear?'

'Yes, sir,' they said.

'Good luck, DC McLeod. Remember your safety matters more to me than a conviction. Are we clear on that?'

'Yes, sir, thank you, sir,' said McLeod and then followed the other three out of the room.

139

Chapter Twenty-Nine

Farrell and Mhairi drove straight through Kirkcudbright. He'd already checked that Lord Merton was in residence. The secretary had sounded reluctant to make an appointment, but he'd been insistent. They carried on for a further fifteen minutes before coming to the imposing grounds of Kincaid House. Driving up through the immaculate grounds, he hoped he was on a wild goose chase and that he would find the housemaid unharmed. However, he couldn't shake off a feeling of foreboding. The house was magnificent, a relic from a bygone era.

'If I'd known we were coming here, I'd have dressed for the occasion,' muttered Mhairi.

He rang the doorbell half expecting to be admonished for not using the tradesman's entrance. A rather stern woman in a navy suit showed him into the drawing room.

Seconds later, Lord Merton arrived. He appeared to be in his fifties and greeted them politely enough, but he looked pale and strained. A noticeable twitch caused his eyelid to flicker, and he quickly averted his gaze from Farrell after introducing himself. He didn't invite them to sit.

'We've received a tip-off that a valuable painting may have been stolen from Kincaid House, sir,' said Farrell. 'I thought I'd best pop out and see whether such an event has already occurred or might potentially occur.'

The man in front of him swayed slightly like he was about to faint.

'Good Heavens! I'm afraid you've had a wasted trip. That is simply not possible. All of my paintings are present and correct and we have quite stringent security measures to keep them that way. Now if there's nothing else?'

'Just one thing, sir. Would it be possible to speak to your housemaid?'

'My housemaid? Good heavens, man, what on earth for?'

'I'm not at liberty to say, sir,' said Farrell.

'Oh, very well. I'll get the housekeeper to send her up. I take it you've finished with me?'

'For the time being, sir.'

'In that case, I'll bid you both good day,' said Lord Merton, leaving the room.

Ten minutes later, there was a light tap on the door and the woman who had let him into the house entered. She, too, looked strained and was clutching a folder to her chest.

'Hello, officer, my name is Susan Dawson. I'm afraid the house-maid is no longer with us. I haven't got round to filling the position yet.'

'What was her name?'

'Poppy Black. She left last week. No notice, just sent us a letter saying she was moving on and wouldn't be back. Why she couldn't have simply told me to my face, I don't know.'

'Did she offer a reason?'

'She's eighteen. People come and go all the time in this line of work.'

'Do you have the letter?'

'Yes,' she replied, pulling out an A4 sheet from the top of the folder.

141

'Known associates?'

'Really, I have no idea. I believe she had a boyfriend; staff aren't encouraged to bring people back to the house.'

'What about a photo?'

'Well yes, she had one taken for her security pass.' She handed him a copy of the pass. Poppy Black had an impish smile and a mass of red hair, caught up in an untidy bun.

'Do you have her current address, as well as her previous one?'

'Yes, they should be in here somewhere,' she said, rifling through the hefty folder. 'Here we are.' She scribbled down the addresses on a piece of paper and passed it across.

'Did you take up references for her?'

'Yes, of course. She worked in Glasgow before she fetched down here.'

'May I see them?'

She flicked through the file and produced two sheets of paper in poly pockets. One of them was on cream stationery that resembled the suicide note, purportedly from Monro Stevenson, and the other was typed on plain A4 printer paper.

'Did you follow these up with phone calls?' asked Farrell.

Dawson was flustered now, a visible pulse beating at her temple.

'Well, no. She was only a housemaid. I had no reason to doubt them.'

'I'm afraid I'm going to need to take these for now,' said Farrell. 'I need to trace this young woman to ascertain that she is unharmed.'

'You think something might have happened to her?'

'Time will tell,' said Farrell.

There was definitely something going on in this house but, if he had no evidence that a crime had been committed, he would have to shelf it for now. It was likely that Poppy Black had been a low-level plant, to gain information for a robbery. A robbery that Lord Merton seemed to have no inclination to either report or prevent. The question remained. Had she scarpered, or had she been silenced for good?

Chapter Thirty

Farrell and McLeod pulled up outside the address given for Poppy Black in Kirkcudbright. It was a very rundown block of four flats and the communal entrance smelled of urine and stale tobacco.

'Poor girl,' said Mhairi. 'Imagine having to come home to this hole at the end of a day working at Kincaid House.'

'No wonder she was vulnerable to a bribe,' said Farrell.

He knocked on the door to her flat. There was no reply and only silence when he put his ear to the letterbox.

'I don't want to bust the door down, in case she's perfectly fine,' said Farrell. 'I don't suppose you have a hairpin in that nest of hair by any chance?'

'Frank Farrell, you say the nicest things. I do, as it happens.' She fidgeted about inside her complicated updo and produced a long pin.

Farrell straightened it out and jiggled it inside the lock for what felt like an eternity. Suddenly, they heard a click.

'Teach you that in the seminary, did they,' said Mhairi.

Farrell threw her a look. The door swung open. Immediately they became aware of an unpleasant smell and an angry buzzing sound that could only mean one thing. Farrell closed the door behind them and pulled on a pair of latex gloves and plastic overshoes. Mhairi did likewise. Slowly they advanced into the flat. The door to the living room opened off the hall. They paused at the doorway. Poppy Black was lying awkwardly on the floor beside a heavy wooden coffee table. There was congealed blood on the side of her head and also some blood on the side of the coffee table. A stepladder had been knocked over, which presumably had been positioned under the central light. A smashed bulb lay near the deceased.

'You buying this, sir? Seems a bit too convenient.'

'Not for a single minute,' replied Farrell. 'Come on, we'd best scarper until SOCO and the police surgeon arrive. Can't risk contaminating the scene.'

As they shut the door behind them, there was an elderly woman with a pinched, grey complexion standing at the open door of the neighbouring flat.

'What's happened to Poppy?' she asked, with a quaver in her voice. 'It's bad, isn't it?'

Farrell glanced at Mhairi, and they walked over.

'I'm afraid so,' said Mhairi. 'May we come in?'

The old woman sagged against the door, and they helped her into the flat and sat her down on a threadbare sofa. Mhairi sat beside her, and Farrell filled the kettle and made her a cup of strong tea. The flat was cold, bare and none too clean.

'I'm sorry to tell you that Poppy is dead,' said Mhairi, enfolding a gnarled arthritic hand in her own.

'How can she be? I don't understand.'

'She appears to have fallen off a stepladder and banged her head,' said Mhairi, choosing her words carefully.

The old lady's rheumy eyes spilled tears as she gulped at her tea.

'Did you know her well?' she asked.

'She would come in and sit with me sometimes. Said I reminded her of her gran. I haven't been able to get to the shops for a while and she'd pick me up a few bits and pieces whenever

I asked. Under all that bluster she was a good lass.'

'Did she have a boyfriend? Anyone call on her recently?'

The old woman pursed her lips.

'There was a boyfriend a while back. Lennie, I think she called him. He barged past me on the stairwell once, knocked me clean off my feet. Just carried on up like nothing happened. She sent him packing a couple of weeks ago. I've not seen anybody since.'

They took their leave of the neighbour and went round the other two flats, but no one was in. They then climbed back into Farrell's car after making enquiries of the remaining two neighbours. No one had seen or heard a thing.

'We've got to catch this bastard,' snapped Mhairi.

'He'll slip up sooner or later. It's only a matter of time.'

They sat in bleak silence until they saw the SOCO van pull in to the kerb. The mortuary van wouldn't be far behind.

The police surgeon arrived right on cue. It was Dr Allison. There were only two police surgeons on call locally. They got out of the car and walked over to meet him.

'One of your patients again, Doctor?' asked Mhairi.

'No, not this time.'

They led the doctor up to the flat. As he saw the flies swarming over the slightly bloated corpse, he flinched but walked over to her, feeling for a pulse.

A few minutes later, he rose to his feet and formally pronounced life extinct.

'I'm afraid that I can't give you any worthwhile estimate as to time of death on this one,' he said. 'The pathologist will have a better idea.'

SOCO moved past, setting their equipment up in the hall.

'I reckon this has been staged to look like an accidental death,' said Farrell, joining them inside.

'If that's the case then they've done a bloody good job,' said Janet. 'You're sure?'

'As sure as I can be,' replied Farrell.

They got to work processing the scene. After a while, Janet motioned to Farrell to come over. She pointed at the floor behind the coffee table.

'It's been moved,' she said.

The track marks on the carpet told their own story. The coffee table had been moved at least 12 inches to fit the scenario.

Phil was gathering up the remnants of the electric bulb. He scrutinized them carefully.

'It's not a match for the light above,' he said. 'The right size and shape but the wrong clip.'

'The killer must have brought it with him,' said Farrell. He looked in the kitchen drawers but found no other bulbs. There were no empty packets in the bin either.

Eventually, the body was loaded into the van, to be accompanied by PC McGhie, who had been summoned from the local station.

Farrell and Mhairi looked around the gloomy flat in silence. Poppy's bedroom was surprisingly childlike with stuffed toys on the bed and Disney pyjamas. There was a nightlight plugged into the wall. She had nothing of value. A life lived on the margins of society, snuffed out before it had even really begun.

'Whoever did this is one cold bastard,' said Farrell. 'He's willing to kill anyone who gets in his way.'

146

Chapter Thirty-One

It had been a long, tiring day. Mhairi could feel the beginnings of a headache as she walked out of the station. Now that there had been another death she was worried sick about the upcoming assignment. She kept seeing the crumpled body of Poppy Black. If anything were to happen to her, it would break her parents. They had already suffered the loss of her brother.

'Mhairi, hold on a minute.' Farrell came up behind her. 'A word …?'

He opened a door into an empty room, and she went inside and flopped down on the seat in front of the desk.

'You know I'm not happy about this Ivy House assignment,' he began.

Her expression softened. She could see he was worried about her.

'I'm going to get them to give you a normal mobile with a fake contract and it will have all the usual social media nonsense you young ones like. We'll make it close enough to your usual phone, so you'll need to hand that into the Tech boys to copy stuff across. I'm going to get a fake phone myself and do likewise. I'm your cousin, Darren, who lives in Edinburgh. That way you can text or phone me any time.'

Mhairi grinned, her mood lifting.

'Thanks, sir. That would definitely help.'

'Off you go then, lots to do tomorrow,' said Farrell.

'I'm meeting Ian for a bar supper, but I'll make sure I get an early night.'

'Ian! I forgot about Ian. What are you going to tell him?'

'Just that I'm on special assignment. It'll be fine. It wouldn't occur to him to go to Kirkcudbright.'

Mhairi arrived home and felt the energy drain from her as the reaction set in to her day. Although she was excited about her upcoming assignment, she was also worried about getting too close to Patrick Rafferty. This was the last thing she needed. Guilt twisted within her. All she wanted to do was climb into her PJs, pour a large glass of wine and have a TV dinner, while catching up on *Coronation Street*. She opened a sachet of food for Oscar and then collapsed onto the sofa, looking longingly at the TV. She really wanted to cry off, but this might be the last time she got to see Ian in a while. Shouldn't she be running out the door in her best finery then, instead of feeling ... what exactly? She was just wiped, that's all. With a sigh, she peeled herself off the sofa, before she got too comfortable, and padded through to the shower.

An hour later, she was ensconced at a table for two in a cosy country pub at Kingolm Quay. Ian was regaling her with a funny story about his wayward sister. Normally, she would have laughed like a drain, but she was bone-tired and struggling to appear interested. Her thoughts seemed to ping back to Poppy Black and the forth-coming assignment like they were sewed on to a piece of elastic.

Suddenly she became aware of a lull in the conversation. She must have zoned out completely. Her eyes fell to her plate, and she realized she had simply been moving the food around instead of eating it. Ian had finished his meal. She raised her gaze to his and, to her horror, she could feel her eyes fill with tears.

'Ian, I'm so sorry. I don't know what's wrong with me tonight.'

He gently placed his hand over hers on the table.

'Hey, there's no need for tears. If you'd rather not see me again, just say. I'd be disappointed, but I promise I won't throw myself off a cliff,' he said.

'It's not that,' said Mhairi, squeezing his hand. 'You know what my job is. Sometimes it gets overwhelming and fills every nook and cranny of my life. The truth is, I'm exhausted and there's no end in sight. This is the first time in a long while I've even tried to have a relationship for that reason.'

'Would it help to talk about it? I know a bit about what's been going on. I presume you're embroiled in the two murders Sophie Richardson has been banging on about.'

'You know I can't say anything, but thanks for the offer. I'm sorry to have been so out of it tonight. I might not even be able to see you for a while, as I'm going to be on special assignment.'

'Come on,' he said, motioning for the bill, 'let's get you home. Somebody needs an early night.'

Once back in Primrose Street, he bundled her off to bed.

'Drat, my phone's nearly out of charge,' she muttered.

'I'm going to stay up for a bit and watch telly,' said Ian. 'Give it here and I'll stick it on in the living room for you. I'll pop it beside your bed later.'

'You'll let me know if anyone rings?'

'Of course, I will.'

He dropped a kiss on her forehead, switched off the light and left the room. Mhairi lay in the dark for a few moments then switched on her bedside light. Yawning, she delved in to her briefcase at the side of the bed to go over her case notes. There must be something they'd missed. Her eyes grew heavier. She scowled and rubbed them. Within minutes, the report she was reading had slid to the floor and she was snoring gently.

Chapter Thirty-Two

Farrell couldn't settle. Usually able to subdue his inner turbulence, he felt agitated beyond endurance. He'd tried to pray but it felt like nobody was home. Music often provided solace, but he felt more like AC/DC than Gregorian chants tonight and that would only ramp up his mood further. A run? Too risky. He'd done his usual five miles before going in to work. Didn't want to pull a hamstring. A copper was no use if he couldn't chase criminals. What then? He felt the walls were closing in on him. Glancing out of the round window looking on to the estuary, he noticed the tide was in. He had it. Grabbing a few extra layers and his heavy duty woollen coat, he went downstairs to the kitchen to make a flask of coffee and headed for the car. On nights like this, he wished he had something with a bit more revs than his dumpy Citroen. Resisting the urge to spin his wheels on the gravel like a boy racer, he drove up the lane and turned left, towards the coast.

With the car heater fighting valiantly against the frosty fingers on his windows, he skirted the town to take the Dalbeattie Road. Half an hour later he reached the quiet beach of Powillimont. As he'd expected, his was the only car. Pulling onto the grass at the end of the bay, he turned off the ignition and left the relative warmth. The waves crashing ferociously against the rocks calmed him, along with the salty tang of the sea and the fishy smell of seaweed. He clambered down until he could walk along the shoreline, his way lit by the silvery gleam of a full moon.

He recognized now what had been bugging him. It was the feeling that his friends were all heading into danger and into outcomes that he couldn't control. It was one thing putting himself in jeopardy, that was something he got a buzz out of, if he was honest. It was quite another watching junior officers walking into hazardous situations. The death of Poppy Black had really rattled him. It smacked of cold, predatory ruthlessness. Someone who didn't operate inside the norms of human behaviour. He could understand impulsive crimes, fuelled by anger, a momentary rush of blood to the head. But both Monro Stevenson and Poppy Black had been killed in cold blood. It made the murderer that much more unpredictable. He hoped that Lind wouldn't be too distracted by what was going on with Laura. The thought of Mhairi having to insinuate herself into the company of that degenerate artist, Patrick Rafferty, made him clench his fists in impotent rage. She talked a good game, but he knew she wasn't half as tough as she liked to make out. She could be drugged, raped, or anything behind those walls, and he would be sitting tight while she ran the gauntlet of all that risk.

He was worried about Dave Thomson as well. Not that he wasn't shaping up nicely. More that he was a bit too keen. Might make him push a bit hard and take excessive risks. Hopefully, being paired with Stirling, who was the most risk-averse copper Farrell had come across, would rein him in a bit.

According to the not so subtle hints that Mhairi had been dropping, Kate seemed to be drawn to that art critic, Lionel Forbes. Normally she was even more reserved than he was. However, Forbes might well be slowly and inexorably creeping under her guard. He felt a tinge of something unaccustomed pierce him. He couldn't be jealous, could he? Since when did he have those kinds of feelings for Kate? Shocked at the direction his thoughts were taking him, he sat down on a flat rock and poured a cup of steaming coffee. Now that he had stopped, the cold stole over him like anaesthetic. He wished it could numb his mind as well as his body. The water looked dark and deadly as it spit foam at the rocks. He shivered despite his warm coat.

Before Monro's murder, he had felt himself drifting away from his earthly ties again, like a ship that had slipped its mooring. Whether it was simply a reaction to all that had gone on last year or not, he didn't know. Since then, though, he had felt himself being drawn back reluctantly into the temporal world and its very concrete problems. He would not be able to decide where his future lay until the three murder cases had been solved. The family of the victims deserved answers.

Chapter Thirty-Three

DI Moore could not remember a time when she had felt more flustered. She was in a taxi heading for Primo Piano in Dumfries in a grade one tizzy. What on earth had possessed her to agree to meet Lionel Forbes for dinner? He was simply a consultant on a case she was working, she reminded herself. After all, Farrell had dated that forensic psychologist they were working with last year, hadn't he? Yes, screamed the voice of reason and look how well that turned out? She shouldn't be so thrown by a simple invitation but, it had been so long, she wasn't quite sure how to react. It's only a meal, she told herself firmly on exiting the taxi. Keep it light and professional and you will come out of this unscathed.

Inside, she glanced around the warmly lit interior until she spotted him in a corner. He stood as she approached, helped her off with her coat and slid the chair out for her, before seating himself.

'Kate, what a charming dress, how lovely to see you!' he exclaimed.

'Lionel, how kind of you to invite me! This is one of my favourite restaurants.'

An attentive waiter hovered round them until they had selected from the extensive menu.

'Can I offer you something from the wine list?' Lionel asked.

'Aren't you driving?' she asked. Way to sound like a copper, Kate, she chided herself.

'No, as it happens, I've an exhibition to review at Gracefield Arts Centre tomorrow, so I'm staying the night in the Cairndale Hotel.'

'Well, in that case, I'll have a glass of red wine, please,' she said.

He ordered a bottle, and there was a slight lull in the conversation.

'So, what do you like to do in your spare time, Lionel?'

'My biggest passion, aside from art, is gardening. Not so much the weeding, pruning, mowing and whatnot but the plants themselves. They can be things of extraordinary beauty and complexity. I've created a small zen garden to escape into. I need to get out there and do some pruning before spring.

'I was attempting to cut back a rather large Buddleia today which nearly had my eye out,' he said, pointing to a livid scratch near his eye.

'Ouch,' she laughed. 'How did you get started as an art critic? Were you ever an artist yourself?'

'I dabbled a little when I was younger, like a lot of young men. I graduated art school but soon realized that I wasn't suited to life as a penniless artist. I then did a Masters and slowly carved out a reputation as a serious reviewer, culminating in columns in the broadsheets and publication of a number of books on aspects of the art world.'

'Do you still paint?'

'When the mood takes me. What I do is not for public consumption, however.'

'Oh, that's a shame, I would love to see some of your work,' she said then felt her skin flush under her make-up. What is wrong with you, Kate? she berated herself in the awkward silence that followed. Asking to look at his etchings?

Lionel gave her a charming smile.

'Believe me when I tell you, you wouldn't thank me for it, my dear.'

'I used to paint watercolours. These days, it's hard to find the time.'

'Or the weather,' he said. 'You can't beat having the scene you are painting right in front of you.'

'You must make a lot of enemies in your line of work?'

'Goes with the territory. Nobody wants bland reviews. Not even the artist. Artists thrive on controversy. They want a strong visceral reaction to their work. It garners them more exposure.'

'I'm guessing not all of them take it well?'

'You could say that ...'

'Nothing recent, I hope?'

He looked uncomfortable.

'Simply someone venting. I'd rather not ...'

'Tell me,' she demanded, slipping back into professional mode.

'I thought this was a dinner date, not an interrogation,' he snapped.

She'd come on too strong. A man like him wasn't used to feeling like a victim. Deliberately softening her voice and body language, she tried once more.

'I'm sorry ...' she began, but he immediately reached across the table and placed his hand over hers.

'No, I'm sorry, forgive me. It has been rather weighing on me.'

'When did it start?'

'Not long after I moved down here, so about four years ago.'

'What form do the threats take? Letters? Phone calls?'

'At first it was letters, quite laughable really. The old cliché of words cut out of a newspaper. Appears to be a reader of *The Times* newspaper, quite clearly aggrieved by a review I had written.'

'Have you kept them?'

'Well, no. I simply scrunched them up and threw them away. Didn't really give it much thought. They were abusive rather than threatening. Along the lines of "Who do you think you are?" That kind of thing.'

'And then?'

'The phone calls started. Not that often, perhaps once a month.'

'Male or female?'

'Impossible to tell. The voice was muffled, as though speaking through some sort of filter. The tone switched to downright threatening. "You're going to be sorry you started this" … "I'll be behind you when you least expect it." "Better get your affairs in order."'

'Are you sure the letters were sent by the person who made the calls?'

'There's no way of knowing. How many enemies can one man have living in a backwater like this? That said, it's unlikely to be someone down in this neck of the woods. Anyone could find my details on LinkedIn or any one of a variety of platforms.'

'Do you have a list of all the reviews you have done?'

'I could probably compile one from old diaries, but I think you've got quite enough on your plate without worrying about me. I don't want to add to your burden.'

'Nonsense!' she said. 'It would set my mind at rest. I would be particularly interested in reviews that are unflattering to the artist and also linked to this area.'

He held his hands up in mock surrender.

'Very well, DI Moore, I'll do as you ask. Now do you think we might talk of something a little more pleasant before I lose my appetite altogether?'

'Of course,' she said. 'And do please call me Kate. As you so rightly pointed out, I'm not on duty.'

They busied themselves with ordering the meal and then sat back and regarded each other. Kate felt herself starting to relax as the red wine warmed her. He really was a very attractive man, she thought. She had always been drawn to cultured men. The only other person she had been this attracted to in recent years was Frank Farrell, but she had no intention of acting on it.

Her beef stroganoff was cooked to perfection. Half way through, Lionel ordered another bottle of wine. She was starting to feel a little light-headed by now and filled up her water glass. At this rate she was going to have a rare hangover in the morning. Then, without warning, the question she always dreaded.

'Do you have any children?'

She could feel the heat flood her face and paused a fraction of a second too long before replying.

'No, do you?'

His warm brown eyes crinkled in concern and again he reached across and laid his hand on hers, giving it a light squeeze, before removing it.

'Two, a boy and a girl, both in their twenties. They went to live in France with their mother after we divorced some years ago.'

'That can't have been easy.'

'No. So, Kate, what else do you enjoy doing when you're not working?'

She was grateful for the swift change of subject.

'I love to travel,' she said. 'I've been known to go to Venice for the day, when I'm feeling particularly hemmed in by the confines of the job.'

'For the day?' he laughed. 'My, that's keen. Do you speak Italian?'

'Enough to get by,' she smiled. 'That day, I came back with a beautiful painting I found in a tiny gallery there.'

'How wonderful!' he smiled.

'Want to know the best bit?'

'Go on.'

'It was Valentine's Day. There I was on a day trip to Venice, as the only singleton on the plane, beside all these loved-up couples.'

He laughed out loud, causing the glances of others to briefly flick their way.

'I do admire a woman possessed of an independent spirit.'

He lowered his voice and topped up her glass.

'Talking of art, how's your investigation going?'

'I can't really talk about it but, suffice to say, I think we're on the verge of a major breakthrough.'

'That's wonderful news, Kate. Be a real feather in your cap if you break this case.'

'I often wonder whether forgers are real artists or simply technicians, incapable of original thought,' she mused.

'It takes incredible skill to replicate the brush strokes of an artist, not to mention replicating the materials used,' he said. 'It'd also require a complete mastery of the medium through years of study. Only the most accomplished artist could have any hope of producing anything but the most pedestrian facsimile.'

'Yes, I can understand that, but a forger might not have the imagination and feeling to become successful in his own right. In such cases aren't they just an opportunistic parasite feasting on the flesh of the artist's work?'

He looked momentarily taken aback by her vehemence.

'I've never really thought about it,' he smiled. 'But, you're right of course. The mechanical art of copying the work of another bears no merit compared to the spark of original creation.'

They were the only diners left in the restaurant by this time. After insisting on settling the bill, he helped her into her coat. She felt a shiver of desire as his bare fingers touched her neck and hoped he hadn't noticed.

As she turned to face him she felt almost mesmerized by the intensity of his gaze.

'Would you care to join me for a nightcap back at my hotel?' he asked.

Chapter Thirty-Four

DS Stirling trudged about the rundown farmhouse with a glum expression. Dressed in his gardening clothes, so as to look the part, he winced as he thought back to the tongue-lashing his wife had given him before he left on this assignment. Vera had been less than impressed that he was effectively going undercover at this late stage in his career, leaving her to cope alone with his elderly mother, who had recently moved in with them and wasn't renowned for her sunny disposition. He shivered as he stuck the kettle on. There was no heating in the damn place. If the forgery gang didn't get him, the cold probably would.

'Dave,' he yelled out the back door, 'fancy a cuppa?'

DC Thomson appeared from round the side of the tractor he had been tinkering with, looking alarmed.

'Sir, er, shouldn't we use our undercover names all the time, just in case?' he whispered.

Stirling rolled his eyes but had to admit the younger officer was right.

'Yes, lad, I suppose you're right. The last thing we want is for you to fail to answer to your name.'

'Mine's milk and two sugars then, Gordon,' said DC Thomson, with a grin.

Stirling resisted the urge to box his ears and poured the tea into two chipped mugs. They sat down at the pockmarked wooden table. Thomson put his new phone between them, and they both stared at it, willing it to ring. They had been at this malarkey for about a week now, and despite sending a text to Shaun's former contact in the gang, no message had been received. The real Shaun was stashed away in a safe house for the duration, with his family having been told he was off partying in Ibiza with some girl he had met online. 'If only …' had been his glum response.

'I don't understand it,' said Thomson. 'Why haven't they called?'

'Could be a number of reasons,' said Stirling, still struggling to wrap his tongue round the name Shaun. 'They might not have another painting ready yet, for one. There's been plenty of heat surrounding the finding of Ailish Kerrigan and the murder of Monro Stevenson. If they've got wind that Poppy Black has been found then that might unsettle them too.'

'Even if they do know Poppy Black's body has been discovered, as far as they're aware we've bought the accidental death, so they won't realize we're on to them.'

'It would have been a different story if the young lass had had any family,' said Stirling. 'It would seem there's no one to miss her.'

'At her age, I would've been in the same boat,' said Thomson.

'Aye, well there's plenty that would miss you now, lad. That Mhairi McLeod would be weeping and wailing like a banshee, so she would.'

Thomson laughed.

'I reckon you're right. Proper bosses me about, so she does.'

'I bet they're hanging fire until the initial fuss has died down. Then they'll be in touch. They might even have eyes and ears on us here, watching and waiting for us to slip up.'

'I can't believe the owner let us move in here,' said Thomson.

'Aye, well it wasn't entirely out the goodness of his heart. He's getting paid rent for as long as we need it. This place had been on the market for months, with not a nibble from a buyer.'

'I feel sorry for the old boy that used to live here,' said Thomson. 'All that thankless toil, eking out a living, then his son sticks him in a home and tries to sell the farm from under him.'

'How's that tractor coming along?'

'All oiled and ready to go. I run the engine for a few minutes every day, just in case. Don't want it seizing up at a critical time.'

'I'm seeing a whole new side of you, Davie boy,' said Stirling, grinning. 'Never had you pegged as knowing your way round a bloody tractor. With you being sent away to school, I reckoned your hands would be soft as a lassie's.'

'I grew up on a massive farm not far from here. My dad was a widower, worked his way up to farm manager.'

'So, how come you never went to the local school then?' asked Stirling.

'My dad was killed when I was eight. Got on the wrong side of a combine harvester.'

'Hell's bells,' said Stirling. 'I'd no idea.'

'The farmer felt responsible for me, I suppose. Sent me away to school in Edinburgh. In the holidays, I worked on the farm.'

'Like leading a double life,' said Stirling, topping up their tea from the teapot on the table.

'Exactly like that,' said Thomson. 'Turned me into a bit of a chameleon, I suppose.'

Aye and a mite too easy to please, thought Stirling. No bloody wonder.

'Are you sure there's no one round here liable to recognize you?'

'Positive. Like I say I didn't mix with the local kids because I was away at school. Then, in the holidays, I was always working. Anyhow, with the new hairdo, I doubt anyone would recognize me. Have to see if blondes really do have more fun?' he said, lightening the mood.

'Aye, that Shaun is a fan of the bleach, for sure,' said Stirling with a matching grin. 'You wouldn't look out of place in *Ibiza Uncovered* with a hairdo like that.'

'Maybe I'll keep it,' said Thomson. 'Imagine the Super's face!'

The smiles slipped off their faces when the phone on the table vibrated. Thomson snatched it up and read the text out loud.

'"Collect item from usual location tomorrow. Take tractor to graveyard Dundrennan Abbey. Place that package and previous package in flower trough Alan Blake. Payment on completion".'

'We're on,' said Stirling, reaching for his mobile and hitting the speed dial.

After he had imparted the necessary information to DI Moore, they sat back to await her instructions, no longer in the mood for conversation.

162

Chapter Thirty-Five

As she arrived at Loreburn Street early in the morning, Mhairi scowled to see Sophie Richardson and her crew outside the station again. As if that wasn't bad enough she saw a different media truck glide into the car park opposite. Ailish's murder had all the right ingredients for a media feeding frenzy. Fortunately they hadn't yet got wind that Poppy Black had been murdered as well. The post-mortem had confirmed their theory. Bartle-White had stated that the blow to the head had been with a blunt object and couldn't have been caused by simply falling against the table. The blood must have been smeared on the table afterwards. The pressure was on. Marching into reception, she faltered on catching sight of the hooked nose and hooded lids of the woman sitting there. Moira Sharkey, tabloid journalist and muckraker extraordinaire. The cold predatory eyes raked over her, but she knew there was only one person she was here to see and that was Frank Farrell.

She was hanging up her coat in the locker room when a junior officer came looking for her.

'DI Moore wants you in the small briefing room. Something's going down.'

She rushed after him, heart thumping.

DI Moore had assembled her core team in the forgery investigation along with DCI Lind. The mood was sombre. There was no knowing what would befall DC Thomson if something went awry with the plan, or his cover was blown. Poppy Black's murder had shown them just how far the forgery ring was prepared to go.

'Mhairi, grab a seat. We've recently heard from DS Stirling that the forger has taken the bait and sent DC Thomson fresh instructions. He's to pick up another package from behind the grave at St Cuthbert's Kirkyard, Kirkcudbright and deposit it and the Hornel recovered from the tractor in a trough at a named grave in Dundrennan Abbey Graveyard.'

'When?' asked Mhairi, feeling the tension squeeze her innards.

'Tomorrow. No time specified. Can you stick these up on the wall for me?' she said, handing a pile of assorted maps and photos across.

Mhairi placed the most recent ordnance survey map on the wall in the small briefing room, along with pictures of the pick-up point at St Cuthbert's Kirkyard, Kirkcudbright and also the graveyard at Dundrennan Abbey.

'The location for the drop off poses some significant problems for us on the surveillance side,' DI Moore said. 'For starters, at this time of the year, and on a Tuesday, there are unlikely to be many visitors. There's no CCTV and we've no way of knowing if the person collecting the painting is already in position.'

'What about substituting an officer for the person selling tickets, ma'am?' asked Mhairi.

'Too risky, for all we know they've been paid off already, which would be tipping our hand.'

'I suppose the same rationale applies to a grave tender or any employee,' said Mhairi.

'It's possible this painting is a dummy run, to see whether Shaun got caught and cut a deal,' said DI Moore.

'Are you suggesting that we let Dave go in with no backup whatsoever?' asked DS Byers.

There was an awkward silence.

'Yes, I suppose I am. And, no, I don't like it anymore than you do,' said DI Moore, the worry lines snaking across her forehead lending credence to her words. 'I have a feeling that this might be some sort of a test with terrible consequences for failure.'

Farrell groaned on hearing that Moira Sharkey was still waiting in reception. He'd hoped she'd got fed up and left. Now he was going to have to see the wretched woman. They had a long and complicated history, dating back from when he was a young priest and a serial killer had targeted him in the confessional. She was never one to let the truth get in the way of a good story. Admittedly, she had given him a useful tip-off in the twin abduction cases last year, but she'd wrung an exclusive out of him first. He loathed her with a very ungodly passion.

'Fine, send her up,' he said, slamming the phone down with more force than necessary.

He didn't have long to wait.

'Come in,' he shouted, as she pecked at the door.

'Ms Sharkey, this is an unexpected pleasure,' he said through gritted teeth. 'Won't you sit down?'

Her hooded eyes were as dark and malicious as ever, and she took a seat.

'Looks like your team is up to the neck in it again, DI Farrell. What's this I hear about another murdered girl? Poppy Black?'

Farrell kept his face impassive. How could she possibly know anything about that? Who had blabbed? If this got out, it would alert the murderer they were on to him, and he might well flee the area before they figured out who he was.

'If you're referring to a case of accidental death, we would ask you to refrain from reporting anything until the family has been informed.'

'I hear that there is no family,' she smirked.

'Where are you getting this from?' snapped Farrell.

'Steady, Inspector. You know I'm not at liberty to reveal my source.'

'What do you want?'

'A little quid pro quo. You know how I love to help an officer of the law. I'm also not entirely enamoured of the bitch in the car park outside.'

'Sophie Richardson?'

'I'll keep my mouth shut, providing you give me an exclusive when it all goes down. I want stuff that no other reporter will get access to.'

'What can you give me to sweeten the deal?' asked Farrell.

'I'm working on that. You know how resourceful I can be.'

'You keep quiet about Poppy Black, get me something useful that I don't already have and I'll get you your exclusive,' he said.

She held out her skinny fingers with painted red talons, and Farrell shook her hand, trying to hide his revulsion at her touch.

Negotiating with this woman always left him feeling slightly tainted.

Chapter Thirty-Six

DI Moore woke abruptly, her heart racing. She had been plagued all night by dreams of DC Thomson meeting a gruesome end, while she stood by, rooted to the spot, like a formless ghost, powerless to intervene. She glanced across at the leonine face next to her on the pillow. She hadn't planned to have him stay over after their supper last night. It had been less than a week since their first dinner date. However, he had been very diverting, and she had needed the distraction. He had sensed something was worrying her and tried to get her to open up, but she had managed to convince him her stress was all down to impending job losses in preparation for the formation of Police Scotland. She hadn't realized she had it in her to be such a good actress.

It wasn't like her to throw caution to the wind like this, but she felt it was good for her, as though she was slowly learning to trust again. She left a note for Lionel, asking him to put the snib on when he let himself out and thanking him for a lovely evening. She could feel the heat in her cheeks as she recalled exactly how lovely.

She slipped out of the house like a wraith into the early morning mist. In her sports gear and carrying her work clothes in a suit bag, she was first in line at the gym when it opened at

6 a.m. She never saw her vigorous workouts as an indulgence, but as a way of hanging on to her equilibrium.

An hour later, her muscles trembling but her mind steady, she slipped behind her desk, determined to grab the day by the throat and not relinquish her grip until DC Thomson was safely back at the farm in one piece.

Unaware of DI Moore's silent vigil in Dumfries, DS Stirling and DC Thomson were sitting around the kitchen table at the farm, warming their hands with steaming mugs of tea. Farm tractors were generally out early and so, to attract as little attention as possible, DC Thomson was to set off just before seven heading for Dundrennan Abbey. The last thing he wanted was to get caught up in rush hour traffic heading for the larger towns in the area. He had picked up the package last night from behind the grave in St Cuthbert's Kirkyard under cover of darkness, but it was in oilskin sealed with red wax. The seal had Latin inscribed on it and was very distinctive. It would be impossible to replicate at short notice. It looked like something a notary public might have used in years gone by. They had sent digital images across to Dumfries, and they'd be trying to source a facsimile now. He also had the previously recovered Hornel with him which, fortunately, hadn't had a seal.

'Drive carefully,' said DS Stirling. 'The last thing you want is for the tractor to be involved in an accident like before.'

DC Thomson nodded. Despite his brave words to the Super and DI Moore, Stirling could tell that the lad was nervous. And no bloody wonder. Out there without backup, arse to the wind. Too exposed by far.

'Relax, Sarge,' he said, standing up. 'It's most likely just a dummy run to check that Shaun Finch hasn't been turned by the coppers. I'll be back inside the hour, and you can fry us up a storm.'

'On that old thing?' said Stirling, casting a glance at the ancient

168

range that had defied all his attempts to light it. 'Dream on, laddie.'

DC Thomson walked out to the yard and hauled himself up into the tractor. It was freezing cold in these bloody things, so he was well padded. It felt good to take action. All the sitting around had been doing his head in and, much as he liked Stirling, he wasn't the most interesting conversationalist in the world.

He started the engine and put it into gear. His heart was racing with adrenalin. He was going undercover. How cool was that? Okay, admittedly a Maserati would be better than a tractor but, hey, this was Dumfries and Galloway.

He gave a jaunty wave to DS Stirling, framed in the doorway. Turning the wheel, he put his foot on the accelerator and drove out of the yard.

The quiet country roads were virtually deserted. Occasionally he passed a tractor driven by a pimply youth or a hunched old man and tapped his cap in greeting. He narrowly avoided hitting a young deer that slipped across the road in front of him. Deep breaths, Davie boy, he told himself. Deep breaths. As far as he was aware he wasn't being followed. His senses felt heightened. The smell of the moist earth and hedges was overpowering. Almost as if he had turned into a vampire. Everything somehow more vivid, like the colour palette had been intensified.

After a few miles he reached the village of Dundrennan. Some people were out walking their dogs or buying milk from the corner shop. Not far now. Easy does it. His heart was hammering so loudly he fancied he could almost hear it over the roar of the tractor. He carried on through the village then reached the car park adjacent to Dundrennan Abbey. There was nobody about as the abbey didn't open for admissions until 10 a.m. He jumped down and stretched, as though he was just away for a wee stroll to ease his cramped muscles. He pulled up the hood of his fleece. If Shaun were to be believed, he'd never met directly with any of the forgery gang, but that didn't mean they hadn't followed him and had an idea of what he looked like.

The graveyard beside the abbey was still cloaked in tendrils of morning mist, which made it harder to see into the distance. He opened the gate and strolled casually up and down the rows of headstones, until he saw the one he was looking for. It had a rectangular stone trough with small holes along the length of the stone lid where flower stems could be placed. With a quick glance to left and right to check that he was unobserved he slid aside the heavy lid, observing that the holes had been sealed from the inside with clear plastic. He pulled out both packages from inside his fleece and placed them in the deep trough before sliding the lid back into its normal position and standing up quickly. Forcing himself to walk normally he returned to the tractor and started up the engine. As he turned it along the road he had come, he was startled to see someone in his mirror. A shadowy hooded figure came out the graveyard and watched him for a moment or two, before melting into the darkness. They had been in there with him the whole time. His skin prickled with sweat.

When he turned into the farmyard that was providing their temporary home, Stirling pinged out the door like a jack-in-the-box, clearly relieved to see him.

They said nothing until they were both in the kitchen. Stirling handed him a mug of sweet steaming tea and he gulped it gratefully, the reaction starting to set in now.

'Weren't you just itching to open the bloody thing?' asked Stirling.

'Too right. It could be anything from a forged painting to a *Star Wars* poster for all we know.'

'DI Moore is trying to source an identical wax and seal for any future deliveries. I told her you made it back in one piece. She snatched up the phone on the first ring,' he chuckled.

'There was someone there,' he said. 'I wasn't aware of him

until I was driving away and caught him in my mirror, but I think he wanted me to see him. To know I'd been watched.'

'Description?' asked Stirling, flipping open his notebook.

'He was dressed in black with a hood up. White face. Tall, medium build. Sorry, not much to go on.'

'Are you sure it was a male?'

'I assumed it was a man but, looking back, there's no way I can be sure, now you mention it.'

'Any sign of a vehicle?'

'No, he left on foot. Must have parked it elsewhere. I couldn't see if he had the packages, but they were probably stuffed up his jacket.'

'Well, that's the first one under your belt. Hopefully, we can manage some surveillance for the next time, assuming the collection and drop-off points remain the same.'

'Now then, Sarge, what about that fry-up? I'm starving.'

'Sausage, egg, and tattie scone coming up, lad. But you're going to have to work your magic with the range first.'

Chapter Thirty-Seven

Farrell walked briskly to the front of the MCA room and took his seat beside Lind and Moore. Lind gestured for him to proceed. Only the core investigative team were present. As he was about to speak the door at the back flew open and DS Byers rushed in, looking frazzled. Normally someone who prided himself on his appearance, he was sporting non-designer stubble and his shirt was stained at the armpits. Lind motioned to a chair beside him at the front in recognition of the ridiculous amount of work Byers had been doing coordinating the information flow in the various enquiries. Thus far he had been exceptional.

'Things have been gathering pace in all three investigations,' said Farrell. 'We now have a fourth investigation, the suspicious death of Poppy Black, the housemaid at Kincaid House. It's likely she has been involved in passing information pertaining to the security of some valuable paintings there, which might or might not link back to the forgery ring in Kirkcudbright. It also bears similarities to Monro Stevenson's murder. Premeditated and staged to look like an accident in the home. The preliminary post-mortem results indicate she may have put up a fight. Tissue samples were obtained from under her nails, but they don't appear to be a match for any DNA samples in the database. Given these circumstances I have been appointed SIO.'

'Any relatives in the picture?' asked DS Byers.

'She has no known relatives, as she was abandoned into the care system in Glasgow as a baby. It is essential that we keep this on the down-low to avoid tipping off the perpetrator that we're on to him. I'm going to get Andy Moran to stick it in the local paper as an accidental death meantime.'

Farrell felt momentarily light-headed. Events were spiralling out of control. With an effort he brought himself back to the room. Had he taken his lithium this morning? He couldn't remember. With everything going on he was running on fumes. He sat down heavily in the front row. Lind stepped up.

'Kate, did you liaise with SOCO in relation to the marks found beside the body of Ailish Kerrigan?' he asked.

'Yes. They confirmed that the marks were wholly consistent with an easel placed alongside the deceased.'

'This makes it likely that she was murdered by someone within the local art community. And not just anyone,' Lind said, his face sombre. 'A crime of passion is one thing, but it's staggering to think that having murdered her and disposed of the body, the person then saw fit to take the risk of returning to paint beside the remains. Possibly a number of times.'

'It would take a fair amount of strength to haul a dead body out to that location and then up the hill,' said Byers. 'Would you say that points to a male perpetrator, sir?'

'More likely than not, unless two people were acting in concert; but I'd like to keep an open mind on gender for the time being. A woman could have managed it with a quad bike and trailer,' replied Lind.

'Didn't that woman in the art gallery, Janet Campbell, say that Paul Moretti paints dead things?' asked Mhairi.

'Yes, she did,' said Farrell. 'It's something we should look into but the other artist, Mike Halliday, didn't seem to put much store by it. He thought it might be Moretti's way of getting her to stop poking her nose into his business.'

'Maureen Kerrigan has thankfully been keeping a low profile. I'd worried that she might try and get too involved in the investigation, possibly putting herself in harm's way,' said Lind. He motioned to DI Moore.

'DS Byers, I hear you've been burning the midnight oil,' she said. 'Are we any closer to finding a match for the seal and wax that was used for the package?'

'Not yet, ma'am. I consulted a specialist antiques auctioneer in Edinburgh, and they confirmed that it was similar to an old notary public's seal. Apparently, this area is littered with them. Virtually every legal firm in Dumfries and Galloway will have these dotted around as ornaments or gathering dust in their safes. Modern notaries don't use them much.'

'What about the Latin words?'

'*Qualis artifex pereo.*'

'Have you had a chance to dig into that yet?'

'Yes, ma'am,' he said, running a hand through hair you could fry chips on. 'It means, "What an artist dies in me".'

'DS Byers has been doing sterling work across these diverse operations, but I'd like a volunteer to assist him with further work, as required?'

Mhairi stuck her hand up.

Byers nodded and shot her a grateful look. They were really missing the input of DS Stirling and DC Thomson. Who knew how long they would be stuck out in the sticks on special assignment?

DI Moore swiftly concluded the briefing, and the team filed out looking pale and tired. Even with additional officers from the outlying stations, they were severely under resourced for these investigations. Everyone was feeling the strain.

Lind approached Farrell as he was gathering up his papers.

'Can you hang on a minute, there's something I need to ask you?'

'Sure,' said Farrell. 'What's on your mind?'

Lind waited until the last of the stragglers had left and then turned to him.

'This thing about the easel,' he said. 'I don't like it. It has all the hallmarks of a complete nutter.'

'It rather sounds like it,' said Farrell. 'Hopefully, the press won't get wind of it; they'd have a field day.'

'I was thinking of reaching out to Clare Yates and asking her to consult on this one.'

'I see,' said Farrell.

'She was tremendously helpful with that case last year, but I wanted to make sure having her around again wasn't going to cause any difficulty for you?'

'Water under the bridge,' said Farrell. 'No point going to the hassle and expense of getting someone down from the Central Belt, when we've got her expertise on our doorstep.'

'Great, I'll give her a call then.'

Farrell nodded in what he hoped was an enthusiastic manner and left the room.

In truth, he was less than enthralled at the prospect of having Clare Yates around again. Last year they had become deeply involved, and when he was at his most vulnerable, she had completely bailed on him. It had cut deep. He would have to maintain a professional distance and hope for the best.

Chapter Thirty-Eight

Mhairi sat at her dressing table applying make-up. It felt weird now making herself attractive to appeal to another man, one that wasn't Ian. Even though it was all for work, she couldn't help but feel like she was betraying him. The fact that she found Patrick Rafferty so attractive didn't exactly help matters either. She was going to have to convince him to trust her without letting matters get out of hand.

With a last slick of red lipstick, she was done. She was meeting him in The Smuggler's Arms at 8 p.m. and aiming to get the last bus back to Dumfries at 11 p.m. She'd gone for a dressed-down look of skinny jeans and a leather jacket, with a tight black top.

Farrell had offered to drive her there and would be lurking about somewhere until she was ready to come back home, just to be on the safe side. She also had some mace spray in her bag.

The doorbell rang, and she grabbed her bag and flung open the door. Her face fell.

'Ian! What are you doing here?'

'I thought I'd surprise you,' he said, his expression tightening as he took in her attire. 'I thought you were planning a quiet night in. I'll let you get on.'

'Wait,' she said, grabbing him by the arm, 'it's not what you think. I have to go out … to a work thing.'

'I could wait for you to get back,' he said. 'Keep Oscar company?'

Mhairi felt her face flush. This was not what she needed right now.

'Look, Ian, I'm sorry. I probably won't be back until late. Let's do something at the weekend?'

'Fine,' he said, turning away, but not before she had seen the look of hurt on his face.

She was still at the door, watching his receding back, when Farrell pulled over in his beat-up Citroen. No one could accuse Frank Farrell of being flash.

She jumped in to the passenger seat and they were off.

Yet again, the job was taking a toll on her personal life. She winced as she thought about Ian's defeated expression as he walked away.

'You OK?' Farrell asked her, shooting her a concerned look.

'I'm fine,' she replied, flashing him a smile. She resolutely put Ian out of her mind and brought her focus back into the present.

Stealing a sideways glance at her boss as he drove, she noticed a muscle twitching in his jaw. His skin was pulled so tautly over his cheekbones it looked all but translucent. She hoped he was looking after himself. He had come so close to mental collapse last year that it had scared her.

'What are you going to do to amuse yourself in Kirkcudbright?' she asked.

'First off, I'm going to pop down to Stirling and Thomson, see if they're driving each other crazy yet. Then, I'm going to wander about, maybe grab a fish supper.'

'No one can say you don't know how to party, sir,' she teased.

They pulled up round the corner from The Smuggler's.

'Now, remember, Mhairi, it's just a drink. I don't want any heroics. Do I make myself clear?'

177

She shot him a sketchy salute and climbed out of the car, watching as the Citroen disappeared from sight.

As she walked into The Smuggler's Inn, she was pleasantly surprised. Instead of the grubby den of thieves she had been expecting, it was warm and cosy, filled with the aromas of home cooking. The mahogany bar and gantry was adorned with real-ale pumps and bottles of spirits. Two old boys were playing dominoes and there was a log fire taking the chill off the evening. Once her eyes adjusted to the gloom she spotted Patrick Rafferty waving at her from a table near the fire and sauntered over to join him.

'Mhairi, I half thought you might stand me up,' he said as he got to his feet and kissed her cheek. 'What can I get you?'

'A vodka and Coke, please,' she replied, slipping off her jacket and noting his appreciative glance, before he walked to the bar.

She sat with her back to the wall, as she waited for him to return, so she could see who else came and went.

Mike Halliday was sitting near the door with an attractive dark-haired woman, who Mhairi thought looked vaguely familiar, but couldn't quite place. She gave him a small wave, but he turned away, ignoring her, to concentrate on his companion. Charming she thought. Mind you, maybe his girlfriend was the possessive type.

Patrick returned with the drinks and two packets of crisps. Gleefully, she pounced on the cheese-flavoured ones.

'Do you, know,' she said, 'these crisps are the only thing keeping me in Dumfries and Galloway. I've never seen them anywhere else.'

'A cheap date and easy to please,' he said. 'Loving it so far!'

So, he had a sense of humour? Maybe this wasn't going to be so bad after all. And, she had to admit, he was easy on the eye. You do know that you're working! snapped the sharp internal voice that sounded uncannily like her mother.

178

'Why on earth did you flee Ireland and come to a full stop here?' she asked. 'I thought artists were meant to starve in garrets somewhere romantic like Paris or Rome. Kirkcudbright? Not the most obvious choice, surely? Cheese crisps notwithstanding.'

'We came across on the ferry from Stranraer and hitched as far as here. That night, we were having a beer in a pub when Hugo and Penelope waltzed in. I still remember how they seemed to light up the place. We got talking. When I mentioned I was an artist and that we were effectively running away to be free spirits, they offered to let us stay for a few nights. When I saw Hugo's studio I was in awe of his talent, in awe of everything about him I suppose.'

'How did Ailish get on with them?' asked Mhairi.

He shot her a sharp look then seemed to relax again.

'She was up for it at first. Thought they were so sophisticated, a million miles away from her puritanical upbringing. Plus, we were in love.'

His mouth twisted, and she realized that he had been profoundly affected by the discovery of Ailish's remains. The news had leaked out to the press not long after they had visited Ivy House. The headlines had cast Patrick in the role of villain. He was now enduring trial by social media.

'I'm sorry,' she said. 'I shouldn't have mentioned her. We can talk about something else.'

'No,' he said. 'It's fine really. It helps to talk. She was murdered. I still can't get my head round it. I don't know who else I can trust.'

'It's a lot to take in.'

'Ever since she left, I liked to imagine her now and then, maybe in Spain against a cobalt blue sky, maybe in a souk in Morocco. She always had a smile on her face and those long dark curls. To think that all that time she was lying alone in a shallow grave in the middle of a firing range ... it makes me want to hit something.'

He drained the rest of his pint and went to the bar, his hands hanging loose by his sides, clenched into fists.

Mhairi picked up the remains of her vodka and Coke and drained it. Things had taken a darker turn and she didn't know how to get them back on track. He was either a consummate actor or his grief for Ailish was real. That didn't mean he was innocent of Monro's murder though. Or the forgery, for that matter. She longed to ask him if he knew Poppy Black, but didn't dare.

A draft of air caught her attention and she glanced up. Mike and his lady friend were heading out the door. This time he gave her a small wave. Maybe she had imagined him blanking her earlier.

Patrick returned to their table. He was swaying slightly on his feet and she wondered how much he had had to drink before she got there. She decided he was too wound up to take the conversation back to Ailish.

'Do you know a local artist called Mike Halliday? The guy who was sitting over there with the brunette.'

'That wasn't just a brunette,' he said, sounding bitter. 'That was Maureen Kerrigan, Ailish's sister.'

'Oh,' said Mhairi, somewhat at a loss. 'Why didn't you go over and speak to her?'

'Because she hates my guts,' he said. 'Blames me for her sister's death along with everyone else. And she's not wrong.'

He glanced at Mhairi's frozen expression and laughed. It wasn't a nice laugh.

'I don't mean I killed her, although, I'm flattered to think that you thought I might,' he said with heavy sarcasm.

'Patrick, I didn't …'

'If I hadn't treated her so badly by taking up with Beth, she wouldn't have left. This is my fault. I know it. And Maureen does too. She wants my head on a plate and I'm half inclined to give it to her.'

Mhairi stared at him in dismay. At this rate there'd be no second date and she'd have blown her chance to get the inside scoop on The Collective. She had to turn things around.

'You can't change the past. All you can affect is the present and the future. If you could wave a magic wand, Patrick, what would you be doing five years from now?'

'I'd be away from this bloody lot, that's for sure,' he said. 'I'm going to stick around until Ailish's killer is found. That's the only way to honour her memory. Then I'm off. I might give up painting altogether. I don't think I have the stomach for it anymore.'

'And here was me thinking you were desperate to paint me,' she said, trying to lighten the mood.

He turned and gazed at her intently, which made her blush.

'I meant what I said. You have an expressive face.'

'With my clothes on?'

'If you insist,' he said. 'Who'd have thought that a big scary detective like you would be terrified of a bit of life modelling?'

'Hey, less of the big!' she joshed, relieved that his mood had improved. They chatted about safer topics until she realized that it was nearly time for the bus back to Dumfries.

'I've got to head off now, before I turn into a pumpkin,' she said.

'I'll walk you to the bus stop.'

'Sure,' she said, groaning inwardly. Now she wouldn't be able to get a lift back with Farrell but would have to trundle all the way on the bus.

The bus stop was deserted, but she knew that Farrell would be lurking somewhere.

Suddenly, Patrick took her in his arms and kissed her so deeply it sent shivers all the way up her spine.

He grinned at her when he finally released her.

'You're good people, DC Mhairi McLeod,' he said and then whispered something in her ear that caused her cheeks to flame, before walking away.

As if things hadn't been complicated enough already, she thought, biting her lip as the bus came into view, hoping that Farrell hadn't seen what had happened. It was bad enough that she had to kiss Patrick. The worst thing was that she had enjoyed it. She thought of Ian's sad face and the guilt made her feel sick to her stomach.

Chapter Thirty-Nine

Farrell was parked in a side street facing the bus stop. His jaw tightened as Mhairi got on the bus. That kiss suggested that she was getting in too deep. As he was about to start the car, he noticed a shadow shift in his peripheral vision. Someone slipped out a shop doorway and moved off, walking quickly. They were wearing a hoodie. Farrell thought about checking it out but decided it was most likely nothing. He turned on the engine and drove behind the bus containing Mhairi all the way back to Dumfries. Parking across the road in the Whitesands until the last few passengers straggled off, he then flashed his lights. Spotting him, she hurried across and jumped in the car.

'Home?' he asked, putting the car in gear.

She nodded. Her face pale and tense. He decided not to mention what he had seen. Driving through the town he headed for her flat in Primrose Street, then pulled in to the kerb.

'You'd better come in,' she said, sounding bone-tired.

'It'll keep to the morning.'

'No, it's best if I tell you now, while it's still fresh in my mind.'

He followed her into her comfortably messy flat. The cat flap banged and Oscar stalked in. They settled down with their mugs of coffee.

'He's really cut up about Ailish,' she said. 'I'm convinced he's got nothing to do with her murder. No one could be that good an actor.'

'You'd be surprised,' said Farrell. 'Stay on your guard. I take it you managed to strike up a rapport? I … er … was parked near the bus stop.'

'You could say that,' she said, her face flaming.

'Be careful, Mhairi. I don't want you getting in over your head. Boundaries can become blurred in no time.'

'Don't worry, I can handle it.' She abruptly changed the subject. 'Maureen Kerrigan was in the pub with Mike Halliday. They didn't stay long.'

'I didn't know those two were friendly,' said Farrell. 'Okay, good work. I'll get off now and let you rest.'

As he drove away, he hoped that this assignment wasn't going to put a spoke in the wheel of her new relationship. It had taken long enough for Mhairi to find someone she could trust after her fiancé had ditched her shortly before her wedding. That had been for doing her job as well. Patrick Rafferty was just the type of irresistible charmer she could do without right now, especially if he turned out to be implicated in murder or a forgery ring.

Driving home, the rain came on, matching the greyness of his mood. As he parked outside the cottage, he could tell that it was high tide by the water encroaching on the banks at the foot of the lane.

Fumbling with the key, he heard a plaintive meow from the other side of the door. Henry was not a fan of the rain. He would have checked out the back of the house through the cat flap and be hoping that the front door world would be nice and dry for him.

The cottage felt cold and sterile. These cases had meant that he was out all hours and hardly ever home. Although fatigue had crept into his very bones, he forced himself to sit up for a while with Henry, who was purring away noisily, while having a small nightcap and listening to some classical guitar.

Suddenly he jolted awake. There was someone banging at the front door. Confused and disoriented, he moved a disgruntled Henry off his knee. It was nearly 1 a.m. Who could be calling on him at this time of night?

He ran downstairs to the front door and opened it a crack, ready to slam it shut again if necessary. Seeing who was on the other side, he hastily swung it wide. It was Lind.

'John, what's wrong? What are you doing here at this time of night?'

His friend was still in his rumpled work suit and his face looked grey and clammy. He had a deep gash above his right eye that was oozing blood.

'Frank, I'm sorry for landing on you like this. I had nowhere else to go.'

'In you come, whatever's going on, we'll figure it out.'

Once his friend was settled on the couch with a tumbler of whisky, Farrell lit the fire, closed the curtains and switched the lamps on. The shadows receded as the cottage looked warm and welcoming once more.

'Laura and I … well, we had a fight. A bad one.'

'All couples fight, John. It's a normal part of …'

'Not like this.'

'What happened to your head?'

'She threw a plate at it.'

'I'm sure she didn't mean …'

'Then she threw another one. And another one.'

'Had she been drinking?'

Lind laughed mirthlessly.

'When is she not, these days?'

'What about the kids?'

'Staying with my mother, thank God. I've had to tell her we've been having a few problems. At her age she shouldn't have to be worrying about my shit. So I can add crappy son to the ever-growing list of areas in which I'm letting my family down.'

'Your mum would've soon figured it out anyway. And she's as fit as a flea.'

Farrell had fond memories of Margaret Lind. She had given him more succour than his own mother had, growing up, that's for sure.

'Would it help if I had a word with Laura?' asked Farrell.

'I doubt it. She had a few choice words to say about you too, Frank.'

'Did she now?' said Farrell, tensing as he wondered what was coming next.

'Told me you spoiled her fun on a night out, took her home and put her to bed. Thanks for the heads-up, by the way,' Lind said with a hint of bitterness.

'Some low-life predator was skulking around. Laura and her friend were a bit the worse for wear. I thought I'd better intervene.'

'Why the hell didn't you tell me she was making a fool of me all over town?'

'I think you're blowing this a bit out of proportion, John. It was one night, that's all. No harm done. I didn't want to cause any trouble between you, that's all.'

'You know the worst thing?' Lind said, his voice breaking as he strove for control. 'She told me she married the rebound guy. After all these fucking years she says that to me. Can you believe it?'

This was worse than he had thought.

'She was lashing out, trying to hurt you. That's all it was.'

'I thought that she'd got over you. I really did. But since you came back to the town …'

Farrell didn't like where this was going.

'It's got nothing whatsoever to do with me, John, and everything to do with losing the baby. She's angry and depressed, not herself. Surely you can see that?'

186

'I don't know what to think anymore,' his friend said, his teeth starting to chatter in spite of the fire as the reaction set in. 'Can you honestly tell me that you weren't tempted?'

'I would *never* …' said Farrell.

'That's not the same thing,' said Lind.

'Laura and I were still teenagers when we split up,' said Farrell. 'Even if I hadn't gone away to the seminary, we most likely wouldn't have lasted. It's you she chose to marry.'

'I know you did nothing to encourage her,' said Lind, attempting a smile. 'I wouldn't be here otherwise.'

'You're going to have a shiner tomorrow,' said Farrell. 'Talking of shiners, do you remember that time we had a punch-up with those two boys from Glasgow? Self-styled hard nuts?'

Lind flexed his knuckles as though remembering the pain.

'Sent them hame greetin' for their mammies. And you were an altar boy the next day, looking like something from *Die Hard*.'

'I thought my mother was going to spontaneously combust, she was that mad,' said Farrell, laughing.

They reminisced about their boyhood exploits for a while, until Lind's face had lost some of its tension. He had lost weight, too, his cheekbones looked as if they were trying to come through his skin and the collar of his shirt was far too loose. His old friend was heading for the rocks and Farrell felt powerless to help him.

Although it was already after three in the morning, Farrell knelt for a further hour praying in the privacy of his room, his face a mask of concentration as he reached for the Divine with all the determination he could muster. When at last he opened his eyes again, the walls were bathed in a silvery glow from the moon. A shrill scream rent the air from some hapless creature caught in the jaws of a predator. No matter what our earthly travail, life goes on, thought Farrell, stretching wearily and pulling back the duvet.

It was an answer of sorts.

Chapter Forty

The following morning Farrell dropped Lind off in town to avoid any raised eyebrows at them arriving together. He went looking for DS Stirling and found him heading for DI Moore's office with DC Thomson. Both were still attired in their farming gear and looked tense.

'Mind if I sit in, Kate?' he asked, poking his head round the door. 'It's hard to see where one investigation ends and the other begins at the moment. Safest if we all have an overview of what's going on.'

'I couldn't agree more,' she said, smiling. 'In you come, everyone. Love the clobber, guys. You never know, it might catch on.'

Stirling and Thomson exchanged rueful glances.

'Got your mobile switched on?' she asked DC Thomson.

'Yes, ma'am, always.'

'I decided to pull them both back to Dumfries,' she said to Farrell. 'We can't have two such experienced officers stuck out of the way in a remote farmhouse when we're undermanned as it is. They'll still sleep on the farm for the time being but spend their mornings here doing normal duties. That way, DC Thomson can still be seen out on his tractor.'

'What if there's a tail on Thomson?'

'He goes shopping for small agricultural supplies. All the kind of things you might expect. We bring him here lying down in an unmarked police car.'

'Did Shaun Finch give any idea as to how often deliveries were being made?' asked Stirling.

'It averaged out at one a week but not at a predictable day or time. If a phone call comes in when Thomson's down here, he'll take off straight away. The officers in Kirkcudbright have their instructions. Assuming the exchange takes place in the same manner as before, we should have people ready to tail the pick up next time.'

'Are you planning to lift him at that point?' asked Stirling.

'No, we want to keep him or her under observation in the hope that they'll lead us to the actual forger. Lackeys are two a penny. It's the forger we need to put behind bars. That kind of skill isn't easy to find. It would shut the whole operation down here.'

'It's possible that Monro Stevenson may have been involved,' said Farrell.

'It could explain why he was murdered. Maybe he wanted out and threatened to cut a deal and blab,' said Stirling.

'He also left The Collective around the same time Ailish did,' said Farrell. 'His breakdown came a few months after she went missing. He was obsessed with her. Perhaps he went after her and she rebuffed him. He could even have killed her?'

'A crime of passion is one thing,' said Stirling. 'Dragging her body up to the Dundrennan Firing Range and painting it is a whole different level of crazy.'

'I still feel that the announcement of the shortlist to the Lomax Prize has got to figure in there somewhere,' said DI Moore. 'Could Monro have been so elated by his inclusion and the promise for the future it held that he refused to forge anymore paintings, for example?'

'The Prize Committee have agreed to let us view the shortlisted

189

works,' said DC Thomson. 'They're being held at the Royal Scottish Academy in Edinburgh.'

'Excellent. I'll ask them to send down slides,' said DI Moore.

'Lionel Forbes is already familiar with the work of the artists we're interested in, all apart from Paul Moretti. Strangely, he's never seen any of his work. Rather odd, now I think about it?'

'I've been wondering about him,' said Farrell. 'Given that Kirkcudbright is a small town and all the artists seem to know each other, isn't he a bit too much of an enigma? There was also that throwaway comment by the gallery owner, Janet Campbell, that he paints dead things.'

'You're liking him for Ailish Kerrigan's murder?' asked DI Moore.

'Too early to say.'

'What about his medical condition, sir?' asked DC Thomson.

'He's able-bodied, just allegedly allergic to sunlight. He could paint her by the light of the moon or even take a hurricane lamp with him.'

'You think he might be faking it?' asked Stirling.

'Possibly,' said Farrell. 'To what end though?'

'DC Thomson, I left you in charge of the CCTV footage of Broughton House before you were given your present assignment. Have you passed it off to someone else to take forward?' said Farrell.

'Yes, sir. PC Green was at a loose end with the family not needing her so much now. She's organized a team to go through it all.'

DC Thomson's phone suddenly vibrated, making them all jump. He snatched it up and looked at the text.

'It's a go,' he said. 'I'm to collect the package by two o'clock and drop it off in the same place as before.'

'Right,' said DI Moore taking charge. 'You and Stirling drive back to the farm. We've already filled the boot of your car with farming supplies. I'll contact the officers we have standing by in Kirkcudbright to get into position.'

'Hopefully, this time we'll manage to stick a tail on the pick-up guy and get the next chain in the link,' said Farrell.

'Can't I be there at Dundrennan as a tourist or something? Give the lad a bit of extra cover? None of them have ever met me,' said Stirling.

'As far as you're aware,' said DI Moore. 'They may have had the farm under surveillance and know what you look like. I get that you want to help Dave, but it's simply too risky, Ronnie.'

'I wonder if someone has already dropped off the parcel at St Cuthbert's Kirkyard?' said DC Thomson. 'I take it we have surveillance in place?'

'Yes, but further away than we would like. Hopefully, they'll be able to follow the person depositing the canvas back to their point of origin. There are multiple access points,' said DI Moore. 'The drive from there to the graveyard at Dundrennan Abbey is around six miles.'

DS Stirling and DC Thomson got to their feet, looking tense but resolved.

'Off you go then,' said DI Moore. 'Stay alert, DC Thomson and, remember, no heroics!'

'Yes, ma'am,' he said, and they both turned and rushed out the door.

DI Moore sank back into her seat. Farrell didn't envy her. It was never easy sending junior officers into what could be a dangerous situation.

Farrell waited patiently while she phoned her contact in Kirkcudbright.

'DI Moore, speaking. The operation is a go. Collection by two o'clock and drop off at usual site … yes … keep me updated, please.'

Farrell stood. He'd hoped to bend her ear about Lind but now clearly wasn't the time.

'Let me know if you need a hand, Kate.'

'Thanks Frank, will do,' she said, reaching once more for the phone with a distracted look on her face.

Chapter Forty-One

Farrell tracked down PC Green and her team of four constables, who were all sitting in front of their computer screens, like zombies, watching endless CCTV footage.

'How's it going? Much in the way of repeat visits? Any by the artists we gave you photos of?'

'I was about to give you a shout, sir. The main repeat visitor, so far, is Monro Stevenson,' said Rosie. 'I've isolated and copied the frames in which he appears. It would've taken us a lot longer without the facial recognition software.'

The young man who strode about Broughton House in the footage with such vigour and confidence had no idea that his life would soon be extinguished. He seemed fascinated with the paintings, snapping occasional digital photos and making copious notes.

'None of the other artists you mentioned made an appearance over the six months apart from Hugo Mortimer, but he was there just the once and didn't take such a keen interest as Monro Stevenson.'

'Mortimer didn't linger in front of any particular painting?' asked Farrell.

'Not really, sir.'

'Lionel Forbes, the art critic, visited a couple of times too,' said PC Green.

'I didn't know you were keeping an eye out for him as well,' said Farrell.

'DC McLeod added him, sir.'

'Did she now?' said Farrell. Mind you, it was hardly surprising, given that he had made a particular study of Edward Hornel. Probably writing a freelance article for some arty magazine.

'Good work, Rosie, keep me updated on your progress.'

'Yes, sir,' she said, rubbing her neck and bending her eyes to the screen in front of her once more.

His next port of call was PC Calum McGhie, who was splitting his time between the Dumfries and Kirkcudbright stations.

'Any luck in tracking down the locksmith?'

'Yes, turns out Stevenson used a Dumfries firm: Neil Benson is his name.'

'Did he tell him why he needed the extra security?'

'I'm afraid not, sir.'

'Another dead end then.'

'He did mention that he was also asked to fit improved window locks on all the windows.'

'Seems a bit excessive,' said Farrell.

'Especially in Kirkcudbright, sir. The local criminals aren't exactly sophisticated.'

'Until now,' said Farrell.

He headed off for the canteen. They hadn't got a lot of sleep last night. He'd fortify himself with coffee and a Mars Bar, then go and tackle Lind. He really should take a couple of personal days to try and sort out his marriage, but Farrell knew there was no point in even suggesting it, with his team embroiled in such active investigations.

Grabbing two coffees to go and a couple of Mars Bars, he swiftly ascended to Lind's room, where he found his friend and boss staring at the papers on his desk as though he couldn't read English. His black eye was colouring up into a gothic riot of purples and greens.

'Get you a few chains and a ripped T-shirt and you can start a punk revival band,' he joked.

Lind didn't react. It was as if his words hadn't penetrated. It must be some kind of delayed shock. Farrell had never seen Lind look so out of it. At this rate it would get back to the Super and that wouldn't do at all! He made a snap decision.

'Come on, grab your jacket, we're going to Kirkcudbright,' he said in a tone that brooked no argument.

'What? Why? I can't possibly …' Lind stuttered, slowly coming back to life. He reached for the coffee and gulped it down.

'DC Thomson is doing another pick up this afternoon, so we're in play with the forgery op. Won't hurt to be on hand if the proverbial hits the fan.'

'Same place as before?'

'Yes, and drop off. I think the first one was just a dummy run to check Shaun Finch hadn't rolled over.'

'It was a gamble letting it run with no backup for the lad.'

'I know, but it looks like it paid off,' said Farrell. 'I also want to have another crack at Paul Moretti,' he continued. 'The owner of that gallery, Janet Campbell, said he used to paint dead things. I reckon we need to look into him further. Kate's holding the fort here. Plenty to get on with. You up for it?'

'Be better than moping about here, I suppose,' Lind said with a mirthless smile.

Before Farrell turned the key in the ignition, he glanced at his watch and took out a pill from the container in his jacket pocket, washing it down with a slug from his water bottle.

Lind glanced at him.

'How's your health been? Sorry, I've been so caught up in my own problems, I hadn't even thought to ask.'

'Fine,' said Farrell. It was a relief in a way that the team now knew he'd been close to another breakdown last year. 'Still on a maintenance dose of lithium and probably always will be.'

'When was your last check-up?'

'The end of December. I'm having them six monthly instead of yearly for the time being. Reassures the brass, if nothing else. Plus a wee day out in Auld Reekie never hurt anyone.'

'For what it's worth,' said Lind, 'I reckon I'd have been driven barmy if I'd had to face what you did last year. Three murders and a forgery ring feels like a walk in the park compared to that, eh?'

'Aye, but we're not done yet. Tell me that when we've got everyone bang to rights,' said Farrell.

His phone pinged.

'Get that will you, John?' he said, thinking it was probably an update in relation to the case.

Lind grabbed the phone. Silence.

'Well?'

'It's Laura. Since when have you and Laura been text buddies?'

'Since never,' said Farrell, hoping Lind believed him. 'Read it out then. Don't keep me in suspense.'

'"I need to see you",' intoned Lind robotically. '"Call me".'

Farrell sighed. This was just peachy. Now Laura was trying to drag him into the middle of their mess too. He hoped Lind realized it was nothing more.

'Look, John, don't you think you and Laura should sit down together with a counsellor or something? Relationship mending is not my strong suit.'

'I've already tried that,' said Lind. 'She walked out. Maybe if *you* suggested it …?' he said with more than a hint of bitterness.

'I'll think about it,' said Farrell, suddenly aware that he was grinding his teeth. The pair of them really did need their heads knocking together.

They drove in stony silence until they reached Kirkcudbright.

Chapter Forty-Two

'We should visit the gallery first, speak to Janet Campbell,' said Farrell. 'She's a nice enough woman, loves to gossip. I reckon we'll get more out of her if you turn on your usual charm.'

They parked by the harbour. The tide was in and the fishing boats long gone. Determined seagulls stalked those tourists unwise enough to be eating food from the nearby chippy. A short walk brought them to the gallery. A sleeping tabby cat lay on a cushion in the mullioned window. Janet Campbell was chatting with a couple of tourists. Farrell and Lind walked a bit up the road giving her the space to close the deal, and then turned and went in when they saw the beaming couple exit with a rectangular package wrapped in brown paper. At least she'd be in a good fettle then, thought Farrell.

'DI Frank Farrell,' she beamed, as the tinkling bell announced their arrival. 'I was wondering if you'd be back to see me. And who's this gentleman with you?'

'DCI John Lind,' he said, advancing to shake her hand.

'Someone's been in the wars!' she said, peering at Lind's black eye. He was temporarily lost for words. Farrell rescued him.

'Chasing criminals isn't without its dangers,' he said.

'Goodness!' she exclaimed, suitably impressed. She rushed to the door and turned the sign to 'Closed'.

'I've been rushed off my feet all morning. It's time I had a break anyway.' She plopped down on a stool behind the desk.

'I've been meaning to call you, DI Farrell. I had Maureen Kerrigan in here yesterday asking all sorts of questions about Ailish. Who her friends were? Did I know of any bad blood between her and anyone else? I answered them as best as I could, poor lass. However, I don't think it's safe for her to be poking around on her own like this. Who knows what hornet's nest she might stir up?'

'Thank you for letting us know,' Farrell replied. 'You're right to be concerned.'

'May I ask how long your gallery has been in Kirkcudbright?' asked Lind.

'I've been here upwards of thirty years and my father was in here before me. He died young, bless him, so I didn't have much choice really.'

'Are you an artist yourself?'

'I went to art school but, what with running the business and looking after my mother, I never really gave it a proper go. I still paint for pleasure though. It's relaxing.'

'Do you exhibit your work for sale?' asked Farrell.

For the first time they glimpsed the steel behind the amiable facade, as her voice hardened.

'I did in the beginning. I had a big exhibition at a gallery in Edinburgh when I was twenty-five. My mother was so proud. I sold a few pieces on the night. Everything seemed to go so well. The people attending were so complimentary.'

Her face twisted in remembered pain.

'What happened?' asked Farrell.

'Lionel Forbes happened. That man ruined my life. He wanted to make a name for himself as an art critic and he decided to unleash his vitriol on me. I was savaged, totally hung out to dry. That was me put in my place. And here I have remained,' she said, belatedly trying to inject a somewhat dismal note of humour.

197

'You must have been less than thrilled when he ended up in this neck of the woods, then,' said Farrell.

'Dreadful man, walks about like he's God's gift to art. If he stuck his nose in here I would probably throw something at him.'

'Do you have any pieces in your gallery by the artists up at Ivy House?' asked Lind.

'I might have a piece left by Penelope Spence. She's really rather good. A sculptress in the main, but she also paints.'

She disappeared through the back, returned with a bust, and placed it on a tall plinth.

It was a handsome face that bore more than a passing resemblance to Hugo Mortimer. Smiling in anticipation of their reaction, she removed it and held it out to them. Looking down on it from above, there was a woman's face inside the head, trying to claw her way up from the depths with skeletal fingers, her lips drawn back from her teeth in a scream or a snarl, it was hard to say. Farrell shuddered. It was unusual for him to have such a visceral reaction to a piece of art.

'Good, isn't she?'

Both men nodded in agreement.

'I don't know why she didn't enter this piece for the Lomax Prize. Despite being so talented she seems to prefer to stay in the background. I've a waiting list for her pieces from serious collectors. She doesn't like me to exhibit them in the gallery. I'd best put it away before she catches me showing it off. Have my guts for garters she would.'

'You've been incredibly generous with your time,' said Lind. 'Before we leave you in peace, I wanted to ask you about Paul Moretti.'

Instantly, Janet wrinkled her nose in distaste.

'You mentioned previously to DI Farrell that he paints dead things,' said Lind.

'Yes.'

'Can I ask exactly how you came about this information? Was it from Moretti direct?'

'No. Moretti had left the studio flat and Mike Halliday was in the process of moving his stuff in. I was preparing an inventory so we could get on with signing the lease, when I came across a few of his canvasses in the cupboard. It gave me such a turn. Moretti had shown me a painting before, even had the temerity to suggest I might want to sell it in the gallery, but the four in that cupboard were on a whole different level.'

'I know this might be difficult but it's very important. Could you describe the canvasses to us?' said Lind.

'It was a foal.' Her eyes filled with tears. 'It looked like it was dying. There were a number of other canvasses, each showing a further stage of decomposition in grisly detail. Utterly vile.'

'Do you know what became of them?'

'You'd have to ask Mike Halliday. I don't know if he left them in the cupboard or tried to get them back to Paul Moretti. He said he'd take care of them, whatever that meant.'

'How long ago was this?'

'About three years ago. That's when Mike moved into the studio.'

'Thank you, Janet, you've been most helpful. I'm sorry we had to make you remember that unpleasantness,' said Lind.

'How did you find Moretti as a person?' asked Farrell.

'I didn't really have much to do with him. He was very quiet and introverted. Could hardly get a word out of him, rarely made eye contact. I don't know how much was down to his condition or his personality. He was always so muffled up in scarves and whatnot, there could have been anyone underneath.' She shuddered.

As they walked out of the gallery, Farrell glanced at his phone. There was a message from DI Moore, which he showed to Lind. The forgery operation had been a bust. DC Thomson had gone to the pick-up site, but there was no parcel there. He'd hung about for a while, then went back to the farm with a view to trying again later, should there be another text.

'I don't like it,' Lind sounded worried. 'I hope they're not on to us. We can't keep everyone on standby indefinitely. I reckon they're still not sure whether Shaun is a plant or not. We need to figure out a way to earn their trust.'

'How about if he reports back that he saw someone watching the pick-up point?' said Farrell. 'That might allay their concerns.'

'Good idea,' said Lind. 'He could even suggest an alternative site and then we could have the surveillance sorted before they even check it out. I'll run it past DI Moore, see what she thinks. I'll meet you down by the harbour.'

Chapter Forty-Three

While Lind went off to phone DI Moore, Farrell wandered round the side of the gallery. He smiled and nodded at Mike Halliday, who was saying goodbye to an attractive dark-haired girl. They made a handsome couple. He kept walking until he reached the harbour wall. The beauty of the sun glinting on the sea against the backdrop of pastel-coloured cottages afforded a painful contrast with the evil deeds that had been done in this place.

Lind interrupted his reverie.

'I've spoken to Kate. She's going to pop out and visit Stirling and Thomson incognito with Mhairi this afternoon. They're also going to scout for possible pick-up sites that would give us a slim but not too obvious advantage in terms of terrain.'

'Depending on how we get along here, we could perhaps meet them at the farm,' said Farrell. 'Before we tackle Moretti, let's pop in on Mike Halliday and see if those canvasses are still there.'

There was no sign of the girl when they walked back up. Mike Halliday was sitting on his customary bench with a cup of coffee. A wooden summerhouse displayed a number of his canvasses, scenes of Kirkcudbright in the main. A couple of middle-aged women were selecting two paintings, with much agonizing. Halliday piled on the charm and they happily paid and had their

201

purchases wrapped, before leaving. Farrell and Lind had waited patiently to one side, not wishing to disrupt his business.

'Doing a roaring trade, there,' commented Farrell.

'It keeps the wolf from the door,' said Halliday. 'I didn't expect to see you again so soon, DI Farrell.'

Farrell introduced Lind, who was staring down at the open sketchbook on the bench.

'That's some shiner you've got there,' said Halliday. 'Looks painful.'

'Kick-boxing,' said Lind, shooting him an unfriendly look.

'Right,' said Halliday, with a hint of a smirk.

Farrell jumped in, not sure why there was a sudden undercurrent of hostility shooting between the two men.

'The reason we're here is on the off-chance that the canvasses by Paul Moretti are still in your cupboard?'

Halliday's expression tightened.

'Let me think,' he said. 'I might still have them. He certainly never came to claim them. I probably piled my own stuff in on top. Might take a bit of time to excavate them, that's assuming they're still here.'

'We're in no rush, but it might help with one of our lines of enquiry,' said Farrell.

'I'll see what I can do,' said Halliday, disappearing into the cottage. 'Give me a shout if any customers come in,' he called back to them.

Ten minutes later, Halliday re-emerged carrying four canvasses wrapped in oilskin. He slowly unwrapped them, then propped them up against the wall of the summerhouse. Farrell blanched but said nothing.

'Whoever painted these is one sick bastard,' Lind exploded. 'You're not going to tell me this fucking shit is art, are you?' he said to Halliday, who looked at him, stony-faced, as well he might. Lind was bang out of order, shouting the odds when the guy had only produced the canvasses at their request.

Farrell cast an apologetic glance Halliday's way. He nodded, seeming to bite back an angry retort of his own.

'We need to see if we can learn anything from these that might help the investigation, John.'

Lind reluctantly swivelled his eyes back to the four canvasses.

'Whoever painted this abomination has no imagination whatsoever,' he snapped. 'Hell, even I could torture something and photograph it. Where's the skill in that? It's a record of suffering, not art at all. Crude rubbish.'

Farrell did not entirely agree with him, but kept quiet, not wanting to inflame his normally mild-mannered friend any further. Although the subject matter was grim and disturbing, he rather suspected that it had been executed with a surprising degree of skill. He could almost smell the heaving flanks of the sweaty young foal, slick with sweat. However, it was the terror in its eyes that was so realistic. If Moretti had painted this, he was a very fine artist, and in all likelihood a psychopath.

The first canvas was the worst. In that one the foal was still alive. In the second picture, the spark of life had been extinguished. A light frost covered its body and the shackles had been removed. The third picture showed it decomposing, the eyes had been pecked out and the bloated carcass become infested by all manner of things. Other animals had clearly feasted on the remains, which were now only an echo of the life that had once animated it. The fourth canvas showed merely the skeleton, with a few remaining pieces of fibrous tissue attached.

'Are you sure it was Paul Moretti who painted these?' Farrell asked Halliday, who was also looking white with anger and as if he was struggling to control his reaction to the scenes before him.

'I can't say for sure,' he said. 'They're unsigned and I'm not familiar with his work. It was my landlady who said they were his, when I was moving in and she found them in a cupboard. I just covered them up and forgot about them, to be honest.'

'Christ, I don't know how you sleep at night under the same

roof as these,' said Lind. 'Give me a nice watercolour like those you're selling here. Now that's what I call art.'

'Thank you,' said Halliday in a flat voice. Probably still hacked off by Lind's outburst.

'Is there any reason you didn't return them to the artist?' asked Farrell.

'I figured if he wanted them he'd come knocking. Hardly my job to chase him all over town.'

'We're going to need to take these with us,' said Farrell. 'I assume you have no objection?'

Halliday's face was still pale under his tan. Mind you, thought Farrell, artist or not, those pictures were enough to turn anyone's stomach.

'Sure, glad to be rid of them,' he said with a smile. 'I'll wrap them up for you.'

Chapter Forty-Four

Mhairi sank into the front seat of her Renault Clio, panting with exertion. She'd only had thirty minutes' notice that she'd be driving DI Moore to the farm at Kirkcudbright and she'd had two months' worth of rubbish to get rid of, not to mention clearing all her assorted belongings into the boot. Her boss had very high standards. Standards, which Mhairi acknowledged guiltily, she did not share. She'd changed into a pair of worn denims, hiking boots and a faded sweatshirt, as per instructions. She would act the role of Dave's girlfriend, if anyone was sniffing around. The prospect of that leaving DI Moore paired with Stirling caused her to snort with laughter.

'Something funny?' asked DI Moore, through the open window.

Dammit, how did she do that? Her boss always seemed to catch her on the hop.

'Er, just recalling a scene from *The Big Bang Theory*, last night,' she improvised wildly.

'Oh? Which one?' asked DI Moore, with a hint of a smile.

'Er, just a second, I'd better check the water level,' said Mhairi, leaping from the car.

Her boss was wearing jeans and a fleece with her hair up in a ponytail. She looked a lot younger when she wasn't wearing her starchy work suits.

Mhairi made a show of examining the water, then jumped back in, turned the ignition, and roared out of the police car park.

'What do you think went wrong, ma'am?' she asked. 'I can't help worrying that they're on to us and DC Thomson could be in danger.'

'They do rather seem to be always one step ahead of us,' said DI Moore, sounding worried.

'I can't see how the real Shaun Finch could have got word out to his family. As a condition of walking away from this, he's been in protective custody with no devices from the minute we arrested him,' said Mhairi.

'I'm fairly sure he hasn't had the opportunity to leak something, although you can never be absolutely sure.'

'What about any of the experts we've instructed?' said Mhairi, choosing her words with care.

'None of them have been told about the undercover op. Besides, there's only Lionel Forbes, so far, as being pertinent to the forgery operation.'

'Oh, right,' said Mhairi.

'Something to say, DC McLeod?'

'No, ma'am.'

They drove in silence for a few miles.

'Is DCI Lind okay, ma'am?' asked Mhairi.

'Yes, as far as I'm aware. Why do you ask?'

'I noticed him leaving with DI Farrell this morning. He seemed to have hurt his eye and not his normal self ...'

DI Moore said brightly, 'Oh that! Yes, he can be so clumsy. I believe he's been having trouble with allergies. Probably forgot his antihistamines.'

You do know I'm a detective? Mhairi wanted to shout at her.

'Ah, that explains it,' she said instead.

Half an hour later, they were drawing into the farmyard. Mhairi was pleased to see Farrell's dumpy blue Citroen.

Leaping out of the car, she headed straight for the kitchen. Inside, the mood was grim and, as she reached the table and saw the canvasses laid out on it, she knew why.

'Bloody *hell*!' she exclaimed, before sitting down abruptly.

DI Moore, hot on her heels, said nothing but her face tightened in anger.

'What *is* this?' asked Mhairi.

'They were found in a cupboard, when Michael Halliday moved into the studio flat attached to Janet Campbell's gallery,' said Farrell. 'She maintains they must have been left behind by Paul Moretti. He'd asked her to sell a painting of something dead before but nothing on this scale. Just a brace of pheasants or something,' said Farrell.

Mhairi caught DI Moore sending covert glances in Lind's direction, clearly shocked by the state of his face. Lind was avoiding eye contact with her. None of this boded well, she thought.

'So, your thinking is that whoever killed Ailish may have painted her in the same manner as this?' asked Stirling, looking like he wanted to punch someone.

'Let's not jump to conclusions,' said Lind. 'It's a pertinent line of enquiry, but not the only one.'

'Are you planning to haul Moretti in for questioning?' asked DI Moore.

'Not yet,' said Lind. 'I'd like to have the paintings analyzed first to see if we can glean anything else off them that might be useful. Kate, perhaps you could invite Lionel Forbes into the station to give them the once-over? See if he's ever come across anything like this before?'

'I'll get on that right away. Let's wrap them back up for the time being. We need to do everything by the book in case these ghastly things wind up as exhibits in court one day,' she said.

DC Thomson had been tight-lipped and silent thus far. Mhairi, who was sitting beside him, bumped him with her shoulder.

'Don't worry, Dave. The two cases are totally separate. Whoever painted these or killed Ailish is a complete psychopath.'

'You don't know that for sure. In fact, we don't know bloody *much*!' he said and stormed out the back door.

'He doesn't mean it,' said DS Stirling at once. 'The lad's feeling the pressure. He was all psyched up and then left high and dry.'

'Did he send the text along the agreed lines?' asked DI Moore.

'Yes, went for a bit of a whiny faintly pissed-off tone. He also said he'd had a feeling he was being watched, when he visited the pick-up point, but couldn't be sure. He said he knew of another place that was better but didn't specify,' said Stirling.

'They didn't bite?'

'Not yet.'

At that point DC Thomson marched back in, eyes wide with excitement, his earlier outburst forgotten.

'I've heard from them. They've agreed to the new pick-up. I've been texting back and forth. I've to deposit the Hornel painting recovered from Shaun along with another package.'

'When?' asked DI Moore.

'Thursday morning at 6 a.m.'

'Great, that gives us two days,' said Stirling.

'They said it was a big job and I'd be paid double.' He paused. 'They also said I'd better not screw it up or I'd have a target on my back.'

'A big job?' mused Lind. 'I wonder what that means?'

'It could mean any number of things. It could mean there are several paintings, or one high-value one,' said Farrell.

'It hopefully also means they have no idea we're on to them,' said DI Moore. 'We have to make sure that all uniformed police stay off the streets in Kirkcudbright until this goes down. However, I want additional Dumfries Officers posing as tourists and locals to give us sufficient troops to mobilize, if necessary.'

'We'll have your back, Dave, don't worry,' said Mhairi, squeezing his arm.

Chapter Forty-Five

Farrell and Lind returned to Kirkcudbright and parked down a side street near the sheriff court. It was only mid-afternoon, but Farrell felt a wave of exhaustion sweep over him. They'd had nothing to eat since breakfast. Time to refuel.

'I'm just going to grab us a couple of rolls and coffee from the deli across the street. Give you time to figure out how you want to approach Moretti.'

Despite his lean physique, Farrell had always performed better with food in his belly.

Once back in the car, running scared from the marauding seagulls, Farrell took a large glug of coffee that tasted a whole lot better than the muck down the station.

Lind did likewise and fell upon his chicken mayo roll like he hadn't eaten for a week.

'Moretti is a bit of a strange one,' said Farrell. 'It goes way beyond his medical condition.'

'Do we have anyone objective vouching that he even has a medical condition?' asked Lind, energized by the caffeine.

'No,' said Farrell. 'You think he might be faking it?'

'No idea but it should be pinned down. He could be the murderer, hiding right under our noses, or he could be completely innocent.'

'Either way, we need to do a bit of poking around,' said Farrell.

They left the car where it was. Crossing the High Street, they walked up the hill until they reached the cottage at the top.

Like before, the heavy drapes were drawn and the house was deathly still. Farrell rapped heavily on the door. The sound echoed through the building, but there was no answer.

'So where is he then, if he's unable to go out during the day?' said Lind.

Farrell shrugged. They waited a few minutes longer then turned and retreated back down the path.

'We need to find out if he owns the house, or if it's rented,' said Farrell. 'Right now, this man is a ghost. We don't have a single piece of substance on him.'

'Apart from the fact he was shortlisted in that competition,' said Lind.

Farrell contacted the station to speak to Byers.

'Can you do a full background check on Paul Moretti, last two known addresses: Studio Flat, Kirkcudbright Art Gallery, and Lavender Cottage, Silvercraigs Road, both Kirkcudbright. I want every last grain of information you can find. Dig deep. It could be crucial to the girl's murder. Cheers. Heading back now.'

At the station in Dumfries, Farrell posted a briefing for 5 p.m. His brain was whirling with all the possible permutations and combinations of the cases. Potentially they could all be linked or completely separate. Until some of the missing pieces clicked into place, they would have to continue operating in the dark.

PC Rosie Green knocked and stuck her head round his door. He motioned her in.

'I didn't realize that Fiona Murray worked at Broughton House too, sir,' she said.

'Neither did I,' said Farrell. 'She certainly gets around. Cleaners often have more than one job, though.'

'Perhaps. Most of the time her activity seems what you would expect, tidying, polishing, mopping floors.'

'Go on.'

'But in this one bit of video, I saw her down where the safe is in the basement office.'

'And?'

'At first I didn't think anything of it. She was emptying the bin, polishing the desk, but then she started to look a bit furtive and I realized she was over by the large safe in the corner.'

Farrell quickly went down to the computer suite with her. PC Green called up the footage in question.

Fiona Murray kept up a convincing pretence of dusting and polishing right the way across the room, but then sank to her knees and quickly opened the safe. She removed a metal-coloured tube and substituted it with an identical one, which she withdrew from her large bucket of cleaning materials. She then quickly closed the safe and stood up, still flicking with her duster as she moved towards the door. The whole process had taken only half a minute. Had PC Green not been so eagle-eyed and conscientious, they might never have known.

'Great work,' he told her. 'This could be the breakthrough we're looking for. Make sure you're at the briefing at 5 p.m. DI Moore will be well made up when she hears this. She should be back in the building in another half hour or so.'

'There's something else,' she said, fingers flying over the keyboard. 'On the 28th of December, there was clearly a special delivery to Broughton House. An armoured security van pulled up at 8 a.m., before the place is open, and unloaded something. Look at this, sir.'

Farrell stared at the images on the screen. Two security men wearing helmets, flanked a third man in a suit carrying a large cylindrical metal tube. They were escorted inside by two women, one of whom locked the door behind them. Five minutes later the two security guards and the man who had been carrying the package reappeared and departed in the security van. The whole operation had taken less than fifteen minutes. With the level of security and the tense stance of the staff, glancing nervously all around as the package was escorted inside, he doubted very much that it was a Hornel painting. What had really been stolen from the safe and why hadn't the National Trust reported it?

Chapter Forty-Six

As Farrell entered the room, Lind put the phone down. His grey complexion was only relieved by the darkening hues of the blues around his eye.

'That's the search warrant requested for tomorrow morning,' he said, running his hand reflexively through his thinning hair.

'I wonder if Moretti's done a bunk?' said Farrell. 'Depending on what we find when executing the warrant, I reckon we need to detain him for questioning as soon as possible. I'd just like a bit more to strengthen our hand than the assertion of one gallery owner. At the moment, all he needs to say is that the paintings were there when he moved in as well. Difficult to disprove.'

'Agreed,' said Lind. 'We also need to know if his purported medical condition is genuine or simply a convenient smokescreen.'

There was a knock at the door and Byers stuck his head round.

Lind waved him in to join them, and he pulled up a chair beside Farrell.

'Byers, have you managed to pin down Moretti, yet?'

Byers sighed and shook his head.

'Man's a bloody ghost. Officially he doesn't exist. No social security number or trace of him anywhere in official records.

Something well off, there. Be a bugger to trace if he's done a runner.'

'You can say that again,' said Farrell. 'If he's been faking his medical condition, all he has to do is remove the scarves and walk away. Mhairi and I visited him and didn't even get close enough to know what he looks like under all those layers.'

'Could be sitting in the staff canteen and we'd be none the wiser,' muttered Lind.

'Did you contact the organizers of the Lomax Prize?' asked Farrell. 'I assume he had to give them some kind of brief bio to go along with the submission?'

'Yes, but it drew a complete blank. The judging was blind. Bios were only to be produced after the shortlist was announced, to prevent bias. In any event, he's withdrawn his work from the competition.'

'Despite being shortlisted?' said Lind.

'I know, right?' said Byers, scratching his head. 'Who does that?'

'Someone with something to hide,' said Farrell. 'The question is what? Do we have an image of the original piece?'

'No, due to the fact it was withdrawn, the trustees say that they had to delete all digital images on the instructions of the artist.'

'Is the entry still with the organizers?' asked Farrell.

'No, it was couriered back to Moretti two days ago,' said Byers. 'Apparently it was brilliant, but disturbing.'

'It's a long shot,' said Farrell, 'but it might be worth having a local copper go round and speak to all staff involved, see if any of them snapped an image on their phones when no one was looking. Guarantee anonymity.'

'Sounds like you're liking this guy for the murder of the girl,' said Byers.

'Her name's Ailish Kerrigan,' snapped Lind, causing Byers to sit up in surprise.

'Too early to say,' said Farrell sending Byers a warning look.

214

'He's certainly a person of interest, if his links to the paintings in Janet Campbell's studio flat can be proven.'

'It would be premature to say anything to Maureen Kerrigan for now,' said Lind.

'Does she have long dark hair?' asked Farrell.

'Yes, why do you ask?' said Lind.

'I saw a dark-haired young woman with Mike Halliday today in Kirkcudbright,' said Farrell.

'Dark hair isn't exactly uncommon in these parts,' said Lind.

'Even so,' said Farrell. 'Whether that was her or not, I hope she's not poking around, asking questions. Especially now that it's at least a possibility that we're dealing with an out-and-out psychopath.'

'True, I'll give her a ring. Try and get her to at least relocate to Dumfries for the time being,' said Lind.

'Have you spoken to Clare Yates yet, in relation to gaining some insight into the mind of the killer?' asked Farrell, trying to keep his expression as neutral as possible.

Lind glanced at his watch and looked horrified.

'About that …'

His words were interrupted by a knock at the door.

'You've got to be kidding me,' muttered Farrell.

'I asked her to swing by to give her thoughts on the paintings we recovered today,' Lind said, looking awkward.

Byers made heroic efforts to control a smirk trying to escape as he stood up with the other men.

Lind strode to the door and opened it wide. There on the other side was his former girlfriend, even more gorgeous than the last time he had seen her. Her smile slipped as she took in Lind's ruined face and then Farrell standing awkwardly behind him. Lind took control.

'Clare, thanks so much for coming in. I thought we might be more comfortable in the conference suite. I'll arrange for the paintings and coffee to be sent up there.'

'Excellent,' she said, sending a strained smile of acknowledgement in Farrell's direction. She walked off with Lind, who was managing to dredge up a superhuman amount of small talk as they went.

'Awkward, much?' said Byers, in his usual tactless manner.

Farrell sent him a glare, which should, by rights, have turned him into a pillar of salt, and marched off in the opposite direction.

He knew Lind had done the right thing in calling Clare in. He had thought he wouldn't be affected by seeing her again. He was wrong. It had devastated him when she called time on their relationship last year. He'd been considering leaving the priesthood and seeking a papal dispensation to be released from his vows. However, she hadn't wanted to take on his considerable baggage and, in all honesty, he couldn't blame her. As he walked along, all he could feel was the imprint of her body in his arms like a phantom limb. The faint vapour trail of her perfume left hanging in the corridor taunted him. He had to get out of here. Fast.

Chapter Forty-Seven

Lind sat opposite Clare Yates in the conference room. There was an awkward silence as he realized that he had exhausted his supply of social chit chat. The coffee and paintings had yet to arrive. He knew that she was wondering about his bruised eye. Dammit, that was the thing about psychiatrists, they sat there in silence until you rushed to fill it, revealing God knows what in the process. He had used the technique himself to great effect in the interview room, but never had the tables reversed, until now. Just as he was on the verge of cracking wide open and muttering something unconvincing about walking into a door, he was saved by a tap on the door.

PC Green came in with the labelled paintings, closely followed by one of the admin staff, bearing a tray of coffee that she placed at the far end of the table.

'Thank you, both. Rosie, I hear you've been doing sterling work with the CCTV footage.'

'Thank you, sir,' she said, carefully depositing the paintings on the oval table in front of them. 'I'd best get back to it.'

Carefully, he removed the paintings from their protective covering and laid them out in front of Clare, who was sitting opposite. Reflexively, she gasped, her hand shooting up to her mouth.

'Takes your breath away, doesn't it,' said Lind. 'And for all the wrong reasons.'

'Such ferocity,' she murmured, struggling to regain her composure. 'The suffering of that poor animal. Trapped on its back like that. Those eyes … turned towards the artist …'

'The other three appear to document the moment of death and subsequent stages of decomposition,' said Lind. 'What do you reckon?'

'Well, I'm no expert on art,' she said, 'but I think that whoever painted these pictures is most likely a psychopath. A lot of planning and effort has gone into this endeavour.'

'Assuming you're right, is it possible that the perpetrator might move on to kill a young woman in the same fashion?' asked Lind.

'Well, yes, God forbid, that's entirely possible. Cruelty to animals, as I'm sure that you're aware, is one of the predictors for someone evolving into a murderer, even a serial killer. How long ago were these painted?'

'No clue. According to the gallery owner they were left by Paul Moretti, a previous tenant. We've got a warrant for his arrest, but he's disappeared into thin air.'

Lind reached into the folder he had brought with him and took out a picture of Ailish Kerrigan's remains in situ. Clare studied it carefully.

'I'm wondering,' said Lind, 'if it's at all likely that the same person who painted these pictures may have conducted a similar study on the deceased. Look,' he said leaning over the table, 'see these marks here …? We're wondering if the murderer set up an easel in the clearing.'

'How long ago did this girl go missing?'

'Three years,' said Lind.

'Then we have to face the possibility that the killer may strike again or, indeed, they may have already done so.'

'You reckon there might be other canvasses like this out there, only with human remains as their subject?'

'There could well be,' she said. 'From what you told me on the phone, these ones were only discovered by chance in a remote location. It's possible that painting his victims in this way might be a pattern of behaviour for him that is very ritualistic. He probably feels a compulsion to repeat it.'

'What do you think about the fact that the dead foal is a male?' said Lind.

Clare looked again at the painting of the desperate animal.

'I should have noticed that. It does muddy the waters a little as to the underlying motive, assuming we are talking about the same perpetrator. Of course, the means and opportunity may have influenced the choice, but I doubt that, somehow.'

'Any guesses as to what might have been going on in the perpetrator's head when he was doing these paintings?' asked Lind.

'Could be a number of things,' she said. 'Assertion of mastery and complete dominion over a living thing? Has it been possible to establish whether the deceased girl was sexually assaulted?'

'No,' said Lind. 'Impossible to say.'

'I'm not getting any overt sexual imagery looking at the picture of the foal again. Another possibility is that cruelty isn't the main motive at all.'

'What then?' asked Lind.

'Well, think of the medium he's chosen to record his crimes in? I think it's entirely possible that he's a megalomaniac, who sees this as great art and is out to make a name for himself.'

'Then, he's deluded,' said Lind.

'Not necessarily,' said Clare. 'I hasten to add that I'm in no position to evaluate the art, but I wouldn't be surprised if it was considered well executed. It has an undeniable power about it.'

'What nutter would want these hanging on their wall?' said Lind.

'You'd be surprised,' she said. 'Overseas collectors on the dark web would pay an absolute fortune for human images like this.

I remember reading a paper on an analogous matter fairly recently.'

Lind leaned back in his chair and sighed, feeling weary to his very bones.

'And I thought the world us coppers inhabited was dark,' he said.

After he had shown her out and returned the paintings to the evidence room, he returned to his office. He'd been putting it off long enough. It was time to phone his wife and see if he could salvage anything from the wreck of his marriage, before it completely foundered.

The phone went straight to voicemail. He didn't leave a message. It looked like he was staying another night with Frank then.

Forcing his mind away from his domestic problems, he went in search of DI Moore. Perhaps she could get an indication from that art critic as to how much skill had gone into producing those monstrosities. He tapped lightly on the open door. She was bent over some bulging files, her brow furrowed in concentration. Looking up she smiled wearily, motioning him to take a seat.

'John, what can I do for you?'

'That art critic of yours.'

'Lionel Forbes?'

'Yep, that's the one. Just how expert is he?'

'Very. Why?'

'And you can vouch for him?'

'Of course. I checked him out thoroughly before inviting him to consult in the first place. Nothing in his background gave me cause for concern.'

'I'd like you to show him the pictures we recovered. Ascertain if he's seen anything like it before, or if there's any clue as to the identity or ability level of the artist.'

'You really think that the same person might have painted our dead girl?'

'All supposition at the moment but, yes, I think that's a distinct possibility,' said Lind.

'I'll ring him and see how soon he can come in here,' she said.

Lind moved to get up, but she reached across the desk and laid her hand on his. He froze.

'John,' she said, 'your face ... what happened?'

'It was the funniest thing ...' he started to bluster.

'John, it's me you're talking to ... what really happened?'

Lind sighed and dropped back in the seat.

'Don't overreact. It was a plate. Laura. She flung it in my direction. I'm sure she didn't mean ...'

'Has she ever done anything like this before?'

'No! Of course not! We have a good marriage. She's not like that.'

'You've both been through a lot, I know that ... but still, John ... it's spousal abuse.'

'I'm handling it,' he said, uncomfortably aware that he wasn't handling it at all.

'If you need any help ... with anything ... don't hesitate to call on me.'

'I won't,' he said with a quick smile, getting to his feet. 'Let me know what Lionel makes of the paintings. We could really do with a break in this case.'

Lind headed back to his office. The desk was overflowing with paper. All four investigations were gathering momentum and he was starting to feel like he was being sucked under by an undercurrent of fatigue. There was some time before the last briefing of the day. He couldn't allow his marriage to founder on the rocks of his career, like so many coppers before him. It was time to put up a fight for his family. Everything else would have to wait. Grabbing his jacket, he left the building and swiftly drove home.

* * *

Letting himself quietly in the front door, he stood and listened. The familiar sounds of the house welcomed him back. The kids were still staying with their granny. He could hear a muffled noise coming from the lounge. Opening the door he saw Laura curled in a ball on the sofa sobbing wretchedly into a cushion. Without even thinking about it, he rushed over and scooped her up into his arms.

'John,' she sobbed, 'I'm so sorry. I don't know what's happening to me. I'm turning into a monster. Look at your poor face. You must hate me.'

'Shush,' he soothed. 'As if I could ever hate you. It's a rough patch. All marriages hit them.'

'I love you,' she sobbed, louder now.

'I know you do. And I love you. I think we might need some help figuring stuff out though.'

'Counselling?'

'Can't hurt,' he said, smiling at her.

'You hate the idea of spilling your guts to strangers,' she said.

'True. But I hate the thought of losing you more.'

'Ever since I lost the baby I've felt filled with a murderous rage. The only thing that dulls it down is alcohol. I look at you sometimes, John, and I feel like I hate you; like you've abandoned me and left me to go through this all on my own.'

'I have to work, Laura. I have to keep people safe.'

'You didn't keep me safe,' she said.

They remained sitting there, each lost in their own thoughts, as the sun set and the shadows lengthened.

222

Chapter Forty-Eight

Farrell's alarm went off at 5 a.m., as usual. At least he'd had a decent night's sleep, because Lind had returned home to try and repair his marriage. He resolved to keep well out of Laura's way as he didn't want to unsettle her further. It was likely that she felt drawn to him due to their shared history and also because he represented a time when she was carefree, before her life had spiralled downwards and she became mired in grief.

He pulled on his running gear and headed up the lane. As his feet slapped down rhythmically on the road, he tried to empty his mind of the cases troubling him, but images kept slipping through like some jumbled slideshow. The face of Monro's girl-friend, Nancy, was in there. Her expression in the photo reminded him of something, but who or what? The more he probed, the hazier the image became, until he had to let it slide away.

It was replaced by the face of Maureen Kerrigan. She hadn't returned Lind's calls yesterday. If she started poking around, asking too many questions, the killer might decide to silence her for good. The shadowy form of Paul Moretti crept in next. Farrell was frustrated and annoyed that they hadn't gone after him quicker. Worse, they had no clue what he even looked like. He had been hiding in plain sight and no one had even thought to question it because of his alleged condition. If those paintings really were his, he could be out in the daylight stalking his next victim, with no one being any the wiser.

Then there was the forgery ring, operating with seeming impunity right under their noses. He was worried that young Davey wouldn't have the experience to handle himself, if everything went belly up. He was convinced both Monro Stevenson and Poppy Black had been murdered to ensure their silence. He would never be able to forgive himself if anything happened to one of his junior officers. Lind was doing his best, but clearly wasn't at the top of his game at the moment due to his domestic strife. What it really boiled down to was that Farrell must carry the whole situation on his shoulders and keep everyone safe. He prayed that he would be equal to the task.

Back in the cottage, he fed Henry and had his usual power shower. He then lit the fat creamy candle on the low table and knelt facing the small wooden crucifix above. Closing his eyes, he tried to push out the ugliness in his head, as the familiar scent of beeswax from the heated candle rose up in the air. His breathing slowed and gradually he lost all sense of himself. His soul reached up towards God, the well-worn incantations slipping through his mind like smooth pebbles. After half an hour, the pain in his knees reminded him it was time to focus on the temporal plane once more. Grimacing, he made the sign of the cross and got to his feet, with less grace than he would have liked. At this rate, he would have to give in and get himself a kneeler, like some old codger.

A few minutes later, dressed in one of his identical black suits and a grey shirt, he was tucking into scrambled eggs and toast, having already taken his lithium. Henry lazily stretched and stalked out into the garden, causing a group of small birds to scatter noisily.

With a sigh, Farrell locked up the house and folded himself inside his dumpy blue Citroen. He couldn't continue to go on, caught between two worlds like this. He was going to have to make a decision: return to life as an active priest, or commit to his career in the police and undergo laicization. To remain as he was would be tantamount to moral cowardice. He had been dodging his spiritual adviser, Father Joe Spinelli, for a few months now as he knew he would ask the kind of searching questions he hadn't been ready to answer. He felt doubly guilty because the elderly priest, who lived in Edinburgh, was becoming frailer and might not be with them for much longer.

At the station, they had a conjoined briefing at 8 a.m. Lind was looking less tense about the face, Farrell noted with relief. He signalled to Farrell to start.

'Byers, have we got the search warrant for Moretti's place?'

'Yes, sir, courtesy of a very grumpy sheriff last night,' he said, waving a sheet of paper in the air.

'Excellent, Mhairi and I will head out to Kirkcudbright to execute that first thing.'

'What about Moretti?' asked Byers. 'I hear he's disappeared into thin air.'

'Looks rather like it,' said Farrell. 'The Kirkcudbright lads have been keeping a discreet eye on the property and there's been no apparent activity.'

'I take it there's no way he could slip in and out from the rear of the property?' asked Byers.

'No, the garden backs on to a sheer crag. You'd need proper climbing gear to tackle it.'

'Hopefully, we'll find something of interest in the property itself,' said Farrell. 'Who was looking into the staff administering the Lomax Prize?'

PC Rosie Green's hand shot up.

'Only one person admitted taking a digital image before deleting them. The officer who spoke to her sent it to me this morning.' She bent over her iPad and in a few seconds the image

225

appeared on the whiteboard on the wall. It was stunning and shocking in equal measure. It was impossible not to have a strong reaction to it.

'Isn't that …?' asked Mhairi.

'Hugo Mortimer,' said Farrell.

There was silence as they all stared at the image. The canvas was huge and showed the handsome patrician features of Mortimer staring into a mirror, full lips curled in a smile, but with a bacchanalian image reflected back. Two small horns were budding from his head. He stood clothed in faded jeans and an artist's smock but with bare, misshapen feet. A man's neck was crushed under one foot and a woman's under the other. A naked young woman with long dark hair knelt before him in supplication, but her face couldn't be seen. There were what looked like claw marks down the tightly bunched muscles of her back. The approach towards Mortimer was littered with broken naked bodies, lifeless glassy eyes staring into infinity. It was without doubt the best and the worst painting Farrell had ever seen.

'Moretti painted this?' said DI Moore, sounding shocked.

'Apparently so, ma'am,' said PC Green.

'Could that be Ailish, sir?' asked Mhairi, pointing to the kneeling girl and voicing what they were all thinking.

'I bloody hope not,' Lind replied. 'Let's not get carried away. It's just a painting remember, not a literal depiction of actual events.'

'Hopefully,' said DS Byers.

'Even so,' said Mhairi. 'If it's meant to depict Hugo Mortimer, could it also imply he had a relationship with Ailish, or worse than that, raped or killed her?'

'Can you imagine if it had won?' said DI Moore. 'Hugo Mortimer would have been a laughing stock. Paul Moretti and he must have some serious bad blood between them.'

'I'll call Clare Yates in on this,' said Lind. 'See what she makes of it, because I'm at a complete loss. I reckon this is another one

226

for Lionel Forbes as well, Kate. I don't know about you, but I can't even begin to fathom what's going on between all these artists. Even allowing for artistic temperament, this seems … extreme. You'll have to swear him to secrecy, mind. Moretti can have no idea we've stumbled upon this image.'

'He's coming in later,' DI Moore said. 'I'm sure that we can count on his discretion.'

Farrell noticed Mhairi stiffen slightly. She glanced away, refusing to meet his eyes. What was that about? he wondered.

'PC Green, I want you to get the police in Edinburgh back out to the Lomax Prize office. They're going to need to seize that phone as evidence, pending us finding the original painting,' said Lind.

'We need to detain the housekeeper, Fiona Murray, for questioning,' said Farrell. 'Mhairi and I can pick her up on the way here from Kirkcudbright. I reckon she knows way more than she's been letting on. Unfortunately, I suspect she'll clam up and request a solicitor as soon as she knows we have her on the CCTV removing an item from the safe.'

As they were all dispersing, Lind turned to Farrell and muttered under his breath.

'I don't like it, Frank. I don't like it at all. Keep me looped in on each and every development in these cases. I have a feeling more lives could be at risk.'

Chapter Forty-Nine

As they were leaving Dumfries, Mhairi's phone beeped. It was a text from Ian suggesting they meet up that night. A worm of guilt twisted within her. She'd been fobbing him off ever since she'd met up with Patrick. Ian deserved better.

Farrell glanced across at her.

'Problem?' he asked.

Honestly! Sometimes she could swear he could see right into her soul.

'Just a text from Ian,' she said, her voice flat.

'I see,' he said.

'I'm meant to be meeting Patrick tonight. He's invited me to Ivy House for supper. Give me an opportunity to sniff around a bit, pick up on any undercurrents.'

'Why didn't you say anything at the briefing?'

'I'm telling you now, aren't I?'

Farrell looked worried. She didn't blame him, but she was as sure as she could be that Patrick wasn't involved in any of the crimes they were investigating. His feelings of guilt and grief over Ailish had seemed genuine. She hadn't detected one false note.

'I hate to bring it up, but are you sure your judgement isn't being impaired? You seem quite drawn to him.'

Mhairi snorted in derision, but her thumping heart told a different story.

'He's someone I'm using as a source of information to further the case. I'm going out with Ian, remember?' she snapped.

'Then perhaps you'd better text him back,' said Farrell.

'I will do. Later.'

They continued in silence until they arrived in Kirkcudbright. Farrell parked the squad car outside Lavender Cottage. They walked up the stone path to the door, and Farrell knocked loudly.

'Police! Open up!'

They could hear the sound echoing down the hall inside, but there was no response.

Farrell tried the door. It was no surprise to find it was locked.

'Shall we bust it down, sir?' asked Mhairi.

'I doubt that'll be necessary,' said Farrell, producing the key from the inside of a stone planter.

'How did you …?'

'Prayed to St Anthony. Works every time,' he said with a triumphant glint in his eyes.

'Hmm,' muttered Mhairi, as Farrell swiftly opened the door.

They both stood motionless in the long dim hall. A mantel clock chimed the hour, making them jump. The air felt stale, as though it hadn't been disturbed for days. At the rear of the hall, they could see a strip of light under the closed door. They moved towards it, checking the four doors opening off the hall on the way. Each room had heavy drapes drawn across the window. The furniture was old and dilapidated, as though it had been plucked randomly from a charity shop. Mind you, he was a bloke, thought Mhairi.

Reaching the end of the hall they opened the door and their eyes widened in shock.

'What the hell?' said Mhairi, turning to Farrell, who was looking as surprised as she was. They were standing in a bright open-plan studio space, flooded with natural light from a skylight. There

229

were canvasses everywhere in various stages of composition. A number of them looked familiar but Mhairi couldn't pinpoint why. DI Moore would know. She was the culture vulture in the station. Carefully, she took digital images of all the art work she could see. A few were signed Aaron Sewell. There were none that resembled the horrendous images they had recovered from his previous flat.

'It's clear to me now that Paul Moretti is simply a disguise, probably created because he's someone reasonably prominent in the local community,' said Farrell.

'I'm going to look in the wardrobes,' said Mhairi. 'Might give us some clues as to his real identity.'

The bedroom was to the front of the house. The bed was neatly made. She felt under the pillow, but there were no pyjamas. She rifled through the bedside table. There were a couple of pairs of black lacy underwear stuffed in the back of the drawer behind a couple of pairs of boxers and some grey socks. There were very few clothes in the wardrobe. The whole place had the vibe of a creepy hotel room, rather than somewhere someone actually lived. There was a reading light and a few scuffed paperbacks. Try as she might she could find nothing to suggest an alternative identity for Moretti. She headed for the bathroom next. There was only one toothbrush and no obvious signs of a woman's presence. Moretti clearly had good taste in bath oil, she thought, opening the expensive bottle to take a sniff. Not the kind of thing you'd use if you suffered from an allergic skin reaction. There was no emollient cream in sight. The whole illness thing had clearly been a big con, she thought, cross with herself for having been taken in.

Farrell stuck his head round the bedroom door.

'Have you found the painting from the competition yet?' she asked.

'No sign of it.'

'Do you think that the real Paul Moretti might be someone we've already met?' she asked.

'Quite possibly,' said Farrell.

His face was strained and Mhairi guessed that he was beating himself up as much as she was for letting him slip through their fingers.

'I'm off to do the sitting room. I'm going to keep the curtains drawn, just in case we're being watched,' he said.

They continued with their search, taking care to leave everything exactly as they found it in case Moretti returned.

The writing bureau in the living room contained an untidy jumble of papers and bills, nothing remarkable. However, Mhairi's probing fingers struck lucky as she nudged a small lever, which opened a secret compartment at the back of the drawer. She extracted a number of letters addressed to Aaron Sewell.

'That's the name on some of the canvasses,' said Farrell peering over her shoulder, ready to swoop with an evidence bag.

'Do you think that they're one and the same person?' asked Mhairi.

'Impossible to say,' said Farrell. 'If Moretti is simply another artist, then why all the subterfuge? It doesn't make sense.'

'Who'd have thought painting pictures could be such a nasty business?' said Mhairi.

'Where there's money there's a motive for murder.'

'I haven't found any paperwork to suggest Moretti had a bank account. What do you suppose he lived on?'

'Probably income derived from his main identity, Aaron Sewell,' said Farrell. He pulled out his phone.

'Byers, can you look into the artist Aaron Sewell for me? That may be the real identity of Paul Moretti. I also want his financials run down. The fact that Sewell's correspondence appears to come here, and that there are canvasses signed by him in Lavender Cottage, should give you sufficient cause. Cheers.'

They gave the property a final check before locking the door and replacing the key.

'Where to now, sir?' asked Mhairi.

'I think it's time to pick up Fiona Murray and see what she has to say for herself. But before we do that, we're going to pay Broughton House a little visit and see what they've been storing in that safe.'

Chapter Fifty

Farrell and Mhairi parked outside and walked up the stairs of Broughton House. To the right of the entrance was a table with a middle-aged woman taking money for tickets and guide-books.

'Are you members of the National Trust?' she enquired.

'No, I'm afraid we're here on police business,' said Farrell, producing his warrant card.

Immediately, her demeanour changed and her eyes flicked nervously from one to the other.

'Oh, er, how can I help you, officers?'

'And you are?'

'Jemima Jones,' she almost whispered. Her face looked clammy and pale.

'Is there somewhere a little more private?' asked Farrell, aware of a group of tourists shamelessly earwigging while pretending to look at a display cabinet.

'Yes, we can go to the office. I'll just give Lucy a nudge to cover the desk.'

They made their way downstairs, with Farrell ducking to avoid banging his head, and were shown in to a tiny room that immediately felt crowded, once they were all inside.

'I'm sure you know why we're here,' Farrell said. He then paused and looked at her expectantly.

Jemima shifted in her seat. Her glasses were starting to steam up.

'Er, no, I'm really not sure …' she tailed off.

Farrell sat back and folded his arms, his gaze uncompromising. The silence lengthened until Jemima cracked wide open.

'Look it wasn't my decision not to report it.'

'Go on,' said Farrell.

'The National Trust told us to take delivery of a very valuable painting. It was just to be for a few nights, until they could put in place the necessary insurance and courier arrangements to take it back to Lord Merton's estate at Kincaid House.'

'You said, "take it back". Had it been stolen? Restored?'

'I'm not supposed to say anything. I could lose my job.'

'I should think that's the least of your concerns right now,' said Farrell, standing up. 'Maybe we should continue this in Dumfries, at the station?'

'No! Please, sit down. I'll tell you what I know. I didn't want anything to do with it. I hoped that it would all work out okay if I just kept my mouth shut.'

Farrell glanced at Mhairi who looked as baffled as he was.

'Why don't you start at the beginning?' he said.

'The painting had been stolen from Lord Merton's country seat at Kincaid House.'

'When was this?' asked Farrell. 'I'm not aware of any report to that effect.'

'It was never reported,' she said. 'It was a Turner and worth millions. The family notified the insurance company and were advised to sit tight pending a ransom demand. The ransom was paid by the insurance company and the painting delivered locally, which is where we came in. The National Trust knew we had a safe here and thought that the painting could sit tight with us until all the necessary arrangements were put in place.'

'Is it still in there?' asked Mhairi.

'Yes, of course. The manager and I are the only one with keys,' she said.

This was worse than they had thought. A lot worse. Farrell pulled up the footage on his phone of Fiona Murray opening the safe and removing a cylinder. He had no doubt that Jemima's shock and dismay were genuine.

'I don't understand. That's our cleaner. What's she doing?'

Abruptly, she jumped up and raced down some steps to the basement, with Farrell and Mhairi in hot pursuit. Opening the door to a somewhat larger office this time, with a key she pulled out from around her neck, she rushed over to the substantial safe in a corner of the room and opened it. Her relief was almost palpable as she pulled out a metal tube from the stacked art works inside. Quickly she opened the tube and carefully extracted the contents.

'See, it's still here!' she exclaimed. 'I don't know what's gone on, but there's obviously been a huge misunderstanding. This is the painting, I'm sure of it,' she said, looking up at them with hope flaring.

'It could be,' said Farrell. 'I hope that it is. But I'm afraid there's been a skilled forgery ring operating out of Kirkcudbright for a while now. It's possible the painting was stolen and a copy returned. You left before the bit where Fiona placed an identical cylinder back in the safe.'

'But, Fiona can't be involved. She's just the cleaner; I never would have imagined she could do something like this.'

'Do you know where she is now?' asked Mhairi.

'I've no idea. She doesn't come in until after we're closed for the night. Her references were spot on. She produced a Disclosure certificate as well.'

'Do you still have the documentation?' asked Farrell.

'Yes, it'll be in her file.' She dashed over to one of the cabinets, pulled out a slim file and handed it to him. Inside was a very decent-looking Disclosure certificate and glowing references from Monro Stevenson and Hugo Mortimer.

'We're going to need to have the painting examined by an expert as quickly as possible.'

'I'm afraid all this is way above my pay grade,' Jemima said. 'I'll probably lose my job over this. I'll contact the National Trust and get the name of someone you can liaise with.'

Farrell felt sorry for her, but the cleaner should never have been allowed the run of the building when no one else was there.

'How did she get access to the safe key?' he asked. 'I'm assuming it wasn't hanging on a hook somewhere?'

'No!' she said, then looked puzzled. 'Actually, I've no idea. I keep my key on a chain round my neck, where no one can see it. The only other key is in a locked drawer in my desk.'

'I don't suppose you've had reason to have a locksmith or joiner in the museum, recently?' he asked.

'Well yes, as it happens,' she said, surprised. 'Fiona reported that the hinges on the office door were starting to …' She buried her head in her hands. 'Dammit, I've been a fool, haven't I? It's my fault. She recommended a joiner and I never thought twice about it.'

'These people have been fiendishly clever,' said Mhairi. 'All you did was place your trust in the wrong person.'

'I take it you instructed Neil Benson from Dumfries?' asked Farrell.

'Yes, he came early in the morning, just two days after we received the painting.'

'One final thing before we go. I want you to say nothing about this to anyone. Is that absolutely clear?' said Farrell.

She nodded.

'We're at a very crucial stage in the investigation and lives could be put in jeopardy if they twig that we're on to them. I'll phone the contact you gave me in the National Trust and explain everything that's transpired.'

Again, she nodded.

'We'll be in touch,' said Farrell. 'Here's my personal mobile,' he said handing over a card. 'Any problems give me a call. If we don't get hold of Fiona Murray by the time the museum closes, I'll send in a couple of undercover officers, ostensibly working on a restoration project to make sure there are no problems overnight.'

Chapter Fifty-One

Farrell and Mhairi drove to the harbour and grabbed two take-away coffees. Sitting on a bench overlooking the sea, they mulled over their options.

'What do you think, sir? Should we call in reinforcements to hunt for Fiona Murray?'

'We'll track her down ourselves. We now know that she's potentially implicated in everything but the murder of Ailish Kerrigan. Even if she's not involved in what happened to Monro Stevenson, she's definitely in tow with the forging ring. If we flood the area with officers and go in mob-handed, not only might we never catch the real villains, but we put DC Thomson's life in jeopardy too.'

'But if we arrest her won't that put the wind up them?'

'Not if we get her to talk, and cut a deal for her to walk if she delivers everyone else's head on a plate.'

'We need to lose the squad car then, sir. Doesn't exactly come with stealth mode.'

'We'll try her home first,' said Farrell.

Ten minutes later they were outside Murray's modest flat. There was no answer to the doorbell. Farrell peered through the letterbox. There was no mail lying on the carpet, so she hadn't done a runner yet.

They looked for a spare key, but their target was too switched on to be caught out that way. As a result of the CCTV footage they had a search-and-entry warrant, but Farrell didn't want to leave any trace of their presence, so busting the door down wasn't an option. He stared at Mhairi intently.

'What?' she asked.

He held out a hand.

Mhairi rolled her eyes but fished out a hairpin for him. After a few seconds, the lock yielded. Inside, it was still in immaculate order. There was nothing in the way of home comforts in evidence. Everything was plain and functional to the point of sterility. The only adornment was a small picture of the Virgin Mary in the middle of the mantelpiece.

'It's well seeing she cleans for a living,' whispered Mhairi. They both slipped on latex gloves and methodically went through the flat, room by room. It felt almost monastic, thought Farrell.

'There's no family pictures,' he said. 'A woman her age, that's a little unusual.'

'It feels really impersonal,' said Mhairi, 'as if she's not emotionally invested in the place.'

'Got something,' said Farrell, feeling under the thin mattress. He pulled out a large plain padded envelope and emptied the contents on the bed. There was £10,000 in cash and a photo of a beautiful young girl in school uniform.

Mhairi studied it intently.

'Isn't that Ailish Kerrigan?' she asked.

'It could be,' said Farrell. 'But as I understand it, Fiona Murray didn't start working up at Ivy House until months after Ailish went missing. She couldn't possibly be implicated in her disappearance.'

'Maybe she stole the picture from Ivy House. Could be she's been digging around into Ailish's disappearance to gain some leverage, perhaps blackmail the killer?' said Mhairi.

'Well, if that's the case she's a woman who likes to live dangerously,' said Farrell.

Suddenly, they heard the scrape of a key in the lock.

They stood behind the bedroom door until Murray had entered and closed the front door behind her. She moved into the kitchen, and then Farrell and Mhairi stepped out, standing between her and the exit.

Murray choked back a scream and sagged weakly against the kitchen units.

'You scared the bejesus out of me! What the devil do you think you're doing? How did you get in here? You've got no right ...'

Farrell handed over the search warrant, which she studied closely.

'Fiona Murray, you're under arrest for stealing a painting from the safe at Broughton House. Anything you say will be noted down and can be used against you in a court of law. Do you understand?'

She nodded, her expression unreadable.

'We're going to take you to Dumfries police station now for processing. I'm not proposing to put cuffs on if you can assure me you're not about to do a runner,' said Farrell.

'I hardly think I'd get very far,' she said.

He waited with her in silence while Mhairi retrieved the patrol car.

Back at the station she was processed by the Custody Sergeant. She declined the services of a solicitor. The only visible reaction from her was when he lifted out the photo from the envelope.

'That's mine,' she snapped. 'Give it to me!'

He ignored her and continued noting the item down in the property register.

'Cell 5,' he said, escorting Murray to the door and ushering her inside.

'Keep a close eye on her,' said Farrell.

'Will do, boss,' he replied.

Chapter Fifty-Two

Farrell and Mhairi did a swerve into the canteen and grabbed coffees and sandwiches. It was already well past lunchtime.

Ten minutes later and they were hurrying up the stairs to the conference room, where the team were assembled.

Farrell quickly brought them all up to speed on the morning's events.

'She's obviously a part of the forgery gang,' said Lind. 'That much is self-evident from her actions at Broughton House.'

'I doubt she's involved in the creation of the forgeries,' said DI Moore. 'She's no studio space, as far as we're aware. I think her role is more likely to be logistics, moving things around and whatnot. A cleaner is a perfect vehicle for that. Access all areas yet practically invisible.'

'You mentioned a photo?' said Lind.

Farrell produced the evidence bag, and Lind inspected the image through the clear plastic.

'Yes, that's Ailish Kerrigan all right. I'm sure of it,' he said. 'It doesn't make any sense though.'

'Unless, she discovered someone in the forgery ring was involved in her murder and has been putting herself a wee insurance packet together,' said Byers.

'Given her clear involvement,' said DI Moore, 'I reckon the forgers have to be located within Ivy House. Some or even all of them may be implicated.'

'Monro himself may have been a participant, for all we know,' offered Farrell.

'I'm fairly sure Patrick Rafferty isn't involved in Ailish's disappearance,' said Mhairi. 'He seemed genuinely surprised and distraught about her murder. The forgery ring may well be a different matter.'

'We still don't know the real identity of Paul Moretti,' said Byers. 'Can you guys remember anything at all that might help us measure him up against the known players we've come across so far?'

Farrell and Mhairi glanced at each other in frustration then shook their heads.

'Like we said before. It was early days in the investigation. He wasn't a suspect. We'd no reason to doubt his allergy to sunlight condition, as the gallery owner, Janet Campbell, had effectively vouched for it,' said Farrell.

'It was virtually dark,' said Mhairi, 'apart from one very low energy bulb in a corner.' He was sat down the whole time, so we can't take a guess at his height. As to his build, he had so many layers and scarves on, it's almost impossible to tell with any degree of certainty. But if I had to take a punt, I would say he's of slight build. If he was fat, he'd have taken up a lot more space on the sofa. Now that I think about it, I reckon he might be quite tall, as I do remember his legs extending quite a way towards us.'

'That gives us a bit more to go on,' said Lind. 'I take it Moretti's apartment is still under subtle surveillance?'

'Yes, the local Kirkcudbright boys are handling that,' said Farrell.

'My money's on Hugo Mortimer,' said DI Moore. 'He was effectively banished by his peers years ago and has been living a dissolute life down here, yet he manages to pull it out of the bag and get shortlisted for a major competition. Clearly, he must have kept painting up a storm, yet no exhibitions for years? Maybe he was honing his skills, forging all this time. How else are they keeping that show on the road up there?'

'He's an arrogant sod, as well,' said Byers. 'Forging would appeal to his ego.'

'Possibly,' said Lind.

'What's the plan for Fiona Murray, then?' asked Farrell. 'Get her to roll over on the others in exchange for immunity?'

'I'd be happier with that, if I can be assured that she's not involved in any of the three murders,' said Lind. 'I'll give Ailish's sister Maureen a ring. It might be worth giving her a peek at Murray to see if she knows of any connection between her and Ailish. Murray does have an Irish accent, but we're so close to Stranraer that's hardly unusual.'

'It can't hurt,' said Farrell. 'Give you a chance to fire that warning shot across her bows as well in relation to poking around playing amateur detective.'

'True. Now we're starting to have an idea of what we're up against with regard to her sister's murder, I think she needs to be formally told to back off for the time being.'

'That'll give Murray a bit longer to stew in her own juice before we interview her,' said Farrell.

'You'll all remember that we've got young Davey out there undercover. I need to know if it's safe to put him in play tomorrow, or whether to pull him and Stirling out of there pronto,' said DI Moore.

'I suggest you and Farrell conduct the interview, Kate. That way, we should be able to cover all the angles of the various investigations. I'll observe from the room next door. I'll sound out the procurator fiscal in advance as well, to get an idea of the scope we might have for a plea deal to force her hand. Much depends on how much she can lay out for us,' said Lind.

DI Moore glanced at her watch.

'I've got Lionel Forbes coming in shortly to assess the paintings recovered from Janet Campbell's studio flat. I'll also ask him to look at the digital images of Moretti's entry for the Lomax Prize. See if he thinks they could possibly have been painted by the same person.'

Chapter Fifty-Three

DI Moore felt unusually flustered as she waited for Lionel Forbes to arrive. Unable to settle, she paced up and down, before taking a small compact out of her bag and applying a fresh coat of lipstick. Her blue eyes were glittering, and she was as jumpy as a basket of frogs. This really wasn't like her at all. She had to pull herself together, or someone at the station would notice that the resident Ice Queen had defrosted into a soggy mess. A sensible calm woman of thirty-six should most definitely not be behaving like a giddy teenager, she told herself sternly. It didn't help.

A knock at the door heralded the arrival of the paintings and the digital images. Carefully, she slipped on gloves and lifted them out of their wrappings and placed them face up on the table. Her skittish mood immediately dispersed as she took in the suffering of the foal displayed on canvas. She laid the digital image of Paul Moretti's entry for the Lomax Prize beside them.

There was a light tap on the door and PC Rosie Green showed in Lionel Forbes and then left. Immediately he strode over to her and took her in his arms. She stiffened in his embrace, and he drew back at once, regarding her quizzically.

'What's the matter?'

'We can't,' she said, feeling unwanted heat rise in her face. 'It's not appropriate.'

'That's not what you said last night,' he said, with a wicked grin.

There was another knock at the door.

What now? thought DI Moore, striding over to open it. Mhairi stood in the doorway.

'I wondered if I might sit in, ma'am?' she asked.

'Yes, of course, in you come,' Moore said, not sure whether to be relieved or sorry.

'Good afternoon, sir,' said Mhairi.

Her unaccustomed formality told DI Moore that she didn't like him. Well, she barely knew him.

Business-like now, she motioned them round the table further into the large room.

Even Lionel Forbes looked shocked when he first beheld the paintings, but then he spied the image painted by Moretti and laughed out loud.

DI Moore glared at him.

'Sorry,' he said, clearly struggling to compose himself, 'it's just so clearly meant to be a send-up of that idiot Hugo Mortimer. If this got out, he'd never recover. He'd be a laughing stock!'

DI Moore was now tight-lipped with anger. What had got into him today? She glanced at Mhairi, whose expression was studiedly neutral.

'The reason I invited you to come here was to ascertain whether the paintings of the foal and the digital image beside them could feasibly have been painted by the same person.'

Forbes cleared his throat and took out a magnifying glass from his briefcase. He sat down at the table in front of the first painting in the sequence. Then he flipped open a notepad and, without saying another word, got to work. He didn't seem particularly repelled by the subject matter, thought Moore; but presumably, in his line of work you became accustomed to seeing all sorts.

Moore glanced at Mhairi. This was clearly going to take some time.

Eventually, just as both women had reached the outer edge of their patience, Forbes looked up.

'Well, I can say one thing categorically. The same artist did not paint the pictures of the foal and the picture of Hugo Mortimer. Obviously, I would've preferred the original painting to work from, rather than a digital image, but I'd be prepared to stake my reputation on it nonetheless.'

This was not what they wanted to hear. DI Moore looked at Mhairi in consternation.

'How do you know?' she asked.

'Well, the brushwork, for starters. Artists tend to have little tells in their style if you know what to look for. Both extraordinarily talented, however.'

'Whatever floats your boat,' muttered Mhairi, earning a glare from DI Moore.

'Is there any possibility you could hazard a guess at the identity of either of these artists? There's a strong likelihood that they're local to the area, so you might possibly have come across their work before,' said Moore.

For the first time, Forbes's eyes slid away from hers. He knows something, she thought, digging her nails into her palms. But, if he does, why doesn't he say anything? The pause lengthened.

As if becoming aware he had waited too long, Forbes cleared his throat.

'Sorry, I've been standing here racking my brains, but nothing is coming to me. To the best of my knowledge, I've not seen the work of either of these artists before.'

Mhairi was staring at him through narrowed eyes.

Maybe he didn't want to share any unsubstantiated suspicions in front of a junior detective. After all, his own professional reputation was on the line if he got it wrong, thought Moore.

She was uncomfortably aware that she was starting to make excuses for him.

'Which is the more talented of the two?' Mhairi asked, her stance challenging.

'I couldn't possibly say without having the principal canvas from Moretti in front of me.'

'Doesn't the subject matter bother you at all?' asked Mhairi.

'It's not something I would choose personally,' he replied. 'However, the degree of skill in the execution is extraordinary. Art is meant to shake you out of your comfort zone. If you want pretty pictures, then go to the likes of Mike Halliday.'

'Thanks so much for coming in,' said Moore. 'We won't take up anymore of your valuable time. Let me show you out.'

Mhairi looked close to losing her temper. She really could be most intemperate at times, thought DI Moore, giving her a severe look on the way out of the door.

Chapter Fifty-Four

Mhairi pelted along to Farrell's office and stood fidgeting with impatience in the doorway, until he glanced up from what he was doing and noticed her.

He smiled and motioned her in. He was looking a little frayed around the edges, she thought. His near breakdown last year had affected her more than she had let on and she had kept a beady eye on him ever since.

'Mhairi, come in and tell me what's on your mind, before you blow a gasket,' he said.

How to begin? She didn't want to cast any aspersions on DI Moore, that's for sure. Farrell cleared his throat and stared at her.

'Come on, Mhairi, spit it out. I haven't got all day. What's bothering you?'

'I don't think that Lionel Forbes is on the level, sir,' she said.

'How so?' asked Farrell, putting down his pen and sitting back in his chair.

'I think he knows something he's not letting on in relation to Moretti's competition entry. I think he's seen his work somewhere before, so he might know his real identity.'

'If that was the case then why wouldn't he simply say?' asked

Farrell. 'He could always hedge his bets and indicate he wasn't entirely sure.'

'I don't know,' she admitted. 'There's something else. I'm worried he's somehow targeted DI Moore and inserted himself deliberately into the forgery investigation.'

'DI Moore is a very smart capable officer who can take care of herself,' said Farrell. 'If his behaviour was as off as you think in the meeting she'll already be raising the same questions in her own mind.'

Mhairi looked unconvinced.

'Yes, sir. Please don't tell her I said anything?'

'I won't. I know it came from the right place. Where would we all be without you to keep an eye on us, Mhairi McLeod?'

'Really, sir,' she said standing up to leave. 'I have absolutely no idea.'

She could hear him chuckling as she marched down the corridor.

Once back at her desk, she hadn't made much of a dent in her paperwork when DS Byers popped his head round the door.

'Mhairi, we've finally managed to track down Nancy Quinn, Monro Stevenson's girlfriend. I'm about to interview her. You can sit in if you want.'

'Sure,' she said, jumping to her feet and putting her jacket back on. 'Where's she been hiding herself all this time, Sarge?'

'Spain, apparently. She was seen in Kirkcudbright this afternoon by PC McGhie, trying to get into the cottage of the deceased. He detained her at once.'

'There's something doesn't add up about this girl,' said Mhairi. 'Hardly enacting the role of the grieving girlfriend, is she? Not been near the parents, according to PC Green.'

'I gave up trying to figure out women a long time ago,' said Byers.

'Clearly,' muttered Mhairi under her breath. Byers smirked.

Why did she always let him wind her up like this? Pushing her irritation to one side, she opened the door to the interview room and walked in.

The young woman seated across the table was undeniably beautiful with a golden tan and blonde sun-streaked hair. She looked like she'd stepped out of a surfing ad. Mhairi instantly felt lumpy and dumpy and straightened in her chair.

Byers set up the tape and introduced them both and the interview commenced.

'I must caution you that anything you say will be noted down and can be used against you in a court of law. Do you understand?'

'Yes.'

'Can you state your name and date of birth?'

'Nancy Quinn, 5th August 1988.'

'Please confirm your whereabouts on the evening of Sunday, 6th of January 2013?'

'I was home alone.'

'When was the last time you saw Monro Stevenson?'

'The Friday night before he died. We went out for dinner to celebrate him being shortlisted. He stayed the night at mine. When I woke up in the morning, he was gone.'

'At 12.15 p.m. today you were discovered round the back of the cottage rented by Monro Stevenson, attempting to break in. Would you care to tell us why?'

'I would hardly call it breaking in.'

'You were jemmying the back window with a crow bar,' said Byers.

'I was lucky there was one lying nearby. Look, I was simply trying to get my stuff back. There was no one around. It couldn't hurt Monro, so I decided to give the window a little help.'

'What items were you looking to obtain?' asked Mhairi. 'You weren't living there. As I recall, you didn't even have a toothbrush, never mind a drawer.'

A flash of anger, immediately tempered with a phoney smile.

'Items of an intimate nature,' she said, sizing Byers up from under her long lashes.

To his credit, Byers remained impassive. Maybe he wasn't as big a sucker for a pretty face as Mhairi had thought.

'Please detail the exact nature of the items concerned,' he said.

'There were sketches, a portrait he had painted of me ... in the nude,' she said. 'I didn't want them to fall into the wrong hands. Monro would have wanted me to have them, I'm sure.'

'There were no such items in the inventory of contents,' Byers said.

No, but there was a nude painting of another girl, thought Mhairi. A dead girl.

'Did Monro ever talk to you about any former girlfriends, people he'd been in love with before the two of you met?' asked Mhairi.

'No, nobody,' she said, but the tightening of her lips told Mhairi she was lying.

'I heard he had a thing for a beautiful dark-haired girl at one time,' Mhairi said. 'In fact we recovered a painting of her from the cottage. Did you ever see that when you were staying over? You did stay over, right?'

'Of course I did,' Nancy shot back with narrowed eyes. 'He was an artist. I didn't expect him to sit painting a bowl of fruit every day.'

'How did you meet the deceased?' asked Byers.

'At a gallery event in Kirkcudbright,' she said.

'Which gallery was that?' asked Mhairi.

'The Tolbooth, down the High Street. I was admiring one of his paintings, not realizing he was the artist. He introduced himself and we arranged to meet the following night for dinner.'

'Could you confirm the date for us?' asked Mhairi.

'Yes, around the middle of December last year,' she replied.

'What is it you do for a living?' asked Byers.

'I'm a postgraduate student at Glasgow School of Art.'

'Specializing in?' asked Byers.

There was an awkward pause and, for the first time, she looked cornered.

'Art restoration.'

Byers didn't miss a beat and quickly segued into another question, as though her reply had been of no consequence. Mhairi cast about in her bag for a tissue like she hadn't picked up on the significance either.

'Is there any particular reason why you haven't visited Monro Stevenson's family since he died?' he asked.

Again, she looked uncomfortable.

'I didn't really know them that well. I had a feeling the mother in particular wasn't that keen on me. It seemed easier for all concerned if I simply stayed away.'

'In Spain?' said Byers, injecting a note of incredulity.

'I needed to get away from the memories,' she said with a not-quite-convincing catch in her voice.

'Made lots of new ones, in Spain though, judging by your Instagram account,' said Byers.

'Look, are you going to charge me with anything or not?'

'We'll ready the paperwork and then you'll be released without charge, on an undertaking not to go near Monro Stevenson's cottage again,' said Byers.

'Thank you,' she said, obviously relieved.

'Interview terminated,' said Byers.

Mhairi and Byers both stood up and left the room. They headed along the corridor until they were out of earshot.

'I'm afraid your "To Do" list just got longer, Mhairi.'

Mhairi flipped open her notebook.

'I need you to contact Glasgow School of Art and get information on both her undergraduate and postgraduate studies in restoration. We need The Tolbooth's CCTV footage from the night of the exhibition in December. Be interesting to see who else she talks to when she's there, particularly if it's any of our potential suspects.'

'What about obtaining a warrant for her phone records?' asked Mhairi.

'Eventually, but I think we need a bit more evidence yet. I don't want to tip our hand too soon. I also need some deep background done on her, with a view to discovering any family or social connections between her and any of our players in Kirkcudbright.'

'You reckon she was a plant sent to keep an eye on Monro Stevenson, sir?' asked Mhairi.

'I think it's a strong possibility,' Byers replied.

Chapter Fifty-Five

Lind was feeling the strain. Tonight was his first marriage counselling session with Laura and he knew that if he failed to turn up on time their fragile truce would shatter. Come what may, he had to be there. He flicked through the reports on his desk from Farrell, Moore, and Byers. Things were really starting to hot up on all the investigations. However, they still lacked much of the key information they needed. One of the crucial facts they were missing was Moretti's real identity. If they could only pin that down, then perhaps the other pieces would start to slot into place. They had removed various items from the cottage to obtain samples of his DNA. Hopefully, he would show up somewhere in the system.

Byers had run into a brick wall when digging into the identity of Aaron Sewell, the signatory of several canvasses in Moretti's cottage. Apparently, he was very in vogue and making big waves commercially but looked down on by the art establishment. He too was a ghost. No press interviews even. His own agent, a public-school type from Edinburgh, didn't even know his real identity. Part of the mystique, he had burbled enthusiastically on the phone. Bloody inconvenient more like, thought Lind. His agent paid all sums due into an offshore bank account that prided itself on its discretion. Any contracts or paperwork were sent by email to an IP address for an internet café in Dumfries, but could also be accessed remotely. Lind had put the Tech squad on it hoping the guy might have slipped up somewhere.

Farrell had discovered a common link between the forgery case and Monro Stevenson's murder. Both had used the same Dumfries-based locksmith and joiner, Neil Benson. He would be detained and questioned tomorrow, depending on the outcome of DC Thomson's operation in the morning. The biggest decision he had to make today was whether to sanction DC Thomson going into play. It now appeared at least likely that, instead of a forgery, he might be transporting an authentic near-priceless work of art. The restoration unit at the National Trust had said it would take time to determine whether the painting in the safe at Broughton House was a forgery or not. If it was genuine, it was more than valuable enough to kill for and he didn't want the young officer's blood on his hands.

There was a light tap on the door.

'Come in,' he called.

In walked Maureen Kerrigan.

Lind stood up and invited her to sit.

'Thanks for coming down, Maureen,' he said.

'PC Green said you've got a woman in custody who was carrying around a picture of my sister?'

'Yes, her name's Fiona Murray. She's got an Irish accent. Does the name mean anything to you?'

She shook her head decisively.

'No, nothing. Do you think she's involved in the death of my sister?'

'Highly unlikely,' said Lind. 'We're questioning her in relation to another unrelated matter. I gather you might have been poking around a bit, asking questions?'

Maureen's pale skin flushed.

'Well, do you blame me? No disrespect, but the police don't seem to be making much progress. I need to find out what happened to my sister. I owe her that, at least.'

'Of course I don't blame you. However, without going in to detail, things have taken a somewhat sinister turn. Another young woman has been murdered, though we're not releasing the details yet.'

'Do you mean Poppy Black?' she asked.

'Where did you hear that?'

'I was in The Smuggler's Inn with Mike Halliday. That TV reporter, Sophie Richardson, was in there talking to Billy Ryan, the barman.'

'What was said?'

'That the girl had been found dead and it looked like an accident, but she had information in her possession suggesting that she had been murdered.'

Lind's heart sank. Could they possibly have someone leaking stuff to the press?

'What did the barman tell her?'

'Nothing. He was as tight as a clam. After she'd gone, a man came in who looked a bit of a hard nut. He wasn't from round here. I heard Billy tell him Poppy Black might have been murdered and to watch his back.'

'Did anyone notice you listening in?'

'No, I was careful. None of that seems to be relevant to what happened to my sister, though.'

'A person of interest in relation to your sister's murder has disappeared but could still be in hiding locally. We don't know what this person looks like. You might even have come across him already.'

'I've not come across anyone I could believe capable of murdering my sister,' she said.

'Please believe me when I say that often the most evil people are those you would least suspect. I'm asking you to back off completely for your own safety. After all, if anything happens to you, who will obtain justice for your sister?'

She scowled at him.

'That's emotional blackmail.'

'Yes, it is, but from the purest of motives. I simply want to keep you safe at such a delicate point in the investigation. Perhaps it would be better if you stayed in Dumfries rather than Kirkcudbright for now?'

'I'll move in with Mike Halliday. He's 6 feet 4 inches of pure muscle. It'll be like having my own personal bodyguard.'

'How well do you know him?'

'I know him well enough. He was a friend of Ailish's. She used to hang out with him when she got sick of that lot up at the big house. I met him the first time I came over, after she went missing. He was as convinced as I was that something bad had happened to her and she hadn't just run off. We've remained in touch ever since. He's been my eyes and ears over the years. He's just as keen as me to find out her fate and I wouldn't like to be in their shoes when he does.'

'So you're not a couple, then?'

'I didn't say that,' she said, folding her arms.

'Sorry, didn't mean to pry. My interest is only confined to keeping you safe, Maureen.'

She softened.

'I know that, really I do! But you don't need to worry about me. I promise I'll be careful.'

Lind's phone rang.

'Maureen's with me, we'll be right down.'

'I take it PC Green explained that we'll be in a room adjacent to the interview room, with a one-way mirror so that you can get a good look at the woman.'

They walked downstairs and into the designated room. Maureen moved to the window and stood stock still, frowning in concentration. She suddenly swayed on her heels. Then, just as Lind was stepping forward to check she was okay, she pushed past him and ran out of the room.

Wrong-footed, he pursued her. Instead of running down the corridor, as he expected, she wrenched open the door to the interview room. She rushed over to Fiona Murray and slapped her hard across the face, before a shocked Farrell and Moore managed to intervene.

'How could you, Mam?' Maureen screamed. 'What were you thinking?'

Fiona Murray sat, as if carved from stone, with the imprint of Maureen's hand etched across her cheek.

'What on earth is going on?' exploded Farrell.

'That woman's real name is Margaret Kerrigan. She's Ailish's mother. And she used to be mine, too,' Maureen added bitterly. 'Please, take me out of here. I can't bear to be in the same room as her.'

Chapter Fifty-Six

Farrell and Moore settled back down in their chairs. Fiona Murray sipped slowly from a glass of water with shaking hands. The interview had been suspended when Maureen Kerrigan burst in, and Farrell switched the tape on again.

'Interview resumed at 4.15 p.m. I must remind you that you're still under caution and anything you say can be noted down and used against you in a court of law. Do you understand?'

'Yes.'

'Do you deny that you're the mother of both Maureen and Ailish Kerrigan?' he asked.

The dough-faced woman before them looked conflicted as though, even now, she was still considering brazening it out.

DI Moore leaned forward and spoke softly.

'I know it must have been a shock, Margaret, your daughter bursting in here like that.'

Suddenly, the fight seemed to go out of her.

'It's a long time since anyone called me that,' she murmured.

'So, for the record, your name is Margaret Kerrigan,' said Farrell.

'Yes. I was beside myself when she went missing. I knew straight away something bad must have happened to her. She was headstrong, but she was a kind girl. There's no way she would have sent a text saying she was heading home and then never contacted us again.'

'Why didn't you mention anything about your intentions to your family?' asked Farrell. 'They must have been worried sick.'

She shrugged.

'Looking back, I think I had a bit of a breakdown. I spoke to the local Garda, but they seemed to take the view that if Ailish had chosen to run off and live in sin with some fellow in Scotland, that was her lookout. Maureen contacted DCI Lind and he told her that given her age and no evidence of foul play, his hands were tied, although he did list her as officially missing at least.'

'I can understand you coming over here to ask a few questions,' said DI Moore. 'But what possessed you to assume a false identity and leave your existing family not knowing if you were alive or dead?'

'I was crazed with grief and guilt too. I'd said the harshest things before she left. The last words she heard from me on this earth were "May you rot in Hell, you little whore". I'd give anything to take that back.'

She paused and took a drink of water, her hands still shaking.

'Anyway, when Maureen showed me the text I was overjoyed. It felt like I'd been given another chance. But she never arrived. The weeks dragged on. Then one night I was sitting in the kitchen. I'd reached my lowest ebb. I considered ending it all, God forgive me. The only thing that stopped me was the thought that I would never see my precious girl in the afterlife. I decided to investigate her death myself. It was all I had left to give her. I picked up my bag, put on my coat, slipped out the house and disappeared. As soon as I got off the ferry, I invented a new identity and jumped on a bus to Kirkcudbright. It didn't take me long to obtain some bogus identity papers off the internet. Good cleaners are hard to find these days. I bided my time until there was an opening at Ivy House and in I went.'

'The painting of Ailish in Kirkcudbright Art Gallery. I assume it is you that pays to keep it on the wall there?'

'Yes, I hoped someone might see it and remember something. I like to visit it every so often.'

'So far, so understandable,' said Farrell. 'But how did you get from there to being part of a forgery ring?'

Murray stiffened. Farrell held his breath. Then, her shoulders lowered, as her whole body seemed to exhale.

'I don't suppose it really matters what happens to me now. One of my daughters is dead and the other will never forgive me.'

'You don't know that,' said DI Moore. 'She may well come around, once she learns the reasons behind what you did. Helping us now will surely count in your favour?'

'Maybe. My initial intention was to get into Ivy House and poke around, try and find out if anyone there was likely to be connected to Ailish's disappearance.'

'And?'

'It was like Sodom and Gomorrah. The thought that my lovely girl had been caught up in the midst of it all near broke my heart. That Patrick Rafferty, turning her head and filling it with nonsense, then discarding her in favour of another model, like she was less than nothing. How I didn't go for him with a meat cleaver, I do not know. Hugo Mortimer was the worst of the lot. He seemed to swing both ways. Nothing was off-limits sexually. How Penelope Spence could stand it, I really don't know. He would do stuff right in front of her. Cruel bastard, he is. Oh, she would pretend to be just as depraved as he was. Always letching after Monro Stevenson, for example, but it was a huge act. He told me he called her on it one night. She completely froze. All she wanted was Hugo. No accounting for taste, I suppose.'

'And Ailish?' prompted Moore.

'It seems that she left in a strop after catching Patrick with a new model. The more I dug around, the more convinced I became that whatever had happened to her must have occurred after she had left Ivy House.'

'How did you get mixed up with the forging ring and who else at Ivy House is involved?' asked Farrell.

Murray looked like she was being pulled apart by some internal battle.

'Things have changed now, Margaret,' said DI Moore. 'You must see that.'

'I've been working for them in the last couple of years,' she said. 'Not on the art front. Can't paint to save myself. I was more concerned with distribution, moving things around from A to B.'

'Who else is implicated?' asked Farrell. 'You might as well give it up, Margaret. You have a daughter that still needs you. If you cooperate to the fullest extent possible, that will count for a lot with the Crown Office.'

'I didn't set out to become a criminal, you know,' she shot back. 'I was a good God-fearing woman before Ailish was taken from me. You don't earn much cleaning. I'd rent to pay; things were getting desperate. Then Hugo asked me to do a few off-the-book jobs. Said there was good money in it for me, if I kept my mouth shut. It didn't take me long to figure out what they were up to. Over time I earned their trust.'

'So Hugo Mortimer is the forger?' asked DI Moore.

'Yes, although he brought in Monro Stevenson on some of the jobs, like the Hornel painting. Said the boy was a unique talent. He was a bit jealous of him. When he found out that the boy had been shortlisted for that major art prize as well, he was like a bear with a sore head all week.'

'Were you friendly with Monro Stevenson?' asked Farrell.

'Yes, I suppose you could say that. I didn't meet him, until after he'd had his breakdown and left Ivy House. I sensed that he'd simply lost his way for a while, like Ailish. He liked to talk about her, though he never knew I was her mother. He was a good lad at heart. I couldn't believe it when I walked in that morning and saw him like that …'

Her face contorted, and Farrell produced a clean handkerchief and passed it to her.

'My, you're old school,' Murray said. 'Used to be one of the hallmarks of a gentleman, that.'

'It still is,' said DI Moore, trying to lighten the mood, while Murray blew her nose and composed herself.

'How did you come to clean for Monro as well?' asked Farrell.

'Monro had advertised in the local paper, so I applied.'

'Margaret, did Mortimer ask you to spy on Monro? Report back any rumblings of discontent?' asked Moore.

Tears spilled as she nodded, her expression one of abject misery and regret.

'For the tape, please,' said DI Moore.

'Yes, God rest his soul. That snake asked me to spy for him.'

'Did Monro know?' asked Farrell.

'No, he thought he could trust me.'

'Had Monro seemed particularly troubled of late?'

'He'd been a bit off for a few weeks. I think he felt trapped by what he'd got himself mixed up in. Being shortlisted gave him hope. He was the happiest I'd ever seen him, even talking about moving somewhere else, making a fresh start.'

'Was there anyone else at Ivy House involved in the forgery ring?' asked Moore.

'No, only Hugo Mortimer. No one else knew, not even Penelope. Hugo might have been the forger, but he certainly wasn't running the show.'

'Who was then?' asked Moore.

'All I know is that he was local. Even Hugo was afraid of him.'

'Think, Margaret,' urged DI Moore. 'There's more riding on this than you know. Another young life could be in jeopardy, if we don't figure this out in time.'

Farrell coughed a warning to prevent her saying anymore on the subject.

'Do you know if the ringleader was an artist himself?' he asked.

'I haven't a clue. I don't think he forged the paintings, from what I gathered, but he was certainly the brains behind the operation. I think that he's dangerous as well.'

'What makes you say that?'

'Anyone who can scare Hugo Mortimer to that extent has to be pretty hard.'

'What about Paul Moretti?' asked Moore.

'Bit of a weirdo. I bumped into him once, when I was leaving Ivy House. I almost tripped over him coming out of the gate. I apologized, but he completely blanked me and slunk off. Quite creepy, the way he was skulking about up there at that time of night. The only things beyond the house are the graveyard and the woods.'

'Is Moretti friendly with anyone local, as far as you're aware? He's a person of interest and we're keen to speak to him,' said Moore.

'Keeps himself to himself. Even has his groceries delivered. Proper hermit. I don't know a single person who has ever seen his face.'

'You know that you were caught on camera removing a package from the safe at Broughton House?' said Farrell.

'Yes,' she sighed. 'The camera is usually switched off. I forgot to check it.'

'On whose instruction did you do that?'

'Hugo Mortimer's, though I gather the order came from the boss.'

'Were you told what was in the package?' asked Moore.

'I knew it was a painting and that it would be labelled in a certain way.'

'That painting was stolen from a big house in the area and was being stored at Broughton House temporarily, while the National

Trust negotiated with an intermediary for its safe return,' said Farrell.

'I assume that you substituted a forgery in its place?' said Moore.

'Yes, Hugo didn't sleep for weeks getting it done.'

'Was Hugo Mortimer or his boss involved in the original heist?'

'Hugo Mortimer wasn't as far as I'm aware. I have no idea about his boss.'

'That must have netted you a nice little bonus,' Farrell said.

'I know what I've done is wrong,' she muttered. 'But I figured it's a victimless crime. I don't go around hurting people. The copies are so good, odds are no one would even know they're not looking at the real deal. Where's the harm? A picture's a picture, right?'

'You're either being completely naive or utterly disingenuous,' said DI Moore. 'Genuine works of art matter. Each piece is unique.'

'Well, I've never been one of those arty farty types,' she snapped. 'If it looks like a duck, quacks like a duck, then it's a bloody duck as far as I'm concerned.'

'Did it ever occur to you that Monro Stevenson may have been murdered by either Hugo Mortimer or the person he works for?' asked Moore.

'No. Not for one minute. You don't think Ailish's death could be anything to do with that lot, after all? And there's me working for them all that time … Holy Mother of God, please no …'

'Ailish's murder was almost certainly not linked directly to the forgery ring. It appears likely that she was murdered by an artist, but that's all we are at liberty to say right now,' said Farrell.

Farrell glanced at Moore and she nodded.

'Margaret, we're going to take a short break now. Someone will be in to offer you some refreshments. Interview suspended,' said DI Moore as they both stood up and left.

Lind was waiting for them outside and motioned them both into another room so that Fiona Murray couldn't overhear.

'I reckon we've got a leak,' he said. 'Someone has blabbed about the circumstances of Poppy Black's death to Sophie Richardson.'

'That's all we need,' said Moore. 'But how do you know?'

'Maureen Kerrigan heard her mouthing off to the barman in The Smuggler's. He in turn passed the information along to some hard case from Glasgow.'

'Leave it with me,' said Farrell. 'I have an idea.'

Back in his office he picked up the phone. Time to make a deal with the devil.

'Moira … About that exclusive … there's something I need you to do for me.'

Chapter Fifty-Seven

The mood in the briefing room was tense. Fiona Murray's account of events had blown open the forgery ring. All they needed was the identity of the ringleader. Monro Stevenson's involvement seemed beyond doubt now and it was likely that it had got him killed. The Super slipped in and took a seat at the back just as Lind held his hand up for silence.

'As you've all no doubt heard, we have Fiona Murray in custody, aka Margaret Kerrigan, and the mother of Ailish Kerrigan. She's confirmed that Hugo Mortimer is the principal forger. He was assisted at times by Monro Stevenson who forged the recovered Hornel painting.'

'Are we bringing Hugo Mortimer in for questioning then, sir?' asked DS Byers.

'No. We want to have a crack at discovering the top man first. Murray doesn't know the identity of the ringleader, but he's meant to be a nasty piece of work. He might even be implicated in the murder of Monro Stevenson.'

'What about the murder of Ailish Kerrigan?' asked Stirling. 'Any possible link there?'

'None as far as we're aware. The mother seems fairly certain that Ailish wasn't murdered by any present or past occupants of

Ivy House. I doubt she'd let them off the hook or have got embroiled with them to the extent that she has, if she had any lingering doubts.'

'Is there nothing else we can do to track down Paul Moretti, sir?' asked Mhairi.

'I was wondering about that,' said Farrell. 'Murray mentioned almost tripping over him when she was coming out of Ivy House. Given that his medical condition is clearly bogus, I believe the reason his disguise is so elaborate is because he's already well known both to us and to others. Is it possible he's one of the residents of Ivy House?'

Everyone fell silent as they considered this.

'I'm meeting Patrick Rafferty there, tonight. He's cooking me dinner,' said Mhairi. 'I can hopefully get a proper look at them all.'

'Watch out for things like their walk, scent, build, mannerisms. Have your actual encounter with Moretti to the forefront of your mind as you think about all these different facets. If anything strikes you then DO NOT, I repeat DO NOT, act on it or betray any sign that you are on to them,' said Lind.

'I'll take a run down there tonight, make sure I'm on hand, just in case,' said Farrell.

Mhairi shot him a grateful look. Those pictures had really freaked her out. She'd put money on it not being Patrick, but you never knew.

'I think we also need to speak to the gallery owner, Janet Campbell, again,' said Lind. 'The pictures were discovered in her flat, but I don't think we've adequately pinned down the timeline for them being deposited there.'

'Good point,' said Farrell. 'I mean, for all we know, they could have been in the flat when Paul Moretti originally moved in.'

'I'll speak to her in the morning myself,' said Lind. 'We want everyone on the ground in Kirkcudbright first thing tomorrow. DS Byers, with the assistance of PC Green, will be needed here to coordinate and manage the flow of information. We've drafted in officers from the whole of the area, who will all be in plain clothes and posing as tourists.'

'DC Thomson is to proceed as planned, then, sir?' said Stirling, looking worried.

'Yes,' said Lind. 'Tomorrow we're going to follow the trail in the hope that it leads us to the ringleader and we can shut it down for good.'

'What about Fiona Murray, sir?' asked Mhairi. 'Surely, if word has got out about her arrest, they may suspect she's blabbed, which could put tomorrow's operation in jeopardy?'

'I heard back from the procurator fiscal a few minutes ago,' said Lind. 'He's authorized us to make a deal. She returns to Ivy House saying she was charged with attempted theft, but we don't realize the painting in the safe is a forgery. She'll be released on bail and have the paperwork to back it up. In exchange, she'll be immune from prosecution, provided she testifies against them when required.'

'Do you reckon she'll go for that, sir?' asked Mhairi.

'She nearly bit my hand off,' said Lind. 'Plus, I think she's hoping that if she cooperates with us it will earn her brownie points with her remaining daughter.'

'What about Maureen?' asked DS Stirling. 'We can't have her running amok, causing havoc in the midst of all this, surely?'

'She's assured me she'll stop poking around. She's going to lie low at her boyfriend's house.'

'Can we trust her?' asked Moore.

'I think so,' said Lind. 'She's had a lot to process, but the thing that matters most of all to her is finding her sister's killer. She'd do just about anything to avoid getting in the way of that.'

'Right, I think that's everything for the time being. I want everyone to go home and get an early night. Tomorrow's going to be a demanding day. Unless, there's anything you want to add, sir?' he asked, addressing the Super who had sat motionless at the back of the room.

The Super stood up and walked to the front.

'These cases have tested us to our limits. I would urge everyone to be alert at all times. Take nothing for granted. We are up against ruthless and cunning adversaries. I want everyone to stay safe. No gung-ho, tactics. Is that clear?' he said, glaring at Farrell and Mhairi in turn, both of whom tried not to look offended.

'DS Stirling?'

'Sir?'

'Keep your eye on DC Thomson in so far as you can. Please convey to him my appreciation of his efforts to date.'

'Will do, sir,' replied Stirling.

The meeting broke up, but there was none of the usual good-natured banter on the way out the door. Everyone was feeling the pressure and, by this time of the night, was running on fumes rather than fuel.

Lind glanced at his watch, and Farrell saw him wince.

'Need to be somewhere, John?'

'Marriage counselling. I'm running late. Hardly gets things off to a great start.'

'Grab your stuff,' said Farrell. 'My car's at the top end of the car park. I'll wait outside the door.'

Lind rushed away, and Farrell was sat behind the wheel as he emerged from the station. They got to the community centre at five minutes past seven. Laura was standing waiting with a face like fizz.

'Good luck,' muttered Farrell as Lind hurriedly got out of the car.

He had an hour to kill before he picked up Mhairi at eight. Just long enough to grab a haggis supper from the Balmoral Café and head back to Kelton, to sort out his furry pal. As he drove past St Margaret's, he noticed a smattering of people entering for evening Mass and wished he was able to join them. His soul craved peace, but none was to be found for the foreseeable future.

Chapter Fifty-Eight

Farrell turned into his lane at Kelton and parked outside the cottage. The smell of the haggis supper soaked in salt and vinegar was making him salivate in anticipation. As he let himself in, Henry pounced on his feet, purring ecstatically. Poor cat must be ravenous. Just as well he hadn't gone for the fish or it would likely have been wrestled from his arms by a crazed feline. Despite the fact there was still some dried food in his bowl, Henry had clearly tired of waiting for his tea, as there were the remains of two mice on the kitchen floor. That was the disadvantage of a cat flap, sighed Farrell, scooping up the leftovers with a paper towel and wiping the floor with disinfectant. Henry sat back and watched him, a slightly miffed expression on his face.

Finally, with Henry chewing happily on his meaty chunks, Farrell got stuck into his own tea, washed down with a can of Irn Bru.

He then dashed upstairs for a quick shower to wash away the grime of the day, both mental and physical. Throwing on jeans, a jumper, and a scuffed leather jacket he gave a definitely plumper Henry a few minutes' attention before leaving the house once more.

* * *

Mhairi was waiting for him outside her flat, casually dressed and with her hair in a ponytail.

'Sorry, I'm a few minutes late,' he said. 'I had to sort out Henry.'

'Don't apologize. If looks could kill, I'd be dead already. Oscar hates me being out so much at the moment.'

They drove in companionable silence until they reached Kirkcudbright. Farrell parked at the harbour, so that Mhairi could maintain she had arrived on the bus and had to get the last bus home.

'Now remember, don't take any unnecessary risks.'

'I want to get inside Mortimer's studio and bedroom, if I get a chance,' said Mhairi.

'The only way I can see that happening is if he's out for the night. If you do get in, don't linger. We're looking for any signs he's copying another artist's work, or wax seals. Take images of his paints even. Also, anything tying him to the murder of Monro Stevenson, such as those sheets of cream notepaper or the missing glass. It's possible he was also behind the murder of Poppy Black, so look for any packets of bulbs, evidence of forged references for her etcetera.'

'What are you going to do while I'm at Ivy House?' asked Mhairi.

'I'll have a drink in The Smuggler's, see who's about and what's being said, then I'll take a quick run out in the car to see DC Thomson and go over things one more time for tomorrow's op. After that, I'll swing by and watch the entrance to Ivy House until you re-emerge. I'll be behind the wall across the road. As good a way as any to put away the evening.'

Mhairi picked up her bag and bottle of wine and opened the door.

'Be careful,' Farrell said. 'Be on your guard and trust no one. I'll expect you out the door by 11 p.m. at the latest.'

'You worry too much, sir,' said Mhairi with a cheeky grin, but they both knew she was rattled.

Farrell watched her until she disappeared from view. Then he exited the car and walked up to The Smuggler's in the centre of town. It was fairly quiet and no one paid him any mind as he ordered a pint of low-alcohol lager and sat in a dark corner. As his eyes grew accustomed to the gloom, he noticed Maureen Kerrigan with Mike Halliday. He had his arm around her and they were deep in conversation. Fortunately, she didn't recognize him.

The door swung open and, to his surprise, in walked Penelope Spence. She was slumming it tonight, he thought. She wore an expensive-looking scarf and a trendy hat. Her clothes were ostensibly casual, but the tailoring shrieked expensive. Was she meeting someone? He raised the paper he had brought for concealment. Thankfully, she hadn't spotted him. She turned away from the bar, carrying two whiskies. Looking neither left nor right she headed upstairs. As he slowly lowered his newspaper, he noticed that he wasn't the only one who had clocked her. Mike Halliday had his eyes locked on her ascent, with an expression that could only be described as hostile.

Farrell glanced at his watch. It was already 9 p.m. If he was going to nip out to the farm and get back to meet Mhairi he would have to shift some. Maybe whoever Penelope was meeting was already there? Where was the Gents? He took his glass back to the bar and was gratified to be directed upstairs.

There were three doors opening off the first-floor landing, with the toilets right at the end. Making sure he was unobserved, he placed his ear against one door. There were voices inside, but he couldn't make out what they were saying. He opened the door and took in the assorted home-knitted sweaters and anoraks around a table littered with coffee cups and pictures of trains.

'Sorry,' he muttered, before withdrawing.

The next room was empty, which left one remaining possibility. He heard someone coming. He immediately bent over to tie his shoelace. As he straightened up he saw a man's back disappearing into the remaining room, but he had no idea who it was. He crept forward and applied his ear to the door. No joy. They must be talking in hushed voices. Again, he glanced at his watch. If he barged in unannounced there might be unexpected repercussions. Given what was going down tomorrow, far better to walk away and stick to his original plan.

By the time he returned downstairs Mike Halliday and Maureen Kerrigan were gone. He had intended to strike up a conversation, as he was fairly sure that Halliday would have noticed the man head upstairs. It looked like nothing much got by him. Clenching his jaw in frustration, he quit the pub and walked back to his car.

The darkness became more and more impenetrable as he neared the farm. The stars twinkled cold and remote above. His window down, he inhaled the myriad frost-tipped scents of the night. A scream pierced the air. Another small furry life snuffed out by a ravenous bird of prey.

Confident that he had not been followed, he dimmed his headlights and turned into the farmyard.

He turned off the engine and tapped lightly on the door. Stirling let him in. He was drawn and tense. Farrell already knew from their last major case that he was someone more comfortable policing from an office than out in the field. DC Thomson seemed nervous but game for the upcoming challenge. He smiled reassuringly at him.

'One more day to go, Davey boy, then we're pulling you out of this hellhole.'

'Thank Christ, for that, sir,' he said, then reddened.

'Och, you'll be bopping the night away in The Venue or Chancers by the weekend,' said Farrell.

'I've gone right off the countryside,' said Stirling.

'I take it you've had no more texts,' said Farrell.

'Not a thing,' said Stirling. 'The Operation seems to be a go.'

'Has DI Moore been in touch to update you on today's developments?'

'Aye, that she has,' said Stirling. 'I couldn't believe it when I heard about Fiona Murray. Some carry-on that.'

'You're sure she won't tip them off?' asked DC Thomson.

'As sure as I can be. She's going to walk completely if she cooperates, so that's a huge incentive, not to mention the need to build bridges with her remaining daughter. A bit more challenging if she's stuck behind bars in Scotland.'

'Walk the lad through it one more time,' said Stirling.

'Go and pick up the painting from inside the ventilation shaft at the disabled toilet down at Kirkcudbright Harbour. It'll have been deposited there by Fiona Murray, who'll have swapped the real painting back from the forgery and placed a tracker within it. Drive the tractor forty-eight miles to Morrisons, in Stranraer. Take the package and deposit it in the boot of an empty Ford Escort, registration number, SH61 DYF, for which you'll have been given a spare key. Then collect the brown envelope with your pay-off, lock the boot, and saunter into the store café with a paper under your arm. Order a cooked breakfast and remain there for one hour exactly. When you leave, simply return to the tractor and drive back to the farm, where you'll await further instructions.'

'Do you reckon they'll lead you to the ringleader?' asked DC Thomson.

'I certainly hope so, but either way we're going to pick up Hugo Mortimer tomorrow. Once he's in custody you guys can make your way to the station in Dumfries.'

He glanced at his watch. Time to move, so he could intercept Mhairi.

He shook DC Thomson's hand on the way out.

'Good luck, lad, play it safe and by the book and you'll be fine. We'll have your back, never fear.'

* * *

It was completely dark by the time he left. Driving as fast as the hairpin bends would allow, he made it to the harbour in Kirkcudbright in record time. Quickly he walked up to Ivy House. Checking he was unobserved, he slipped over the wall into the wood opposite and concealed himself behind a tree from where he had a good vantage point. He didn't have long to wait. A figure was coming up the hill. Something about the build and gait seemed familiar, even though it was dark. As they reached the entrance to Ivy House, Farrell noticed that the face was completely obscured by a scarf and a beanie hat. It was Paul Moretti. Suddenly he stopped just before the entrance to the drive where he was partially shielded by an overgrown shrub. Farrell held his breath, staring intently. What was he up to? The scarf was unwound and placed in a backpack. The hat came off. He still couldn't see the face. Then, as the figure straightened and pulled on a different hat, Farrell's heart nearly stopped. It was Penelope Spence. She casually glanced to her left and right then entered the driveway to Ivy House.

As soon as the thought popped into his head he knew it to be true. Penelope Spence was Paul Moretti. The more he thought about it, the more it made perfect sense. He almost laughed out loud. That picture of Hugo for the Lomax Prize. Payback with knobs on, if she'd had the nerve to go through with it.

The smile left his face abruptly. He couldn't, try as he might, see Penelope Spence as Ailish's killer. If it wasn't Moretti, then who could it possibly be?

277

Chapter Fifty-Nine

Mhairi looked up and smiled as Patrick handed her another bottle of beer. She had an hour before she had to leave, and she hadn't had the opportunity to accomplish anything. Patrick, true to his word, had cooked her dinner, which they'd ate in his room, some exotic Thai number. Mhairi had always been drawn towards guys who could cook. Self-preservation, her mother would have remarked caustically. It didn't help that he was gorgeous as well. Or that he was funny and interesting to talk to. Ian's face floated into her mind accompanied by a pang of guilt. Get a grip, Mhairi, she told herself sternly. Patrick could also be a criminal master-mind, or a twisted killer. How on earth was she going to get the chance to go snooping? He hadn't left her side since she arrived.

'Right,' he said, sitting down beside her on the couch. 'Let's get down to brass tacks.'

She tried to hide her alarm and edged away from him slightly. He laughed.

'Mhairi McLeod. While I would have no objection whatsoever to jumping your bones, I'm not fool enough to think for one minute that's why you're here.'

She gave him an awkward grin.

'I'm sorry, Patrick. Under different circumstances ...'

278

'I'll accept those crumbs of comfort,' he said. 'Look, everything changed here for me when I learned about what had happened to Ailish. The only thing I know for certain is that I had nothing to do with her death. Monro Stevenson was hardly my favourite person. Give him a bloody nose? Sure, if I'd had a few beers, I might have been tempted. But blow his brains out? Not in a million years.'

'Have you noticed anything suspicious?' asked Mhairi. From what Fiona Murray had said, he had no clue that the forging had been going on right under his nose. However, things were at too delicate a stage to risk confiding in him.

'We used to have an open studio policy in the house. Everyone would drop in on each other and discuss their work in progress. In the last two years, that's changed. I still keep my door ajar, but Hugo and Penelope have become really secretive about what they're working on. Maybe the Lomax Prize has something to do with it. All I can say is that the climate in the house has changed and I don't know why. That woman, Fiona Murray, creeps around like a witch's familiar.'

'How so?' laughed Mhairi.

'She's often in a huddle with Hugo and, a couple of times, they've stopped talking when I come in. I don't like it at all. I'm going to stick around for a while, see if they catch Ailish's killer. I feel I owe her that.'

'What then?' she asked.

'Maybe do something radical like go home to Ireland and become a teacher.'

'The return of the prodigal son,' she said.

'You could say that. Look, what were you hoping to accomplish tonight? Tell me! I can help or cover for you while you have a snoop around.'

She could be walking into a trap, but her intuition said he was genuine. She didn't want to leave empty-handed as she didn't know when she might get an opportunity to return.

279

'OK, I want to get into Hugo Mortimer's studio and bedroom.'

'How long will you need?'

'Ten minutes. Does he know I'm here?'

'He knows I've a friend round, but he doesn't know it's you, and no one's poked their noses out of their rooms all night.'

'How do we get him out then?'

Patrick thought for a minute. Then he went to his studio next door and brought back a power drill. He unscrewed one side of a bracket pinning a bookshelf loaded with art books. It sagged alarmingly.

'There's a bathroom two doors down from Hugo's. Go in there and lock the door. I'll ask him to come and hold the end of this while I fix it.'

Mhairi nodded and they quietly made their way upstairs. She slipped into the bathroom and locked the door. Patrick thumped on Hugo's door.

'Hey, man, I need your help. There's a wee dram in it for you.'

She heard Hugo's door open.

'Good God, Patrick. Do you really have to make such a din? Some of us are trying to work you know.'

'I need a quick favour. The bracket on my bookcase has come away from the wall and the whole thing's about to collapse. Won't take long, I promise.'

'It had better not. I'm at a critical stage in my latest work,' Mortimer said but she heard them both moving down the hallway.

Feeling sick with nerves she slipped from her hiding place and into Hugo's studio. Glancing around, she snapped the works in progress that she could see, but nothing leapt out as a potential forgery. She also photographed all the paints and materials around. Still no sign of him returning. She slipped into the bedroom next, her heart thumping unpleasantly. Quickly, she scanned the room, but couldn't see anything of interest. Time was passing. She fought the urge to rush and focused, looking more slowly. Still nothing. She was about to let herself out of the bedroom when suddenly she froze. Footsteps. Hurriedly, she squeezed under the bed, praying she wouldn't have to remain there indefinitely. There was a large black portfolio bag beside her. Fortunately, Hugo went back into his studio. She slid out the case and photographed the contents. This would do nicely. She slid it back under the bed, quietly slipped out of the room, and ran lightly down the stairs.

Patrick was waiting for her in the shadows under the stairs, with her bag and coat. She gave him a quick hug as he opened the front door for her.

'I always found Nancy Drew sexy,' he muttered in her ear, causing her to blush. 'One of these days I'm going to immortalize you on canvas.'

Like you did with Ailish? The words popped unbidden into her mind, causing her heart to miss a beat. She swiftly made her way down the drive.

No doubt, Farrell was lurking somewhere in the trees across the road, but she simply walked on down the hill. He would soon catch her up if he was there. Glancing back at the house, she saw a figure silhouetted against the light from an upstairs window. Who it was, she was unable to say, but it made her feel uneasy. She could feel their eyes boring into her back as she continued on her way.

Chapter Sixty

Farrell caught up with Mhairi as she reached the car, breathing heavily. He hadn't left his hiding place, until the person watching Mhairi had drawn the curtains.

'Steady on, sir, you'll have a heart attack,' she scolded.

'Wait until you hear what I've got to tell you,' he puffed, opening the car door. Mhairi got in and they pulled out of the car park heading back to Dumfries.

'In your own time,' she grinned.

'Penelope Spence and Paul Moretti are one and the same.'

Mhairi's shock mirrored his own.

'What? You can't be serious?'

'Oh, but I am. I saw her walking up the hill to Ivy House. She'd a hat on with a scarf wrapped round her face and it was dark, but then at the gate, she pulled it off and I got a clear view. Think about it, the painting of Hugo, the women's underwear in the cottage, her slight build and height?'

'All this time, she's been running around right under our noses,' said Mhairi.

'We've been chasing a ghost all along.'

'But why on earth has she created this other identity? It doesn't make sense.'

'I think it makes perfect sense,' said Farrell. 'Remember those canvasses signed by Aaron Sewell? I've always wondered how that lot up at Ivy House manage to live the way they do. She muttered something about an inheritance, but I reckon if we scratch the surface that'll turn out to be another whopper. Basically, she supports them by getting her hands dirty and being a grubby commercial artist,' said Farrell.

'Hell, if I could paint like that I'd be shouting it from the rooftops, not trying to hide it,' said Mhairi.

'There's a lot of snobbery within the art world. She'd be despised by her peers for selling out and painting for the masses. Ridiculous really, but there you have it. Hugo would have a complete fit and no mistake,' said Farrell.

'And being a forger is somehow better?'

'Perhaps in his mind it is. I think it panders to his ego, as well as boosts the coffers. How did you fare this evening?'

'Patrick helped me get inside Hugo's studio and bedroom. I got everything I could, but it was a close shave at the end.'

'Patrick helped you? You told him?'

'I did what I had to do to get the job done,' she said, looking her boss square in the eye. 'My instinct tells me he's not involved with any of it.'

'As long as you're sure …?'

'Completely. I took digital images of all the canvasses and work I could see in Hugo's studio. I haven't a clue what images I've got there, as I was working so fast I didn't have time to process what I was seeing. I found his sketches of the missing Turner painting in a folder under the bed. I didn't see anything sadistic though, nothing similar to the foal pictures. That would have jumped out at me.'

'I don't like Hugo Mortimer for the murder of Ailish,' said Farrell. 'I could see him being implicated in Monro Stevenson's death, if he was threatening to blow the whistle on the whole forging operation or trying to disengage from it. But the murder of Ailish and those paintings of that animal are a whole other layer of evil.'

'You'd think you would instinctively sense that you were in the presence of a psychopath, wouldn't you?' said Mhairi. 'Like the primitive part of your brain should recognize evil and warn you somehow?'

'Would that it were that easy? Real evil often hides behind the most affable of facades. Psychopaths can learn to mimic social norms.'

'As if I wasn't creeped out enough already,' said Mhairi.

They drove the rest of the way in silence, each preoccupied with their own thoughts. Mhairi kept going over Patrick's parting words to her about immortalizing her on canvas. He had been involved with Ailish right up until she disappeared. Could he have followed her after she stormed out and killed her in a fit of rage? If so, then maybe that tipped him over the edge and he tried to make sense of it all by turning her into a work of art? A way to render Ailish immortal in his eyes? She'd been so sure that he was innocent. Was she still?

'Would you like to come in for a coffee?' asked Mhairi as they turned into Primrose Street.

'Just a quick one, then,' said Farrell. It was going to be a long day tomorrow, so he didn't want to be home late.

Once in her flat, he had to wait while Oscar was placated. Farrell wandered into the tiny but cosy kitchen and stuck the kettle on.

Mhairi arrived to take over a couple of minutes later.

Sitting on the couch, he took a sip of her offering and pulled a face.

'What on earth is this?'

'Camomile tea,' she said with a smirk. 'I reckoned if we both had coffee, we'd be pinging off the walls all night.'

She uploaded the images from her phone on to her work laptop and sat beside Farrell on the couch, so they could go through them. As she had previously indicated, there were no grisly ones whatsoever, which tended to back up their theory that Hugo wasn't involved in Ailish's murder.

'Wait a minute,' said Farrell. 'Let's see that ink drawing again. Does it remind you of anyone?'

Mhairi studied it closely. It was a tasteful nude of a young woman. Her expression was inscrutable. She started to shake her head, but paused.

'She does look familiar. I feel like I've seen her before.'

'You have,' said Farrell. 'It's Nancy Quinn, Monro Stevenson's girlfriend.'

'But that makes no sense,' said Mhairi. 'They hadn't been going out long. She completely denied knowing anyone from Ivy House, past or present, when she was interviewed.'

'There's more. Find that image of Hugo Mortimer that Paul Moretti, sorry, Penelope Spence, painted.'

'Do I have to? It's totally gross. He's not exactly Daniel Craig.' She pulled up the image.

'Now look at it side by side with the ink drawing of Nancy Quinn. Concentrate on their faces,' said Farrell.

'Like I'd want to concentrate on anything else,' muttered Mhairi. 'Oh wait a minute …'

'What do you see?'

'She has his nose and eyes. Is it possible they could be related? God, my head is spinning at the implications. I mean, would you paint your daughter naked? Euch, don't even answer that!'

'It's possible (a) they might not in fact be related (b) he might not know they are related (c) she might not know they are related or (d) neither might know they are related,' said Farrell, ticking the options off on his fingers one by one.

'I don't buy "d" for an instant,' said Mhairi.

'Me neither. My money is on her having tracked him down. There's no way to guess at her motives.'

'This is going to send Penelope Spence into a meltdown if she ever finds out,' said Mhairi.

'Agreed. First thing in the morning can you write up a full report on your work tonight? DS Byers can action what information in it he can, while the rest of us head out to Kirkcudbright to support DC Thomson and try and crack open at least one of these damn cases.'

'What should we do about Nancy Quinn?' asked Mhairi.

'Ask Byers to arrange to keep tabs on her informally. I don't want her brought in until tomorrow's op is safely concluded, in case she's in cahoots with them.'

'There's something else,' said Farrell, shifting in his seat.

'Sophie Richardson was sniffing around The Smuggler's. She appears to have become privy to some information about Poppy Black's murder.'

'How? The official line is that we're treating it as an accidental death.'

'There's no easy way to say this, Mhairi. I'm afraid that you're the source of the leak.'

Stung, she jumped to her feet.

'How can you say that? I would never ...'

'Ian is a journalist,' said Farrell. 'It's true that he's on a sabbatical to write a novel, but Moira Sharkey said that he's been feeding Sophie Richardson information for a price. She, in turn, has a source in Sophie Richardson's camp, which is how she found out.'

Mhairi sat down heavily.

'I didn't say a thing to him about work. I wouldn't. I do remember one night I fell asleep in bed reading the preliminary post-mortem report on Poppy Black. He could have read it when he came through. How could he? I trusted him!'

'I'm sorry, Mhairi. Her source did say that he'd followed you to Kirkcudbright one night and saw you with another man.'

'Patrick Rafferty,' she sighed.

'Maybe that's what made him decide to do this.'

'I don't care what his reasons were,' she snapped. 'I never want to see him again. I'm so sorry, Frank. I'll talk to the Super in the morning.'

'No one else needs to know,' he said. 'If I were you, I'd simply chalk it up to experience.'

She let him out, then slumped on the couch, still reeling. Picking up her phone she sent Ian a final text. Then deleted his number and blocked him. It was done. She'd been wrong about Ian. Could she have been wrong about Patrick too?

Chapter Sixty-One

DI Moore knew she shouldn't have accepted Lionel's invitation
to come round for a late supper, but she was so out of her mind
with worry about tomorrow she had seized upon the distraction.
He'd looked at her quizzically, when she'd asked if she could stay
the night. But when she said she had some routine business in
the area tomorrow morning he'd happily acquiesced. She wasn't
sure if her colleagues, particularly Frank and Mhairi, would
approve of her mixing business and pleasure in this way, but she
was surely entitled to some kind of a life outside work. It had
been a long time since she had met such an interesting and, let's
admit it, attractive man as Lionel Forbes.

Usually reserved and reticent, he had a way of enlivening her
and drawing her out of her shell that she found most liberating.
It was time that she allowed herself to live and love again after her
husband's devastating betrayal twelve years ago. Shot when she was
attempting to arrest an armed robber, she had been robbed of the
chance to have children. Even now, all those years later it still caused
a catch in her throat, when she thought about how ruthlessly he
had excised her from his life, like so much dead wood. At least he
had moved out of the area finally, so she didn't have to see him
with the new younger improved version and their adorable children.

Children that by rights should have been hers. She didn't know how, as she never talked about it, but somehow Lionel had managed to draw all this poison out of her tonight, aided and abetted by copious amounts of red wine. She was both scared and exhilarated by her own daring. What was happening to her?

The bathroom door opened and Lionel came and joined her in the bed. He smiled at her and took her in his arms. As their lips met, she felt her body and finally her mind forget itself in the moment.

She awoke with a start just after three. Her head was thumping, and her mouth was dry. Good Heavens, she was turning into Mhairi McLeod. They'd be swapping hangover tips at this rate. This would never do. She was far too old to have her head turned by a man in this way. She glanced over at Lionel. He was lying on his back, snoring gently. That's what must have woken her up. She slipped out of bed and grabbed his dressing gown off the hook. It was too late to go home. She would just have to quietly prowl about, until she could reasonably come back in to grab a shower without looking like a mad woman.

Padding around in her bare feet, she set about exploring. She was curious about Lionel. He had a way of deflecting her questions in relation to his background in a way that seemed perfectly reasonable at the time, but at three in the morning, could feel like he was trying to hide things from her. Now that she was more emotionally invested in him, she had to tread cautiously. She didn't want the rug pulled out from under her again.

She started in the living room, putting on a table lamp and enjoying the freedom of checking out his photos and knick-knacks unescorted. There was a picture of an elderly couple who must be his parents. They looked quite bohemian, she was amused to see, and much less formal and serious than Lionel. Moving along the mantelpiece, she saw a family grouping. An unsmiling Lionel, aged about ten, stood a little apart from a younger version of his parents. They had their arms looped around a smiling golden-haired child, who looked to be about eight years old. The family resemblance was unmistakable. Funny, Lionel had never mentioned he had a younger brother. Maybe something had happened to him? He'd already told her that both his parents were dead. Killed in a car accident abroad some years ago. Probably too painful to talk about. Feeling guilty, but unable to stop herself, she drifted like a wraith into his study.

Aside from a fine collection of books, many of them on art, there were numerous carefully chosen pieces placed around the room, the majority of which she too would have been pleased to choose. Walking past the back of his desk to examine one of these in closer detail, she noticed a piece of thick cream paper poking out of a closed desk drawer. With shaking hands she slowly slid it open. What she saw there made her heart almost stop. How could she have got it so wrong? She hurriedly closed the drawer leaving it the way she had found it. Where was her phone? Thankfully, she'd left her handbag in the lounge. Moving through there, she bit her lip as she slowly extracted it from her bag, every rustle deafening to her heightened senses. She slipped back into the study and gently pulled out the drawer once more to photograph the contents. Quickly she sent the images to her work email account and quietly closed the drawer, leaving it exactly as she found it. On her way back through the kitchen she pulled out a glass from a cupboard and left it on a work surface. Heart hammering, she crept back to bed, sliding her phone under her pillow. There, she lay, on her side, trying not to shake with fear at the implications of what she had just seen. When he woke up in the morning she was going to have to pull off the acting job of her life so that he didn't suspect she was on to him.

She awoke as Lionel placed a steaming mug of coffee and some toast on her bedside table. She must have fallen asleep. Forcing herself to smile at him, she gave a lazy stretch.

'Breakfast in bed, you're spoiling me,' she said.

'What were you up to last night?' he asked, watching her with a guarded expression.

'Oh, sorry, did I disturb you? I woke up with a thumping headache. Too much red wine. I should be old enough to know better,' she laughed. 'I went to the kitchen and got a glass of water and managed to track down some paracetamol in the bathroom.'

She had left the glass on the surface in the kitchen, hoping he would notice it. His expression relaxed. He was fully dressed already, and it was only gone seven.

'I hate to rush you, but I've got to head up the road to Glasgow soon. I've a meeting with an editor about another art column.'

'I've got an early start myself,' she said, sipping the coffee and trying to force the toast down her closed throat.

'Oh, anything interesting?'

'I wish. Staff appraisals at the local nick. This job comes with so much red tape I feel strangled by it some days.'

'Really? I would've thought your time would be too valuable to spare you with everything that's been going on.'

Oh yes, and you'd know all about that, she thought.

'It won't take long. Sadly, all our investigations seem to have hit a wall. Hopefully, we'll catch a break soon. I'd really pinned my hopes on you having come across the artist who painted the foal,' she said, watching him closely.

'I'd love to know their identity too. An incredible talent.'

She was unable to hide a flicker of distaste.

'Don't get me wrong. I was as appalled as you by the apparent suffering of that poor creature, but art has a way of transcending such considerations,' he said.

'Anyway, I'll just pop in the shower so I don't hold you back any longer,' she said, forcing herself to smile.

He reached for her, but she nimbly evaded him. As she closed the bathroom door she saw anger tighten his jawline. She needed to get out of here, and fast.

291

Chapter Sixty-Two

Farrell and Lind were breakfasting at the cottage in Kelton. They stared at each other morosely over their cereal and coffee. Lind had spent another night sleeping on Farrell's couch. He had been sitting in the garden waiting for him when he returned from Mhairi's flat. Laura had lost her rag in marriage guidance and stormed off. Lind had gone after her and they'd had a massive row. She'd asked him to move out and was threatening to change the locks. He had never seen Lind looking so down. It was like he had no fight left in him, and he was going to need plenty if he was going to turn this around, thought Farrell.

No wonder there was such a high rate of attrition with marriages in the force. That said, he still thought Laura was behaving irrationally. It's not as if Lind was running around on her. All he was guilty of was trying to do his job and make the world a safer place for their kids to grow up in.

'Right,' said Lind. 'Let's get this show on the road. Kirkcudbright here we come.'

Farrell's mobile rang as he stood up.

'Hey, Kate, we're just heading out now … are you sure? … How did you? … OK … park yourself at the local nick until we get there …'

'Tell me,' said Lind, who had been fidgeting with impatience throughout.

'Basically, Kate has discovered that Lionel Forbes is implicated in the murders of Monro Stevenson and Poppy Black. He's almost definitely our missing link in the forging case.'

'But how did she …?'

'She was staying the night at his place and couldn't sleep.' He felt a lurch of anger at the thought of Kate with that creep. 'She went for a poke around and discovered a sheet of cream paper in a drawer that matched the suicide note, some red wax and the seal stamp used for the forged paintings. There was also a packet of bulbs with one missing, most likely the one we found in Poppy Black's flat. She took digital images of it all, but she didn't dare remove it and bag it up to avoid compromising the op today.'

'You mean she and him?'

Farrell nodded.

'Is she all right? Did he twig she was on to him?'

'Yes, she's fine. She thinks she pulled it off.'

'Bloody hell,' said Lind. He thought for a moment, once more the capable officer and man that Farrell knew him to be. Thank God his focus was back, thought Farrell. They would all need to pull together as a team today.

'Right, Frank, you head off to the station and brief Byers on these latest developments. I see no reason to mention that Kate was staying the night, for the time being. She was simply at his for dinner to discuss something pertaining to the case, when she inadvertently noticed the paper poking out the drawer, which aroused her suspicions and further investigations. Got it?'

'Loud and clear,' replied Farrell.

Lind's phone rang. Laura's name flashed on the screen.

'Aren't you going to get that?' asked Farrell.

'It will have to wait. In the meantime, I'll head off down to Kirkcudbright and liaise with DI Moore. I want to make sure DC Thomson has all he needs to wrap up this operation today. I have a feeling we won't get another bite at this particular cherry.'

Farrell locked up. The cold damp fog made the early morning darkness even more impenetrable. Hopefully, it would lift later. Lind's engine was already running, his window down.

'See you later,' said Farrell, as he walked by and slid into the Citroen.

He followed Lind to St Michael's Bridge then waved him off to the left as he continued straight on. His stomach churned, and he had a feeling of foreboding he couldn't shake off. He wished he was heading straight to Kirkcudbright like Lind. If they got really lucky they might wrap up both the murder of Monro Stevenson and the forgery ring today.

Once he entered the station he swiped through the door and took the stairs up to the MCA room two at a time. DS Byers looked like he had been in there most of the night and clearly hadn't even had time to shave.

'Thank Christ one of you is here,' he exploded, when Farrell walked into the room. 'There's a limit to what I can get done on my own.'

'Sorry, Mike. I know you've been run off your feet in here. With the investigations overlapping like they have, you've been doing the work of three men, and I reckon you're the only one among us that could have kept all the plates spinning.'

Byers looked mollified.

'DI Moore and DC McLeod were working their socks off last night,' said Farrell. 'Have you got the stuff they sent you yet?'

'Regular Cagney and bloody Lacey, that pair,' grumbled Byers.

'I need you to get a search warrant for Lionel Forbes's place, but we won't execute it until we see how the chips fall today. I don't want to alert any of them prematurely that we're closing in.'

'That background you requested on Nancy Quinn? Turns out she was adopted. She's estranged from her adoptive parents. Broke off all contact with them when she went to Glasgow School of Art. Her adoptive parents have no clue as to the identity of her natural parents but said she had become obsessed with tracing them before she left. Social services have confirmed that her birth parents are Hugo Mortimer and Penelope Spence.'

'Did you see the picture Mhairi found in Hugo Mortimer's studio?'

Byers grimaced.

'Do you think he knows? I mean he's a bit of a lech, but to paint his own daughter like that? Turns my stomach, it does.'

'He might,' said Farrell. 'Equally he might not. It could all be part of some twisted revenge plan she has for him. Time will tell.'

'This bloody lot should have their own reality TV show.'

'Can you bring the Super up to speed?' asked Farrell. 'I'm about to head off to join the others in Kirkcudbright.'

Byers looked distinctly unhappy at the prospect, but he nodded reluctantly.

'What do you want me to do about the whole Penelope Spence/ Paul Moretti issue?' he asked.

Farrell thought for a moment.

'Nothing right now. I'm as sure as I can be she's not implicated in any of the four crimes that we're investigating. As far as I can figure, the whole disguise was simply a ruse to hide from Hugo the fact that she was getting her hands dirty as a successful commercial artist.'

'And yet, it would be her money keeping the whole sordid set up afloat,' said Byers shaking his head in disgust.

'Depending on how today shakes down, I'm going to get her in, tell her we've figured out her little game and see what she knows about the origin of those paintings in Janet Campbell's rented studio. If she didn't paint them, then she might have an inkling of who did,' said Farrell.

Chapter Sixty-Three

'You ready, lad?' said Stirling, pacing around the farm kitchen. The cold and damp seemed to have permeated their very bones.

'As ready as I'll ever be,' said DC Thomson.

'Now, remember, I'll be at the Farmers' market in Kirkcudbright and then drift off to The Smuggler's for the afternoon. That way I'll be close by the pick-up point at the harbour. We've flooded the market with plain-clothes officers, dressed to blend in with the tourists and locals. DCI Lind, DI Moore, and DI Farrell will all be centrally located and in constant touch with everybody.'

'I still can't believe that Lionel Forbes is involved in all of this. We're going to look like a right bunch of wallies when it gets out he was consulting on the case,' said DC Thomson.

'His credentials were impeccable, and expertise of that kind isn't easy to come by down this neck of the woods. Plus, he was no doubt keen to insert himself into the investigation.'

'Weren't he and DI Moore …?'

'At the end of the day, she was the one who cottoned on to him and was able to get us the vital evidence we needed to bring down the whole operation. Took guts, that did.'

'I'm just glad she's okay.'

'Let's hope so, lad. Right, are you ready to get going?'

'Locked and loaded,' Thomson replied, with an attempt at levity.

'Now remember, we have trackers on the tractor and inside the tube containing the painting. Sergeant Forsyth and the fire-arms team are also in the local nick on standby, just in case. In so far as it's ever possible to say, we've got your back.'

DC Thomson nodded.

'Right, Sarge. I'll be off then.'

'If all goes according to plan, we should be out of this bloody hellhole for good, tonight,' said Stirling. 'Can't wait to sample the wife's cooking again.'

'It's got to be better than yours, Sarge,' said DC Thomson. 'Reckon I'd die of malnutrition if we have to keep this cover going much longer.'

'Cheeky bugger,' replied DS Stirling. 'I'd like to see you try.'

They fell silent once more.

'Right, off you go, lad. I'll wait ten minutes then drive my car in. Be over before you know it.'

DC Thomson nodded and left the kitchen. Minutes later, the tractor roared into life. Stirling immediately texted DI Moore that Thomson was in transit, then stood motionless until the sound diminished to nothing. He was getting far too old for this bloody lark. His nerves couldn't take it. He was already on diaz-epam and beta blockers from the doctor, following on from the case last year.

Sighing, he locked the door behind him, walked over to his car and turned on the ignition.

DC Thomson trundled along until he reached the centre of Kirkcudbright. As it was the Farmers' market, there were tractors and trailers everywhere, which was good camouflage. He parked up at the harbour and strolled to the pick-up point in the disa-bled toilet near the Tourist Office. Locking the door behind him, he removed the grille from the ventilation shaft and reached up to pull the tube out, placing it inside his rucksack. He returned to the tractor and fired up the engine. Although it was still freezing, his checked shirt was welded to his back with sweat and he was struggling to control his breathing. Over the shirt was a bulletproof vest and on top of that a sweatshirt and a baggy hoody. Easy, Davey boy. Screw this one up and you'll never hear the end of it. He consciously deepened his breathing until the anxiety receded, then indicated and pulled out. All he had to do now was keep his cool until he reached the rendezvous point in Stranraer.

The package would be exchanged for the money in the car park at Morrisons. He would then get the hell out of Dodge and those above his pay grade could deal with it.

Relaxing now that he was leaving the town behind and heading out into the open countryside, he settled further down in the uncomfortable seat. He had a fair drive in front of him. Suddenly his phone pinged. He snatched it from the seat beside him and broke out in a sweat once more.

'Change of Plan. Proceed to M74 Services Johnstonebridge. Await further instructions there.'

Shit, this wasn't good. The whole surveillance op was geared to an intercept at Stranraer. Most of the Dumfries manpower was holed up in Kirkcudbright and beyond. There was bugger all left in Dumfries, never mind the tiny station of Lockerbie, which was the closest to his new destination. He grabbed his other phone and quickly texted DI Moore. Oh well, it was out of his hands in any event. Just go with the flow, Davey boy, he muttered. Just go with the flow.

Chapter Sixty-Four

'Dammit!' shouted DI Moore.

Farrell, Lind, and McLeod glanced at her in alarm. Moore was not one for losing her cool. All four of them were holed up in a tiny office in Kirkcudbright nick, laptops and phones in front of them. DS Stirling was still in the town maintaining his cover, just in case.

'They've only gone and changed the rendezvous point to Johnstonebridge Services. The majority of our resources are committed in the wrong place, leaving DC Thomson without adequate backup. We don't even know if they're ultimately headed to Glasgow, Edinburgh or down the M6 to bloody England,' she said, throwing her chair back to pace around the room.

Lind was already on the phone to Byers, relaying the new intel.

'We need to think about this,' said Farrell. 'Is it even possible that DC Thomson is simply a decoy and that the real painting has been, or is about to be, picked up by someone else? We need to maintain some officers in this area to cover all eventualities.'

'Wait a minute,' said DI Moore, calmer now.

'Lionel Forbes told me this morning that he was headed up to Glasgow to speak to an editor about doing a new arts column for their paper. Perhaps he's handling the exchange himself?' she said.

DI Moore texted DC Thomson immediately.

'Lionel Forbes may be handling exchange himself. Await further instructions.'

'We've got the warrants in place,' said Lind. 'DI Moore and I will nip round to Lionel Forbes's house. Fiona Murray can let us in with her key. I doubt very much that he's there, but we may garner some clue as to his intentions and obtain evidence in relation to the murder and forging ring that he's yet to destroy. Kate, did you happen to get his licence plate before you left?'

'Yes, he drives a silver Mercedes, registration number, LF1 ART.'

Lind keyed in the details to Byers, asking for the car to be traced and discreetly tailed.

'Frank, you and Mhairi head to Dumfries at the double. DC Thomson's tracker should keep you informed of his whereabouts. He'll be much slower than you in the tractor. I'm going to send half the firearms team back as well, but retain the other half here, in case we're being led on a wild goose chase,' said Lind.

Farrell and Mhairi swiftly packed up their stuff and left the room.

A few minutes later, Lind and Moore were standing outside Lionel Forbes's handsome townhouse. They knocked on the door. It immediately swung open and Fiona Murray let them in. Her face was expressionless as usual.

'He's not here. I've no idea when he'll be back,' she said.

'Where are you meant to be today, Fiona?' asked DI Moore.

'Working at Ivy House. I told them I was popping out to get some supplies.'

'Well, I suggest you pick them up and get back there,' said DI Moore.

Murray nodded, her skin pulled tight as a drum over her cheekbones. The strain was starting to tell on her.

'Not long to go until this nightmare is over for you, Fiona,' said Lind. 'We need you to keep it together for another few hours. Can you do that?'

She nodded and walked towards the door.

'I'll leave you the key. I doubt I'll be needing it again.'

Once she had left, Moore and Lind got to work. The wax seal, paper and bulbs were no longer in the study desk. Neither was the silencer. Lind glanced at his watch and ran to the back door. Rolling up his sleeves he emptied the wheelie bin. They discovered the missing items double-bagged and taped right at the bottom. There was something else in the bag. A heavy torch with traces of dried blood on it.

They had just retrieved them when they heard the unmistakable sound of the bin lorry approaching.

Lind straightened up, mopping the sweat off his face with a hanky.

'Bloody hell, that was cutting it fine.'

Abruptly, DI Moore turned on her heel and headed back into the house and up the stairs, with Lind following. She entered the bedroom, her face flaming as she noticed the unmade bed she had just left a few hours ago. Lind said nothing as she flung open the wardrobe and stared around wildly, then dashed into the en suite.

'What is it?' asked Lind. 'Speak to me, Kate.'

'He's not coming back,' she said.

'What? Are you sure? You said he was meant to be heading to Glasgow. Perhaps he's intending to stay a few days?'

'No, he's taken too much for that. I think he's going to collect the painting himself and flee abroad with it. I've been all through his desk and there's no sign of a passport anywhere. He must have been waiting to pull off this last big job before running.'

'Think, Kate. Apart from the silencer in the drawer, did you see any evidence that he owned a gun?'

She thought hard but eventually shook her head.

'No evidence that I saw, but he would hardly tell me. He may well have access to a gun. There was no record of Monro Stevenson ever having a firearm. Lionel Forbes must have shot him with his own gun, then left it there in the hope it would be passed off as suicide. He could have another.'

She gnawed her bottom lip.

'This means that DC Thomson is in far more danger than we realized, if he's tying up loose ends before running,' said Lind. 'If Forbes is doing the exchange himself, he might twig that we swapped the real deal back with the forgery. He's bound to open the package. It means the difference between a life of luxury and a life of penury.'

'I'm not worried about that,' said Moore. 'According to the experts, the forgery was so skilful that it required scientific analysis to reveal it. Even Forbes wouldn't be able to tell.'

'What if he finds the tracking device?' asked Lind.

'That's a bigger problem,' she said, looking worried. 'The package is sealed shut but if he opens it and roots around he'll find the tracker. It's small but visible.'

Lind got on the phone to DS Byers and imparted the latest information. He then rang Farrell.

'You're going to have to run point on this, Frank. I can't get down there in time. I need you to get to Johnstonebridge Services ASAP. Uniforms know to give you a free pass. DS Forsyth is already en route with half the firearms team. We've got back up converging from Lockerbie and Moffat stations. Thomson is about fifty minutes out. He's waiting to hear that you guys are in position. Hurry!'

'Will do,' replied Farrell, his knuckles white on the wheel as he pushed his clapped-out Citroen to the max.

Chapter Sixty-Five

Lind pulled his phone out once more.

'Fiona? We need one more favour. We'll be at Ivy House in five minutes. Can you unlock the front and back doors for us and then get the hell out of there? We won't come in until you are down the drive. We'll make sure your cooperation today is included in our report to the procurator fiscal.'

'Will I pull DS Stirling in as well, sir?' asked DI Moore.

'Yes, and draft in two squad cars to take Hugo Mortimer and Penelope Spence separately into custody. I don't want them to have any opportunity to communicate with each other, once we've arrested them.'

They met DS Stirling and the uniformed officers outside the driveway to Ivy House, the squad cars having been parked out of sight. Within five minutes, Fiona Murray left the building carrying her shopping bag. She sailed past them with her head held high and carried on down the hill, as though they didn't exist.

'She's one tough cookie,' whispered DI Moore to Lind.

'She's had to be,' he replied.

Stirling and DI Moore each crept round the back of Ivy House, while Lind and two uniforms headed for the front door.

They didn't give the usual warnings because the element of surprise was crucial. The last thing they wanted was for Hugo Mortimer to alert Lionel Forbes that their cover had been blown. All of them were already familiar with the layout of the large Victorian house due to the floorplan prepared by Mhairi.

Stealthily, Lind and Moore crept up the stairs. The house was silent apart from the sonorous tick of the grandfather clock in the hall. As they got closer to Mortimer's room, they could hear the sound of laughter, one male and one female. They paused outside and listened. Then Lind pulled out his baton and gently turned the handle. Fortunately, it wasn't locked and the three of them advanced rapidly into the room.

'Police, put your hands in the air. Stand up and face the wall!' Lind yelled, throwing a dressing gown over to the scantily clad young woman in the bed.

'That's Nancy Quinn,' Moore said to him.

'What the hell do you think you're playing at?' shouted Mortimer, scrambling to his feet.

Quinn did as she was told, saying nothing.

'Hugo Mortimer and Nancy Quinn, you are both being placed under arrest for forgery and conspiracy to commit murder. You are not obliged to say anything, but anything you do say will be noted down and can be used against you in a court of law. Do you understand?'

'What? Conspiracy to commit murder? You can't be serious. Take me in by all means, if you must, but this young woman has nothing to do with any of this,' said Mortimer.

'I think we'll be the judge of that, sir,' said Lind, fastening handcuffs on the pair of them, after they'd been allowed to throw on some clothes.

They marched Mortimer and Quinn downstairs, where they met DS Stirling and PC McGhie walking out with Penelope Spence, also cuffed.

'Why on earth have you arrested Penelope?' asked Mortimer, looking baffled.

Spence glared at both him and Quinn as she passed.

'You old fool. She's young enough to be your daughter,' she hissed.

Quinn smirked.

'It's not what you think,' muttered Mortimer.

It's not what you think either, thought Lind.

As they were leaving, Patrick Rafferty emerged from the kitchen, coffee mug in hand.

'Er, what about me?'

'What about you?' replied Lind.

'Aren't you taking me in too?'

'Have you committed a crime?'

'Not that I'm aware of.'

'Then, enjoy your coffee,' said Lind, walking past him.

'I'll head back to Dumfries with this lot, if that's okay, sir,' said Moore.

'I've just got one or two loose ends to tie up here, then I'll be right behind you,' said Lind.

Chapter Sixty-Six

Farrell and Mhairi pulled into the car park at Johnstonebridge Services. They both had standard-issue vests on, which would afford them some limited protection. Farrell was armed with a Taser and he told Mhairi to keep to his rear. They could see the tractor and trailer across the huge car park, but there was no sign yet of Lionel Forbes. Perhaps he wasn't going to do the handover himself after all. Glancing around, his practised eyes soon spotted members of the firearms team strategically placed. DC Thomson looked vulnerable perched high in his tractor. As he'd been instructed by Farrell, he climbed down, looking bored and lit up a fag. He had a folded copy of the *Daily Record* with him and glanced at the headlines. Good lad.

'Here he comes,' muttered Mhairi, shrinking down in her seat. As instructed, DC Thomson didn't react to the sight of the silver Mercedes pulling up beside the tractor. After all, he wasn't meant to know what Lionel Forbes looked like.

Farrell and Mhairi crept out of their car and, using the cars between them for cover, slowly moved towards Forbes. They could see Sergeant Forsyth and three of his officers also advancing stealthily.

Forbes wound down the window of the Mercedes and spoke

to DC Thomson, who looked suitably startled. Thomson climbed up into the cab and, looking furtive, jumped back down and handed over the package through the window in exchange for a brown envelope. He then casually hauled himself into the tractor.

Farrell breathed a sigh of relief and instructed the officers to hold their positions. He ideally didn't want to make a move until DC Thomson was out of harm's way.

Forbes then opened the tube in the car and examined the contents.

This was exactly what he hadn't wanted to happen. Farrell held his breath as he waited to see what Forbes would do. A muzzle poked out of the window of the car and a shot was fired, DC Thomson toppled to the ground and rolled under the tractor.

Mhairi contacted the nearby ambulance.

'Officer down, possible GSW. Await instructions to approach.'

Sergeant Forsyth shot out the tyres of Forbes's vehicle as he gunned the engine. The car slewed at an angle then came to a halt. There were a few screams from distant members of the public, who were diverted away from the action.

Mhairi reached the tractor and dived underneath. She found DC Thomson, white as a sheet and clutching his chest, but the vest had taken most of the impact of the bullet.

'Bloody hell, Davey, you gave us a right bloody scare,' she muttered, mussing his hair. 'Stay put for now. Help's on its way.'

The car was now surrounded on all sides by heavily armed officers. Farrell was passed the megaphone by one of the armed-response team.

'Give it up, Forbes. You're completely surrounded. Exit the car with your hands up,' he shouted.

There was no movement. The car was now surrounded by DS Forsyth and his firearms team. Suddenly, the car door opened and a leg appeared, followed by another. Forbes slowly stood up and turned to face them, his hands raised, still holding the gun in his right hand. The urbane mask had slid from his face to be replaced by one of feral savagery.

'Place the gun on the ground, slowly, then come back up to a standing position with your hands raised in the air,' said Farrell.

Forbes bent forward in slow motion as if to comply but at the last second the gun swung up fast.

'Go to Hell!' yelled Forbes, as he was taken out in a hail of bullets.

Farrell ran over to the tractor and reassured himself that DC Thomson, though badly bruised and shaken up, wasn't seriously hurt. He waved over the paramedics.

Mhairi was still by his side.

'Mind if I go with him in the ambulance, sir?' she asked.

'As if the poor lad hasn't suffered enough,' he said.

DC Thomson managed a weak grin. He looked like he was slipping into shock as the reality of what happened started to sink in. A dose of DC McLeod was just what he needed.

Farrell waited until SOCO arrived and the crime scene had been processed. He felt a wave of fatigue move through his body, as the adrenalin left his system. He was grateful that Lind had managed to keep DI Moore in Kirkcudbright while they took Forbes down. Even so, she didn't let people into her life very readily and he knew that this miscalculation on her part would cause her anguish for some time.

Chapter Sixty-Seven

At the harbour in Kirkcudbright, Lind slumped back in his car with relief. All officers safe and accounted for. Although Lionel Forbes had been killed, no blame could possibly be attached to the officers under his command in the circumstances. He had been given every opportunity to surrender but had chosen instead to aim his weapon. DC Thomson was being kept in for a few hours' observation, no doubt being driven mad by Mhairi clucking over him.

Laura suddenly popped into his mind. He thought of his four kids and felt a hard lump in his throat. He had to get through to her. Farrell and Moore could take up some slack for a bit. He got out his phone.

'I'm sorry. Home early tonight. Can we talk? I've never stopped loving you. Not for one single minute all these years. X'

Feeling a sense of peace settle within him, he suddenly remembered he had meant to stop by the gallery and have another word with Janet Campbell on the subject of the canvasses. The other cases might be all wrapped up, but he still had to catch Ailish's killer. They now knew that Penelope Spence was Paul Moretti but, although she had obstructed the police investigation by her actions, her motives had been personal rather than criminal in intent.

He stooped as he entered the gallery, the bell tinkling to announce his arrival. Janet rushed to greet him, her homely face split wide by a smile.

'DCI Lind. This is a lovely surprise! What can I help you with today?' she asked.

He smiled back at her.

'If every member of the public was as helpful as you,' he said, 'our jobs would be an awful lot easier.'

'What about a cuppa?' she asked.

'Thanks, but I'm afraid I have to be getting back to Dumfries, nice though that sounds. The reason I popped by is that we've discovered that Paul Moretti didn't paint those canvasses that Mike Halliday found in the cupboard.'

'And you're sure about that, are you?' she asked, her face clouding.

'Yes, completely. What I need to know is whether you personally looked in that cupboard before Mike Halliday took entry as a tenant?'

'Well, no, I didn't. I pay a cleaner to go in at the end of every tenancy. They throw out any rubbish left and give it a deep clean. You know what these artist types can be like. The cupboard has a lock, so I suppose it's possible it was overlooked. The paintings could have been in there for quite some time. I don't think anyone ever asked me for the key, until Mike moved in.'

'Was the cleaner somebody local?' he asked.

'No, I'm afraid it's one of those companies from Dumfries. It's somebody different every time they come. I'll look through my files and forward the details, just in case.'

'Who was the tenant before Paul Moretti?' asked Lind.

'Let me see, that would be Elizabeth Morley. Lovely lady. Makes beautiful jewellery. Very refined.'

In other words, a dead end, thought Lind. He thanked her and left.

He was walking by the tail end of the building, when he glimpsed Mike Halliday sitting on his usual bench. He remembered that the last time he was here he had admired some of Mike's paintings. There had been one in particular that stood out, a painting of Caerlaverock Castle where he and Laura had their wedding photos taken. On impulse he decided to see if it had been sold.

'Hey Mike,' he said. 'Just wandered by on the off-chance you still had that painting of Caerlaverock Castle for sale? It might earn me some brownie points with the wife.'

Halliday leapt up, a friendly grin on his face.

'DCI Lind. I hear you boys have been busy today. Care to share?'

'No can do, I'm afraid. Anyway, you know what small towns are like. Janet will probably be able to give you chapter and verse before I've even got back to Dumfries.'

He laughed and disappeared inside to re-emerge with the painting five minutes later.

'This the one you're after?'

'Perfect,' Lind replied. He paid the modest price happily.

As Halliday was wrapping it for him, Lind felt his spirits rise. Laura was going to love it. It would remind her of happier times.

'Now this is what I call art,' he said appreciatively, as he took the parcel. 'Not like that sick crap that came out from your cupboard. Even I could do better than that and I'm all but colour blind.'

Halliday laughed.

'Best stick to the day job then.'

'You're not wrong there,' replied Lind walking away in the direction of his car. As he opened his wallet to put away the change, he noticed that Halliday had given him an extra tenner by mistake. He swung round but the door was already closed. If he didn't give it back to him now he would forget all about it. There was no answer to his knock. He tried the door and found it unlocked. He would leave the money on a table inside.

Entering, he walked into the sitting room. The interior was larger than it had looked from the outside. Maybe Mike had gone to take a nap upstairs. Best not to disturb him. Putting the money on the coffee table, he turned to leave. He stopped. Maybe he should leave a note? He pulled out a pen and cast around for a scrap of paper. His eyes widened as he saw a pair of ankles poking out from behind the couch. Leaning over, he saw Maureen Kerrigan's terrified eyes staring up at him. She was bound and gagged.

Suddenly, he felt a huge thump to the back of his head. As he sank to his knees, he caught a glimpse of the furious face of his attacker. Everything faded to black.

Chapter Sixty-Eight

As soon as he got back to the station, Farrell went in search of DI Moore. He knew she would have been informed of the shooting by now and he was worried about how she might be coping.

Tapping lightly on her door, he walked straight in.

'I come bearing caffeine,' he said, waving the plastic cartons at her.

She gave a small smile, though he could see from the pallor of her face that she was struggling to keep herself together.

'Frank, come in, just what I needed.'

He closed the door behind him and sat opposite her.

'I'm sorry how things turned out with Forbes,' he said. 'For what it's worth I wasn't crazy about him, but I didn't have him pegged for a murderer or some kind of criminal mastermind either.'

'Thanks, Frank, kind of you to say. My instincts are usually pretty spot on. Guess I only saw what I wanted to see.'

'Don't beat yourself up about it. Only myself, Lind, and Mhairi knew there was anything between you, other than police business, and that's the way it's going to stay,' he said.

'Mhairi knew?' She groaned.

'Yep. It was hate at first sight,' he grinned. 'Full McLeod heckles.'

'She's going to make a bloody good detective, that one.'

'I can cover if you want to get off home. I'm sure Lind will be back any minute.'

'Thanks, Frank, but I prefer not to be alone with my thoughts. Not yet anyway. I'd rather keep busy.'

'Right then. I've fixed the last briefing for 8 p.m. That hopefully gives us enough time to mop up what forensics can be processed in-house and interview Hugo Mortimer, Penelope Spence, and Nancy Quinn.'

'How about I take the two women with DS Stirling?'

'Fine by me. I'll tackle Mortimer with Mhairi. Have you seen her? Or perhaps I should ask if you've heard her?'

Moore pointed to the left.

'The noise and commotion proceeded that way,' she smiled.

'Excellent,' said Farrell, turning to leave.

Sure enough, he hadn't taken more than a few steps when he heard Mhairi's voice coming from the sergeant's room, regaling them all with the events of the day.

'DC Thomson was incredibly brave,' she continued, as he stood in the open doorway. 'He maintained his cover until the bitter end. I'm taking up a collection for him.' She shook a biscuit tin. 'Dig deep, it's not every day one of our lot gets shot in the line of duty.'

Everyone in the room crowded round her, eager to contribute.

Farrell coughed, causing her to jump.

'In your own time, Mhairi.'

'Coming, sir,' she said, shutting the tin which was now stuffed with notes.

Once they were walking along the corridor, he handed her a twenty.

'Stick that in your tin.'

'Thanks, sir! Where are we going?'

'To interview Hugo Mortimer. DI Moore and DS Stirling are handling the other two.'

314

'He's off the hook for murder at least,' said Mhairi.

'He'll still do significant jail time for the forgery, though,' said Farrell.

'He won't have heard that Lionel Forbes is dead yet, will he, sir?'

'No, he's had no access to communications of any sort. Everyone in the custody suite has been told to zip it.'

A text pinged and Farrell glanced at his phone and frowned. It was from Laura.

'Heard there's been a shooting on the news. Is John OK? He's not picking up. Worried sick.'

That's odd, he thought. He knew they'd been having difficulties, but John didn't have a vindictive bone in his body and wouldn't want her to worry. He texted.

'Nothing to worry about. He wasn't there. Still in Kirkcudbright.'

The reply pinged back in an instant.

'Thank God. Tell him to come home when you see him.'

Chapter Sixty-Nine

By the time they reached the custody suite, Mortimer was already sitting in one of the interview rooms, flanked by two burly uniforms.

'Thanks, guys, we'll take it from here,' said Farrell, switching on the recording device and attending to the usual formalities.

Seen under the harsh lighting, Hugo Mortimer was a ruin of a man. He reminded Farrell of *The Picture of Dorian Gray*. Years of excess and selfishness were written in the lines of his still-handsome face. Undaunted, he sent a roguish smile in Mhairi's direction. Playing along, she flashed back one of her own. Only Farrell could see her fists clenched under the table.

'For the record, can you confirm you've declined your right to legal representation?' he said, sending Mhairi a warning look.

'Let's just get on with this, DI Farrell. Some nonsense about alleged forgery, I believe?'

This guy was too cocky by half, thought Farrell. Time to wipe the grin off his face.

'So, how long have you been sleeping with your daughter?' he asked, launching the grenade.

Mortimer turned white, then shook his head as if to rid himself of what had just been said.

'What the bloody hell are you talking about?' he snapped.

'Are you telling me you don't have a daughter?' said Farrell.

Silence.

'Well?' pressed Farrell.

'I may have a daughter, but you're wrong. We've never met. I could never …'

He looked so sick that Farrell almost felt sorry for him.

'We have established that Nancy Quinn is your biological daughter.'

'But why would she? How could she? Oh my God, does Penelope know?' He sank his head into his hands and groaned.

'Not yet, but I'm sure she'll find out one way or the other. We have evidence that she was obsessed with you and insinuated her way in to your life,' said Farrell.

'Did she ever contact you, ask to meet?' said Mhairi.

'Yes, on her eighteenth birthday. I told her I wasn't interested. I'm not proud of it.'

'Did you ever tell Penelope she'd got in touch?' he asked.

'No, why would I? It was finished business as far as I was concerned. I didn't want Penelope getting all steamed up about it.'

'I take it you knew she was Monro Stevenson's girlfriend?' asked Farrell.

'Yes, it was no big deal. I'm polyamorous myself.'

'Is that what they're calling it these days?' muttered Mhairi.

Farrell glared at her and nodded towards the tape recorder. She looked abashed.

'What did Monro have to say about it?' asked Farrell.

'He didn't know.'

'Bet he wouldn't have been quite so willing to forge for you, if he knew you were cavorting with his girlfriend?' said Farrell.

Mortimer looked wary once more.

'I don't know where you're getting this forgery business from. I'm an artist, not a forger.'

'Takes money to bankroll a place the size of Ivy House,' said Farrell. 'And yet, you seem to have no discernible income stream?'

'Penelope has enough money from an inheritance to keep us comfortable,' he said.

'So you sponge off Penelope, while flaunting your polyamorous lifestyle right in front of her? You're quite the catch,' snapped Mhairi.

'Oh, please,' said Mortimer. 'Save me from the moral rectitude of the great unwashed.'

'What if I were to suggest to you that there is no inheritance?' said Farrell.

'What do you mean? Of course there's an inheritance. We've been living off it for years.'

'What if I were to tell you that Penelope Spence is the real identity of Aaron Sewell, the incredibly successful commercial artist?'

Mortimer went slack-jawed.

'No way, I don't believe you. It's not possible.'

'Oh, but it is,' said Mhairi. 'She also goes by the name of Paul Moretti.'

'That freak? No way!' shouted Mortimer, thoroughly rattled now.

'Bit of a shock to discover that your bohemian lifestyle has been funded by the graft of a successful commercial artist,' said Farrell.

'I can't believe she kept it from me all this time,' he said.

'We know all about the forgery ring,' said Farrell. 'Arrests have been made and the stolen painting has been recovered.'

'I'm delighted for you, DI Farrell, but I can assure you that it's nothing to do with me,' Mortimer said, folding his arms.

'What if I were to suggest to you that Lionel Forbes has laid it all out for us. How you were the boss and he was only involved giving advice on the periphery?'

Mortimer's jaw tightened, but he said nothing.

'You really think that a man like Lionel Forbes wouldn't throw you under the bus to save his own skin?' mocked Farrell. 'I didn't have you figured for being that naive.'

Still nothing. Farrell continued, hoping the bluff would pay off.

'Forgery is a serious offence, but it doesn't top murder, of course.'

'Murder? I didn't murder anyone!' said Mortimer.

'We know that either you or Lionel Forbes murdered Monro Stevenson,' said Mhairi.

'What if I were to suggest to you that Lionel Forbes might be willing to testify that *you* murdered Monro, because he wanted out of your little racket and threatened to spill the beans?'

'He said that? Lionel said that?'

Farrell remained impassive.

'That bastard! I know nothing about any murder. Yes, I might have copied a few pictures, but where's the harm in that? Lionel was the hard-ass, not me. I'm an artist. I simply relished the challenge.'

'And the money?' said Farrell.

'It was a victimless crime. The money wasn't to be sniffed at but I'm sure Lionel creamed off the lion's share. He was the brains behind the whole thing. All I did was paint pictures. That was the beginning and end of it. There, are you satisfied?'

'So, what you're really saying is that you were Lionel's tame artist in exchange for some pin money?' said Mhairi. 'Penelope's sounding cooler by the minute.'

Farrell pushed over a piece of paper.

'I want details of every picture you've forged, along with approximate times and dates. If it matches up with the information already in my possession, then I'll consider whether to indicate to the procurator fiscal that you cooperated with us.'

Mortimer picked up the piece of paper and started writing.

Chapter Seventy

Penelope Spence sat ramrod straight in her chair. She could have been carved from stone. Across the table, DI Moore and DS Stirling glanced at each other.

'We can't help you if you don't talk to us,' said Moore. 'I understand that all of this has come as something of a shock.'

'You think?' shot back Spence.

'You yourself are not in any significant bother here,' Moore pressed on. 'You're entitled to call yourself whatever you want in Scots law, as long as it's not for a fraudulent purpose.'

Spence's shoulders relaxed a little.

'The worst you're facing is obstructing a police investigation. I think it's entirely possible that, if you cooperate fully from this point on, the procurator fiscal might let you walk.'

'I intend to cooperate,' she said. 'I had no intention of getting caught up in all this mess. When the police seemed to be focusing their attention on me I panicked and was scared to return to Lavender Cottage in case I was arrested.'

'DI Farrell mentioned that you met a man upstairs in The Smuggler's Inn. Can you confirm who that was, please?'

'Miles Prescott, the Edinburgh agent for my Aaron Sewell identity. He thinks I'm simply an intermediary.'

'You've told us you didn't know Hugo Mortimer was involved in this forgery ring,' said Moore.

'I still can't believe he would rip off other artists in this way.'

'There's something else we really need your help with.'

'Go on.'

'We're still investigating the murder of Ailish Kerrigan. At first, we thought your alter ego, Paul Moretti, might have done it,' said Moore.

Spence let out a nervous laugh.

'Why on earth would you think that?'

'Because of these paintings,' said Moore, signalling to DS Stirling to unwrap them.

The horror that flitted across Spence's face was clearly genuine.

'These are revolting,' she muttered.

'Can you remember if they were in a cupboard in the studio that you rented from Janet Campbell when you moved in?' asked Moore.

'I'd have got rid of them if they had been.'

'Janet Campbell assumed they were yours, because you'd asked her to sell a painting of some dead stuff that she thought was pretty gross too,' said Stirling.

'That was only a painting of a dead brace of pheasants I picked up in a charity shop to deter her from poking around in my business,' she said.

'So you haven't seen any other work locally that could potentially have been painted by the same artist?' Moore asked. 'We believe the murderer could still be in the area.'

Spence pulled the paintings towards her and frowned in concentration as she studied them for several long minutes.

'I can't be completely sure, but the uncompromising nature of the pieces and something about the brushwork point to Mike Halliday.'

'Mike Halliday?' said DS Stirling, surprised. 'Isn't he the one who paints the pretty pictures for tourists?'

'He's also the one who lied to us about the paintings being in the cupboard when he took over the studio,' said Moore.

'He applied to join The Collective a few years ago and had to submit some work,' said Spence. 'He was undeniably talented, but he got off his face with us one night and the stuff he came out with was a bit freaky. We didn't want to live with him. Patrick Rafferty handled it. Said we didn't feel his work was of a sufficiently high standard. We could hardly say we simply didn't like him! He took it hard, I gather.'

'Is there any chance you might still have his submission, or was it returned to him?'

'I'm not sure. I can find out,' she said.

'Thank you,' said Moore. 'You've been most helpful.'

She hesitated, then switched off the recording device.

'Interview terminated,' she said.

'There's something else you need to know. This may be hard to hear.'

'Go on,' said Spence.

'That young woman who we brought in with Hugo?'

'What of her? Floozies come and floozies go,' she said, compressing her lips into a straight line.

'Now Hugo had no idea of this, whatsoever, until we told him, but it appears she may be your daughter.'

Spence went white and swayed in her seat. DI Moore poured some water and handed it to her.

'It appears that she contacted Hugo when she turned eighteen. He sent her off with a flea in her ear, saying that neither of you wanted anything to do with her.'

'He had no right,' she said, silent tears running down her face.

'She was determined to insinuate herself into your lives, in some bizarre form of revenge.'

'We were very young. I was besotted with Hugo. I wanted to keep her. I thought he would come round once he met her. She'd only been in the world one hour when he gave me an ultimatum.' Her voice broke. 'I chose him.'

DI Moore summoned PC Rosie Green, who had been waiting nearby.

'I have to leave you now with PC Green. You can stay here while we process your release on police bail and ascertain how the fiscal wishes to proceed.'

'I'm getting out?'

'Yes,' said Moore. 'You won't be allowed to go back to Ivy House yet, or have any contact with certain individuals, but subject to that, you'll be free to go.'

'What about my daughter?' she said, as if the word was stuck in her mouth. 'Can I see her?'

'The best I can do is relay to her that you knew nothing of Hugo's rejection and would like to see her. It won't be allowed until the legal process has concluded, however.'

'Thank you,' she said. Suddenly, she reached out and grabbed DI Moore's hand, taking her by surprise.

'I mean it. I'm in your debt.'

'Great interview, boss,' said DS Stirling, as they walked away along the corridor.

Moore smiled wearily. It had been a long and harrowing day and they were nowhere near done yet.

Farrell intercepted them as they were leaving the custody suite. He looked tense.

'Any word from Lind?' he asked.

'No, isn't he back yet?' asked Moore.

'No one's seen or heard from him since the arrests in Kirkcudbright this morning. Something's wrong. I'm sure of it. I need to get down there.'

'Agreed. We also need to arrest Mike Halliday for the murder of Ailish Kerrigan. Seems the canvasses were his after all. You'll need a fair-sized team with you, as he's clearly dangerous. The

323

only thing we have going for us is the element of surprise. We need to get to him before he realizes we're on to him,' said Moore.

'Halliday? Are you sure? He seemed so harmless,' said Farrell.

'Yes. Sure as I can be anyway.'

'Wait a minute, didn't you say earlier that Lind planned to visit Janet Campbell at her studio? Perhaps he discovered something and Halliday nobbled him. Shit! We need to get down there, right now,' he snapped, spinning on his heel.

DI Moore grabbed his arm.

'Yes, we do. But you need to take a breath first.'

At first Moore thought he was going to shrug her off and bolt. But, slowly, he regained his control and nodded. She let go.

'Here's what we're going to do. You head down to Kirkcudbright with Mhairi.' She looked at DS Stirling and hesitated.

'I want to go too, ma'am. I know the locale best after my undercover work. I won't rest until I know the DCI is safe,' Stirling said.

'Good to have you,' said Farrell, knowing how much it had cost Stirling to place himself in harm's way once more.

'I'll tell the Super, hold a briefing for everyone else and run the show with Byers from the MCA room,' said Moore. 'I'll send DS Forsyth and the firearms team down behind you for backup. I'll also get PC McGhie and the Kirkcudbright boys back in play.'

'Can you handle Laura?' asked Farrell. 'I need to stay focused.'

'You got it,' she said. 'Now go!'

Chapter Seventy-One

Lind woke up with a start. It was pitch-black, and he had no idea where he was. He was lying on his back on a hard, uneven surface. He tried to move his arms and legs, but they met with resistance and he heard the clank of metal on metal. Shit, he was shackled. Not good. He could hear a muted roar and realized he was near the sea. He licked his lips and tasted salt. The earth smelled damp and there was a musty smell. Seaweed? His teeth chattered with the cold. His clothes had been removed. Fear flared within him as he remembered that he was being held captive by Ailish's killer.

Chapter Seventy-Two

Farrell had driven to Kirkcudbright like a maniac, Mhairi, pale and quiet beside him. Stirling followed in another car behind, having scooped up DC Thomson. He had discharged himself from hospital and insisted on coming. DS Forsyth and his team were meeting them at the harbour.

It was already dark, and they slid like shadows through the still night, until they reached the studio where Halliday lived. Farrell felt sweaty and nauseous, the fear for his friend gnawing at his guts. The strain of the last few days was beginning to unravel his mind and he prayed silently for the strength to see him through the coming ordeal. He had to save Lind or die trying. Failure wasn't an option.

The property was surrounded. Shrouded in darkness there was no sign of activity within. Janet Campbell had been evacuated out of harm's way by PC McGhie. Bracing himself, Farrell gave the order to advance. The firearms team burst the door open, and Farrell and Mhairi ran in the door behind them.

It didn't take long to establish that the flat was empty.

'Shit!' yelled Farrell, punching the wall in frustration.

DS Stirling and DC Thomson ran in a few moments later.

'The shed and summerhouse are empty, boss,' reported Stirling.

Farrell swayed on his feet, suddenly light-headed. He could see Mhairi staring at him anxiously. They were all waiting for him to direct them, and he had nothing. He sought divine inspiration, but the murderous rage he was feeling blocked that avenue. He examined the interior minutely looking for a wisp of a clue. Anything that might tell him where Halliday had gone. Nothing. There wasn't even an unwashed coffee cup. How could the lair of a crazed psychopath look so unremarkable? His men had fallen silent. He could feel the heat of their suppressed impatience, like bloodhounds waiting to be unleashed. Taking one of the powerful torches, he went out into the yard. He stood there and slowly directed the torch in an arc, praying for something, anything, to leap out at him. It felt as though the world was holding its breath.

Suddenly, he had it. The last time he had swung by with Lind, there had been a boat and trailer in the yard. They had gone, along with Halliday's black Land Rover.

'He's taken the boat,' he yelled. 'Down to the harbour.'

They ran straight there, and after a few minutes' search they found the Land Rover, tucked down the side of a parked lorry. The harbour master's office was closed, but there was an emergency contact number.

Farrell rang it at once.

'DI Farrell, here. I need to know when Mike Halliday launched his boat tonight. He's abducted one of our officers. That's good to know … Do you know what kind of boat it is?'

Farrell hung up. 'He couldn't have launched before 6.15 p.m., because the tide was too low. His boat's a twentysix-foot motor boat, painted blue and white. Stirling, can you liaise with the coastguard? We need a boat launched and standing by, as well as a search-and-rescue helicopter.'

'On it, boss,' said Stirling, tapping at his phone and turning away.

'There's a few large caves the other side of the Dundrennan Firing Range,' said Mhairi. 'Because of their location, no one ever

327

goes there and they're pretty much only accessible from the sea. As Ailish Kerrigan's body was found within the range and he's familiar with the area, perhaps he could have gone there?'

'It's worth a shot, Mhairi. Go and tell Stirling to pass that on to the coastguard.'

A few minutes later, Stirling and Mhairi returned to the group.

'If there's no other leads, it might be worth heading down that way ourselves, sir,' said Stirling. 'The farm Thomson and I were occupying is nearby and the caves might be accessible from the cliffs. We could use the farm as a base of operations meantime.'

'Good idea,' said Farrell. 'Mhairi, can you contact the military, explain what's happening and ask some of their men to rendez-vous with us at the farm, bearing ropes and tackle for a possible cliff descent.'

Mhairi, too, busied herself on her phone.

Farrell wandered off to the water's edge as everyone started getting in their vehicles. As he looked up at the enigmatic face of the moon turned towards him, he hoped and prayed that Lind was still alive and able to gaze upon it too.

Chapter Seventy-Three

Lind woke up with a start, his eyes skittering around the cave. He was still shackled and so thirsty his tongue was stuck to the top of his mouth.

'Water,' he croaked.

Halliday sighed in annoyance. Lind could hear a pencil scratching across the paper on the easel.

'Keep still will you. I don't have long to get this right. There's really not much point in me giving you water. It will only prolong the inevitable, but I suppose if it will shut you up and let me get on …'

Halliday walked over to him and dribbled some water into his mouth from an open bottle.

Lind gulped greedily. His head felt woolly and swollen. He needed urgent medical attention, but could see no way, shackled as he was, to gain the upper hand in the situation.

He knew Farrell would be looking for him by now, but he could already feel the sands of time running out. His thoughts drifted off again, to Laura and the children, and he took refuge in their company as his eyes closed once more. Suddenly, he heard the drone of a search-and-rescue helicopter coming closer. For a moment, hope flared within him. But the sound soon receded into the distance, until all he could hear was the scratch of the pencil as he retreated deep within his mind.

Chapter Seventy-Four

Farrell came off the phone, his eyes glittering. He looked manic, thought Mhairi, and she worried that he was going to break down under the strain of the night's events.

'That was the coastguard,' he said. 'They think they've located the boat, pulled up on the shore not far from here. As instructed, they didn't linger, so that Halliday doesn't realize we've got the drop on his location.'

'So he's hiding in the caves then?' said Mhairi.

'There's only one really deep one, apparently, so my money's on them being in there. We need to move out now,' said Farrell.

'Wouldn't it be safer to wait until first light?' asked Stirling.

'Yes, but we're not going to,' said Farrell. 'We don't know if Lind's still alive, but I'm not going to sit here in the warm while he's down there with that nutter. Because of the danger, I'd like to call for volunteers only. We're going to have to make the descent over the cliffs in the dark, with the help of the two army boys Mhairi was able to rustle up. Anyone who feels unable to do that can wait here with my blessing.'

'DS Stirling, we'll need a senior officer to liaise between the various parties,' he said, giving the older man a respectable out.

'Bugger that, sir,' said Stirling. 'You can count me in for this one. DC Thomson has already been in the firing line today, so I reckon he's the one who should man the base.'

'Agreed,' said Farrell. 'DC Thomson, you've won the respect of every man and woman in the team today, but I'm afraid you have to sit this one out.'

DC Thomson glared at him but shrugged in capitulation. He wasn't fit enough yet and knew he would only slow them down.

'Right, that's settled,' said Farrell. 'Radio silence, please.'

They crept over the wiry long grass towards the cliff edge. The two military men had come well equipped and motioned to them to stay back, until they had selected the best place to descend. Mhairi felt sick with nerves. It was a long way down and she had never abseiled before. Well, she was just going to have to bloody suck it up. Anything for the DCI.

Farrell went first. He gave her the thumbs up as he lowered himself backwards over the cliff, then disappeared from sight. Stirling went next. His legs were visibly shaking, which made her feel a bit better.

Soon, she was waved over and strapped into the harness. There was a roaring in her ears as she stepped off into the inky void. Initially she panicked and nearly wrenched her arm from its socket by trying to stop her descent. But then she remembered the instructions and let out the rope, bit by bit, until her legs finally connected with the rocky shore below. Farrell's strong arms grabbed her and helped her shed the harness. Hopefully, the noise of the waves crashing against the shore would have drowned out any noise they made coming down.

DS Forsyth and two of his men made up the six to advance into the cave. Guns cocked, the firearms team advanced, solid professionals to the core. Mhairi crept forward at Farrell's heels, her baton held at the ready.

Suddenly, a man ran out of the cave, heading for the boat. He was clutching a sketchpad. The closest member of the firearms team took aim.

'Stop, Police!' he yelled. 'Put your hands in the air!'

Halliday slid to a halt as the moon came out from behind the clouds. His teeth were bared, and his eyes glittered with rage. He looked feral. Crouching low, he attempted to run for a rocky outcrop.

A sharp retort rang out, and Halliday toppled to the ground. He lay there unmoving. Sergeant Forsyth ran over, felt for a pulse and shook his head.

Farrell was already running into the cave with Mhairi and Stirling close behind him. The interior was cavernous, the walls lit with flickering light from a number of storm lanterns.

Mhairi let out a cry of distress. Lind's body looked lifeless. His eyes were closed and there was blood pooled under his head.

'John! We're here buddy, stay with us,' yelled Farrell running forward to his friend. He felt for a pulse. It was faint, but it was there.

'He's alive, but only just,' he yelled. 'Hurry!'

The two army boys came running with the spinal board and blankets they'd had strapped to their backs during the descent.

'They're going to take him to the neurosurgical unit at Glasgow,' Farrell shouted over the noise of the approaching chopper. It was unable to land but they managed to winch up Lind successfully. It then turned inland, the sound of the rotor blades receding into the distance.

Silence fell once more, aside from the rhythmical pounding of the waves. Farrell sat down abruptly on a rock, a spent source, as the power drained from his limbs. Mhairi felt light-headed herself. It was almost too much to take in.

Nobody spoke for a few minutes. Feeling her teeth start to chatter with the cold Mhairi approached her boss.

'What now, sir?'

Farrell looked broken, like he was on the verge of collapse. He didn't reply.

She nudged him with her toe. He had to snap out of it. He was the senior officer and decisions had to be made.

His head lifted, and his expression sharpened. He was back.

'McLeod and Stirling need to stay with the body, pending the arrival of SOCO at first light. You can take shelter in the cave, and the army lads can lower down sleeping bags, blankets, and food before they leave. A plastic tent will also be provided, which can be erected over the body to protect it from the worst of the elements.'

'You'll be all right?' he asked, looking at Mhairi.

She didn't reply, staring past him at Halliday's boat pulled up on the shoreline.

'Mhairi?'

'There's someone in the boat!' she shouted, taking off at a run. Farrell spun round and followed her. As they got closer they could see it was Maureen Kerrigan. Although she was bound and gagged, she'd managed to shuffle into an upright position. She was cold and shaking, but otherwise unharmed. They quickly freed her. She clung to Mhairi, sobbing.

'I saw DCI Lind being taken away. Is he going to be OK?'

'I don't know,' said Mhairi. 'He looked pretty bad.'

The army officers took Maureen away to winch her up the cliffs to where DC Thomson was waiting. Farrell turned to Mhairi.

'Are you sure you'll be OK until morning?'

She stepped up and hugged him.

'We'll be fine, sir,' she said. 'I'm sure DS Stirling has plenty of war stories to pass the time. Let us know as soon as you hear anything about the DCI.'

'You got it,' said Farrell, turning to stride away.

Chapter Seventy-Five

Farrell was bone-tired. He opened the gate and walked up the path to Lind's front door, his heart heavy with the knowledge that Lind might never return home. The dawn chorus was already starting up, as the sun crept over the horizon sending out rosy fingers of light.

The door flew open before he rang the bell. Laura stood there before him, her face swollen with tears. Without the need for words, he enfolded her in his arms. After a few moments, she pulled away and invited him into the warmth. They sat together on the settee, surrounded by memories of happier times.

'I still can't believe it,' she said. 'Yesterday, he was fine and today they say he might never wake up again. I can't comprehend it. It's too huge.' She started to cry once more, and Farrell passed her a handkerchief.

'He suffered a heavy blow to the head that caused a bleed on the brain,' he said. 'They'll have a better idea of his prognosis when the swelling subsides. For now, it's in the hands of God.'

'I wish I had your faith,' she sniffed. 'I've tried to pray, but all I feel is emptiness pushing back against me.'

'If it's any consolation, I can assure you that I've been praying loud enough for both of us,' said Farrell with a wan attempt at a smile.

'All those stupid arguments,' she wept. 'What was I thinking? It all seems so pointless now. The things I said to him ...' She beat at herself with her hands in a torment of self- loathing.

'Hey,' said Farrell, reaching across to grab her hands. 'He loved you. He knew you loved him. The rest was just a bump in the road. Part of living and loving is rowing. He needs you to be strong for him now. Are you going to take the kids to see him today?'

'Yes, my mother's taking us all to Glasgow later. The doctors think it might help for him to hear our voices. I've told them that Daddy's hurt his head and is having a big sleep so the doctors can make it better. I have an aunt in Edinburgh. She's said we can all stay up there with her until things become clearer.'

Farrell stood to go.

'If you need anything, Laura, anything at all ...'

'You'll be the first to know,' she said.

Somehow Farrell managed to drive himself home. It was fully light now, although the curtains were still drawn as he crunched down the path at Kelton. The River Nith at the foot of the lane was still and calm. Henry roused himself sleepily from his basket near the Aga and wound around his legs. Everything was the same, yet different.

He walked slowly upstairs to his bedroom and closed the door. Then he lit a large beeswax candle, faced the small crucifix on his wall, sank to his knees, and prayed for the life of his friend with an intensity he had never known.

Acknowledgements

I would like to thank my brilliant editor, Finn Cotton, for keeping me twisting like a fish on a hook until I could answer all the awkward questions including the exact nature of a Haggis Supper! This book would be a pale imitation of the finished product without his skill and diligence. Thanks are due also to my copy-editor, Janette Currie, and the rest of the team at Killer Reads. I would also like to thank the cover designer, Dominic Forbes, for his eye-catching and original cover.

Writing can be a lonely occupation, but I am truly blessed to have the support, friendship and encouragement of Moffat Crime Writers and my Crime and Publishment gang. I would also like to thank my book group, Dumfries Readers, for their encouragement and enthusiasm. My friend, Barbara Witty, deserves a special mention for her role as my unofficial publicity assistant with a salary payable in cakes. A great number of bloggers have kindly either reviewed my books or hosted me for guest posts. I would like to thank each and every one of you for your support, which I deeply appreciate. Special thanks must go to Kelly Lacey at Love Books Group for doing such a great job organizing my blog tour. Finally, last, but never least, a huge thank you to Guy, Alex and Jenny for your unwavering love, tolerance and understanding. It is never easy living with a writer who has lost the plot!

KILLER
READS

DISCOVER THE BEST
IN CRIME AND THRILLER.

SIGN UP TO OUR NEWSLETTER FOR YOUR CHANCE
TO WIN A FREE BOOK EVERY MONTH.

FIND OUT MORE AT
WWW.KILLERREADS.COM/NEWSLETTER

Want more? Get to know the team behind the books,
hear from our authors, find out about new crime and thriller
books and lots more by following us on social media:

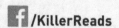 /KillerReads   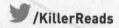 /KillerReads